THE THIRD PITCH

ROBERT ALLEN STOWE

Black Rose Writing | Texas

The author grants the final approval for this literary material.

First printing

ISBN: 978-1-68433-802-3
PUBLISHED BY BLACK ROSE WRITING
www.blackrosewriting.com

Printed in the United States of America
Suggested Retail Price (SRP) $19.95

The Third Pitch is printed in Georgia

*As a planet-friendly publisher, Black Rose Writing does its best to eliminate unnecessary waste to reduce paper usage and energy costs, while never compromising the reading experience. As a result, the final word count vs. page count may not meet common expectations.

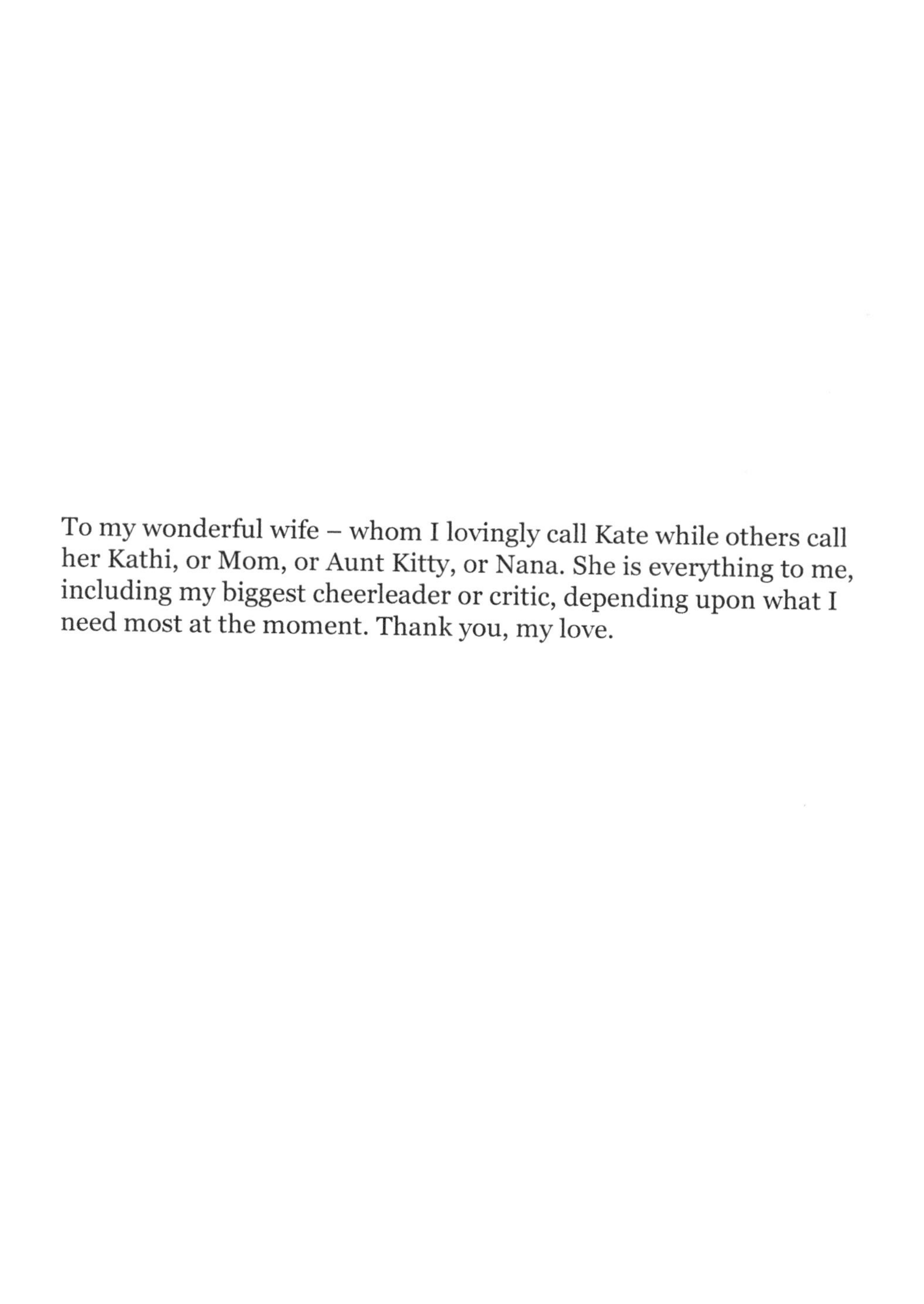

To my wonderful wife – whom I lovingly call Kate while others call her Kathi, or Mom, or Aunt Kitty, or Nana. She is everything to me, including my biggest cheerleader or critic, depending upon what I need most at the moment. Thank you, my love.

ACKNOWLEDGEMENT

Many thanks to those who served as pre-readers, editors, grammarians and muses: my brilliant and beautiful daughters Paisley and Lauren, Gene Pahlmann, Brant Jones, dear friend Jim Tripp, fellow author Rick Thorpe, and especially my life-long friend and fellow author David Allen Edmonds. If there are any grammatical errors, mistakes or non-sequitors, it's all their fault.

THE THIRD PITCH

PITCH NUMBER ONE

Monday, June 20:

Charlie Franklin sat uncomfortably in a hard-backed chair facing the massive dark oak desk of His Eminence Phelan Cardinal Maroney, his leather chair empty. Monsignor Wesley Leonard, an arrogant and too young monsignor ushered Charlie to his seat. Self-satisfied, the monsignor left him alone.

Charlie looked around the room. The City of Cleveland had always had an Archbishop overseeing the Catholic diocese, but Maroney was the first Cardinal ever assigned to the city. The interior of the office was fitting for such an important prelate. Highly polished, almost-antique furniture, subdued lighting more fitting in a funeral parlor, the faint scent of bee's wax candles in the air even though no flames could be seen. Subdued Gregorian Chant piped in from unseen speakers completed the mood that Cardinal Maroney wanted his guests to experience – benign calmness mixed with an apprehension bordering on dread. On the wall behind the desk was a massive cross constructed entirely of mirrors. Each cross beam a foot wide and three feet in length both across and down. No ghastly statue of a crucified human affixed, rather you saw yourself in the mirror, in the cross, on the cross. At least that's how Charlie reckoned the artist intended it to be interpreted.

"Impressive," Charlie thought to himself, "and intimidating". He wouldn't have wanted a stick of the Cardinal's furniture for his own apartment, and certainly not the mirrored cross, but then his tastes ran more toward the lazily comfortable. He looked again at the cross, at his reflection, and estimated that so many heavy mirrors probably made the damn thing weigh at least 500 pounds.

The Monsignor said the Cardinal thanked Mr. Franklin for agreeing to come to his office this Monday morning, and that the Cardinal wished to speak to him personally as soon as he finished some important business in chambers. Now, Charlie saw himself as a fairly experienced individual, but his past up-bringing as a good little Catholic boy left him slightly threatened around any ordained cleric, and an invitation to come to the Cardinal's office – well, that was like an order from the President of the United States, or something. You can't refuse a call like that. Charlie had seen Cardinals on TV, but he'd never seen one in person, and certainly never been in one's presence.

Charlie bemusedly wondered if they finally figured out that he drank the altar wine back in grade school. He'd probably have to do penance for that one, he grinned inwardly. There really was no other reason for him being summoned. He no longer attended Mass, no longer even considered himself among the true believers. There were too many unanswered prayers and too many personal losses to give credence to a mystical overseer. Such fantasies are best left to the multitude of unrealistic artistic renderings.

Charlie had done a few good things during his life, and, yes, some bad things, but no one really could trace the bad deeds back to him, certainly not the Cardinal. Yet, here he sat, at a loss to figure out why he was in the Cardinal's office in the Chancery building behind but somehow attached to the main Cathedral, sitting in a stiff chair that was beginning to feel worse than a church pew the longer he sat there.

Charlie Franklin was a licensed attorney, although he seldom appeared in a courtroom anymore. He primarily focused on helping clients avoid embarrassing situations, especially those created by their own misdeeds. Sometimes it was politicians, sometimes business leaders, always it was someone who had something to lose if their misdeeds became publicly known. Sometimes the misdeed was technically illegal, but most of the misdeeds were simply immoral. Charlie turned down helping prospective clients who were trying to avoid prosecution for a felonious act. He did have a few scruples, after all. If the client had a past criminal record – well, he could consider that in the past. He just wouldn't help them avoid another prison sentence.

Some people called him a Fixer. He hated that term. It was fairly accurate, but he hated the concept just the same. He preferred to think of himself as an Advisor to the Rich and Powerful, and he was handsomely rewarded for his ability to assist and advise his clients in staying out of the glare of public scrutiny. He was good at his profession, even though he never got any acclaim once the case was resolved. He preferred it that way. True, there were times, in the dark of a sleepless night, when he allowed self-pity to creep in, admitting that he was actually helping bad people do bad things. But he'd bring himself back by remembering that there were many good people that just made one bad mistake and needed a second chance to make amends, too. And then there were the times when he did what was required for his client and willingly accepted the fee, only to then quietly and anonymously lay the evidence of wrongdoing at the feet of law enforcement. That always made him feel better about himself.

Which is why he was puzzled by the invitation from the Cardinal. It didn't seem right that a high-ranking member of the clergy should need the kind a work for which Charlie was known. Even more, how would a Cardinal even know to contact him? Something didn't feel right about this. Perhaps this was all about him drinking the altar wine when he was twelve after all.

Behind the wall holding the mirrored cross and looking through the one-way-mirror glass of the vertical transept, a tall, portly man dressed in red got his first glimpse of Charlie Franklin seated in front of the desk. "You're sure this fellow can pull this off effectively?" the Cardinal asked. "He doesn't impress me very much. He's, well, a bit frumpy, don't you think?"

"Better that he doesn't look that competent. He'll get less attention," replied the Monsignor.

"Tell me again about his background before I go in there."

"Yes, your Eminence." The Monsignor rifled through his notes. "Born Catholic, poor family in an old neighborhood on the Southeast side of the city; attended St. Aloysius College Prep, but since fallen away from the Church. Remains a bit in awe of anyone in a clerical collar. Never married, but has had several female companions."

The Cardinal chuckled, "Haven't we all?" Then turning and bowing to the Monsignor, "Present company excepted, Wesley, but you do have George." He waved the discussion away, "Please go on about Mr. Franklin."

The Monsignor continued, "Graduate of Marshall Law School; employed soon after graduation by Sloan and Sloan, those renown ambulance chasers. He learned much of his trade from them. Broke out on his own to – shall we say – assist Walter Morrisey in his Congressional bid. You will recall that Mr. Morrisey had some ethical and moral issues that needed to be settled quietly and covertly. Mr. Franklin was instrumental in aiding Congressman Morrisey to a successful election."

"Very impressive, that bit of work," acknowledged the Cardinal, "but that was a decade ago. What's he done since?"

"The people that recommended him to me were reluctant to say. But they swear that they use him whenever the occasion necessitates and are never dissatisfied."

The Cardinal looked out again through the one-way mirror, "I don't know. He looks like a frightened choir boy out there. This is such an important bit of work ..." He turned quickly to the Monsignor, "What will happen if this turns out to be badly managed? How do we keep our name out of it?"

The Monsignor put down his notes and went to the dressing table to get the Cardinal's *zucchetto*, what the Cardinal preferred to call his red beanie. He affixed it properly on the Cardinal's head. "The less you know, the better. But to put your mind at some ease, we know he has no close next of kin. We will ensure that no one in the Chancery is implicated. He will either achieve success or we will be free to explore an alternate path without any repercussions."

The Cardinal looked hard at the Monsignor. "That is all well and good, but I still say he does not look up to the job." He crossed the room to the wet bar and poured wine into a gold chalice, draining it in a few short gulps.

The Monsignor shook his head. "I am told you will think him to be naïve, weak, that you will think he does not understand what you wish him to do. Those who recommend him felt the same way at first. Don't be deceived. And don't give him more information than what we rehearsed earlier. Tell him to expect a message from me providing all the details he will need to complete the mission."

The Cardinal rubbed the Monsignor's close-cropped buzz-cut hair. "Wesley, I know full well the importance of this mission. After all, it is my future we're talking about. Don't worry. I won't disappoint you."

After sitting in the hard-backed chair for so long a time, Charlie was startled to his feet when the door to the Cardinal's chambers flew open. He nearly knocked the chair over backwards as he rose, legs half asleep. The large heavy-set man in red cassock literally charged into the room, the Monsignor backing away with the door to avoid being run over.

Monsignor Leonard said, "Your Eminence, may I introduce Charles Franklin, the man you wished to see. Mr. Franklin, His Eminence Phelan Cardinal Maroney." The Monsignor left and closed the door behind him.

"Your Eminence," bowed Charlie.

Extending his hand, the Cardinal said, "So kind of you to meet with me, Mr. Franklin. Please join me at these more comfortable chairs by the round work table. The desk area is so terribly formal, don't you agree?"

Behind the wall the Monsignor tsked, "Already changing the script." He adjusted his own seat to look out a side corner of the two-way mirror and switched the recording system to gather the discussion from the area chosen by the Cardinal. Fr. Leonard had been with the Cardinal for several years, although he never felt secure in his role in the diocese, as the then Bishop Maroney spoke to him only seldom, and seemed to wince when he did. But over the past many months, Wesley Leonard saw a different side of his senior cleric. He didn't quite understand the change, but welcomed his new role and wanted to believe that he had become the Cardinal's most trusted and efficient aide. Wesley was elevated to Monsignor while Maroney was still an Archbishop, just a few weeks prior to his own elevation to Cardinal.

With the coronation coming, Archbishop Maroney's attitude seemed to change. He grew more affable, more liberated to speak his mind. He shared his thoughts with Wesley. He told Fr. Wesley Leonard that he had great plans that would take both of them to high places.

Father Leonard, now Monsignor Leonard, was thrilled to have been plucked from obscurity at such a young age, promoted ahead of many more worthwhile and senior priests. And the Cardinal forgave the scandals that had hounded Father Leonard in the past and even permitted him to continue to fraternize with George, as long as he maintained discretion. The Monsignor would do anything for Maroney. He believed the Cardinal now trusted him implicitly, even though he was unclear as to what the great plans mentioned by the Cardinal might be, or his own expanded role.

The Cardinal continued talking to Charlie Franklin, "I prefer to be as comfortable as possible. I spend enough time on my knees, you know." Both men chuckled. "If you don't mind, I'd like to get to know you a bit. I may have a job for the right person and before I simply offer it to someone with whom I'm just now meeting, I prefer to know that the person is the right one. Is that acceptable to you?"

"Of course, Your Eminence. I fully understand." Charlie nodded rapidly. His heart was racing and his mouth was dry. "And I hope you will excuse me if I appear nervous. I've never spoken to a Cardinal before. I'm not sure if I should fall on my knees, confess my sins, or prostrate myself."

The Cardinal bellowed out a hearty laugh, "Oh, my word! Please make yourself at ease. I'm just a man, like yourself, talking to a fellow man about an opportunity for a mutually satisfactory arrangement. Understand, I've done some research, asked around about you, done a little homework, since this project is, shall we say, sensitive, especially for someone in my position."

Charlie didn't question the Cardinal about who he may have spoken to. Charlie knew who he had done work for in the past and none of them could be called saintly. Which meant the Cardinal had reached out to the underbelly of humanity to get a recommendation about his work.

From a pocket in his red cassock, the Cardinal produced a small notebook and pen. "Now, as I hear it, you are a baptized Catholic?"

Charlie blinked, "Yes, that's true."

"You attended St. Aloysius College Preparatory School?"

"Yes. And managed to graduate," Charlie joked.

"Indeed. With a 3.6 Grade Point Average. That's impressive for such a demanding school."

Charlie sat back, "Wow! I don't even remember that. You have done your research!" Charlie's warning senses were on full alert.

"You successfully passed the bar exam and are a licensed attorney?"

"Yes. Marshall Law School, class of 1998." Charlie's smile was fading quickly. He didn't like where this was headed. But he tried not to show his concern.

"Do you have any associates who work with you, and must they know the details of your work?"

"I tend to work alone. Partners ask too many questions and can actually make easy jobs messy. I do have a receptionist who serves as a secretary. Adds to the image of professionalism," he added as a weak joke. "But she seldom knows any details of my cases."

"I'm told you never married and you have no close relatives still alive?"

Charlie shook his head. "There are a few distant cousins I haven't seen in several years. As for a wife, I never found the right woman." He wasn't about to tell the Cardinal about the one love who rejected his proposal during law school. Let's see if he brings her up. If he does, thought Charlie, I'm walking out now. Some things are best left private.

The Cardinal continued, "I understand. Sometimes no decision is better than the wrong decision." He looked at his notes, "You are no longer a practicing Catholic? Why is that?"

Charlie bristled, "No offense intended, Your Excellency, but that's between me and ... your God."

"Your Eminence."

"What?"

The Cardinal smiled, "You said 'Your Excellency'. The proper greeting for a Cardinal is 'Your Eminence'."

Both men sat back in silence for a few very weighty seconds. "I do not wish to pry, Mr. Franklin, but as a Man of God, if I can be of assistance in mending your relationship with the Almighty, I must offer my hand."

Charlie's face went expressionless, one of his best defensive weapons. "I'll let you know if either of us needs your help."

"Either of you?"

"Either me or the Almighty."

The Cardinal smiled and nodded, "Didn't intend to strike a nerve, Mr. Franklin. I've been told you are capable of quietly resolving sensitive matters for important people so that no one is even aware that something may have occurred. Is that so?"

"Your Eminence, if I were to respond to that question, I'd either be lying or admitting to a potentially illegal or more likely immoral activity on behalf of a client. I neither wish to lie to an ordained priest nor admit to any such activity, felonious or not. So, with all due respect, I prefer not to answer."

"I was warned not to underestimate you, Mr. Franklin. Bravo. Alright, then. Let me tell you a little about what I may need from you."

"OK," said Charlie, "mind if I take some notes of my own?" He pulled a notepad and pen from his sport coat pocket.

Now it was the Cardinal's turn to be defensive. "Certainly, certainly. Although if we reach an agreement, we will provide all the details of the project at a later time." He regained his composure, "You see, I was blessed to be born into a wealthy family. For a long time, my family collected ancient art, artifacts, documents of all kinds. It was something we did as a family, not to be pretentious, simply as our own kind of hobby, if you will."

Charlie said, "Wow! That's some hobby. I bet it got expensive."

"Well, after all these years of accumulating, it is priceless, I suppose. My brother keeps it all vaulted away. It would be unseemly for me to have any of the collection in my own possession."

"I can see how that might be awkward, raise eyebrows, I suppose."

"Yes. Indeed. I still dabble from time to time, can't help myself. I've become aware of a document that my brother would dearly love to have. It would complete a collection he has been gathering for many years. I wish to make it a present to him on his birthday."

"What a nice gesture," said Charlie with a smile.

The Cardinal leaned forward conspiratorially, "Here's the thing. As I mentioned before, it would be unseemly if I simply picked up the document from the dealer, what with the news media and such. And a secret negotiation linked to my name likewise runs the risk of becoming known and might appear to be scandalous, even though quite innocent. What I hope to do is make the purchase as anonymously as possible, with someone unassociated with me actually receiving the parcel."

Charlie nodded and asked, "Shall I assume that is why you asked me here today? Am I to be the recipient?"

"Exactly so. But if the recipient – you, in this case – is asked any questions, they must be willing to retain my anonymity. I have been told that you can be trusted to keep confidences."

"I've made a practice of protecting my clients. A good lawyer knows when to say something and when to keep his mouth shut. I doubt you'd have received a recommendation to contact me if I had failed to do so in the past. You should note that I haven't asked you who recommended me – and I won't. Mainly because I don't want to know, nor do I wish to acknowledge who may or may not have been a past client."

The Cardinal's face showed he was impressed. "Well said. You are proving the recommendations are correct. You are a very smart fellow." The Cardinal was practiced in disarming people with compliments. Charlie gave an "aww shucks" smile to show the Cardinal he succeeded. "Well then. Are you interested in being my secret emissary to gather my brother's birthday present?"

"You said your brother's collection included ancient art and artifacts. A lot of that kind of stuff is protected by the foreign countries where they were found or where they originated. Possessing those kinds of things can be dicey, even illegal, depending upon what it might be. Can you assure me that the item you want me to get for you is not – shall we say – a hot item? I don't want to run afoul of Interpol, or worse."

The Cardinal waved off the suggestion. "Heavens, no. My family was well aware that there were unscrupulous dealers selling both real and fake art or even antiquities that were problematic with the authorities. We actually turned a couple of nefarious fellows in when we came across them. No, we only make purchases that are legitimate." The Cardinal chuckled, "Although, I must admit, there were times when a transaction took on a kind of 'cloak and dagger' attitude. Added to the mystique, I suppose."

Charlie looked thoughtfully at his empty note pad. "There are a couple of other matters we haven't touched on." He looked up at the Cardinal, "Will this project require any international travel? I have a passport but ..."

The Cardinal waved his hands. "Oh, no, no. The parcel is ... here in the United States. Further details will be provided later."

"Uh huh. OK, that's good. About how long do you envision needing my services for the immediate acquisition? I need to balance out the rest of my schedule – other jobs, appointments," Charlie lied. "Of course, my confidentiality will remain in effect even after the immediate job is over."

"Aha. I had not considered that you might have other business to attend to. Of course. Well, I imagine that acquiring the, um, parcel and returning it to me will take a few days, no more than a week I should think. Would a week present any conflicts with other business, other matters you are tending to?"

Charlie pulled out his cell phone to give the appearance of checking his calendar. It was empty. "One week. Yes, I believe I can fit that in." He pocketed the phone, "That brings up one further matter. My fee."

The Cardinal feigned shock and put his palms to his chest. "Dear heavens! Are you really going to charge a man of the cloth for requesting such a small favor?" The Cardinal's face widened into a smile. "Of course, dear fellow, of course I expected to pay your fee. Let's see – if I enlist your services for one week, what would you charge?"

Charlie took a casual attitude, "Well, if this were straight lawyer work, the going rate is about $250 an hour. That would be ten grand for one week of forty hours. But this is different, won't require digging through law books and composing briefs. But it sounds like there may be a little bit of travel involved and it still requires my time. So, let's say we call it $6000 for the week, plus any expenses incurred. Half up front plus an expense line."

The Cardinal was a bit shocked, "Whew. That is slightly higher than I anticipated. Hopefully it won't take a full week. Alright. I assume you would like a contract?"

Charlie raised a hand. "No! No contracts. You want anonymity? Don't put your name on a piece of paper. And if you don't have an untraceable checking account, make it a money order or straight cash. Send the initial payment with your instructions. When I've procured the package, I'll return it directly to you. I will contact the Monsignor to request an appointment for – let's call it 'spiritual enlightenment'. You can put that in your calendar to avoid suspicion in the future."

In the chambers the Monsignor placed a quick call. "George? You ready? They're about to break up the meeting. Try not to let him see you following him."

The Cardinal was surprised but satisfied. "Why, you seem to have thought of everything and very quickly. I am pleased that we have come to an agreement. My brother will be very excited to receive his gift. Thank you." He rose and rang a bell on his desk. A few seconds later the Monsignor entered. "Monsignor Leonard, would you be so kind as to show Mr. Franklin the way out? He has kindly agreed to be of service to The Lord."

• • •

Back in his chambers, the Cardinal awaited the Monsignor's return. He motioned to him to pour them both wine in the golden chalices. "I think that went extremely well," said the Cardinal.

The Monsignor tilted his head. "Your brother's birthday present? That was not in our practice script."

"I came up with that on the spot. Pretty good, eh?"

"As long as he bought it without hesitation, it should be OK. I do wish you had followed the plan closer. I didn't get a good camera angle on him from where you sat."

The Cardinal waved the criticism off. "He's as naïve as new-born kitten. You got the audio though, correct?"

"Yes. Not much in it, but I liked that he doesn't want a contract. That plays right into your hands."

The Cardinal jumped forward in his chair. "I know! That was almost too much to ask for. There's no tracing it now." He sat back, "Is George tailing him?"

"Yes. He'll report in shortly as soon as he's certain where Franklin's is headed. We expect he'll just go to his office."

"Alright. I'll come see you in a few hours. But now I'm going to my chambers. Marie is due to arrive shortly. When we're done, I may have to hear her confession again."

• • •

Charlie paused as he left the chancery, taking a deep breath of the cool air freshening off Lake Erie. It made a mid-June day feel like late Spring. He passed through the iron gate bordering or protecting the entire compound. Flowering bushes interwove with the eight-foot wrought iron fence. The juxtaposition was ironic: sweet-scented flowers against an iron wall. Was the intention to be welcoming or forbidding? He shook off the thought and walked briskly toward his office. That was a strange meeting, he thought to himself shaking his head. He headed South on East 12th Street toward Chester Avenue.

At a corner a few blocks away, a stocky figure in a darkened doorway said, "Hey, Wiseguy, gotta buck?" The voice was unmistakably Moe Howard, late of Three Stooges fame. Charlie stopped dead in his tracks and stepped toward the curb away from the figure.

Another voice, "Aww, Moe. Ya' scared the guy!" It was Larry Fine's voice, also one of the Stooges.

"Shaddap you maroon!" Moe replied. The lone figure of many voices emerged onto the sidewalk. He was filthy, badly needing a shave, and his clothes were nothing better than rags. His nearly bald head had close-cut greying stubble along both sides.

Curly came to life, "Aww come on! All we want is a cuppa coffee."

Moe again, "Why I aughta..."

Charlie looked up and down the street, seeing only a lone figure, stopped thirty yards behind him. He looked at the Stooge impersonator and quietly said, "You look ridiculous." He crossed the street and yelled, "Get a job, you crazy bum!" He turned onto Chester Avenue continuing a casual stroll toward his office. A block later he entered his office building and bounded up the back stairs to the 2nd Floor.

His receptionist and secretary and once-upon-a-time girlfriend greeted him. "How did it go?"

Charlie shook his head. "Rita, I've had lots of strange meetings over the years, but this one ranks among the strangest. You don't expect a man-of-the-cloth to lie to your face, especially to lie so badly. I have no idea what this guy's really into, but it seems that I'm now somehow in the middle of it."

Rita asked, "Did he notice your lapel pin? Did the recording system work?"

"He never mentioned the pin. I'll check the tape shortly to see if it caught everything. In the meantime, why don't you clear out just in case this thing starts getting weirder than it already is. Who ever heard of a priest needing a front man?"

"Alright, but you be careful, too. I told you this sounded hinky from the start." She gathered her things, "I'll make sure the alarm system is activated at your apartment, then start a big batch of spaghetti sauce. Come home safe – and hungry." As she locked the door behind her, she yelled, "Bring home a nice Chianti!"

An hour later Charlie sat behind his desk making notes on a yellow pad, alternately listening to or rewinding the tape recording of his conversation with the Cardinal. He heard a key being used on the locked main office door. A nearly-bald, stocky figure entered the reception area, then opened the door to Charlie's interior office.

"Where's Rita?" the figure asked.

"Hi, Pete. I sent her home. She's making her spaghetti sauce for dinner at my place. You can come over if you want. I didn't want her around here until we know more about what's going on."

"Given what I saw, that's probably a good idea. But I'll probably miss out on dinner." Pete wiped away some missed shaving soap from the corner of his ear.

"Where did you get that awful outfit? The smell of those clothes lingered for a half a block. And the Stooges' bit was unnecessary, don't you think?"

"Yeah, I saved some rags for just this kind of occasion. I liked the Stooges' bit. Been saving it for quite a while. I suppose you know you were followed," Pete said as he took a seat opposite Charlie.

"I expected that I would be. Someone was a stolen base or so behind me. There's something not right about this whole thing. The Cardinal's not taking chances."

Pete smiled like he had a canary in his mouth. "Someone else is interested, too."

Charlie looked up, "What's that supposed to mean?"

"First comes some amateur from the Cathedral almost stepping in each of your footprints. He was easy to spot. Curly red hair, florid complexion. Stood out like an airplane beacon. Then someone's following him! Watching both of you. The second guy was a seasoned veteran, done surveillance before. Hit them both up for a buck. The first guy ponied up. Here's the bill. Might get a latent off it if we need to." He produced the dollar in a plastic bag.

Charlie was puzzled, "Who's the second guy?"

Pete scratched his balding head, "Dunno. Never seen him before. Not an amateur. Not a cop, either."

"Description?"

Pete screwed up his face, "Dark hair, not quite five-foot-six or so, slim build, dressed all in black. You know, he tried not to talk to me. Not 'go away', not 'beat it'. But he did mumble something. Almost sounded foreign."

Charlie sat back, "What do you mean 'foreign'? From where?"

Pete said, "If I had to swear to it on a bible, I'd have to say it sounded Italian."

Charlie chewed his lip, "You wouldn't come within three feet of a bible, Pete, but if he was Italian does that mean Rocco's boys are somehow up to something?"

"I dunno about that. I've seen the type of guys Rocco employs. Unless he's a new import, this guy didn't have the swagger. I don't think it's one of his guys."

"Interesting. Not a cop, not from the Cardinal, and not from Rocco. What the hell are we into here?"

"Yeah. I know. I mean not knowing makes you crazy. I'm gonna take off through the back. I need a good shower. Want me to do anything?"

"As a matter of fact, yes. His Eminence Phalen Cardinal Maroney mentioned a brother who collects ancient artifacts. Could you do some checking on this brother person to see what we can find out about either him or the collection?"

"Sure thing. See you later, or maybe tomorrow."

Charlie taped his pen on the yellow pad for several minutes as he considered various possibilities. In his line of work, he forms alliances – contacts that are neither always friend nor permanently foe, neither always reputable nor congenitally dishonest, people from various backgrounds who know things – people with whom you share information, offer your expertise, or occasionally trade favors. Sometimes you touch base for your benefit, sometimes for theirs. The only code of conduct between such people is that any information provided must be factual – unless to be factual is inconvenient. You only call on them when you're stumped, never wanting to abuse the fragile alliance nor look incompetent.

In the matter with the Cardinal, Charlie was out of his element and needed a different perspective. He unlocked an innocent looking small drawer in his desk and pushed aside the false bottom, retrieving a cell phone licensed to a virtually unknown and totally fictitious shell company headquartered in a storage shed in the Seychelles Islands. He dialed an overseas number.

The recipient of the call recognized the number calling him. "*Buonasera*. It has been a long time. Why do you call?"

"I have accepted a strange mission. Your guidance would be appreciated."

"*Bene*, if I can, I will help."

"A Cardinal in the U.S., Maroney, wishes my help. Any flags on this man?"

The voice at the other end paused, then said, "Others are likewise concerned over this person. They watch him. Tread carefully. Trust not. All is not what it seems. More to come if possible." With that, the line suddenly went dead. All such calls end quickly, but the abruptness of this one surprised Charlie. He returned the phone to its secret charging location. Looking down at his yellow pad, he recognized that he had traced the outline of three circles. And he realized he was hungry for a late lunch.

Charlie figured one or both of his tails might still be hanging around, but rather than sneaking out the back he went straight out the front of the building. He whispered to himself, "let's see how good these guys really are, and if they're brave enough to go right into the belly of the beast."

He headed back down Chester Avenue and turned toward the busy theatre district. Early afternoon generated patrons seeking discount tickets, stand-ins and extras running toward stage doors in hopes of appearing in a production that night, window shoppers and gawkers mixed in, cabs and cops, a tangle of traffic negotiating narrow streets originally carved for horse-drawn buggies. Charlie chuckled as he weaved this way and that, changing directions, crossing against traffic attracting shouts, curses and policemen's whistles. Once he spotted a dark-haired short and thin man dressed in black looking alertly through the crowd for his quarry. On purpose, Charlie turned back and brushed right past him, drawing him away from the hubbub and down a small side street. Charlie slowed and stopped in front of The Thespian Grill, checking the display menu that he already knew by heart, then entered.

The Thespian Grill was a well-known old hangout, once as famous as Toots Shor's was in New York City, serving decent steaks, chops and seafood. In the old days, stiff drinks were served at an enormous sunken square bar. Some of the dining areas were well-lit for those who wanted to be seen, other dimly lit to protect those who didn't. The best actors who performed in the nearby theaters always had a feature table reserved. Their photos, some as faded as their careers, still hung on the walls. The theater extras had jobs as waiters and waitresses. Celebrities, politicians, athletes, the inevitable newspaper reporters and editors – everybody who was anybody jammed in almost every night, if not for dinner than at least for a drink. The bar was usually wrapped two and three people deep.

But times change. These days the only actors that came in were the wannabe's and use-to-be's, sadly sitting at round tables sharing failures and dreams, whispering about what could've been. The Thespian Grill is still somewhat successful, although the main customer base has shifted to a significantly different kind of clientele. Gone are the brightly lit chandeliers, replaced by small dim lights on each table, dim enough to make you squint to read the menu. Some older folks still go there out of nostalgia. But for those who are famous or infamous, this darker Thespian Grill better suits the reasons for their visits. They've not come in search of quality food or drink, and they certainly hope not to be recognized.

The backroom office is no longer where the owner manages the restaurant. The restaurant manager now works out of a converted mop room near the front door. The backroom area is now the office of Rocco Parmissano, known without affection by the nickname 'The Big Cheese'. Rocco likes to be thought of as the Capo of the city and tries to keep tabs on whatever is going on, whether legal or illegal. Not everyone in his line of work agrees that he should consider himself Capo, and because of that and other casual misdeeds, there's always a certain tension hanging in the air of the Thespian Grill, enhanced by the two large men stationed by the entrance stairs like a pair of Dobermans.

Charlie was a regular patron, welcomed since he had done some covert work for 'The Big Cheese' which required a subtlety not readily available with Rocco's regular crew. He walked down the stairs into the large main dining room which wrapped around the sunken bar. He leaned to the Doberman on his left. "I've got a tail. Let him in, I'd like to see what he does."

The Doberman said, "Sure thing, Mr. Franklin."

Charlie quickly went to the back of the bar so he could face the front. Only two seats were open, one on either side of a balding, middle-aged man wearing an ill-fitting and garishly multi-colored sport coat reading a tout sheet from the local racetrack. Charlie took one of the seats and said, "Hi, Carp."

Without looking up Rico Carponi, local bookie known as The Carp, said, "Hey, kid. How ya' doing?"

The front door opened and a small, thin dark-haired man entered, trying to adjust his eyes to the gloomy interior. "Carp, take a look at the guy just walking in. Know him?"

The Carp raised his eyes from the tout sheet and took a quick peek at the stranger. "Nope. Never saw him before. Someone important?"

"I don't know. Picked him up as a tail right after I took on a job."

The Carp put down the tout sheet and looked at Charlie. "Kid, whatever job you just took, it ain't what you think it is. Take it from Rico Carponi, you got yourself a hot one."

Charlie nodded, then tapped the tout sheet. "Anything I should consider in here?"

The Carp said, "I always love taking your money, kid, but I don't give out hints. You wanna bet, I'll take your action. But based on your past success rate, you oughta stick to football." He got the attention of the barmaid, "Hey, Sally, get this guy a drink. He needs one."

The stranger looked around a bit, then quickly exited the restaurant.

The Carp said, "Your buddy didn't like the smell of the joint, did he?"

Charlie shook his head, "I thought he might be one of Rocco's guys, but it looks like that's not the case. And he's not a cop, either."

The Carp said, "Ahh, don't ya' just love a mystery?"

Sally asked, "You want the usual, Charlie?"

• • •

In the Cardinal's Chambers

The Cardinal rolled over and sat on the side of the bed, sweaty and breathing heavy. "Marie, you are a magnificent wonder. I won't ask where you learned to do that."

A naked Marie jumped youthfully off the other side of the bed, saying, "I've got lots more tricks to show you that will rock your world, 'Philly'. You've been wrapped up in those robes so long you just don't know how good sex can be." She faced the Cardinal and stretched her arms high above her head, smiling as she saw his admiring stare. "I just wish we could go somewhere together so we can really have a fun time," as she kissed his sweating brow. "I'm gonna take a quick shower, okay?" She ran into the bathroom as the Cardinal leaned back into the pillow.

"Philly," he said to himself. "I like that. Phelan, Phillip, Philly. No one else calls me that. Makes me forget who I am and what I'm about. I wonder if I'll be able to take her with me when I make my move. I'll have to look into that when the time comes. Won't be the first time in history. How did the others do it?"

The buzzer beside the bed broke his imagining. He dialed the outer office. "What is it, Wesley?"

"Sorry to bother you, Your Eminence, but George has reported in."

The Cardinal got to his feet, "Oh, good. I'll be out in a few minutes. Ask him to wait there."

Marie began toweling off. "Just a quick rinse. I need to get dressed and meet my girlfriends for an early afternoon cocktail. When can we get back together?"

"Why Miss Carlisle," said the Cardinal with mock shock, "you're not becoming an alcoholic, are you?" He gave her and the towel a huge bearhug.

She twisted away giggling and said, "At least I'm not drinking wine at 7 a.m. every morning like some people I know."

"Oh, the terrible life we clerics must live!" He began to dress. "As for when we shall be able to rekindle our romance, I've got some important business to conduct over the next several weeks. It will require my undivided attention. So please don't be upset if I don't contact you until it has all been resolved."

Marie Carlisle smoothed down her short red dress and played the part of a hurt mistress, "You've got business that's more important than me? What's so special that I have to be without you?"

"Now, Marie. There are times when I've got to be more cautious than usual. I've employed someone to help me with something very special and very secret. He's supposed to be extremely trustworthy but one can never be too sure of fellows you've just met."

"Who is he? What's so important that I've got to stay away from you? Am I supposed to satisfy myself alone? I'll need a lot more batteries."

The Cardinal chuckled, "I'm afraid I can't give you any specifics right now, but I will say it involves my future – and maybe yours, too!"

Her face brightened, "Ooh, does that mean maybe we can go off together? I'd love it if we could do some travelling – I've got some special ideas if we can get naked outside somewhere."

The Cardinal suddenly found himself getting aroused again. He stepped back, "Oh my word! Now look what you've done to me. Yes, I think I'll have to arrange that." He turned around, facing the picture on the wall of the country estate his family owned. Turning back to Marie he said, "Yes, maybe we can find someplace where we can go and be invisible together."

She kissed him and headed for the back exit leading from his room to a secret garden connecting to the main walkway from the Cathedral. "Finish your special secret work quick, sweetie. I can't wait too long."

He watched her leave. "My god, that woman has me spinning. I will take her on a trip somewhere. I've just got to." He threw on pants and a shirt, all that was necessary for a meeting with Wesley and George, and went to his outer office.

"Gentlemen, tell me what we know," said the Cardinal as he took his seat behind the huge desk.

Monsignor Wesley Leonard said, "George followed Mr. Franklin to his office, where he remains now. There were no other people seen entering or leaving the office building. George returned here after watching for the better part of an hour."

"Do you know if there is a back entrance to his office building?" the Cardinal asked George directly.

George gave a wide-eyed glance to Wesley for instructions. His natural ruddiness blushed more at being questioned directly. Seeing no reaction from Wesley, he said, "Your Eminence, I do not know if there are any other doors. I watched from the front."

The Cardinal shot the Monsignor a disapproving stare and said, "I see. So, all that we know for certain is that no one entered or left Mr. Franklin's office building through the front doors for about 45 minutes after he entered. Correct?"

Wesley tried to recover the advantage, "There's no reason to think Franklin will do anything other than complete the assignment you've given him. As you yourself said, he's fairly naïve for someone as accomplished as he is. He takes things at face-value. It's kind of his advantage. The less he knows, the better it is for him – it gives him plausible deniability."

The Cardinal considered and said, "Alright then, what's our next step? When do we give him the instructions?"

George breathed a sigh of relief as his lover protected him. Wesley said, "We're asking him to drive to New York City. Two reasons: first, it's better if there are no airplane tickets where the purchase could be traced; and second, we don't wish the package to be subject to examination or search by the TSA. George has made the appropriate hotel reservations for Mr. Franklin. Per the instructions your contact sent, the meeting time and location where the transfer will take place is included in the instructions to Mr. Franklin. When we are certain all is as it should be, I'll complete the second and final part of the wire transfer for the purchase as you recommended."

The Cardinal nodded, "I like what you are arranging. What about Mr. Franklin's fee?"

Wesley said, "I've accessed the private fund and pulled the $3000 in cash that he wants as the first half of his fee, and I've included another $1000 for his expenses so he can rent a car and pay for the hotel. We'll send the money and instructions to him later this afternoon. If he requires more funds for meals or anything else, I'm sure he'll tell us upon his return."

"If all goes well, it may not be necessary to pay him another cent," sneered the Cardinal. Again, George gave Wesley a wide-eyed stare, this time with even more concern.

• • •

After leaving the Cathedral area, Marie Carlisle sauntered into a nearby coffee shop and ordered a coffee at the counter. She took two sips, watching the door and the street through the plate glass window for any sign that she was followed. She slipped into the restroom and quickly exchanged her light-weight red dress for a short blue skirt and white silk blouse from her large purse. She rolled her long brown hair into a tight bun and pinned it in place. Donning a pair of large sunglasses, she exited the restroom and the coffee shop without returning to her coffee. At a rapid pace, she turned several corners. Seeing no one following her, she slid down a short alley and entered the back door of the Thespian Grill.

Another Doberman stood just inside the back door. "Hello, Miss Carlito," he said.

"Hiya, Tommy," said Marie. "Is Rocco in?"

"Sure is. In the office last I saw."

Another of the Crew sat just outside the office door and nodded to her that she could enter as the green light was illuminated. "Hiya, Rocco," she said, closing the door behind her. Rocco Parmissano sat behind a large wooden desk. His consigliere, Angelo DiFranco, sat on the couch.

"Marie! Good to see you. What's new?" said Rocco.

"I just left the Card. He's up to somethin' strange."

"The Rev? What kinda no good is he cooking up now?"

Marie Carlito sat on the edge of Rocco's desk. There were very few people who could get away with that. Marie was one who could. "I'm not sure what he's got going on. Said he wouldn't see me for a while, had to concentrate on some important business. Said it was super-secret, and it had to do with his future."

"His future?" questioned Rocco. "What future? He's already a Cardinal, making lots of cash under the table, got himself a hot girlfriend ..."

Marie blushed, slid off the desk and took a nearby chair. "He's hired someone to help him with whatever it is. Says he has to be extremely cautious about it. I got the impression that he doesn't necessarily know or trust the guy he's hired. All very weird."

Rocco sat back and folded his arms, "Yeah, very weird. He should come to me if he needs somethin', not hire outside help. He knows how to reach out to me. I kinda like knowin' what's goin' on in my city." He looked at his consigliere, for advice.

Angelo DiFranco had been with Rocco for almost two decades and was trusted for his strategic thinking. He had designed and orchestrated many of Rocco's most successful projects, while protecting Rocco from his impulsive and bull-headed appetites.

Angelo asked, "Marie, do you have any idea who he hired? Or why?"

She shook her head, "No. I quizzed him a bit, told him he was sacrificing some kinky sex for puttin' me off for this guy. But he wouldn't give up anything more than what I told you just now."

Angelo smiled, "You did good. I'm glad you brought this info to Rocco." And then to Rocco, "We need to sit on this and discuss. May be something, may be nothing that bothers us." To Marie, "Stay in touch with the Rev, let us know if he gives up any more info, or if he stays away from you for too long. That may give us more information about whatever he's planning."

Marie knew she was being asked to leave. "Okay, guys. I'll see you soon."

Rocco said, "Hey, Marie. You see Natalie at all these days?"

"Yeah, I'm gonna have a drink with her later."

"Ask her to stop in and see me. She's the Mayor's type and I need him to do me a favor."

Marie smiled as she closed the door behind her.

Rocco asked Angelo, "I can tell your thinkin' somethin'. What's on your mind?"

Angelo said, "This is all very preliminary but, as you mentioned, the Cardinal's in a pretty sweet place right now. What could make a rich, famous, sexually satisfied 55-ish year-old man want something more? And what might that be? There are very few guys you could hire to do something that might improve his future, as he suggested to Marie. I'll look into it quietly and see if that person is anyone we know."

Rocco said, “Just haul their asses in here and ask them direct-like.”

Angelo waved off the idea, “That might spook them into quitting whatever they’re doing, which will likewise spook the Card. We need to let him think no one is wise to him so we can find out what’s what. Like I said, may be nothing to us. But let’s find out before we chase it underground.”

• • •

Charlie Franklin’s Apartment

The buzzer from the suburban apartment lobby got Rita’s attention. She pushed the reply button, “Yes?”

A man in the lobby said, “Package for Mr. Charles Franklin.”

Rita replied, “Leave it and he’ll come retrieve it in a minute.”

“My instructions are to deliver it personally to Mr. Franklin.”

Rita said, “Then come back in half an hour.” She sensed that this latest job would require both Charlie and her to be very cautious. She hated the kind of jobs Charlie took that were borderline – either borderline legal or borderline dangerous. Sometimes, as with the Rocco job, they were both.

Ten minutes later, Charlie rapped on the door with his all-is-well knock and entered. They had developed the A-I-W Knock after Rita became jumpy with the Rocco job and pulled a gun on Charlie one night. “D’ya have the Chianti?” she asked as she stirred the bubbling sauce.

Charlie handed her the bottle saying, “It comes highly recommended.”

She checked the label, “Nice. A guy came by a few minutes ago wanting to personally hand you a package. I told him to come back in a half hour.”

“That would probably be from the Cardinal. He’s not wasting any time, is he?”

Rita turned up the heat on a pot of water. “What the heck kinda job is this? And why did you want me outa’ the office?”

"Why don't you hold off on cooking the pasta until we get the package. We can look it over together and answer that question for both of us. I'll pour us some wine while we wait."

She shut off the stove and leaned against the counter. "Why must you always get involved with something shady? Why not just be a regular lawyer and be satisfied with that? I don't know how much more of this kind of work my heart can take. I get to feeling antsy with these gigs and start making up stories in my head. Then I imagine bad things and I freak out at shadows. Better you make less money and have a regular life."

Charlie welcomed her to sit next to him on the couch with the two glasses of wine. "Rita, you would be bored if all I did was regular legal work. Even more, I would be bored with that, too. You enjoy this as much as I do. I never liked poring over those law books back in college. I can't believe things changed that much when you went through law school during the last few years. Do you want to just write legal briefs all day? Research precedents?"

She sipped the wine, "No, I hated writing practice briefs. But sometimes ..."

"I know," he said, "when it gets dangerous, we both get anxious, but that's what makes us feel alive!"

"As long as we remain alive," she sank back into the couch.

"May I remind you, I don't carry a gun. To do so is to invite someone else to pull out one of their own. You're the only person with a weapon around here, and you nearly used it on me one time!"

"See? I told you I get antsy when the job gets hinky! Maybe you just need to include me in on the details more so I understand all the ramifications. I usually give you good advice."

"That you do, Rita, that you do. OK, with this one you and I are equal partners. But the Cardinal did ask if I had any associates when I worked on projects. I told him I preferred to work alone. So, you're going to have to keep that façade in place."

Rita smiled, "I like that even better. By knowing what's going on but pretending I don't I can be of even more value. You'd be surprised how men like to believe in the 'innocent lady' routine."

Charlie tilted his head, "I'm not surprised that you like that technique. I believe you used it to get my attention in the Blue Danube, didn't you?"

Rita smiled smugly, "My goodness, a lady never tells her secrets."

While still in law school, Rita earned a living as a pretty good jazz singer in the Blue Danube Supper Club. Struggling to make a go of her life, she fell into arrears with the Cleveland Musician's Union, an outfit aligned with the Teamsters. One night she recognized Charlie as someone who had given a presentation in one of her law classes, and grabbed his arm at the bar during one of her breaks. The Union was making threats, she told Charlie, could he offer any advice, any help? She'd be forever grateful, she said. He was smitten by the pretty little brunette and told her he'd see what he could do.

A few weeks later, her past dues were forgiven and she and Charlie had a brief sexual fling. Even though it quickly became apparent that they were not compatible love partners, he hired her to work for him while she studied for her second try at the bar exam, her first try ending in failure. She kept an apartment in the trendy Near West Side while keeping a key to Charlie's east side apartment on Cedar Hill. Occasionally she spent the night there.

They both knew the arrangement wouldn't last forever. Rita was very smart, both book smart and street smart. She would eventually pass the bar and move on. In the meantime, they enjoyed each other's companionship, relied on each other's abilities, and became a fairly formidable team.

The lobby buzzer rang. Charlie leaped up and pressed the intercom button and flipped the camera switch in one motion. The screen on the wall lit up revealing a pink-faced young man with curly reddish-brown hair. "May I help you," said Charlie.

The startled young man said, "Uh, I have a package for personal delivery to Mr. Charles Franklin."

"I'll be right down," replied Charlie, switching off the intercom but leaving the camera on.

"You want my gun?" asked Rita.

Charlie chuckled, "No, you keep that thing locked up. This guy will be no trouble. Be right back."

In the lobby, Charlie showed his identification and accepted the package, no signature was required. The delivery boy turned and stumbled away from the apartment building as fast as a jack rabbit escaping a coyote.

Returning to the apartment, Charlie said, "I believe that was one of my tails from this morning."

Rita looked surprised, "One of? How many tails did you have?"

"Pete said I had two – this guy and one other behind him. This guy is strictly an amateur but Pete said the second guy was a pro. Not a cop, and not one of Rocco's guys either."

"What the hell?" whispered Rita.

"I know. Let's see what the package has in it."

Inside the large manila envelope was a rubber-banded stack of $100 bills with a sticky note saying "first half of fee", a second stack of bills made up of $100, $50, and $20 denominations with a sticky note saying "$1000 for expenses", and two typed-out pages of instructions:

• • •

Mr. Franklin is instructed to drive – not fly – to New York City. He will be receiving a parcel which is very large and delicate. To prevent poor handling by TSA Agents or baggage handlers, it is requested that Mr. Franklin travel by personal auto. A rental car has been reserved in his name at the Avis Rent-a-Car on East 14th Street in downtown Cleveland for pick up on Tuesday, June 21. He will be expected to pay for the rental out of the expense fund.

Mr. Franklin is to check into the Waldorf-Astoria Hotel on Wednesday, June 22. Reservations have been made in his name for a one-night stay. He will be expected to pay for the hotel out of his expense fund.

Mr. Franklin is to meet a person identified as T. K. Constantine in the Bull & Bear Bar within the Waldorf-Astoria Hotel at 7:00 p.m. on the evening of his arrival, Wednesday, June 22. Mr. Franklin is to wear a sport jacket with tie, and place a white carnation in his lapel button to identify himself. T. K. Constantine will contact Mr. Franklin and deliver to him a large parcel.

Since the parcel is delicate, the employer wishes that it be handled with great care to ensure that it is not damaged in any way. Under no circumstances should the parcel be opened by Mr. Franklin, T.K. Constantine or any other person. Exposure to air or sunlight may lead to premature degradation of the item enclosed.

There will be no need to provide any compensation to T. K. Constantine. That has already been handled via a private financial transaction.

Mr. Franklin is implored to drive carefully and not break any traffic laws. The safe return of the parcel to the employer is paramount.

Should any difficulties arise, Mr. Franklin is requested to return to the employer immediately, with or without the parcel. However, he is admonished not to attempt contacting the employer directly by phone. All contact should be completed through M. Leonard.

Upon his successful return, Mr. Franklin is instructed to bring the package directly to the employer, no matter what time of day or night.

Upon the successful completion of the above instructions, the second half of Mr. Franklin's fee will be paid.

• • •

"Well, that clears everything up, doesn't it, Charlie?" Rita threw her hands up in exasperation. "I feel so much better about this job. Nothing seems out of sorts to me, huh?"

"Careful, girl, your sarcasm is dripping."

"It's one thing when you're called on to deliver a message or to cover up someone's dirty stuff. That's the kind of thing you excel at. You do that all the time with no problem. And you do it legally – for the most part – and you do it here locally where you know the lay of the land and where you've got contacts if something goes haywire. But this – this is way outside the bounds of your safety net – and it may even be highly illegal."

"What sounds illegal about it?" Charlie asked.

"Jeez, you can be dim sometimes! First, the 'employer' never identifies himself in the instructions. Kinda odd, don't you think? Second, you're to meet some stranger who knows how to identify you, but you have no way of identifying him, to pick up a package of who-knows-what but sounds like something nobody wants to touch with their bare hands. Could be drugs, could be stolen stuff, could be radio-active, who knows? Third, the whole deal is paid for in cash, which should set off alarm bells in your thick head. They're using you as a mule!"

Charlie grinned, "Calm down, Rita. I also find the whole thing very odd, kind of scary, and it definitely smells like something less than legal is going on here. I just wanted to hear your take on the whole project before I weighed in." He poured more wine. "Let's heat up the pasta while we talk through this – I'm starved."

Over dinner Charlie and Rita mulled the strange instructions and the pros and cons of following them as they were expressed. They wondered what the Cardinal was trying to acquire, and why it was such a secret needing someone like Charlie to retrieve it. If there was something illegal in the package, what would Charlie's legal exposure be? Without a contract with the Cardinal, there would be no way to prove that it was in Charlie's possession only for delivery to someone else.

Following the possibility that the Cardinal was supplying at least a half-truth, they wondered if it actually could be an ancient artifact, possibly old enough and under the protection of International Law which would make its possession highly illegal. Charlie didn't have any contacts in Interpol to help him out if that was the case.

Finishing up dinner, Charlie answered his buzzing cell phone, "Pete?"

"Yeah, Charlie. Got something to share. Can I come up?"

"Where are you?"

"In my car about a half-block away. Makin' sure no one's tailing me or spying on you."

"Sure, come on up. I doubt he's still around but the little red-head guy from this morning delivered a package about an hour ago."

Pete replied, "No sign of him up front. I'll swing around back to make sure he's not still around. Be up in a few."

It didn't take long before Charlie buzzed Pete into the building, meeting him at the front door of the apartment. "Got some left-over spaghetti if you're interested. Take a minute and read through these instructions the Cardinal just sent over."

Pete shook his head, "Nah, thanks anyway. Picked up something to eat on my way over here." He quickly read through the instruction pages.

"You said you had something to share with me," said Charlie, offering Pete a seat as Rita entered the room.

"Hiya, Rita. Yeah. You asked me to look into the Cardinal's brother who's got a collection of antiquities. Well, there is a collection, alright, supposedly a pretty big one. But no one's seen any of it for years, and I guess no one has ever seen the whole collection in its entirety."

"Where's it being kept?" asked Charlie.

Pete smiled, "Wouldn't we all like to know? The family had several land holdings scattered all over the Northeast, with buildings or houses on each of the properties. From what I've gathered so far, no one is sure where any of it is, or whether it's all in one place. But that's not the biggest piece of news."

Rita laughed, "Pete, I can always count on you to bury the lead."

Pete smiled, "That's what my editor always told me. It's what we old investigative reporters call 'the big reveal'. So anyway, the brother's name is Sean Maroney, the only living offspring of the Maroney clan other than his nibs, the Cardinal. That is, if you can call him living."

Charlie said, "Fill in the blanks, Pete. What's that supposed to mean, 'if you can call him living'?"

Pete sat back, "He's in a facility near Akron. No visitors. He's got advanced Alzheimer's."

Charlie sat back hard in his chair and thought for a minute. "Let me piece this together, and check me to make sure we're all on the same page. The Cardinal wants me to pick up some package, maybe an artifact, in New York City to be presented as a gift to his brother for his birthday. He said his brother will really appreciate it, as it will complete one part of his collection. But his brother may not even know his own name at this point, let alone be thrilled over an artifact he doesn't recognize. Because this artifact may gain unwanted attention if it became known that the Cardinal has procured it, he asks me to pick it up as sort of a 'dark drop' delivery. He wants no one to examine it, so I have to drive it back here from New York, avoiding the eyes of the federal workers of the TSA. The person who has it, someone named T. K. Constantine, will find me in a bar at the Waldorf-Astoria day after tomorrow. Interesting that they chose the Waldorf, which is due to close in a couple months for a planned two-year renovation. That makes any follow-up searches for evidence fairly moot. All the fees for my services have been paid in cash. There's no contract or any paper trail on any of this. In the meantime, the Cardinal has sent someone to tail me, and someone we don't know sent someone to tail both the first tail and me. Is that about it?"

Rita said, "I think that pretty much sums it up."

Pete shook his head, "And by the way, Sean's birthday isn't until late September, more than three months from now. So much for the birthday present idea. Why don't you just walk away from this thing. It's way too squirrely." He went to the liquor cabinet and poured himself a healthy bourbon. "Anybody else want some?"

Charlie was bemused, "No, Pete, just feel free to help yourself."

Pete was oblivious, "Thanks, I will."

"No, we're not going to walk away from this one," said Charlie. "We already know too much and I think the Cardinal is more capable of sinning than he is of forgiving sins. If I were to beg off it would hurt both my reputation and possibly my ability to breathe air. We have a rough idea of the game he's playing, given that the cards are coming off the bottom of the deck, so let's work out a strategy to win this deal."

• • •

Tuesday, June 21:

At 10:00 a.m. the next day, Charlie walked the four blocks from his office to the Avis Car Rental lot, claiming the car reserved in his name. The attendant shuffled through the papers on his desk looking for the reservation paperwork.

"Aha! Yes, here it is. Oh, I see your assistant has selected a bright yellow sedan for you, sir."

Charlie tried to hide his surprise, "Really? Was that a young fellow, reddish hair?"

"Yes," the attendant recalled, "he actually did a personal inspection of the vehicle to make sure you would find it suitable."

Charlie smiled, "He's always trying to ingratiate himself to me. Let's take a look at it."

The attendant led Charlie to the lot where the car was parked. Charlie looked it over and announced, "You know, on second thought, I'd like a dark-colored SUV – like that one over there. Can we make that happen?"

The attendant was surprised, "Well, I suppose we can make that change. I'll need to change the paperwork."

"Good. Let's do that. But let's not tell my assistant about the change. He thinks I like yellow cars, but actually, I don't. He's such a nice fellow that I'd hate for him to think he did something wrong."

Thirty minutes late Charlie drove the dark blue SUV off the lot and around two corners to a parking garage a block away from his office. He walked through a back alley to enter the key-locked back door to his office building. Rita was waiting for him.

"Everything OK with the car?" she asked.

"Well, it is now. I took a different vehicle than the one they chose for me. I suspect they put some sort of tracking device on the one I was supposed to take. They're going to get a surprise when that one starts heading to Cincinnati, or someplace."

"Won't that make them suspicious, that you took a different car?"

Charlie mused, "Maybe. But it will take them a couple days to figure out what I'm actually driving, and if there's someone watching for a yellow sedan either going to or coming from New York City, they'll be sorely disappointed. If the Cardinal was just playing nice with the reservation, he won't care. If he's not playing nice – which I suspect is the case – he won't want to mention the switch."

Rita picked up a note, "Pete called. He's all set. Doing a bit more research the rest of today. Said you should google your contact's name. What pops up is not likely who you'll meet."

Charlie gasped, "You mean they used an alias? What's this world coming to when you can't trust a priest?"

"Now who's being sarcastic! By the way, I scanned this place earlier. No bugs, no devices."

Charlie nodded, "Good. Thanks. I'm getting the impression the Card and his team got very little advice and counsel on how to handle this. They're strictly amateur hour in the execution. Nonetheless, we need to be careful given the unknown third party that's taking an interest."

"When are you leaving?" asked Rita.

"In a few minutes. Gotta look a few things up, first. Like – does the Waldorf have a nearby parking garage. When I'm ready to go, I'll ask you to drive me to where I left the rental. I'll get my bags from your trunk and head off. I figure I can almost get to the New Jersey line by early evening. I want to enter Manhattan by noon tomorrow to get my bearings before the Big Meet tomorrow night."

Charlie had the information he needed and he joined Rita in her car, choosing to lay down on the back seat to avoid being seen. Rita pulled into the parking garage and took a ticket. From the back seat, Charlie said, "Third Level, look for a blue Ford SUV parked on the right-hand side." She located the SUV and pulled just ahead of it and stopped, waiting to see if anyone was around.

"Looks empty," she said.

Charlie said, "After you close up the office tonight, pack a bag and stay with a friend for a few days. I'm not sure why, but this all feels very unsettling. I'd rather you weren't alone in your apartment."

Rita whispered, "I'm a big girl. I can take care of myself, but you don't have to give me that advice twice. I was thinking the same thing."

He quickly exited the car as Rita hit the trunk button. He grabbed his suitcase and valise and threw them into the SUV. Without a word, Rita pulled away and exited the garage. He sat for several minutes in the SUV, watching in the mirrors for any sign of a tail. A young couple walked up the ramp giggling to each other. A businessman looked at his watch and searched for his keys, quickly entering a red sedan, late for a meeting. No one else. Charlie started the SUV, left the garage and made his way toward the Interstate heading East.

Three hours later along I-80, he called Rita. "Everything OK on your end? ... Good ... No, no problems for me. Can't see anything that looks like a tail. I'm varying my speeds just to be sure ... What? Oh, yeah, there is something. Find me a cheap hotel near Stroudsburg, Pennsylvania. That'll be a good stopping point around dinner time. I'd rather not drive after dark ... Great. I'll watch for your message ... Thanks. I'll be safe if you'll be safe ... OK, bye."

Around 7:15 p.m. he pulled into the parking lot of an inexpensive but clean-looking, non-descript hotel meant for road trippers. Checking into the room he sent a quick, cryptic message to both Rita and Pete: "all good here". The room had a list of nearby restaurants. He was starved, so he chose one that advertised an up-scale menu and which was only three blocks away. Time to take a little walk, he said to himself, eager to see if anyone would pay any attention to a lone stranger in the early evening hours.

The beef stroganoff was delicious. The two cocktails even more so. Maybe it was the fully satisfied stomach, maybe the cocktails, and maybe the sense that no one knew where he was as he returned to the hotel in the deepening darkness, but his guard was down. Suddenly, he thought he saw a shadow a block away, ducking around a corner. He thought he recognized the shape of the shadow: thin, 5-foot 6-inches or so, looked like dark hair. Maybe. He paused under a large oak away from the lone street light, waiting to see if the shadow would reappear.

How could anyone know I'm here? he thought to himself. I barely know where I am. He crossed the street and continued to the hotel, pausing now and then pretending to scan a house's architecture or a particularly well-shaped sycamore, all the time looking for the shadow.

He entered the hotel and stopped at the front desk. He asked the clerk, "Excuse me, but a friend of mine said he might stop by. I wonder if you've seen him. About 5-foot-6, dark hair, speaks with an accent?"

The clerk thought for a moment then said, "No, can't say as that sounds familiar. But I just got here about an hour ago, so maybe before I clocked in ..."

"Thanks. I'll just catch him next time." Charlie went up to his room, double-locked the door, and settled in for a fitful sleep.

• • •

Wednesday, June 22:

After a couple cups of lousy coffee and a days-old croissant in the hotel breakfast room, Charlie was back on his way, hoping to see a freeway sign for Starbucks. He followed the sometimes-ambiguous signage toward the Lincoln Tunnel, rising into Manhattan just past noon. His timing proved to be awful. Lunchtime in Manhattan meant pedestrian-clogged streets, impetuous cabbies, late-to-arrive delivery trucks, frustrated traffic cops – in all, a melee of people and machines each in a hurry to get somewhere with none of them succeeding.

After the better part of an hour of slipping through tight streets and missing opportunities to advance or turn, he somehow found the Waldorf-Astoria at the corner of Lexington and 49th Street. Pulling up to the valet stand, he rolled down the window and said, "You got a parking lot?"

"Yeah," the valet said, "$45 a day, but you need to go up two blocks and circle back around to enter on 50th."

"Never mind," said Charlie, resigned to let the vehicle rest in the hands of the valet. "How much?" as he handed the keys over.

"You a guest? Special deal today. Thirty bucks plus tip."

"You're a prince," said Charlie gathering his bags and heading into the hotel. He'd been to the Waldorf before, but it had been quite some time ago. The Art Deco opulence always took his breath away. He slowed his pace as he came face-to-face with the enormous bronze and mahogany octagon clock in the center of the lobby.

A bellman brought him to his senses. "Good day, sir. Will you require assistance with your bags?"

"Ah, no, thank you anyway. These are light. Just checking in."

"Right this way, sir," the bellman's arm directing the way, "and let me know if I can be of further assistance."

Charlie couldn't help but rub his palms on the black marble of the registration desk as the clerk brought up his reservation. "You have arrived slightly before the normal check-in time, Mr. Franklin, but we do have a room ready for you, nonetheless. Will the 5th floor be acceptable?"

Charlie smiled, "Yes, that will be quite alright."

With key in hand Charlie scanned the lobby for any recognizable face. Remembering his mission, he returned to the front desk, "By the way, is there a florist on duty?"

"Yes sir, on the lower level."

Proceeding to the elevators, he thought to himself, "OK, Mr. T. K. Constantine, or whatever your real name is, I'm here."

Charlie threw his bags into the room and freshened up quickly. He put on a sport coat, but not a tie, and headed down to the Bull & Bear Bar to get the lay of the land before his evening meeting. He needed a stiff drink anyway after fighting Manhattan traffic.

Entering the bar area, a stocky patron with stubbly greying hair on the sides of an otherwise bald head bumped into Charlie, feigning drunkenness. "Oh, my! Excuse me sir, your royal highness, sir. I think I've had a few, few, few too many." He gave Charlie a huge bear hug, at which point Charlie whispered, "Room 517".

Then for all to hear, Charlie said, "OK, fella, better go get some black coffee," and extricated himself from the hug, proceeding to the bar.

The bartender said, "Our apologies sir, I didn't think he had that much to drink."

"No problem," said Charlie, "he probably came in here half in the bag." He took a stool at the bar to get a feel for the landscape. "How about a Perfect Manhattan?"

The bartender said, "Coming right up."

The bar was generally square shaped with flattened corner points. Uniquely, each side was concave, bending inward toward the bartenders making the square resemble an artistically modified 'X'. The design created conversation groupings for as many as eight patrons at each corner, or in each concave curve. While architecturally odd, the result was the creation of several almost-private areas where business deals could be transacted without other patrons able to eavesdrop. Charlie looked around the room. There were tables and booths along the sides of the room, none which offered much privacy, but which could be used for the package transfer. Lighting was ample, but subdued. Across a half wall, the evening dining room shimmered in opulence. Candle lamps on each table, sparkling silver and glassware perfectly placed. The aromas of early kitchen preparations made Charlie's mouth water.

The bartender returned with his drink. "You'll want to come back tonight for the prime rib. It's the chef's specialty. That's what you are smelling right now. He slow cooks it during the afternoon."

"Thanks for the tip, it's making me hungry already," Charlie said, hoping he might manage to do just that.

Around 4:00 p.m., Charlie heard a knock on the door of room 517 – a sequence of three two-tap raps. He opened the door to let Pete in. "I hope you didn't overplay the 'drunk' scene. They may not let you back in the bar."

"Thought of that," replied Pete. "Brought something for tonight. I'll suddenly have grown some hair."

Charlie shook his head with a wry smile. Pete could be inane at times, but he was always very effective. He had been a highly respected writer at the best city newspaper in Cleveland, first as beat reporter Peter Wasniak, then as the paper's lead investigative reporter. He also wrote a column that appeared irregularly called '*Woz the Wize*', although it did not carry his byline. '*Woz the Wize*' exposed wrong doing, corruption, political and business scandals involving many of the city's more infamous characters. But when he got too close to the truth about a corruption scandal in the Governor's office, his position at the paper was severed. The excuse given was that newspapers throughout America were having a hard time making profits, and Pete's salary was among the highest in the industry, so, 'we're sorry but here's a buyout of your contract – have a nice life'. It must have only been a coincidence that a majority interest in the paper had just been purchased by the Governor's close friend and wealthy ally.

Pete switched gears quickly and began to free-lance into a role he called an Information Provider. Some would call him a Private

Investigator but Pete hated that term. He said he'd never want to earn money as a guy who took pictures of cheating husbands. But there were lots of well-heeled people in town who'd pay good money for accurate information, generally about something secretive. That's where Pete came in. From his newspaper days he had a deep well of contacts, both law-abiding and otherwise, who knew Pete would protect them as his sources, and who provided information in exchange for information that they wanted, either now or later. In the meantime, the well-heeled paid for Pete's services. His annual take quickly became more than double what he made at the paper.

Charlie paid Pete as well as he could, certainly less than he was worth, but Charlie was special to Pete, so whatever he paid was not important. Charlie had done a favor for Pete just after the newspaper incident. The favor was done quietly and without fanfare, with the ultimate result that the corrupt Governor was sentenced to 15 years in a Federal lock-up and the wealthy ally chose to put a bullet in his own brain. A friendship between Pete and Charlie formed instantaneously.

"What do you make of the layout?" asked Charlie.

Pete sat hard on what looked to be an antique chair and picked up the phone on the adjoining table. He unscrewed the mouthpiece and earpiece, replacing both when nothing was found. Eventually Pete said, "There's a nice little park two blocks south of here. I think I'll go for a walk."

Charlie immediately understood. If the Cardinal had put a tracer on the rental car, it was possible he put a bug in the hotel room, too. Charlie had to remember this was a 'road game', he wasn't in his home ballpark. "OK, enjoy", he told Pete. A few minutes later, he put on his jacket and went out for his own walk, finding the park right where Pete said it would be. It was landscaped with irregular islands of trees providing shade amidst the winding walkways, accented with a scattering of isolated marble benches – a relief for the weary. At the rear of the park where it abutted a building, Pete had located a shady bench with a clear view of both pedestrians and street traffic.

"Nicely done, Pete", said Charlie. "I forgot myself back there."

"Yeah, it was probably OK, but it never hurts to be cautious."

"How was the flight in?"

"Uneventful, which is the best kind of flights these days. Got in last night. I'm camped out in the hotel across the street. Not the Waldorf, of course, but pretty nice."

"The Waldorf's a bit stuffy for my tastes," said Charlie. "The Bull & Bear is very cool, though."

"Indeed. Almost too open for a secret meeting with your T. K. Constantine. Did Rita tell you he didn't show up in a google search? None of my contacts here in New York, limited as they may be, have ever heard of him, either."

Charlie nodded, "I'm not overly surprised they used an alias. You're right about the openness of the bar. Kind of hard to conduct a transfer of merchandise in a place that will probably be full by 7:00 p.m."

"I really don't like the smell of this. Too many unknowns. Nonetheless, I'll be sitting at the bar sipping on Coke, or something before you get there. Sightlines are not 360, so if you need me, make some sort of outrageous gesture. Otherwise, I may get bored and switch to bourbon."

"Maybe I'm crazy, Pete, but I don't think this will turn out bad. I'm not sure how I'll get the package, but I really don't expect any curveballs tonight."

"We'll see, won't we, pal?" said Pete. "Go get yourself a white carnation, I'll see you later. Text me an all clear once you've got the package and you're safe for the night. Otherwise, unless I'm needed, I'll catch my flight back tomorrow morning."

They both rose when Charlie suddenly said, "Say, Pete. You haven't seen any sign of my second tail, have you? I thought I saw him in the shadows last night after dinner in Stroudsburg."

Pete stopped and turned to face him, "You think you saw him? Or you think you saw a shadow? Which is it? You said you were not followed out of Cleveland, so how could he know where you might stop? Unless he followed you or he's clairvoyant, there's no way he'd know you were in some small town in Pennsylvania. No one has paid any attention to us here in the park, and I haven't seen our guy since Monday morning. So, if you are still confident that nothing will go wrong tonight, I'd say let's forget about the shadows and light this candle."

• • •

At ten minutes to 7:00 p.m., Charlie maneuvered into the Bull & Bear Bar, avoiding a cluster of six businessmen sloshing toward the dining room. Their departure made a sizable opening at the bar. Charlie selected a stool right in the middle of the gap they had abandoned, leaving a few seats on either side open.

He looked around for anyone who might be paying attention to him, with his inappropriate white carnation in the lapel button of his grey tweed sport coat. He spotted Pete, sipping on a Coke toward the back of the bar. As might be expected, Pete looked ridiculous wearing his cheap hairpiece, but at least the bartender didn't recognize him as the drunk from earlier in the day. Charlie looked at his watch, still short of 7:00 p.m. He always wanted to be punctual, usually arriving early for appointments.

The bartender approached him. "Good evening, sir. May I serve you?"

"Yes," Charlie replied, "Jack Daniels on the rocks, please." Even though Charlie could handle his liquor, he told himself to limit his intake to one or two, at least until the deal was finished.

He sipped his drink and again casually scanned the room. OK, Mr. T. K. Constantine, show yourself, he thought to himself.

Seven o'clock came and went. Minutes continued to tick by. He began to think the deal might somehow have been called off. Charlie casually glanced toward Pete, whose eyes were suddenly locked on the bar's entrance way. Charlie turned to see that every man in the bar was staring at a stunning blonde dominating the entrance, scanning the room. Short blonde hair framing her beautiful face, a low-cut, thin-strapped, very short black dress accentuating her perfectly shaped body, stiletto high heels making her legs look a mile long – no one could take their eyes off her. She smiled at the attention and slowly walked toward the bar, looking this way and that. She grinned and took one of the empty stools next to Charlie.

"Mind if I sit here?" she said in a soft, sultry voice.

Charlie was nonplussed, "No. No, I don't mind at all. Please feel free."

"Are you meeting someone here tonight?" the blonde smiled as she whisked her short bangs away from her eyes.

"Ah, yes. Yes, I believe that I am," said Charlie, suddenly sorry that he had something pre-arranged.

The bartender came over quickly, "May I serve the lady?"

To the bartender, the blonde said, "Vodka Martini, up, very dry." She put her hand on Charlie's thigh and whispered, "I prefer clear-colored alcohol in the summer, Scotch in the winter."

Charlie could only nod in response.

"You said you believe you're meeting someone. Aren't you sure?" she whispered a smile and squeezed his thigh.

Whatever perfume she was wearing had Charlie almost in a trance – the faintness of honeysuckle drawing him in to focus on her green eyes. "Um," he stammered, "I do have an appointment, but the party is late. I'm not even sure what he looks like."

The blonde took a sip of her Martini and licked her lips lasciviously, "Well, maybe you're not actually tied up this evening ... yet," as she gave him a wicked grin.

Despite himself, Charlie was becoming aroused. He chuckled, "Hah, well, let's see what happens and if he shows."

She touched his arm, "My name is Tonya. What's yours?"

"I'm Charlie. Charlie Franklin." Trying to make small talk, he said, "What brings you to the Bull & Bear?"

She sat back and said, "Why, Charlie, I'm here to meet someone just like you. Isn't that wonderful?"

Charlie could only think of one thing to say, and he said it only in his head, Holy Crap! This girl is good! To Tonya he said, "I think it would be wonderful if you were the person I was supposed to meet, too."

Tonya smiled, "I believe in fate. Some things are just meant to be. Here we are, two strangers sitting next to each other having a cocktail in a sophisticated hotel. Each of us has a room all to ourselves – you do have a room here all to yourself, don't you?"

Charlie cleared his throat, "Yes, I do."

"And unless your appointment arrives soon, neither of us has anything to do with the evening, all alone in our rooms."

Charlie tried to keep his head straight and his libido limp, but was having a difficult time with both.

Tonya leaned in toward Charlie resting her elbow on the bar so he could look down her cleavage if he wanted to. He wanted to. "What do you think we should do if the person you're waiting for doesn't arrive?"

Charlie shook his head, straightened up and said, "I'm sure the person I'm waiting for will arrive soon. I need to pay attention. For all I know, he's already here." He adjusted his sport coat to expose the white carnation.

She sipped her drink again, "I'm sorry, I didn't tell you my full name. It's Tonya Katrina Constantine. Most people call me TK."

Charlie's mouth dropped open. He couldn't say a word.

Tonya took the carnation out of his lapel, smelled it and let her tongue touch the various petals. "I hope that doesn't upset you."

Charlie reached for his drink and took a healthy swallow. He steadied himself. "Ms. TK Constantine, it is a pleasure to meet you."

She leaned in and whispered in his ear, "Just because we have business to conduct doesn't mean we can't be pleasant to one another."

Charlie was all but helpless. Of all the possibilities he could imagine, this situation was not one of them. "You're right. We should be pleasant to one another, as long as we can consume our business amicably."

"Marvelous!" she said. "I hope you're as starved as I am. I have reservations for dinner in the next room. Join me." She grabbed his hand, leading him off the stool.

"Wait, let me pay the tab," said Charlie, throwing a $50 on the bar and casting a quick glance toward Pete, who sat with his eyes bulged, his head hard to one side so that his hairpiece was slipping, and his mouth hanging open in a huge 'O'.

As soon as they were seated in the restaurant, TK grabbed the wine list and as the waiter addressed them, she replied, "Please bring us a bottle of this Pinot Noir." To Charlie she said, "I'm assuming we'll have the prime rib they're so famous for. A delicate Pinot won't overpower it."

Charlie was growing more suspicious that this arrangement was somehow way off base. He sat back and said, "Before we go any further, I need to get clear on a few things. You are 'TK Constantine', correct?"

Tonya looked surprised, "Well, yes. That's what I told you."

"And you were to meet someone in the Bull and Bear?"

"I'm so glad it was you," she said, "and not that heavy-set guy with the bad toupee."

"How were you supposed to identify me?"

Tonya smiled, "I was told to meet a man who would have a white carnation in his lapel. By the way, it looked silly on your sport coat. I'm sorry, I think I left the flower on the bar."

The wine arrived and was poured. Tonya tasted it and looked up at the waiter, "Excellent. We'll both have the prime rib. Surprise us with your favorite accompaniments," as she waved him away.

Charlie continued questioning, "And once you've made contact with the man with the white carnation, what were your instructions?"

Tonya smiled that wicked smile again, "I was told I could do whatever I wanted with him." Charlie showed no amusement at the suggestion. "Oh, and to give him a package which he – you, I presume – will take back to wherever he came from." She frowned petulantly, "You really need to lighten up, Charlie. You're too cute to be such a stiff."

Charlie maintained his deadpan expression, "Do you know who gave you the package and the instructions?"

"Why, my boss, silly!"

"Who's your boss?"

Tonya purposely continued playing dumb, "My goodness, don't you know about things like this? It's the person who hired me."

"What's in the package?"

Breathlessly, she said, "I don't know! Can you tell me what's in it?"

"Where am I headed with the package, and who am I giving it to?"

Tonya folded her arms, starting to get angry with the questions, and said, "I don't know where you're going with the package. Let me guess – Boston, maybe? And I assume the package is just for you. Am I right?" She softened her look, leaning into the table conspiratorially, "Look, Charlie. From time to time, I'm employed by unknown people to deliver things. We make sure it's never anything illegal. Sometimes folks want to be anonymous, I guess. We charge a really hefty fee, so I live pretty well doing this kind of work. I find it to be fun, especially when I get to meet someone attractive, like you." She began to rub Charlie's leg under the table with her leg. "But I'm only the delivery person. Let's not make this into something out of a spy novel."

Dinner was served and the conversation slowed into brief pleasantries. Charlie was still uncertain, but he began to think that Tonya really might not know much more than she said. She picked up the check saying it was essential for her firm to pay all expenses to avoid suspicion of financial corruption.

"OK, let's go get that package you seem so eager to have." She grabbed Charlie's hand and led him to the hotel elevator. She pushed the 9th floor button, and, as the door closed, she wrapped her arms around his neck and gave him a deep and prolonged French kiss. She disengaged as the doors opened on the 9th floor and led him to her room. Not a word was spoken. Charlie was trying to quell the excitement in his body and failing miserably. He tried to keep his wits about him, since this was the key reason for the trip, the reason he had been hired by the Cardinal.

She opened the door of her room and led Charlie in. "Take off your shoes and that awful sport coat, Charlie. Relax for a minute." She kicked off her high heels. "I love these shoes, but after a while they hurt." She moved in close to Charlie and undid his tie. "You don't wear one of these too often, do you? You look uncomfortable." She stepped back a few feet from Charlie and slipped the skinny straps of her dress off her shoulders, unzipped the back, and let the dress fall to the floor. She wore no bra, only small, frilly panties.

"What are you doing?" Charlie asked.

She smiled, "Taking my clothes off, silly. What does it look like I'm doing?"

Charlie swallowed hard, "Why?"

She lowered her head and smiled wickedly, "Most men are happy when I take off my clothes. They don't usually ask questions." As she slipped off her panties she said, "You need to get started, too."

Charlie shook his head, "What about the package?"

"Shh!" she said. "I'm getting naked to prove to you I'm not wearing a 'wire'. You need to do the same. Otherwise, there will be no transaction." She approached him and undid his belt, "You don't do this very often, do you?"

"Do what?" Charlie asked, slipping off his shirt.

"Deliver or receive packages. There are certain protocols that are occasionally necessary. I was told to be sure you were not 'bugged'." She pushed his pants to the floor and slid her hands into his boxers. "Mmm. I'm not sure about this. Seems like it could be the biggest, hardest 'wire' I've ever come across." She spun him sideways and pushed him onto the bed, pulling off his boxers. "I need to examine this," she said, jumping onto the bed. "Feel free to examine me any way you want."

Several hours later, Charlie returned to his room, package in hand along with a mildly guilty conscience. He had fully enjoyed his encounter with Tonya, quickly losing his anxiety and engaging with her in full-out lust. Explore as they might, neither found a wire on the other. But now he was wondering if there was anything about the encounter that he'd missed – something which could later be a problem. Around midnight, he sent a text to Pete: "all is well...travel safe". Pete texted back, "You've got some serious explaining to do."

• • •

Thursday, June 23:

Charlie left New York early, crossing into New Jersey around 7:30 a.m., package safely stored in his valise. The package had some heft to it, at least five pounds, just over a foot wide and about 16-inches long, at least four inches thick. Tightly wrapped in several layers of plastic, heavily taped, over a brown butcher-paper wrapping, he could nonetheless detect the edges of what felt like a thick binder through the protective layering. It seemed to hold several dozen pages of some sort of document. He was suspicious of the contents, especially given the melodramatic intrigue of the assignment. But he was not about to pry open even a corner. There was no way to undo even an edge of the package without revealing an entry point. Despite his curiosity, at this point he just wanted to deliver the package and complete the job without further incident.

He drove quickly toward Cleveland while staying within the legal limits and stopping only as necessary for fuel and comfort. Occasionally his thoughts drifted back to TK Constantine. The only word he could find to describe her was "sultry". He knew there were individuals who served as intermediaries between two people who didn't want to be seen meeting. These 'go-betweens' were usually non-descript, average looking people who any witnesses would have trouble picking out of a line-up. He had met a few of them, but never anyone like TK. Having seen her once, no one would have a problem identifying her again. Why would anyone choose her for such a quiet, private transfer of goods? He almost hoped that he would meet her again sometime, and he was fairly certain that he would. Sometimes you just get a sense – a sixth sense, maybe – that a person you just met would show up again in your life when you least expect it, or when you most need to see them again. That was how Charlie felt about TK Constantine. He smiled to himself. Maybe it was just wishful thinking.

Pennsylvania seemed to take forever to pass through. Once in Ohio he was on his home field, and he began to feel better. He made one last gas stop approaching Akron and placed a call to the number given him by the Monsignor. He told him he needed to see the Cardinal for "spiritual enlightenment", and that he'd be there in just over an hour.

The Monsignor seemed both surprised to get the call and excited that the package was on its way. "Oh! It's you! And you have the – parcel – which we discussed?"

"Yes. That's the way it's supposed to work. You give me an assignment. I deliver on your request. Isn't that what you wanted?" asked Charlie, a bit dumbfounded by the response he was receiving.

"Um, yes. Yes, of course. It's just that ... well, we didn't expect you so soon."

"Will His Eminence be there to receive me? I believe my request for 'spiritual enlightenment' can only be delivered through him, personally."

The Monsignor was at a loss for words momentarily, "Um, let me check his schedule ... ", Charlie could hear muffled talk in the background as the phone's mouthpiece was covered. Finally, "Yes, His Eminence eagerly awaits your arrival. An hour, you said? Around 5:30?"

"Give or take a few minutes for traffic."

The Monsignor regained his composure, "Where are you right now, exactly? What route will you be taking?"

Charlie's antennae were suddenly on high alert. "I'm somewhere in Ohio, and I'll be taking the most direct routes from here to you. Have my money ready." He hung up. Before continuing on the road, he called Pete. "How was the flight back?"

Pete said, "I hate airplanes. I inevitably have to sit next to someone uninteresting ... unlike some people's luck when they choose a stool in a bar."

"I'll tell you all about it as soon as I see you. Speaking of which, are you free in about an hour?"

"Can be. What's up?"

Charlie told him about the strange call with the Monsignor. Both agreed it sounded unsettling and made plans accordingly. Pete said, "Maybe they still think you're in the rental with their tracker."

"Maybe," said Charlie, "but the sooner I make the delivery the safer I'll feel."

Arriving in Cleveland, Charlie pulled into the parking garage near his office and found Pete's car on the second level. He moved his bags to Pete's trunk, but brought the package with him to the passenger seat. Without a word, Pete exited the garage and circled the block around the Cathedral looking for anyone suspicious.

Charlie said, "They haven't had time to react."

Pete replied, "Looks clear, but be careful anyway." He stopped at the rear of the Cathedral and Charlie slipped out, moving quickly to the side gate entry to the chancery.

He pushed the communication button at the gate. A few seconds later a voice said, "May I help you?" It was the Monsignor.

Charlie spoke into the device, "I seek spiritual enlightenment from the Cardinal." The buzzer indicated the gate lock was open. Charlie entered quickly, looking behind him and to all sides. He remembered something his father once told him: "A sure sign of panic is when the prey circles around, looking for his attacker." Charlie stood still and gathered his wits, then proceeded confidently to the chancery door.

Inside, the Cardinal watched Charlie's approach on a hidden camera telecast. "He seems way too confident, Wesley," but Monsignor Leonard had already left to admit Charlie. "At least he has the package. We can deal with him later. The package is the most important thing."

The Monsignor opened the door and nodded to Charlie, allowing him to enter. He said, "I'll take the package to the Cardinal."

Charlie held the package close to his chest, "Nope. The deal was that I deliver it directly to the Cardinal, into his hands."

The Monsignor persisted, "But I have your money here in this envelope," pulling a thick, letter-size envelope from his pocket.

"That's all well and good, and I'll be glad to take it once the package is in the Cardinal's hands."

Leaving his eaves-dropping position, the Cardinal entered the room. "Ah, Mr. Franklin! So, you have returned! Wonderful! Is that my package? How dutiful of you to bring it by – I assume you've just gotten back into town?"

Charlie said, "Yes, it's your package, and yes, I just returned from New York City. Here you are."

"Marvelous! I can't wait to open it and view its contents."

"Go ahead," said Charlie, "I'd like to see what I've been carrying around."

The Monsignor jumped in, "That's not possible ..."

The Cardinal interrupted, "Ah, but I wish I could show you, Mr. Franklin. Unfortunately, special precautions must be taken so that the contents are not exposed to excessive environmental factors for fear that permanent damage could result. I, myself, will be forced to put on gloves to handle it in a darkened and sealed room." And then to the Monsignor, "Do you have Mr. Franklin's final payment, Father Leonard?"

Charlie accepted the envelope offered by the Monsignor, "Thank you, gentlemen. If you ever need my help again, feel free to call." With that he waved and exited the chancery, wasting no time clearing the wrought-iron gate and moving toward the rear of the building where Pete's car was idling in the late afternoon shadows.

"No one followed you in or out," said Pete.

"Thanks for checking. Let's do a few laps before I get the rental, just to be sure." He opened the envelope and riffled through what appeared to be thirty, one-hundred-dollar bills. "Payment looks right."

"You gonna tell me about last night?" Pete asked, turning left and right around corners watching for a tail that wasn't there.

"You saw. The blonde was TK Constantine herself – Tonya Kristina Constantine. She had the package. Now it's with the Cardinal."

"That part I figured out. I retrieved the flower you left on the bar. Stupid place to put the microphone. But maybe you didn't want a recording of the, uh, negotiations."

"She pulled the flower. Maybe she knew what it was. She's a pro at this kind of stuff. Checked for a wire and everything."

"That so? Probably had to pull off your shirt as proof, huh?"

Charlie shook his head, "Whatever you're imagining, it's probably real close to accurate. I'd invite you over tonight but I'm worn out." As Pete pulled up to the garage, Charlie said, "I'll call you tomorrow and we can debrief on everything and I'll give you your cut."

Pete opened the trunk and grabbed Charlie's arm, "Be careful and watch your back. That little blonde may have been a distraction to knock you off your game. There's still the issue of who's been tailing you."

"You don't think this is over, do you?"

Pete shook his head, "It's been too neat, too tidy. Given the weirdness of the assignment, the last 48 hours have been too precise. No, this isn't over. Is Rita somewhere safe? We need to keep her there for her own protection."

Charlie stood back from the car, "I told her to stay with a friend for a few days. And she's got a gun. Maybe I should have kept her closer for my own protection."

After returning the rental car, Charlie threw his bags in the back of a cab and headed to his apartment, too exhausted to even think. As the cab pulled to a stop in front of his apartment building, he didn't look around. Had he been more diligent, he might have seen the thin, dark-haired man dressed in black watching from behind a tree across the street.

• • •

In the chancery
Cardinal Maroney fondled the package delivered by Charlie, delicately rubbing the plastic covering as if the wrapping itself was priceless. "I'm taking this into my residence, Wesley. Make sure I am not disturbed."

"Do you wish my assistance," the Monsignor asked hopefully.

The Cardinal clutched the package to his chest and said dismissively, "I'll call you if I require your help." He firmly closed and locked the door of his residence, leaving the insulted Monsignor to tend to the outer office. Hands shaking, he carefully slipped a sharp knife into the plastic. It took some time to cut through the multiple layers protecting the parcel. Torn and ripped plastic began to accumulate on the floor. Eventually he reached the butcher paper, itself wrapped around in several layers. What lay before him took his breath away. A thick binder with a scrolled leather covering, front and back held together with leather thongs. He could only imagine what the dozens of ancient pages inside would look like. He carefully, shakily, lifted the top cover of the binder.

"My God!" he exclaimed. He turned the first page slowly. "What the ...," he blubbered. Turning the pages faster and faster he searched for one page, one document, that would be what he was hoping for. The deeper he dug into the pages, the angrier he became. "Nothing. Nothing here but this trash!" He picked up the phone and called the outer office.

"Yes, Your Eminence?" said the Monsignor.

"Get in here at once!" the Cardinal shouted.

The Monsignor tried the door, locked. He knocked.

The Cardinal, realizing he had locked the door, bolted up from his table and roughly ripped the door open. "It's not here! None of it is here!"

The stunned Monsignor said, "What do you mean? It was delivered just as we directed."

"It's garbage, that's what it is. Come look. All of these pages – lists of the priests accused of sexual abuse from Boston, New York and Philadelphia. Hundreds of them."

Shuffling through the plastic and butcher paper strewn on the floor around the table, the Monsignor went to the book. Each page he looked at carried the photo, biographical information, current address, and list of crimes on priests from the Northeast United States. Some pages carried two or three names, others only one, as the list of crimes filled the page to the bottom. He closed the cover and with mouth hanging open stared at the Cardinal. "What does this mean?"

The Cardinal was furious, "It means we've been had! Someone gave us this – this shit—instead of what we were told we were buying."

"Do you think it was Franklin?"

The Cardinal shook his finger and said, "Sit down, let's figure this out. Would Franklin have been smart enough – no, stupid enough – to have crossed us?"

The Monsignor said, "He's the only one it could have been. He got the package in New York, then switched it before delivering this."

"Too easy," said the Cardinal. "He's the natural place for us to look. I got a message this morning saying the transfer had taken place late last night. Would he have had the time to put together such an elaborate hoax? And what reason could he possibly have to do it?"

The Monsignor shook his head, "He came highly recommended ..."

"Yes. If he is responsible for this, he must know his reputation in this town will be burned."

"But he purposely changed cars to avoid our tracker. Maybe he was angry and this is the payback."

The Cardinal considered, "Or it could be that George just botched the job. Franklin may not even have known about the tracker. Let's think it through from the other side. What do we know about this fellow, TK Constantine?"

The Monsignor thought, "Well, we were given his name in the communication you were sent. We don't really know anything about him. But again, we were told he was very thorough and capable, and of the highest integrity in getting the job done."

"So, we're taking someone's word on this guy, and that guarantee came from someone we also don't really know. Who else is there in this deal that we don't know anything about?" The Cardinal was clearly exasperated. "All I know for sure is that I'm out $6000 for a binder of crap."

"Plus $1000 for expenses," added the Monsignor.

You're not helping," sneered the Cardinal.

Trying to avoid being the target, the Monsignor said, "What about the original dealer? If Franklin did as he was told, and if TK Constantine did as he was told, what about the man who prepared the package in the first place?"

The Cardinal considered the idea. He had not told the Monsignor everything about the deal, just enough to be helpful. "Okay, something I haven't told you."

"I assume there are many things you haven't told me, Your Eminence, but that doesn't change my devotion to you."

The Cardinal nodded, "You're a good man, Wesley. My trust in you is well-founded. The dealer is a person named Merke Edelstein."

"Who is he?"

"She, Wesley. Merke Edelstein is from the Near East. She's a dealer in ancient documents, centuries-old texts. She is the one who prepared the package which I supposedly purchased."

The Monsignor was astounded, "You're dealing with a Jewish woman? You said it was an artifact from the Holy Land. If it is a document, would the Israelis consider it part of their sacred ancient culture?"

The Cardinal sniffed, "I'm not so certain they'd consider it 'sacred', but they likely would not want it to fall into the wrong hands. I don't consider my hands to be the wrong ones."

"Would this 'Merke' person have sent you this," he said, pointing to the binder.

"It appears we will have to make some inquiries. We have three possible candidates for this mess: Mr. Franklin, Mr. Constantine, and Ms. Edelstein. Before we make a rash decision on what to do and to whom, we need to figure out who the culprit is and why."

• • •

Friday, June 24:
Mid-morning the next day, Pete unlocked the office door and found Charlie at his desk looking bedraggled. "I guessed that you could use a coffee and given your appearance it looks like I guessed right."

"Thanks, Pete. I do need that coffee," said Charlie reaching for the cup. "I was on the phone with Rita most of the night going over all the events – she especially wanted to hear the intimate details of my encounter with TK. She thinks it's all hilarious. I kept trying to tell her about your warning that none of this is over. I'm not sure she agrees yet."

Pete shook his head, "Could have predicted that. She may not want to admit it, but she's probably a little jealous and possibly spooked. You two did have a brief fling, and she may feel she has a prior claim. Plus, this has been a strange case from the beginning. She can be one tough lady, but when things get hinky she gets frightened."

Charlie looked up from the un-sipped coffee, "I wasn't looking for something like this encounter with TK. Maybe if I had thought through the different possible scenarios of this job and what I might run into, I'd have been more prepared to fight it off. But, man, this caught me by surprise. Who would associate a babe like that with a job for a Cardinal? Before I knew what was happening, I was staring at a naked gorgeous blonde two feet in front of me."

"Jesus, Charlie, spare me the details. When I saw you two leave the bar, I knew you were toast. Let's allow things to settle down and see if you still have a tail. What do you make of this whole gig? Do you think the Cardinal somehow wanted to ice you once you delivered?"

Charlie finally sipped some coffee, "You know, I'm not sure what he had in mind. I certainly caught his monsignor off guard by delivering the package earlier than they expected. The red-cap didn't want me around when he opened it up – not really a surprise – and he ushered me out pretty quickly. I'm just glad it's over now."

Pete shrugged, "It's not over, Charlie, and you know it. Maybe your direct dealings with the Cardinal have come to an end, but I just have this feeling there's something else going on. For instance, people have been asking around about what the Cardinal is up to. Also, they want to know if I knew what you were up to. One of Rocco's guys called me for information, since that's what I'm known for delivering."

Charlie was surprised, "Rocco!?! What does he care what the Cardinal is doing? Or me, for that matter?"

"Dunno. It was Angelo who called me, and I've never even met him face-to-face."

"Holly crap, DiFranco contacted you directly? Since when does a consigliere make inquiries to an old newspaper man?"

Pete grunted, "I'd prefer you say a former newspaper man and not make me sound as old as ink. I figure they want to keep the inquiries very quiet. Angelo was subtle about it, which is why they didn't let any of the goons make the call. He knows how to ask questions without it seeming heavy-handed. But I definitely got the impression they're interested in what the Cardinal is up to."

Charlie sat back, "What the hell *is* he up to? The story about his brother was a ruse. And why did he need me to pick up the package? Do I look like FedEx? Why the explicit instructions about the New York pick up? And why was the blonde involved? Even if it is only about an old artifact or document, there are other ways, better ways, of handling a transfer of something so valuable. There were too many attempts to track my where-abouts or deflect my attention."

Pete said, "It feels like the package, whatever it is, may be a means to an end. Like maybe he needs the cover that you provide so he can use it to get something else, something that means more to him than a bunch of old documents. If that's the case, it helps explain why Rocco may be interested."

Charlie thought about it for a minute, "You think I should go see Rocco?"

"Hell, no! What would you tell him? What could you tell him? Your reputation is built on keeping your mouth shut. What would you do, say, 'Hi, Rocco, just wanted you to know I took a job for someone – can't tell you who – and it involved – can't tell you what – have a nice day.' He'd love that, wouldn't he? I'd be searching for you at the bottom of Lake Erie."

"Alright, alright. I get it. So, what do I do now?"

Pete said, "You take on the next job and you try to forget about this one for the time being. To wit: I have a feeling you're gonna hear from our dear Mr. Mayor soon, and he'll be willing to pay a hefty fee for your assistance in making a bad story disappear." Charlie looked at Pete over the coffee cup. "A little birdie told me," smiled Pete.

• • •

Saturday, June 25:
Angelo DiFranco knocked, awaiting the green light "OK" before entering Rocco's office. He sat down in a chair facing Rocco, who was analyzing the daily returns from the numbers runners who worked the Hough Avenue area.

"You know, Angelo, we've been makin' more dough on the numbers since the lottery came to the State. My old man fought hard to keep the lottery out. He was afraid it would kill our business. But all it did was teach everyone how the game works, meaning more players and more money for us. We can even use the State's drawing numbers so we don't have to manipulate the returns at the race track anymore. Saves on the expense, draws in more money. What could be better!"

Angelo smiled, "You did the right thing by letting the State boys do their work. They even cleaned up some of the bars and carry-outs where the heaviest action is so even the old grandmas don't mind going in anymore. The nickels and dimes add up quickly. And if one of them hits the number, the whole neighborhood spreads the word and everybody's laying down money."

"Ain't that the truth," Rocco said. "That's another thing my old man was wrong about. He didn't want too many people winnin' 'cause it cut profits. But the conversal is what really happens, the more winners, the more players, and the better profits we make." He put down the analysis report, "So you got somethin' for me?"

Angelo nodded, "Yeah. About the Cardinal. Seems he's looking for some sort of document – may even have found it. Sent Charlie Franklin to New York to retrieve it."

"Charlie Franklin?! He can be pretty pricey for a priest to hire. What'd he need him for?"

"I'm not sure. Charlie can keep his mouth shut, so maybe that's why the Card went so big time. He called a couple political bigwigs to get a recommendation for someone who could get things done quietly, and they all recommended Charlie. What they didn't tell him was that Charlie keeps a back-file on all his clients as a safeguard."

Rocco giggled, "You know, it's funny. I like the guy, even though he could cause me lots of problems with what he's got on us. You just gotta admire Charlie's *cojones* for goin' toe-to-toe with me. I respect that. He knows I could make him disappear; I know that if I do, this place will be crawling with Feds. Stand-off."

Angelo said, "I'm wondering what he'll find on the Card. We're protected from the Cardinal going rogue on us. What we have on him and Marie is probably enough of a threat to keep Maroney in line. But the bigger question is what exactly this delivered document means to the Cardinal, and why."

Rocco sat back, "You know, that fat boy usually comes to me if he's got somethin' he needs taken care of. But he never said a peep about no documents he needs picked up. Which means he didn't want me to know about it. You put that together with what Marie told us and my suspicions get raised. Whatcha' think should be our next move?"

"We wait," said Angelo. "Whatever is going on, this feels like it is only the beginning. We wait, we watch, we listen for chatter. We could call Charlie to come here, but he won't tell us anything we don't already know, and he'd likely be insulted that we thought we could make him talk." Angelo shifted to the other side of the chair, "And there's one more thing."

Rocco hated Angelo's habit of adding 'one more thing' to his advice. "Now what? You know that pisses me off when you do that."

Angelo shrugged off the criticism, "Rico the bookie who sits at the bar, everyone calls him 'the Carp', he reports that on the day Charlie was hired by the Cardinal, he came in here for lunch with a tail. Not one of ours, not a cop, and not from the Cardinal. Rico didn't recognize him. Joey was guarding at the front, he didn't recognize him either, but said the guy looked just like one of his cousins. So, I'm thinking the guy was maybe Italian."

Rocco sat up straight in his chair, "What the hell? You said the papers Charlie picked up for the Cardinal came from New York – you think someone from there was on our turf?"

Angelo shook his head, "If it was one of the New York families, they'd have sent us a complimentary notice that they were sending someone in. That's common courtesy. No, this is something else. Maybe he wasn't Italian, maybe Greek or something. But we need to stay low until we know more."

"I don't like the idea of someone wandering around my city following people into my headquarters without my permission. You check the tape from the front door camera?"

"Yep. No idea who he was. About 5' 5", maybe 5' 6", dark hair, wiry. I'll grab some stills to show you. Anyway, with someone else interested, let's pretend we don't know anything, and see what develops next."

Rocco scoffed, "Won't have to pretend – we DON'T know anything!"

PITCH NUMBER TWO

Wednesday, June 29:
At Charlie's Office

Several days passed. True to Pete's tip, Charlie received a call from the Mayor requesting his immediate assistance in stifling a possible scandal regarding a marital infidelity. It seems that shortly after the Mayor provided cover for one of Rocco Parmissano's activities, he met a lovely young lady named Natalie at a cocktail reception for a business which was thinking of moving their headquarters to town. As the reception ended and everyone departed, the Mayor recognized that Natalie was standing outside. He approached her and offered her a ride in his waiting limo. He escorted her into her hotel and up to her room. An hour and a half later, he took his limo home. Now there was some cover-up needed which required an exchange of cash, some to Natalie and some to Charlie.

After concluding that business the night before, Charlie lazily returned to his office at midday to check for phone calls. He was startled to find the lights on at the reception desk. Coming around the corner was Rita.

"Hey," she said in a voice with no enthusiasm.

Charlie stopped at her desk, "Hey, yourself. Are you OK? You look tired."

"I'm wiped out. Spent the last few nights at Stephanie's. She and I met up with the girls at the Blue Danube for some drinks a few nights ago, and I caught sight of a guy all dressed in black, sitting alone in a dark corner. Didn't match your description – this guy was taller and heavy set, tight blond crew-cut almost looked bald. Steph said he kept looking at me but I don't think it was because he found me attractive. I got this weird sense we were followed home, although I never spotted anyone. So, I sat up all that night with my gun in my lap."

Charlie shook his head, "This is not good. We need to keep tighter contact and security. Is Stephanie aware of the guy in black? Will she watch your back?"

"Not really. She's fun to share a bottle of tequila with, but she ain't no Rambo. I think I'll go back to my place and prop a chair against the door."

"No," said Charlie emphatically, "You gather some duds and stay at my place. The second bedroom is open. I'm no Rambo either, but I'll defend you if you defend me."

Rita demurred, "Look, Charlie, we had a thing for a while, but we both knew we were never going to get married. I didn't want that, never did. You don't want that either. We sort of fell together by accident. You took me in when I needed a place to go. You helped settle me down. We had some great sex together. But, despite my learning how to cook while I was with you, I don't want to be a settled down girl. So, if I'm to move in for a while, let's have a set of rules. I'll stay with you until the coast is clear and I'm ready to go it alone. That may be tomorrow, next week or next month. In the meantime, you and I can come and go with whomever we want, no questions asked and no excuses needed. And if we're home all alone and the mood strikes, we can fuck like bunnies. But when I'm ready to leave or when you say 'get lost', we'll part friends with a hug and a kiss and warm memories. Whadya say?"

Charlie gave a smile, "Very mature outlook. Which one of your friends gave you such insight?"

"When five girls share a couple bottles of chardonnay and a bottle of tequila, wisdom is the likely result," said Rita, "along with a lot of throwing up."

Charlie dropped his head and smiled, "Well, I can't disagree with your assessment. And your new set of rules make sense. But I'd like to add a codicil or two."

"Don't you ever stop being a lawyer?"

"First, for security, you have to let me know where you are going to be. Always."

"Okay, as long as you give me your itinerary, too."

"Agreed. And second, neither of us will bring a sexual conquest back to the apartment – especially Nick. I really dislike Nick."

Rita grinned, "You hate him just because he's a drummer, and drummers are great lovers."

Charlie waved his hands, "Too much information already. Do we have a deal?"

Rita nodded, "Deal. But you have to agree to go into some of the gory details about your encounter with TK Constantine. First, to see if I can pick up any tips for attracting guys, and second, to see if we can piece together what happened in New York."

Charlie shook his head, "I've moved on from that case. No need to go over past deeds and misdeeds."

"Actually, there may be a need. I haven't told you yet. The Cardinal's office left a message on the answering machine. They'd like to see you this afternoon. They said around three o'clock."

• • •

At the Chancery

The Cardinal questioned the Monsignor, "You left the message? Did you insist that he come?"

The Monsignor nodded, "I did leave the message on his answering machine. If he checks his messages, I believe he'll be here. Remember, he still thinks everything with the original delivery was fine, acceptable in every way. There is no way he would conduct his other business and continue life as normal if he suspected something was amiss. The only difference we can see from before the New York trip is that his receptionist has not been seen for a while. She may just be off on vacation."

The cardinal mulled those thoughts, "Perhaps. Perhaps she is on vacation. Perhaps Mr. Franklin knew nothing of the switch of packages. Ms. Edelstein claims it was a mere mix-up and she'd be happy to provide the proper documents we seek – as long as we agree to pay just a little bit more." He rose from his chair and began pacing, "I'm stuck, Wesley. Merke Edelstein has what I want. I must go through her to get the document, despite the fact that I now do not trust her. What if she doesn't deliver again? She might continue to scam me and hold me up for more money. I told her I wanted Mr. Franklin to deal directly with her this time, hoping that might spur her to more accuracy in her delivery. But she declined. She says she only uses intermediaries, preferring to keep her whereabouts unknown."

The Monsignor said, "As you requested, I've made inquiries about her. No one seems to know who she is, or where she resides. Actually, some of the sources I've contacted believe there is no such person, that it is an alias. How sure of her are you?"

The Cardinal continued to pace, "My family used her as the source for many of the antiquities we own. There was never a problem before. Of course, many of the purchases were made by my father. I only made purchases from her on rare occasions, and only with his assistance. My brother, of course, rarely had any contact with her, not that his opinion would mean much today anyway."

"So, what is our plan with Charlie Franklin when he arrives, how are we to instruct him?"

"When Mr. Franklin arrives, if he arrives," said the Cardinal, "we will simply say we have another receipt of – let's call it – the second part of the document. We'll say it was inadvertently separated from the original." He turned to the Monsignor, "How does that sound?"

The Monsignor considered and said, "Plausible. But what details do we provide him? Timetable? Location?"

"Nothing has yet been provided by Ms. Edelstein. We'll simply ask if Mr. Franklin will accept the proposal to be the delivery person again."

"He'll likely be suspicious. What if we add a little investigative work to his role, sweetening the pot while playing to his suspicions?"

The Cardinal sat down intrigued, "What do you have in mind, Wesley?"

The Monsignor smiled, appreciating that his Machiavellian tendencies were being accepted. "Mr. Franklin is known to have many contacts and is able to sort through many complexities. We have some question as to the existence and whereabouts of Ms. Edelstein. Instead of simply using Mr. Franklin as a glorified delivery boy, let's use him for his true strengths. Let him find Merke Edelstein for us. Knowing who she really is and where she resides will give us a wedge against her and prevent her from reneging on the deal."

The Cardinal thought for a moment, "You realize that we will have to ensure Mr. Franklin's eternal silence if he finds her."

The Monsignor nodded. "It is fortuitous that we didn't take any action against him upon his recent return from New York. If we had, he'd be unavailable for this new mission. But you are correct, he will have to be dealt with in a permanent manner – and perhaps, Ms. Edelstein as well."

The Cardinal smiled, "Wesley, you are becoming more and more valuable to me by the day. Do you think George is up to such heinous activity?"

Wesley shook his head, "No, George is far too sweet. But he has some relatives in Boston who are definitely up to the task. I don't believe they are currently incarcerated. They would likely welcome a cash paying job in a different city. Once we have the package you want, we can put it all into motion rather quickly."

"Excellent," he said, heading for his residence door. "Please ask George to invite his relatives to town. It would be best that they learn their way around our lovely metropolis before going to work. Let's put them up in that old hotel we've renovated for homeless people. No one is in it yet, so it should serve as a fine place to board them for a short while." He stopped and sighed, "I've missed Marie these past few weeks, and I want her to be able to come by soon." He opened the residence door only to hear the smoke alarm still screeching. "Damn, isn't that electrician here yet? That thing's been going off for the past four hours."

The Monsignor said, "He's been working on it for quite a while. He said it was a complex unit with three inputs. Shouldn't be much longer."

The Cardinal sighed, "Well, I'll take a 'rosary walk' in the garden to avoid any interruptions. Let me know when Mr. Franklin arrives, or when the electrician is gone."

• • •

At the Thespian Grill

Angelo DiFranco knocked for admission to Rocco's office. When the green light illuminated, he went in. "Hey, Rocco. Just so you know, we've got our guy in the Cardinal's residence right now retrieving the flash drives with the sex recordings. He's putting in new drives for future episodes."

"Good job, Angelo. Wish we could just control things remote-like so we didn't have to go in like this. Raises suspicions, even from a dummy like Maroney."

"I know, but there's just too much marble and metal in the building to be sure we can get a clear signal. Besides, as much as I like the idea of watching Marie in live action, that piece of blubber on top of her would ruin my appetite for days."

Rocco let out a huge laugh to the point where he was coughing on his cigar smoke. "Holy smokes, I almost upchucked. When we get the thumb-thingie, get some choice stills printed. The guys in New York say they need them quick-like." Rocco thought for a moment, "and if you get any of Marie naked without the lardo, print some of those up for me."

Angelo grinned, "Can I have a few, too? Should have the flash drive within the hour. Stills should be available by tonight. Timing OK?"

"Yeah. I don't know why the New York family needs them at all, but I like to be considerate – you know, show some respect. Hey, anything new on that tail what was on Charlie?"

Angelo frowned, "That seems to be tougher than I thought it might be. No one seems to know anything about him. They've seen him tailing Charlie now and again, then he disappears for days. Someone says they saw him coming out of the Cathedral, if it's the same guy. It's almost like he went to Mass, or something. I'd like to have him picked up if we can find him, but he melts away quicker than butter on a steak."

Rocco shook his head, "I don't like this. Somethin's up and I don't have a clue what it is. We got the Card doin' weird stuff, New York wants nasty pictures of him, Charlie Frankin's doin' work for him, and some yahoo who we don't know who-it-is chasin' both of them. Did you reach out to that old newspaper guy, Pete, that Charlie sometimes hangs out with? Maybe he's got some idea."

"Yeah, he's one of the first people I called. It's possible he was one of the first to spot the guy. And he also guessed that the guy might be Italian. Pete thought he might be working for us."

Rocco said, "Well, ain't that the shits? If we find this guy, maybe we give him a job workin' for us. He seems to be better than most of the jamokes we have on the payroll."

Angelo thought for a minute, "Maybe we should put one of our guys on Charlie, not so much to watch what he's doing but to see if we can gather up this other tail. He's pretty slippery, but everyone makes a mistake now and again. One of our guys just might be able to bring him in."

Rocco nodded, "Okay, but let's do one other thing. Let's play nice with the Triunno Brothers and ask if they've got someone that matches the description of this guy. There's probably no reason for them to have a guy workin' this area, but we don't want to start somethin' with them if they got a good reason for the tail. Plus, if it's not their guy, it's only good courtesy to let them know there's an outsider workin' the town. Then again if it is their guy, it may be the first move in a war."

Angelo nodded, "That's good strategy, Rocco. They usually keep their activities centered on the Mayfield Road Hill, but it's smart to bring them into the loop. It's good strategy to open talks with them. They're still pretty upset about other stuff, and you stealing their numbers business in Glenville added salt to the wounds."

"That's just too damn bad. I saw an opportunity and I took it. Could be they want a war. But old man Triunno was asleep in the lasagna lettin' me take Glenville. He can just kiss my ass."

Angelo tried to get him back on a calmer track, "I think Charlie Franklin has done some work for Frank Triunno in the past, so Frank will think we're collaborating to protect a common asset. That will put him at ease when I proffer the inquiry."

"Uh huh," grunted Rocco. "Whatever you said sounds smart."

• • •

At the Chancery

At 3:00 p.m., Charlie Franklin rang the bell at the Chancery door and was immediately let in. The Monsignor offered him a chair in the Cardinal's outer office, again facing the mirrored cross.

The Monsignor said, "Mr. Franklin, so good to see you again. The Cardinal was very pleased with the speed and accuracy with which you completed our last mission. He would like to employ you for another such mission, if your schedule permits."

Charlie filed away the Monsignor's slip of the tongue calling it 'our' last mission and said, "I appreciate the compliment. I didn't expect to get another offer from the Cardinal so soon, but sometimes it works that way. What's the assignment?"

"His Eminence will be out shortly to review his wishes with you," said the Monsignor as he departed into the Cardinal's chambers.

Facing the mirrored cross again, Charlie had the distinct impression he was being watched. He scanned the ceiling, something he had not done during his first visit. There were small alabaster angel's heads at various corners of the oddly cut room, six in all. Each angel's mouth was open as if singing a hymn. Each mouth was wide enough to hold a hidden camera. Charlie smiled, then focused on the cross. Mirrors covered all sides. He wondered – could it be a two-way mirror assembly? If it was real mirrors it would likely weigh over 300 pounds. If it was an assembly of two-way glass, it would not weigh more than about 60 or 70 pounds. He wished he could examine it more closely, but that was out of the question.

Suddenly the door swung open as Cardinal Maroney exploded into the room. "Mr. Franklin, so good to see you again."

Charlie jumped to his feet, "Your Eminence, I didn't expect to be honored by your call again, certainly not this soon after our last meeting."

"Please sit. Yes, it appears I do have another chore for you. Tell me, was the payment you recently received from the Monsignor adequate?"

"Yes, just as we discussed." Charlie made the mental note that an audio recording would put blame for the payment at the Monsignor's feet.

"Excellent. And thank you for the prompt delivery of the package. It's just that – well, it appears – you see, the documents were incomplete."

"Really? I delivered exactly what I was given. If you have an issue ..."

"No,no," interrupted the Cardinal, "I do not believe you did anything wrong, nor is Mr. Constantine at fault."

"Mr. Constantine? Oh, yes, TK Constantine. Well, I'm glad to hear that I'm not being accused of failure to deliver on an agreement. My reputation is at stake in every transaction I am involved with, and I can't have a failure or even a rumor of a failure raising any doubts about my ability."

"No, sir, Mr. Franklin. There will be none of that. I've been in touch with the, um, antiquities dealer who provided the package. It appears an error was made in preparation of the package. But here's where it gets a bit – shall we say, tricky." The Cardinal sat back in his leather chair, "You see, I know the name of the dealer, and how I am told to contact her, but ..."

"Her? Your dealer is a woman, then?"

"Yes. Her name is Merke Edelstein. I have only had a few dealings with her, most of the past purchases were done by my father. Or my brother. Dad has passed away and, since this is to be a gift to my brother, I don't wish to question him. But I've never met Ms. Edelstein, nor do I know where she has her office, or business, or however she may be conducting her work. Since I've purchased an item at a significant expense, and since an error occurred, I feel like I should have a better grasp of the person with whom I'm conducting business."

"I see your point," said Charlie, beginning to sense what he would be asked to do next.

"Just as I interviewed you prior to your employment, I feel the need to know more about Ms. Edelstein. I have been told that you have experience in finding information about individuals in a quiet manner. I would not want Ms. Edelstein to think I distrust her, so I'm hoping she need not know anything about personal inquiries. Is that something you think you could do? Possibly find information about her – her whereabouts, her headquarters, her experience in matters such as this, maybe even a photo of her?"

Charlie took out his notebook and said, "Can you please spell the name so I don't search for the wrong person?"

The Cardinal smiled, "My goodness, you are a marvel. You will do this then?"

"Sure. Finding information about people is one of my chief areas of expertise. Better than being a delivery boy."

"Aha," the Cardinal deferred, "about that. You see, Ms. Edelstein says she will have the proper documents – that is, the remaining part of the document – ready within a few days. She suggests we use the same delivery method as we did on the first attempt, you meeting Mr. TK Constantine in a pre-arranged location. I know you dislike being thought of as a delivery boy, but to keep Ms. Edelstein from reneging on the deal, I have tentatively agreed pending my discussion with you."

Charlie dropped his head, tapping his notebook with his pen. "So, let me understand. You don't necessarily trust your dealer and you want a complete background check done on her. Nonetheless, you've agreed to a deal for a second attempt at retrieval of your artifact, allowing her to dictate the method and means of delivery. Is that it?"

The Cardinal blushed and lost much of his bravado. "Yes. That's the nub of it. Actual delivery details to follow."

It was now Charlie's turn to be in control. "Cardinal Maroney, do you know what a 'rube' is? That's what you sound like. If I were you, I'd find a different gift for your brother. This one is costing you a lot of time, and now a lot more money."

He stood up and leaned over the Cardinal's desk, putting his fists down on the edge, towering over the seated prelate. "If you insist on throwing good money after bad, I have a deal: first, my fee is now $25,000 up front, for which you get information on Ms. Edelstein and the package, and second, I will choose the site of the transfer, which, I assume, will still be in New York City. Third, I need to be able to verify the contents before accepting delivery. Fourth, neither you nor the Monsignor will attempt to track my whereabouts or select the vehicle I will drive. Fifth, tell the little red-haired guy to back off, unless he wants a bloody nose to match his hair color." He looked hard at the Cardinal, whose face was now fully flushed and whose eyes were wide with fear. "Agreed, Your Eminence?"

The Cardinal swallowed hard, and said meekly, "Agreed."

Charlie sat back down as the Cardinal cleared his throat, "I was told not to underestimate you, Mr. Franklin. It appears I errored in assuming you were naïve. Please forgive me my past faults." He straightened himself in his chair, "Your fee is excessive, but given my past transgressions, understandable. Your expertise in these matters, plus your past involvement, makes you indispensable. I promise you will not be followed nor tracked in any way. But as for the verification of contents, I must insist that you not examine the package – the artifact is quite delicate and susceptible to deterioration from air and light."

"Okay," said Charlie, "but you'll not question what I deliver, since it will be in whatever condition it is given to me. What about me selecting the location of the transfer?"

The Cardinal said, "I will attempt to make that demand when I am given the timetable for the delivery."

"Fair enough," said Charlie. "I'll see my own way out – oh, hold on." He shouted, "Hey Monsignor! Turn off the tape machine now!" He glanced at the Cardinal whose mouth hung open. Turning and departing, he said, "See you soon, Rev."

• • •

Early evening, Charlie's Apartment

Rita brought three suitcases and moved into the apartment as if it was hers. Charlie's lifestyle was undergoing an immediate makeover. Pete arrived a half-hour later loaded down with take-out Chinese for them to share for dinner. The plan was to discuss the latest proposal from Cardinal Maroney over fried rice and bites of General Tso's Chicken. Charlie briefed them on what the Cardinal had laid out, occasionally playing back his tape recording of their conversation.

"Jeez, Charlie. I didn't think you had it in you to take on the Cardinal that way," said Pete.

"Why not? He tried to screw me over in a lot of ways last time. I even think he was contemplating offing me," said Charlie.

"Yeah, but you're such a stand-up guy, and a former Catholic, and all. That was a pretty ballsy move against someone one step away from being a Pope, for Chrissake."

Rita chuckled and teased, "Oh, yeah, a real stand-up guy. Not a sinner, like the rest of us. You'd never take advantage of a young blonde in a New York hotel room, would you?"

Charlie said, "Hey! She took advantage of me! I was the innocent victim, remember?"

"I can attest to that," offered Pete, pointing at Charlie. "This guy was dead meat the minute she walked into the bar."

Rita smiled, "I want all the spicy details. Someday I want you to give me a blow-by-blow account – so to speak – so I can learn her tricks."

"Enough!" Charlie shouted, raising his hands to end that discussion. "Let's focus on what's in front of us. Weigh in with your thoughts or opinions. Step one: 25K? Sound agreeable?"

Rita said, "For him to agree to that much, he's desperate. He needs you because he needs the document – or artifact – whatever it is."

"Agreed," said Pete. "He wants the package, he doesn't necessarily want you, but his dealer made you part of the deal, for whatever reason."

"I think the reason may have something to do with Ms. TK Constantine," smarmed Rita. "She'll be the delivery person again, I'm guessing."

Charlie blushed, "Maybe you should come with me this time, Rita, to keep me in line."

"Anyhow," interrupted Pete, "his agreeing to the 25K does show his desperation as Rita says. Are you sure he'll pay up?"

"It's to be an all-up-front payment. If anything gets hinky I can always ask for a bonus before delivery."

Pete said, "What about him agreeing not to track or tail you. Do we take him at his word? The little red-head guy is just a dope, but what if he's got someone else, like the Italian guy?"

"I think 'little-red' is past tense as a tail. I'm betting he'll be happy to exit that line of work. We won't see much of him anymore, except for maybe as a delivery boy," said Charlie. "But the character we're now calling the Italian Guy, He's definitely an issue. Does anyone think he's working for the Cardinal?"

Pete shook his head. "Doubtful. The Cardinal would be hard pressed to find someone that slick to work for him. I think the Italian Guy may be watching the Cardinal as much as he's watching us."

Rita said, "I agree. If the red-head came from the Cardinal, there is no reason for the Italian Guy to be from him, too. And now there may be more than one, if the guy I spotted at the bar was also an Italian Guy, so to speak. No, they're not with the Cardinal but from somewhere else. And that's the problem – we don't know where they come from or who sent them."

"Angelo is certain he's not one of Rocco's boys," said Pete. "He asked me if I knew who he was. My guess is Rocco is also interested in finding out who he is."

"So maybe we just let Rocco do his thing and find out who they are for us," said Charlie. "After all, I don't think any of us is equipped to do battle with these guys, except maybe Rita with her *pistola*."

Rita frowned, "It's a Ruger 9mm. You make it sound like a pop gun."

"I wish you'd get rid of it," said Pete. "You scare me with that thing. Besides, even if you hit someone that won't end anything. I agree with Charlie. Allow Rocco's boys take on the men in black. So far, they've not done anything threatening other than follow you two and watch what you're doing. As disconcerting as that is, it's not illegal. If there's to be violence, let Rocco be the one to do it."

Rita and Charlie looked at one another and nodded. Charlie continued, "Okay, on another topic, do you two think I should demand to inspect the package?"

"Hell, no!" said Pete. "Whatever is in there you don't want to know what it is. Remember, the best adage is 'plausible deniability'."

"I don't know, Pete," said Rita. "Wouldn't Charlie have added leverage if he knows what's inside?"

Charlie said, "I don't think I want to know what's in the package. I get the impression that if I did know, all sorts of people might want me silenced."

"Which is why you want to choose the venue. That's smart," said Pete. "Think they'll agree?"

Rita smiled, "Aw, why not go back to your little love nest? That sounded so cute." Charlie and Pete both glowered at her.

Charlie changed the subject, "Let's discuss this 'Merke Edelstein' person. What do you think is the best way to find out who she is without alerting her that someone is searching?"

Pete said, "I did a quick scan of the internet and found no responses to that name. I know an antique dealer in Miami – did some stuff for my grandmother – he's pretty big in that business. Let me see if he recognizes the name. It's odd enough that someone must have heard of her."

"Good start," said Charlie. "Rita, would you mind going to the library and see if she shows up in any reference books? Let's remember, she may not be on the up-and-up, so finding her may require that we look for someone who buys antiquities illegally – black market stuff."

"Let's back up a minute. Where is a good place for you to set up the meet?" asked Pete. "Does it have to be in NYC?"

Charlie said, "I think we have to assume so, although I'm not sure Ms. Edelstein is actually based there. As you two do your searches for her, let's look into other cities as well. But if the pick up is to be in New York, what's a good spot?"

Pete said, "How about the Empire State Building?"

"No," said Rita. "I've seen *Sleepless in Seattle*. Too romantic." Both men groaned. "Also, there's only one way down unless you jump. How about meeting your girlfriend in St. Patrick's Cathedral?"

Pete started laughing, but Charlie was intrigued, "Talk to me, Rita, what do you see as the benefits of St. Pat's?"

"Well, it's a public setting, although not too visible to prying eyes since it's semi-dark even during the day. There are usually dozens of people inside milling around in a reverent way, providing both cover and a least a little security. If you meet in a pew, the other church-goers will think you're praying, so no one will bother you. There are a lot of exits if the deal gets squirrely. The transaction could take place quietly and in a matter of minutes."

Charlie thought out loud, "Rita, I think your concept is excellent. Secure yet public, quiet yet open. We've been assuming that the delivery person would be TK Constantine. What if it's someone else? How would I recognize them? The white carnation idea was theirs, and it was bogus."

Pete said, "You set the location. Let them worry about the particulars."

Charlie said, "Okay, try this out and tell me where I'm off base. I take an early morning flight into LaGuardia, cab to St. Pat's. I set the meet for 10:00 a.m., or as early as St. Patrick's is open to the public. I make the pick-up, then cab it to a Hertz counter for a one-way car rental back to Cleveland. I can be back here no later than 9:00 p.m., maybe earlier." He looked from Rita to Pete, "There's no overnight hotel, no worries about the Cardinal using a tracker on a car, still no TSA examination of the package. What am I forgetting?"

Everyone sat quietly for a few minutes looking for a possible problem with the plan. Eventually Rita said, "Poor TK. She'll be left in the church feeling awfully horny."

"God damn it, Rita!" both men shouted together as she leaped off the couch running toward the bathroom trailing laughter.

• • •

Thursday, June 30:

Late the next morning, Charlie left his office and walked the several blocks toward Public Square. Every so often he stopped to window shop, especially looking into the windows offering a reflection behind him. He kept seeing men who stopped a half-block behind him whenever he stopped. He thought there were two of them, one on each side of the street. Rather than doubling back to prove his suspicions, he chose to continue moving forward. He didn't want them to think they had been discovered, and he didn't relish an encounter while outnumbered. In the meantime, he made a mental note of their description.

He entered the Terminal Tower Office complex and pushed the elevator button for floor #7. He exited and waited in the hall facing the elevators to see if anyone else got off there. Five minutes passed. No one else exited on the 7th floor. He got back on the next elevator heading up and pushed button #14. Following the hallway around to the right he came to Office #1409, marked "Informational Press Unlimited", with a "IPU" logo beneath the words. Pete had designed the logo himself, and insisted that the letters stood for "I Piss on You".

Charlie touched one long and two short hits on the door bell. Pete's voice grunted, "Whadya want?"

"It's me," was all Charlie said, and the following buzz said the door was unlocked.

"Glad you're here," said Pete, motioning to a chair, "got some interesting tidbits coming in."

Charlie raised his hand to stop the conversation, and with hand motions indicated that he was followed, and by what he thought were two men. Pete nodded, turned on the TV with the sound turned down and picked up a controller beside his desk phone. At the click of a button, the show on TV was replaced by a split-screen view of the hallway outside the door, both left and right. Another click showed a wide-angle view of the area immediately in front of the door. No one was visible in any of the images.

"Don't get many visitors to the 14th floor. My office neighbors are usually on the road. So, if anyone shows up, it's someone who's either lost or up to no good. We'll check periodically. Who do you think was following you, the 'Italian guy'?"

"Didn't look like him, although I couldn't really tell, looking at them in window reflections rather than face-on. Definitely not the red-head. Think the Cardinal could already be breaking our deal?"

Pete shook his head, "I don't think he'd take the risk. You were pretty straight forward when you last met, and like we said, he knows he needs you to make the deal go down. No, I'd wager they're not from him."

"Then, who? Could they be working with the 'Italian guy'?"

Pete sat back and thought for a minute. "You know what? You were able to spot these guys pretty easy, right?' Charlie nodded. "So, they're not really good at their craft, not a pro's pro like the 'Italian guy'. Can you describe them?"

"Nothing special about them. Heavy-set, slacks, open-collar shirts, light jackets, no facial hair, modest haircuts."

"Jackets zipped up?"

"Yeah, I think so, why?"

"Pretty warm out today, don't you think?"

Charlie shrugged, "I guess so, about 80-degrees."

Pete smiled and nodded, "The only people wearing zipped up jackets on an 80-degree day are those covering something underneath. These guys were 'heavy'."

"You mean they were packing? Why would guys with guns be following me?"

"The guns weren't meant for you. They always carry them. I think they're Rocco's boys. I'll bet they aren't even interested in you. They're after the guy that was following you, and those two dunderheads figured the best way to find him was to watch for whoever might be tailing you. Angelo said Rocco was pretty upset that there's an out-of-towner working the area. They probably want to pick him up. But if you were able to spot those two, then certainly the Italian Guy spotted them, too. Don't worry about them. Just let Rocco do his thing."

Charlie sighed, "That's both a relief and somehow disconcerting at the same time. My unwanted gangster protectors aren't worth a shit. That's just wrong on so many fronts." He shifted forward, "You said you had some interesting tidbits. What's up?"

Pete shuffled some notes in front of him, "Yeah. Checked with the antique dealer in Miami. No dice on the 'Merke Edelstein' search. He's making some quiet inquiries for me, but says he knows almost everyone on the East Coast who deals in old stuff and never heard of this woman. Could be that the Maroney Family has been dealing with an alias all along and didn't know it. Or, they did know it and were covering for both that person and themselves. No one can say they're dirty dealing if they don't know who the dirty-dealer even is. I've got some other feelers out, too, but I'm beginning to think there may be no such person as 'Merke Edelstein'."

Charlie said, "But the Cardinal thinks there is such a person, which is why he asked me to find her. If he doesn't know who or where she is, how does he contact her to make purchases? There's got to be someone else involved, an intermediary."

Pete said, "Very good observation my friend, you may excel at this business after all. You're right. Someone else is involved, someone between the Cardinal and this Merke dame, if there even is a Merke dame. But the Cardinal hasn't told us anything about a middle man, has he? What if Merke is the middle man?"

Charlie considered, "He doesn't know Merke, and he thought TK Constantine was a man, not a beautiful little blonde. He's more in the dark than we are, and shelling out big bucks nonetheless. Whatever he's after, it means a great deal to him."

"Yup. A word to the wise: a stupid criminal is far more dangerous than a smart criminal, especially when the stupid guy thinks he's smart."

"So, you think Maroney is dirty?"

Pete rolled back in his chair, "I've seen a lot of righteous guys get caught up in stuff, and lots of bad guys get caught up, too. The righteous guys have a conscience and they try to get straight. Sometimes it works, sometimes not, but they always try to straighten out their mess. The bad guys just dig themselves in deeper, with no attempt at rectitude, no sign of a guilty conscience. They use people as chess pieces, sacrificing them as they go, all to save themselves. Your Cardinal is one of them. He's using you, using the little red-head guy, even the Monsignor probably. You are all his chess pieces and he's willing to sacrifice each of you if it's to his benefit."

Charlie nodded with a grim look on his face, "I've asked this before – should I just walk away from this deal with him?"

Pete said, "You're in too deep and you've got no bargaining chip. You know too much and are a liability if you simply walk away. You're a pawn that's been moved once, and now moved again. You're vulnerable. You need something, some information on the Cardinal, that would make your demise a worse threat than your existence. You know how this works. You've done it before. But walking away right now is not an option."

"And where do you think I can get that leverage?"

"There's something else I've been looking at. Something strange about the brother. Can't put my finger on it, but it needs further investigation. It's an odd thing, how he suddenly got Alzheimer's real bad after years of seeming to be normal. I'd like to get into it, but I'm working three other cases with tight timelines and delivering big paydays. You can use your legal acumen to dig into it more. That and your suave personality may make some headway before your next trip to New York."

"Got it. Speaking of New York, are you OK that I'm going in alone?"

"Trust me, as much as I'd like to see that lovely little blonde again, I've got to get on these other cases. You just go with the plan you've laid out. You'll do fine alone, if last time was any indication. And I do like the plan of meeting at St. Pat's. The more I think about it the better it feels."

Charlie got up to leave, "I do appreciate you helping me even though you've got those other jobs."

Pete waved the thought away, "Gowan, what are friends for? Just be careful. And find yourself a big chip you can lay on the Cardinal's felt table. I think you're gonna need that chip before this game is all over."

Charlie took the elevator all the way to the basement level. Once a train terminal with ticket counters and platforms, the area had been transformed into an indoor shopping mall. The rush of people in the mall made following him difficult, if the two tails were still around. He entered a small coffee shop and took a back booth so he could watch everyone who entered. When he was satisfied with his surroundings, he placed a call to Rita.

"How are things, Rita?"

"God, how I love libraries!" ... (Aside to someone else: "Oh, shut up! I'm not making that much noise!") ... "I need to step out of this area so some of these sensitive types can concentrate. Hold on ... OK, I'm in the lobby. I've been digging all morning through both new and old books – did you know old book dust can make you sneeze a lot – and still no reference to a person named Merke Edelstein. Fun fact – you know what 'Merke' means in Hebrew? Bitter."

"Bitter? I know Merke is an odd sounding name, but what mother names her kid 'bitter'?"

"Exactly my thought. Got some other things I'm looking into. I'll tell you about them later. What are you up to?"

Charlie said, "Just left Pete. He suggested I look into the Cardinal's brother, so I think I'm headed to Akron this afternoon. See you tonight?"

"Sure. Bring us a couple sub sandwiches and some potato chips. I'll pick up some beer on my way home."

"Get me a six-pack that I'll enjoy, not that IPA stuff you drink. And, by the way, watch your back. I picked up another tail or two on my way to Pete's. Could be they won't track you, but just be careful."

"Was it the guys in black again?"

Charlie said, "No, don't think so. Pete thinks they were Rocco's boys trying to spot one of the men in black. But just in case, watch your step."

"'K. You, too. Enjoy Akron."

• • •

Charlie returned to his office, grabbed his brief case and headed to his car. He didn't see either of the two men from earlier, nor did he see anyone else following him. Nonetheless, he had the distinct feeling he was being watched. Maybe it was just a spooky premonition, maybe it was some weird 6th sense, but he'd had the feeling on past jobs and was usually proven correct in the end.

He didn't look up at the old four-story building next to his office. It had been abandoned several years back after the pool hall on the second floor was forced to close. It had been the scene of several nasty and bloody fights, and more than one strange disappearance from time to time. Some people thought the whole structure should be saved as an historic site, since it was rumored that Minnesota Fats had frequently played some big money matches there. Others were not convinced that a location with a bad reputation for illegal gambling, occasional bloodshed, and as the last-known whereabouts of some unsavory individuals warranted being saved and enshrined, no matter who might have been a former client. In the end, the forty or so classic pool tables were not enough incentive to convince the city fathers to shore up the structure, suffering from sagging wooden floors and a sagging reputation. The whole building was scheduled for demolition as soon as the settlement over ownership concluded, acknowledging who would pay for the razing and who then owned the land underneath.

Had Charlie looked up to the fourth floor he might have seen the sun reflecting off the telescope following his every move. It was an excellent vantage point. Someone could watch both entrances to his office building, the parking lot, and even see whether the lights were on or off in Charlie's office rooms. At the other end of the telescope, adjusting the camera lens, was a short, thin, dark-haired man dressed all in black.

On his way to Akron, Charlie kept watch in the rearview mirror. Nothing seemed suspicious. He drove by but didn't visit the facility where Sean Maroney was being cared for. He figured dropping in unannounced might actually alert the Cardinal, since he assumed there was someone at the facility who sent his Eminence regular reports. Instead, Charlie went to the Summit County Courthouse, Records Department. Much of what he was after would be public record. It might take time to locate what he was after, but searching for the information would not appear irregular to anyone watching. He made a mental list of what he needed, realizing he'd only have a few hours to search before the Records Department closed at 5:00 p.m.

He finished his research just as the office was closing. He checked his phone – no messages. He decided to casually walk around the block instead of heading straight to his car. A tail would have to follow him just to see what he was up to. No signs of anyone who looked suspicious. Returning to his car, he turned the air conditioning up full blast. He felt the phone in his pocket buzz. It was a text message from his old friend, Amir Habood. Amir's family ran an Arab-themed grocery store and restaurant with the quirky name of Habood's Foods. He hadn't talked to Amir for several months and he smiled at the chance to refresh their friendship and jab insults at one another, the hallmark of their relationship. He texted back, "In the middle of a case. I'll stop by when I can."

On the way north toward home, Charlie veered slightly off course toward the toney village of Hudson. Swinging down a private dead-end drive on the outskirts of town, he stopped in front of a large estate with a gated driveway. He reached into the back seat for his binoculars, scanning what he could see of the property. There did not appear to be anyone home. He checked the property left and right of the house – lots of manicured bushes and thick trees. Then the binoculars stopped at the far eastern edge of the property, just inside what appeared to be a security fence. It was an old shed, or small barn, almost overgrown by bushes and vines. The vines looked like they were the only thing keeping the shed from falling over. But there was something odd about a heavy-duty power line running from the main house to the shed. The door of the shed was both modern and sturdy, too sturdy for the ramshackle old building. On the left door threshold there was a small electrical box – a key pad controlling a lock.

Charlie smiled and nodded, then turned his car around and headed back, reaching the main road just as a Hudson Village police car was turning into the private drive. Someone did not like a snoop. He headed home, remembering to pick up the sub sandwiches that would be dinner.

• • •

It was almost 7:00 p.m. when he rapped the all-okay-knock and opened the front door. "I hope you brought the subs, I'm starved," shouted Rita.

"I've got your sub if you've got my beer," said Charlie. "Did you get anything out of the library?"

The sat at the table sorting food and beverages. Rita said, "I'm almost cross-eyed from looking at old reference books. I also used the library's computer system to do some searching. I know, I know, Pete already did that. But you know how I am – I don't believe it unless I do it myself. How was Akron?"

"Interesting. I need to do some more digging myself before I reach any conclusions. So, did you find anything?"

Rita took a bite of her sandwich, popped the beer bottle open and nodded. Charlie had to wait as she chewed the first bite and washed it down. "Love that Baked Italian Sub," she said. "Yeah, I found that the woman I now call 'Bitter' does not exist in any printed record. I even looked through an interesting book that talks about fakes and forgeries and antiquity thievery. Nada. My take? It's an alias."

Charlie nodded between bites of his own sub, "Pete agrees with you. His contact in Miami has never heard of her. The antique guy is sending out feelers to his East Coast contacts, but doesn't think he'll find much. And wrap your head around this – if the Cardinal doesn't know who 'Merke Edelstein' is, how does he contact her? There's probably someone between the two, an intermediary. Or the intermediary is Merke herself."

Rita said, "The Cardinal never mentioned anyone else, did he?"

Charlie shook his head, "No. I almost get the feeling that – if there is an intermediary – he doesn't think that person is important. I do. Did you look for 'Ms. Bitter' Internationally? Could she be somewhere in Europe or the Middle East?"

"The books I looked at listed lots of International dealers, maybe not all, but I didn't limit my research to just the U.S. Why did you say Middle East and not just Europe? You got a hunch?"

"I guess when I think of art, I think 'Europe', but with antiquities, I think 'Middle East'. And the Cardinal keeps slipping and saying 'documents', which makes me think of Bible papers."

"Or scrolls," said Rita.

Charlie looked up at her. "Yeah. I guess that would fit the description, too. I hadn't really thought that way, but, yeah, that fits in very well."

"Isn't ownership or possession of scrolls prohibited by International Law?" asked Rita. "They're protected by the Israeli Government, I think."

"You're right. If not by the Israelis, then by someone – the Vatican, maybe. But scrolls are, well, tube shaped by their very nature. What I delivered to him was flat, like a book. And that seemed to be what he expected."

Rita considered, "Unless someone flattened the pages of the scroll, and put it in a kind of book form. He keeps saying the documents are sensitive to air and light. That says they're very old. Whatever he's after, scroll or otherwise, it very well may be illegal to possess. Which is why he needs someone else to pick it up, someone with a reputation for protecting his clients and who can take the fall for the crime."

Charlie put down his half-eaten sandwich and took a swig of beer, "You're trying to ruin my appetite, aren't you?"

"I just think you need to be even more cautious on this than you may have originally thought. I know you're usually very careful, but you generally deal with people who have something to fear, and you have a good idea of what you're walking into. Those factors give you leverage. This is different. He's told you virtually nothing of substance, certainly no truths, and you're treating this just like you're covering up someone's infidelity with a stripper. You need to be more careful with this one than you've ever been before."

"You're very astute. Something about this doesn't feel right, didn't feel right from the beginning. Pete told me to walk away on day one. Should've listened to him. I asked him today if he thought I should walk now, and he says I'm in too deep with no hook on the Cardinal that I can use to protect myself. That's why I went to Akron, to see what I could find out about the Cardinal's family."

"And? Did you get something?"

"Maybe. I did run by the family estate. It's still listed as Maroney Trust property in the county records. Big place, well kept, lawn mown, bushes trimmed. Didn't see any signs of life, though. Kind of a strange place."

"Did you stop in to see the brother?"

"No. I assume that the well-givers have been given instructions to alert the Cardinal if anyone stops by. I don't want him to know I'm poking around. Speaking of which, since you so love the library, could you head back and do one more piece of research?"

Rita threw her head back in exasperation, "Oh, joy! I was hoping I could spend more time in that book mausoleum!"

Charlie laughed, "Maybe you can get most of the information on-line, but for some of it we'll need to check the newspaper archives."

"What am I supposed to be looking for?"

"Find out when the Cardinal became a Cardinal. Timetable, coronation date or whatever it's called. And go back several months before and a few months after he became a redcap to see if there are any general articles about him, especially any sabbaticals or retreats he may have taken, and if anyone joined him."

Rita had a wry smile on her face, "You do have a theory, don't you?"

Charlie smiled back, "Maybe. Tiny pieces of a puzzle. But I need some more info before I know how to fit the pieces together to form a picture, and I don't want to color your vision on the research with wild speculation. Let me just say that I don't think he's on a wild goose chase for some piece of antiquity without having someone else who also wants the same thing."

"Ooh!" exclaimed Rita, "A race for the Holy Grail? I love it!"

Charlie held up his hand, "Maybe a race, or maybe the Cardinal is not the end possessor of what I'm delivering. Maybe he's the go-between to someone else."

"Sweet Jesus! You think maybe the Pope wants something from him?"

Charlie shook his head, "There are lots of high-ranking individuals in the Vatican Curia that stand between Cardinal Maroney and the Pope."

"Okay, I'll get on it in the morning, but I think the library will close at noon with the upcoming 4th of July celebration on Monday. By the way, I discovered something else at the library today. I looked up TK Constantine."

"Are you going to look up all my past assignations? You want my girlfriend's name from the 8th grade?"

She waved her hands, "Not for any prurient interest, I just wanted to see if there's any mention of her anywhere. Also, I looked in the police files of New York City to see if she has a record. Nothing. There doesn't seem to be a person named 'TK Constantine' who anyone cares about. The only member of the Constantine family I could find is

Constantine the Great, Holy Roman Emperor from the 4th Century. He did have children, so I guess she could be related – if that is her name."

Charlie said, "She wasn't that old. Constantine the Great, huh? If you want an alias to make people think twice, pick a name that evokes a thought and deflects attention from who you really are."

"So, what are we going to tell the Cardinal if we can't locate 'Ms. Bitter'?"

"I think we need to create a persona for her," said Charlie. "You've done the most searching for her, why don't you take a shot at making up a decent myth. We'll talk it over with Pete when he's free to make sure your description flies by all our standards."

Rita frowned, "You want to make up a character, lie to the Cardinal? Your 'bad boy' side is coming out."

"Well, he expects us to deliver. He has no idea who Merke Edelstein is, or where she comes from, so I think it only appropriate to let him think we were successful in tracking her down. We'll make her sound exotic and hard to locate, almost mystical so that he doesn't go searching for her on his own. In the meantime, maybe we can get him to acknowledge there's someone else between Ms. Bitter and himself."

• • •

Friday, July 1:

It was late the next afternoon when a message was slipped under Charlie's office door. Working quietly in his inner office, he heard the swish of the envelope on the carpet. He peaked out the window to see the red-headed guy running away from the building.

The letter-sized envelope contained a cryptic note:

"The package will be ready for retrieval within a few days. As was noted previously, it is essential that you avoid examination of the package yourself, and prevent the examination and subsequent exposure by the TSA or any other authorities, since air and light may damage the contents. Ms. Edelstein will consider your recommendation for an alternative delivery location, provided it remains somewhere on Manhattan Island, New York. Please provide your requirements by 2:00 p.m. tomorrow, Saturday, July 2.

Information on the identity of Ms. Edelstein will be expected at that time as well. -- M. Leonard".

Charlie grinned as he recognized that the Cardinal was never referenced in any of their written communications. Whether the Monsignor knew it or not, the indicators would all point to M. Leonard as the sole perpetrator of any criminal activity discovered.

Rita had spent the previous night concocting a description for 'Merke Edelstein' that would both satisfy the Cardinal and scare him off from attempts to reach her. On her way to the library she dropped off a copy to Pete so he could massage what she had composed. He was expected to swing by the apartment that evening.

In the meantime, Charlie was exploring his own theory of the Cardinal's motives. He looked at everything from a number of different perspectives. He had learned a lot from Pete during their time together. Pete always said that when he thought he knew what was going on, he would sit back and considered the ramifications to all the various parties involved. He would say, "Put yourself in their shoes, then play it out. How does it feel? If you don't think it feels right, start again and try looking at it from a different perspective." Understanding how other players might see things often led to enlightening ideas.

Such a process came easily to Pete, a remnant of his days as a reporter. But using Pete's process proved cumbersome to Charlie. He wasn't trained for such deep introspection into someone else's psyche. Nonetheless, it was the best method he could think of to try to ferret out what was going on. Charlie tried to use the process in several other touchy cases where his own exposure was possible. He hadn't always gotten it right, but going through the variables at least helped eliminate the least likely motives of his clients.

So, what was the Cardinal after? What could someone like the Cardinal want? He ran down a list of possible motives on a clean notepad:

Money – Money was the usual goal of most avaricious individuals. Plain old greed. But the Cardinal was a member of a wealthy family, and so far, was able to pay off Charlie handsomely in cash. It didn't appear he had a need for money. Of course, more wealth would be welcomed by anyone, perhaps especially by someone who came from wealth. But what would a Cardinal do with a fortune if that was the end goal? It would be hard to spend without arising suspicions and rumors, and there were no heirs to pass it down to.

Charlie put a question mark next to the 'Money' motive.

Prestige – Being a Cardinal was extremely prestigious on its own. Charlie seemed to recall that the former Archbishop Maroney was elevated to Cardinal just under a year ago. Rita would have the specifics on the timing this evening. What more prestige could someone ask for? Was it simply ambition? Did he want a job in a bigger place? Would a position as Cardinal of New York, for example, carry greater prestige? Probably. But once a Cardinal, why ask for a bigger city with more problems inherently involved? Wouldn't it be better to grow gracefully in your current position than try and supplant the existing and highly regarded prelate of a city in which you had no experience?

He put another question mark next to the 'Prestige' motive.

Power – A Cardinal is a uniquely powerful individual within the Catholic Church hierarchy. They preside over the selection of the next Pope. They are revered by the faithful. What more power could a newly elevated cleric want besides being fully acknowledged as a Cardinal? Sure, there was the pride that accompanied the many powerful positions for a Cardinal within the Vatican, including oversight of the Vatican Treasury, a massive amount of money, larger than the GNP of many medium-sized nations. To hold one of the highly-prized Vatican roles would certainly elevate someone's power. But it is doubtful that a newly appointed Cardinal might be considered for one of these key positions. Perhaps if he could provide a unique document that would be extremely valuable to the Vatican hierarchy, maybe then he could parley that important document into a job within the Vatican.

Charlie put an asterisk next to the 'Power' motive. A pursuit of fame. This one was possible. He went back and added an asterisk to the 'Prestige' motive, too. Power and prestige were usually linked pretty closely together. He continued on with other motives:

<u>Sex</u> – A motive usually reserved for politicians or business moguls, sex was a strong motivator for many men. Charlie had worked for several clients who needed help extricating themselves from odd sexual encounters, both hetero and homo versions. There was even one involving underage male participants. Charlie had worked to get his client safely out of trouble with the press on that one, but then casually and surreptitiously gave all the evidence to the Federal District Attorney wrapped up in a bow. The guy never saw it coming. He has 30 years to life to figure it out now. Could the Cardinal have a sex issue? If he was consorting with anyone, male or female, he wouldn't need Charlie to obtain a package from New York. If 'sex' was the motive, he would want knowledge of his activity kept very quiet, not ask Charlie to go off to New York procuring packages, and certainly not have Charlie investigate Ms. Edelstein.

He put an 'X' next to the 'Sex' motive. Maybe sex was too easy to dismiss, but the facts at hand didn't add up to support of that motive.

<u>Revenge</u> – This was proving to be interesting. Charlie would need more information on any person or persons against whom the revenge was plotted. There just were too many unknowns to pinpoint revenge as a motive for what the Cardinal was doing. Did he have a gripe against his brother? Did he want to wave the document / artifact in front of his brother's nose to show that he had it and his brother would never have it? If the brother had Alzheimer's, he wouldn't even recognize what was going on. Who else would the Cardinal despise? Another Cardinal? Someone else he had a gripe with? Or was Charlie himself the victim of the revenge? Couldn't rule it out, but there didn't seem to be much logic in that, especially given the money coming Charlie's way.

Charlie put a question mark next to 'Revenge'. Couldn't say it was a contender, but couldn't rule it out either. That left one last motive to consider:

A Present / Gift – Was Cardinal Maroney telling the truth? Was all of this simply a matter of giving a gift to his brother who was in failing health, the last act of kindness to put his brother at peace before he died from an awful disease? It could be that he wished to provide the one last piece of a family collection that would make his brother smile one last time. Without knowing how bad the brother's condition had become, how deteriorated his mind might be, it was difficult to entirely rule out this benign motive. However, the list of deceits, the outright mendacity, the tracking device and the 'tail' all predicated against the credibility that Maroney was pursuing the 'package' out of a benevolent and altruistic motive. Perhaps he wanted to complete the family collection for himself, and the story about his brother was simply that – a story.

He put a question mark on the 'Present / Gift' motive. It deserved an 'X' if it was for his brother, but it needed to be considered if the collection was just for himself.

Charlie reviewed the list of motives, stopping at the 'Money' motive. The cryptic note asking for his reply by afternoon tomorrow failed to mention anything about paying the $25,000 fee Charlie was demanding. He'd need to correct that when he stopped in to see the Cardinal tomorrow, and he made the mental note to make sure he received the fee before providing the details on 'Merke Edelstein' that Rita had fabricated.

The only motives which had an asterisk, a star in Charlie's mind, were 'Power' and its corollary, 'Prestige'. He nodded at the thought, but then circled words he wrote next to each: 'What Power / What Prestige?'.

Before heading home, Charlie called for a bike courier to take his hand-written response to the Chancery. It read:

"I will arrive at approximately 2:00 p.m. tomorrow, Saturday, July 2, for Spiritual Enlightenment from His Eminence. I will share my learned knowledge as requested, and provide details on my wishes for the proposed future location. It is expected that the donation to my favorite charity will be available at the time of my visit."—Signed: C.F.

Charlie knocked on the apartment door before entering, just in case Rita had her gun out. He found Pete already there, going over the fake profile of Merke Edelstein with Rita, the table littered with empty beer bottles. "Pizza's ordered, be here soon," said Rita, not even looking up. "Hope you got cash."

"Why, of course, madame. As you wish, madame. Please allow me to provide sustenance for you, madame," deadpanned Charlie.

"A pepperoni for Pete and a veggie for me," she replied, still concentrating on the notes Pete was making.

"Aha. No sausage and mushroom for me, I take it," a suddenly irked Charlie said.

"You can call and order another one," said Pete.

Charlie sat at the table with them. "Just what did I do to piss you two off?"

"We're busy," they said in unison. "Trying to nail down this 'Merke' person," said Pete. Raising his head suddenly, "Hey! We should pronounce her name 'Murky'! That's what this bio looks like anyway – very murky."

Charlie went to grab three beers and the phone to add his sausage pizza to the order. Hanging up the phone, he said, "Got it in before the driver left with the first order. Yours may be a little cold when it gets here."

Rita said, "Yes! Wonderful! I like what you've done there, Pete. That's perfect!"

Charlie said to himself, "Of course my broken leg hurts, but I can't feel it much due to the concussion."

Pete said, "It plays perfectly with what you've already come up with, Rita. A natural progression. It's a great collaboration."

Charlie said, "No, no. I don't need any bandages. The splint I made out of birch bark is just fine, thanks."

Rita looked at Charlie and smiled, "What? Oh, you're welcome."

Pete looked over, "When'd you get home?"

"So, you've got a profile on 'Murky' now? I'm supposed to present it to the Cardinal tomorrow."

"You'll love it," said Rita, looking at her notes. "Let's see. Merke Edelstein is a refugee from Eastern Europe where she is wanted for several bad deeds and various felonies. Currently, she is a recluse in an upstate New York villa, seeing no one. She has hi-tech surveillance surrounding the villa, and lower tech security via guard dogs and several persons with high-powered weapons. She uses her contacts in Europe and the Near East, especially Israel, to procure a wide variety of art, books, artifacts and other items, both legally and illegally possessed and traded throughout the world. She has evaded capture by Interpol, MI6 and the American authorities by using a series of intermediaries who she contacts using a post office box in one of several Eastern U.S. cities, as well as some abroad. She demands high payment for her services, and consequently pays her intermediaries very well, which is why they are happy to do her bidding, asking no questions. What else, Pete?"

Pete said, "Merke is approximately 82 years old, in excellent health, and is a crack shot with a hand gun. Oh, and 'Merke Edelstein' is not her real name. No one knows what her real name is." He smiled, "That should keep the Cardinal from trying to find her on his own. By the way, if he asks how we got this information, tell him you have contacts in the International underground. That'll make him think twice about crossing you."

Charlie said, "Jesus Christ! I think I'm glad I never crossed her path!" He thought for a minute, "Does TK Constantine work for her?"

"Can't get her out of your mind, can you Charlie?" Rita smirked.

He frowned, "I need to know what your bio might indicate because that will be an obvious question the Cardinal may ask."

Pete responded, "The best answer is—we don't know. There is so much murkiness – love that word, now – in Merke's past it's hard to say whether TK works directly or indirectly for her. And remember, the Cardinal still thinks TK is a man, so don't blow that."

Charlie sat back and sipped his beer, "I'm very impressed. You two have come up with a terrific fake person. I'll be able to sell this to the Cardinal with no problem. I wonder though ..."

"What? You wonder what?" asked Rita.

"There is someone out there who is doing exactly what you two have described. I wonder how close to the truth you may be."

Pete and Rita looked at one another, "Wow," said Pete. "Hadn't thought of that. What if we've just described the real Merke Edelstein?" He opened what was easily their fourth beer, handing one to Rita.

Rita's mouth hung open before she began giggling, "Holy shit! We've found her!"

Charlie let them revel in their collective genius for a while. Eventually, he said, "OK, Ms. Nostradamus, what did you learn about the Cardinal? You were going to find out when he was appointed to his position, and whether he had any down-time before or after his appointment, remember?"

"Lighten up, Charlie," said Rita. "I didn't forget. It's just that making up a story about 'Ms. Bitter' is more fun than chasing around the history of a fat old man in a red suit – Oh, my god, I just described Santa Claus!" Again, riotous laughter erupted from Pete and Rita, with no sign that it would stop anytime soon.

Charlie took his beer into the living room and sat on the couch reflecting. He loved it when his two close friends bonded over something. It was even better when they bonded over something they had done together. When the laughter died down to an occasional twitter, they joined Charlie in the living room. Rita was just about to expound on the Cardinal's appointment when the security door buzzer rang. The pizza was finally being delivered. Charlie hoped that some food might soak up the beer and bring everyone back to a semblance of sobriety.

Between bites, Rita explained that the Cardinal was appointed and sworn in just over nine months ago, in the Fall of last year, early October. Almost immediately after taking office, he took a three-week retreat. According to newspaper reports at the time, he claimed it was to "Thank God for the honor, and to come to grips with the heavy weight his new role carried."

Pete reflected, "I vaguely recall some of that. It happened right in the middle of the Councilman's bribery scandal, which had everyone's attention. But I do recall that there was some criticism about Cardinal

Maroney taking what amounted to a vacation instead of hitting the ground running and addressing the needs of the various poor churches in the diocese that were closing."

Rita added, "I saw some of that criticism in the newspaper files I read. They also mentioned he was gone for almost two months last summer, before getting named Cardinal. Some said it was health related, others said it was strictly a vacation. No one was quite sure where he went, but there were rumors that it was to the family compound – maybe to take care of his ailing brother? Another report, a small note actually, had him in the Tuscany Region of Italy. Mostly, the news media didn't pursue any of it, letting him have his privacy."

"That's a lot of time away from his duties in a fairly short time frame," said Pete. "That's like eleven weeks away within a three or four-month window. Curious."

Rita added, "Until I did the research, I didn't know that as Cardinal he was still in charge of the diocese. I always assumed it was like the military – you become a General and then you appoint a Colonel to take over your previous duties. But it's not like that in the Catholic Church."

Charlie asked a question that he seemed to already know the answer to, "What's the difference between a Bishop and a Cardinal?"

Rita answered, "Not much, apparently. At least 'not much' in America. A Cardinal is a Bishop, or more likely an Archbishop, who is honored for their past work with a promotion which allows them to wear a red cap. He gets a bigger stipend, but he has the same responsibilities he's always had as Archbishop – tending to the flock, the priests and the churches of the diocese. Now in Rome, it's a bit different. The Cardinals there all have positions in the Vatican, and manage one of the various departments of the Curia. No one says it out loud, but the Curia Boys make the diocesan Cardinals feel like country bumpkins when they get together."

Pete listened intently, "Huh. Must make those enclaves a bit testy."

"What enclaves, Pete?" asked Charlie.

"You know, when they all get together to elect a new Pope after the old one croaks. The Curia boys probably make the hillbilly Cardinals quake in their boots."

Charlie waited to see if Rita would respond. She did. "It's called a Conclave, goof ball, not an enclave. And they wear slippers, not cowboy boots. Even so, there's an interesting part of this. Not all Cardinals are invited to a Conclave."

Pete was nonplussed, "What? I thought if you were a Cardinal you got to be in on everything, the Vatican Vault, the mysterious library, voting in a new Pope, the whole thing."

"Nope," said Rita, munching on some pizza crust. "There's over two-hundred some odd Cardinals but only the top 120 are admitted into the Conclave to elect a new Pope. And if you're currently in the special 120 but get to be over eighty years' old, you're booted. Too old to be a voter."

"That's harsh," said Pete. So, where does our boy fit in? Too new to be a voter?"

Charlie said, "Yes, he hasn't got his stripes yet. He might never get them, since the Curia Boys control who's in and who's not. He'd have to do something really noteworthy to get that kind of honor, to be added to the Conclave roster."

There was quiet for a few minutes as everyone took bites of their pizza and mulled what had just been learned. Finally, Pete said, "That was a long pregnant pause. Is everyone thinking what I'm thinking, that we may have stumbled across the motive behind whatever it is Maroney's up to?"

Rita put down the fresh piece she had just picked up, "Jesus Christ, you think he's after some ancient artifact to prove his worth to the Curia? Just so he can vote for white or black smoke?"

Charlie looked at the dumbfounded faces before him. "Let's just say that's the leading theory for the time being."

• • •

Saturday, July 2:

The Cardinal nervously drummed his fingers on the table in his residence. He wanted a shot of Scotch whiskey, but knew his breath would be tell-tale as it was still early afternoon and he had just recently conducted the noon mass. His aide, the Monsignor, was frantically counting out the $25,000 fee for Charlie Franklin in his small locked office and was unavailable to provide the Cardinal any calming advice. Not that the Monsignor was very good at giving advice at this point. He only knew as much about the plan as Maroney wanted him to know, which wasn't much, which frustrated the young monsignor and forced him to be more diligent in his duties to improve his standing with the Cardinal.

The Cardinal had promised Wesley Leonard a pleasant and significant future if the plan succeeded, a promise the Cardinal intended to keep only if it fit his needs. Otherwise, Monsignor Leonard would be expendable. Since the young man knew only limited information, the Cardinal hoped he would not be a serious risk once the plan reached fruition. On the other hand, if he sensed the young man was becoming a risk – well, there are ways of dealing with him.

But now, the Cardinal needed someone to talk to, even if it meant his only choice was the Monsignor. He dressed in his full red outfit, including the *Zucchetto* skull cap, and went to the Monsignor's office. He knocked on the locked door.

"Who is it," came a harried voice from inside.

"It's me, Wesley," replied the Cardinal. "No one else is here. Open the door."

The Monsignor cracked open the door and looked around to verify that no one else was nearby. "I'm still counting, Your Eminence. Almost done."

"That's fine. Let me in." The door opened wide to allow the Cardinal to enter, then was quickly slammed and locked. "Slamming the door will show your fear of being discovered all the more notably than if you simply closed the door quietly," the Cardinal admonished.

The Monsignor shook his head, "I apologize, but I've never handled this much actual cash all at one time. I've got five stacks of 50 one-hundred-dollar bills, and I'm re-counting to make sure there are no errors."

"I assume you accessed the diocese treasury for this, correct?"

"Well, not the actual treasury, but the amount we set aside from the Sunday Offerings that was never recorded as being received in the first place. The funds on the table will almost deplete that special 'fund'. We'll need to rebuild it over time."

"Indeed. All will be well moving forward. What do you think Mr. Franklin has discovered about Merke Edelstein?"

The Monsignor finished his counting, "Forty-eight, forty-nine, fifty." He looked up, slightly bewildered, "You only told me about her a few weeks ago. I didn't even know she existed. I can't imagine what he could have discovered that you don't already know. How is it that you don't know more, yourself? You've done business with her in the past, I presume."

The Cardinal shrugged, "I followed the same procedure used by my father. I only made a few minor purchases through her – that small 17th Century painting in my office, for example – and I never thought that I would have this much trouble procuring other items through her."

"Did your brother ever purchase from her?"

"Yes, I assume so, but I certainly cannot ask him anything about her now, can I?"

The Monsignor shook his head, "No, that's out of the question. Well, I just hope Mr. Franklin can help put your mind at ease. By the way, I've asked George to do some checking on Mr. Franklin's secretary who is possibly his girlfriend. George is developing a pretty good dossier on her. I figured it may be helpful to have something on our delivery boy if things don't proceed according to our wishes. And even if everything ends well, having some juicy information on Franklin or his friends may guarantee his cooperation and silence moving forward."

The Cardinal smiled, "I came in here seeking a calming voice, and you have provided me with just what I needed. That is excellent. Very good thinking on your part. Ask George to give me a written report in duplicate, just in case I need to show a copy to Mr. Franklin in the future."

Wesley smiled at being appreciated, "He expects it to be finished in a few days, if that's acceptable. Oh, and his cousin and a couple of his old friends from Boston are here, taking in the city and learning their way around. I've got them in the shelter, as you suggested, and gave them the keys to the old Chevy station wagon that was donated for use by the homeless. Amazingly, it still runs."

The Cardinal stood to leave, "Well done. I don't wish to meet them, but knowing they are nearby is reassuring. I assume they are capable of carrying out any mission we send them on?"

Wesley nodded and dropped his head, "George says they are quite undisciplined and a bit frightening. They each have been incarcerated for various crimes, and are currently awaiting trials for some serious acts. I assume they have violated their bail requirements just by being out of Massachusetts. George thinks they wish to go to Canada with the money they earn from us."

The Cardinal sneered awkwardly, "Just keep them away from me. I look forward to George's report on the girlfriend in a few days." Motioning to the desktop, he said, "Put that money in two large manila envelopes. Make them as flat as possible. Anyone who sees him leave here with such packages will assume there are simply papers inside. If he walks out with a thick envelope that looks like a wad of bills – well, that would look questionable." He thought for a moment, "Perhaps he'll be willing to take only one of the packages until the job is complete. We'll suggest that as our safeguard." The Cardinal chuckled and waved what appeared to be a blessing, "Let me know when Mr. Franklin arrives."

• • •

The Thespian Grill

Angelo received the green light to enter Rocco's office. "Got some nice stills of Marie for you," he said, handing a large envelope to Rocco.

Rocco opened it and pulled out a stack of 8 x 10 glossy images of a naked Marie in various positions. "Marone! We're wasting this on the Cardinal? I'm gonna get a boner just lookin' at these," said Rocco.

Angelo chuckled, "We sent a copy of the flash drive to the New York Family who wanted it. Any idea why they're interested in a Cardinal from Cleveland?"

Rocco continued to page through the photos, "Jesus, what a body. I swear, I'll need to have her dump the Card – I need some'a this, myself. Ah, no, Angelo, I have no idea what the Basili Family wanted with the pictures. Maybe you could do some inquiries, since we so nicely provided what they wanted. Give Pauly Basili a call. I think he serves as the consigliere to his old man, Giovanni. You and Pauly can talk as equals. Find out what you can. It's only fair they share somethin' they know, since we're trying to put pieces together ourselves." He put the photos down, "But make sure they know we're not pryin' into their business. I don't need a New York Family gettin' pissed off and choosin' sides in this town. Hard enough keepin' the Triunnos in their place."

Angelo nodded, "I'll be dutifully cordial. The Basili Family, they run Brooklyn, don't they? Wonder if I can get them to send us some good Italian bread. Hard to find here, anymore."

Rocco said, "Yeah, if it wasn't for Gallucci's, we'd be without anything good to eat. Speaking of keepin' the peace with the Triunnos, whad'ya find out about that tail? Are they in on it?"

Angelo shook his head, "Not only did they not know anything about him, they were falling over themselves thanking us for the courtesy of letting them know that an out-of-towner was roaming around. They said if they spotted him, they'd let us know."

"Ya' know," said Rocco smiling, "Frankie Triunno is actually a good guy. He and I yusta be good friends. It was my old man – and his, too, I suppose – what got into a beef over somethin'. I'd like it if we got along better, maybe two Goombahs doing business together, but separate-like. That'd be nice, don't ya' think?"

Angelo just nodded, "Yes, that would be nice. I think Frank may still be upset about Glenville, though. And that other stuff just won't go away."

"Hey, that was just business. If he couldn't protect his own territory from a take-over, too bad. As for that old stuff – aah, no one gets too worked up over somethin' that happened a long time ago, right? They can't hold a grudge forever, right?"

Angelo said, "Anyway, I asked a couple of our boys to follow Charlie to see if they could pick up the scent on the tail that was on him. Nothing so far."

Rocco looked hard at Angelo, "They lost Charlie, didn't they?"

Sheepishly, Angelo looked at the carpet, "Yeah. Somewhere in the Terminal Tower."

"Jesus Fuckin' Christ! I'm surprised we ever get anything accomplished around here with the goof-balls we've got on the payroll. I mean, I know Charlie is pretty good at his work, and he can shake off a tail when he needs to, but gawd almighty, we send two guys and they don't know how to stay on their man? Doesn't fill me with confidence that I'll be safe walkin' out the back door!"

Angelo raised his hands, "Maybe I didn't make it plain what they were expected to do. I told them it would be an easy assignment, no heavy stuff. So maybe they were too casual about it. I'll talk to them before they go out again."

"Give 'em a message from me – they lose the tail this time and I'll send 'em to count the walleye in Lake Erie. *Capisce?*"

Angelo headed for the door, "Yes sir, boss. I'll get on it."

"Uh, hey, before you go," Rocco picked up the stack of photos, "find out where Marie is. She's not busy with the red cap now. Ask her to stop in to see me. I'd like to, uh, talk to her."

"Yes sir," said Angelo smiling as he exited the office.

• • •

The Chancery

At a few minutes before 2:00 p.m., Charlie rang the buzzer at the chancery gate. He had the microphone pin on the lapel of his sport jacket. He wanted the upcoming conversation recorded and eventually transcribed, protection for whatever might come later. Pete, again dressed as a bum, was across the street in an alcove doorway of an old building where a faded for lease sign hung in the window. The two agreed last night that protection might be needed to secure what they assumed would be a substantial cash payment. Not that Pete carried any type of weapon, but he was a fair to good boxer in his younger days, and even later in life he had to be pugilistic to get out of tough situations as a reporter. Not to be left behind, Rita was in her idling car, hidden around the corner to pick them both up when the transaction was complete. No one asked her not to, so she brought her gun.

Charlie was admitted into the Cardinal's office, where the be-robed man sat in his large leather chair. "Welcome, again, Mr. Franklin," said the Cardinal without a smile. "Since you've already guessed that Monsignor Leonard eaves-drops on our conversations, I've asked him to join us in person for this meeting."

"That will be more convenient for both of us, won't it?" Charlie sat in one of the hard-backed chairs, the Monsignor sliding the other to the side of the desk. "Interesting mirrored cross you have behind you."

The Cardinal glanced over his shoulder, "Yes, a lovely piece. A gift, as I recall. Can't remember from whom. Makes one picture themselves nailed to it, doesn't it?"

"Must weigh a ton, all that mirror and metal."

The Cardinal was suddenly mum on the topic. "Let's discuss our next venture, shall we? As I mentioned to you, the first delivery was, let's say, incomplete. Not your fault," he said waving his hands in absolution, "but, nonetheless, incomplete. Ms. Edelstein assures me that she will correct the error in the next package, which is now ready for pick-up. Are you prepared to make the journey?"

Charlie shifted his weight in the uncomfortable chair. "Are you prepared to pay me for my services?"

The Monsignor spoke up, "I have the offering we agreed to in these envelopes."

The Cardinal laid his hand on the desk close to the Monsignor, a sign to say no more. "You were to provide information on Ms. Edelstein, I recall. Have you been successful in your search for her?"

Charlie smiled, "Indeed. She is a very difficult person to pin down, is she not? I wonder how you communicate with her if you need me to locate her? Do you ever speak to her directly?"

"As you've likely discovered, Ms. Edelstein is a very secretive individual. She prefers that I send her communiques through an intermediary. Primarily, we communicate through telegrams."

"You send these telegrams to the intermediary, I assume," said Charlie. "And the intermediary has a box number, rather than a name. And the telegrams are in a form of code."

The Monsignor shot a surprised glance at the Cardinal. He appeared to not know some of those details. The Cardinal again placed his hand on the desk to settle the Monsignor down, "Well, you seem to know the process well. Now perhaps you understand why I've asked you to find Ms. Edelstein so I might have a clearer line of communication. There has been a great deal of money expended in such a secretive way – it only seems fair that I am able to speak directly to the provider of the goods which I have purchased."

Charlie had guessed well. The Cardinal had no idea who he was dealing with to procure 'the goods', as he described them. "I think it best that you make no attempt to contact Ms. Edelstein directly."

The Cardinal raised up, "My heavens, why not?"

"The lady is, as you have just stated, highly secretive. She lives very much off the grid on an estate in upstate New York. You are not the only person looking for her. So is Interpol."

The Monsignor literally jumped in his chair. "Oh, dear God!"

Charlie said, "Yes, 'dear God', indeed. If you were to reach out to her, if you could even find her, you would put yourself in a great deal of jeopardy. First, I understand she's a crack shot with a hand gun, Ruger 9mm, I've been told. Second, I doubt she is ever without some serious security, whether that be alarms, armed guards, dogs or all three combined. Third, if you located her, she would likely go underground, whether you survived the encounter or not. Fourth, Interpol and the FBI could discover your connection, and there would be questions you probably don't want to answer."

The Cardinal sat back heavily in his chair, making it creak under his weight. "I see. No, none of that would be good. I suppose direct contact is out of the question."

Charlie shook his head, "I don't know what you're really into, Cardinal Maroney, and I don't want to know. Whatever it is, I'd rather stay out of it. I received this information – what little I have given you – from some very unsavory individuals in Europe. I don't reach out to them often, for obvious reasons, but they were surprised I even asked about Merke Edelstein. They know of her, but they stay far away. That's what I intend to do."

The Cardinal sat up, "But you will complete this second mission, per our agreement, won't you?"

Charlie had them right where he wanted. "I'm not sure it's in my best interest to continue with you. There are some very scary people involved and you don't even know who they are or how to contact them. What's in this package I'm supposed to pick up? Ms. Edelstein doesn't deal in mere antiques. If discovered, the contents of the package would create a lot of trouble for whoever possesses it. I don't relish being sent to a Turkish prison, which is where Interpol likes to do their interrogations."

"But we had a deal!" squealed the Monsignor.

Charlie looked at him, "You afraid Cardinal Maroney will send you if I don't go?"

The Monsignor's mouth dropped open as he looked at the Cardinal.

"Now, see here, Mr. Franklin. No, I won't send Monsignor Leonard. I trust you. I need you. You said you wanted to set the meeting time and location. I assume – knowing what you now know about Ms. Edelstein – I assume you will take extra precautions to ensure your own safety. You name your terms. I will send a telegram with explicit details as you lay them out. I will insist that there be no variations to your request." The Cardinal leaned forward and changed his expression, "As far as the contents of the package, I assure you there is nothing illegal within the wrappings, and you will not be in jeopardy if you are searched. The documents, of course, could be damaged if the package is opened."

Charlie frowned and folded his arms, as if considering what he might do. He didn't believe the Cardinal's assertion that the package was innocent. He knew it was likely illegal to possess whatever it was, but then again, he never had the intention of not picking up the package. His pride and curiosity wouldn't let him back down at this point, especially since the warning he gave the Cardinal was all contrived by Pete and Rita. He just wanted to establish the upper hand in this deal and learn as much as possible about what the Cardinal knew. Aside from knowing what he was after, the Cardinal knew very little else. No, this was clearly about a trade – whatever he picked up would be traded by the Cardinal for something else, something Maroney wanted very badly.

Cardinal Maroney grew impatient, "Look. Here. Give me the envelopes, Wesley. No, both of them. Here's the payment you wanted, $25,000 in cash. Count it, if you wish. Feel free. Just retrieve this one package for me and I will not trouble you again."

Charlie took the two manila envelopes and gave them a squeeze. "If there's not exactly $25,000 in here, I won't be delivering any package from Ms. Edelstein."

"It's all there. I counted it three times to be sure," said the Monsignor to both Charlie and the Cardinal.

Charlie sat forward, leaning his elbows on the desk, "Here's the delivery instructions: In three days, Tuesday, July 5th, 10:00 a.m., a tour of St. Patrick's Cathedral in Manhattan will begin. I'll be in the tour. Ten minutes in, I'll duck out of the tour and into a pew, midway in the church. The delivery will take place in the pew. If the delivery person doesn't show within ten minutes of my sitting in the pew, I leave. If I get the package, I'll deliver it later that night." He looked toward the Monsignor who was taking notes rapidly. "You get all that, Wesley?"

A few minutes later, Charlie exited the iron gate, two manila envelopes in hand, and turned the corner, out of sight of the chancery. He walked past Rita sitting in the car, then crossed the street where he sat down in a bus stop shell. Several minutes later, Pete shuffled around the corner, stopping at the car where he spoke to the driver and got in the back seat. Rita did a U-turn in the center of the road and stopped abruptly at the bus stop shell. Charlie rose quickly and got in the front seat. No one followed them as they headed to the apartment.

Across the street, in the third-floor window of the same building with the 'for lease' sign, a short, thin, dark-haired man dressed in black filled a 35-mm camera with pictures of Charlie, Rita in the car, Pete dressed as a bum, and the U-turn departure.

• • •

At the Apartment
Charlie counted out $5,000 and gave it to Pete, then went to the safe hidden in bedroom wall and deposited the remaining $20,000.

Pete said, “You know, Charlie, that’s a pretty stiff tip you just gave me. More than I think I deserve.”

“Sometimes I can only give you a little, sometimes the payday is bigger. As far as I’m concerned, you earned it.”

“What about Rita? You giving her a nice cut?”

Charlie said, “She knows the combination to the safe. She can take whatever she wants or needs at any time. I make sure she’s whole at the end of every gig.”

Rita returned to the living room, “I got you on the American flight at 6:00 a.m., Tuesday morning. Lands in New York about 7:30 – plenty of time to cab it to St. Pat’s. The nearest car rental is a Hertz on 55th between 6th and 7th Avenues. Reserved you a sedan. OK?”

“Thanks, Rita, that will be perfect. That’s what, a four or five block walk from the Cathedral? Should be just fine.” Charlie looked around at his team, “Looks like I’m headed back to New York.”

Pete asked, “Any idea who you’re going to meet? Who’s got the package?”

Charlie shook his head, “Nope. Adventure in travel. It’ll be up to them to locate me. No carnation this time.”

“They may never find you in that big church. What if they don’t show in time?” asked Rita.

“Then I head home without a package and $25,000 to the good.”

Pete sat back into the upholstered chair, “I gotta leave in a few minutes. One of my other jobs is coming to a head this afternoon, but I gotta ask, how did His Nibs react to the description of Ms. Murky?”

Charlie smiled, “It was perfect. When I mentioned Interpol I thought they’d both shit their pants. I told them if they tried to contact her, they’d end up dead or in a Turkish prison. Little Wesley kind of squealed at that.”

Rita said, “Maybe he was squealing in delight at the thought of being the boy toy to a bunch of swarthy prisoners.”

"Be nice, you," admonished Pete. "He's just a sweet boy. No need to make him out to be nasty. What would you say if you thought you'd be the girl toy to a bunch of ... never mind, don't answer that."

"Ooh! I love it when you talk dirty to me, Pete. A bunch of what? C'mon, I need a new bedroom fantasy."

"Back to the Cardinal, please," said Charlie. "I had them convinced that I was going to bail on the gig, which had them in a real panic. I told them I was frightened of Merke Edelstein and what she represented and was ready to pull the plug. At that point, the Cardinal literally threw the money at me and pleaded, saying he'd never bother me again after we finished this job."

Pete smirked, "You believe him?"

"Not for a second. I don't trust a word he says. I think Rita and I need to watch our steps for a few months after this is all over. If things go his way – or even if they don't – he'll try to make sure there is no one left to incriminate him."

"You and Rita need to be careful, huh? How about me, am I just chopped liver?" asked Pete.

Charlie said, "So far, they don't know you've been involved. I don't think you've got anything to worry about. But poor little Wesley, I think the Monsignor is in over his head, and he may find himself in water over his head pretty soon."

Rita said, "Poor Wesley. He goes from being shtupped by a gang of Turkish prisoners to counting crawdads at the bottom of Lake Erie. He doesn't lead a charmed life, does he?"

"Okay, I gotta run," said Pete. "I'll be tied up for the next few days. Leave me a message when you're back safe and sound. When I've got some free time, we'll do a *post mortem* on all of this. Travel safe."

After Pete left, Rita asked, "You're all set for your flight on Tuesday, right?"

"Yeah, I think so. Thanks for everything you've done."

"Cool. Listen, I'm going to spend the next few days with my friends, if you don't mind. Fourth of July, picnic, fireworks and all that. I can be safe with them since it will be a big group, and I don't want to just sit here alone twiddling my thumbs while you head off to New York.

Besides, being with some people my own age feels good sometimes. You can call if you need me for something, but I think you're all set."

Charlie frowned, "Is Nick one of the friends you're going to hang out with?"

Rita blew him a kiss and said, "No questions asked. That's one of our rules, remember?"

"Okay. No questions asked. Check with me occasionally so I know you're OK. I'll send you an all-clear message when I'm back in town."

"Great!" She ran off to pack an overnight-or-two bag. Charlie pulled the bourbon out of the liquor cabinet.

• • •

Independence Day Weekend:
A Sunday with no one around. He seldom had a full day just for himself, free to do whatever he wanted. Charlie reviewed his notes on what he knew to date, and made a list of what he hoped to learn or accomplish in the coming days. Swinging by the office, he retrieved the burner phone and charged the battery. Then he treated himself to a nice steak dinner at his favorite restaurant. But once there, he began to feel lonely, sitting by himself at a corner table, overhearing the muffled friendly conversations and the loving murmurs of the other patrons. Charlie was not given to self-pity, but this was one time he wished he had someone else to talk to, sitting at a table for one in such a fine steakhouse. He mused that his choice of work, his lifestyle, left little room for casual friendships. Too often lately he ended his day by falling into unhealthy self-reflection. Too often he tried to imagine a way out of being a fixer, remembering what it was like in the old days, when his time was filled with enjoyable ignorance. These days, too frequently he ended the day asleep in a chair with a drink in his hand. No, he thought to himself. Charlie Franklin shouldn't be left alone too often. But finding a companion who shared his unique view of the world was not easy.

• • •

Last night he drank himself to sleep. Again. Tomorrow, he was scheduled to catch the early morning flight to New York City, but today he was again free. And again alone. Rita was spending time with her friends, whatever that might mean. Pete was dealing with some big cases with big paydays. Charlie put his self-pity aside and tried to puzzle out the several facts and a few guesses from the previous days, and attempt to put them into some sort of order. The overseas call on the burner had provided some answers and led to some solidification of his theories. What had been foggy unrelated pieces were starting to take shape, but the picture was not pleasant.

He thought about returning the call from his friend, Amir Habood, but decided to hold off until his return from New York. Amir and he could argue and laugh for hours, and Charlie needed the time to consider all the ramifications of his work with the Cardinal. Amir could celebrate the 4th of July without him. He considered trying to find someplace to watch fireworks, but a single middle-aged man wandering around in the dark would look like a stalker or worse among the kids and families settling down to watch the boomers. Instead, he turned on the sports channel and watched a series of baseball games until he fell asleep on the couch.

• • •

Tuesday, July 5:

A fitful night full of what-if-this-happens plans came to a quick end as the 4:00 a.m. alarm roused Charlie to a hurried departure for Hopkins Airport. "My own fault," he said to himself. "Should've never made this a one-day trip." He hadn't wanted to spend the night in New York, even though another night with the Vixen of the Waldorf might be great. Nevertheless, there was just too much danger in the air. Another night with TK might be great, or it might be deadly. And so, here he was, boarding the American Airlines flight due to depart at 6:00 a.m.

At such an early hour, it is rare for a flight to be delayed, and this one was no exception. It even landed early, about 7:20 a.m. He grabbed his only luggage, an over-sized mostly empty briefcase, and headed to the taxi stand. On any normal day at any normal time LaGuardia

Airport was a zoo: streams of people shouting several different languages all heading in different but usually wrong directions; baggage with clattering wheels cluttering the too-narrow walk-ways; odors from day-old food, overly-burned coffee, and unwashed travelers assaulting olfactory senses at every turn; irritable cabbie-masters growling at customers and drivers with equal ferocity. But it was not yet 8:00 a.m., and the city that supposedly never sleeps wasn't fully awake yet either.

He was the third person in the taxi line, an unheard-of luxury at LaGuardia. Looking down the drive he saw dozens of cabs lined up, waiting for their first fare of the day. It looked like he'd get into the city well ahead of schedule. A businessman took the first cab, a woman who he guessed to be an advertising executive got the second. And just that quickly he was on his way to Manhattan. He told the cabby to take him to Rockefeller Center, not wanting to disembark in front of the cathedral in case someone from Merke Edelstein was watching.

He couldn't get over the impact of the description Pete and Rita had evolved for Ms. Murky. After having repeated and memorized the description for the Cardinal, he had come to believe some of it himself. That made him jumpy at the thought of having to deal with someone wanted by Interpol, even though it was all a made-up story. At least he tried to convince himself it was made up. They had done such a great job describing the non-existent woman that Charlie himself had come to believe that parts of it, maybe large parts of it, were actually true.

Even though the morning-after-a-holiday rush-hour traffic had started to build, the cab still managed to deliver him to Rockefeller Center well before 8:30 a.m. It didn't take him long to find a coffee shop for only his second cup of the day. The first, airport coffee at its worst, found a trash can after only a few sips. The only beverage on the plane was a plastic cup of apple juice, the coffee maker on the plane being broken with apologies from the flight attendant. So, he had high hopes for this coffee shop serving the multitudes of workers in the Rockefeller Center tower. He was wrong. More dishwater. Perhaps he could find a Starbucks as soon as the transaction was complete. At 9:00 a.m., he made his way toward St. Patrick's Cathedral to register for the 10 o'clock tour.

It had been a long time since Charlie had been in a church, even longer since he had been to St. Patrick's Cathedral in New York City. He was always awed by the neo-gothic ornamental architecture, the incredibly high vaulted ceiling, the strange omnipresent mixture of whispers and echoes, so faint they could be the hushed haunting hum from visitors of long ago. Throughout the massive structure the sweet-scented blend of bee's wax candles and once-burned incense comforted the cool air.

He was one of the first to register for the morning tour. He sat in the shadows in a rear pew, off to the side, looking over his shoulder as he tried to identify someone who might be his contact. A mother and father struggled to contain their two small children who were intent upon running through the aisles. An ancient woman knelt in a pew, reciting the rosary while shakily fingering her beads. A young couple pointed at statues while casually and quietly conversing in what seemed to be an Eastern-European language – maybe Polish, maybe Czech. A faint swish of garment fabric announced a group of three Dominican nuns in fully covered garb, all black except for a halo of white encircling their faces, as they slowly took in the glory before them. A sad old man, grasping a funeral card from his beloved wife in both hands, pointed it toward the mighty altar so his departed wife could see it through the card. There were others. A young priest, mouth agape, enjoying what was likely his first visit; a group of teenagers all wearing their school colors; several others slowly craning to see the highest points and marveling at the colors of the stained glass. There were, perhaps, three dozen worshipers in all. None seemed likely to be Charlie's contact. None carried a package that could be what Charlie was to receive. He began to think that the deal might have been called off.

As 10:00 a.m. approached, Charlie joined the line forming at the rear of the cathedral, all with tickets in hand to show to the tour leader. He worked his way toward the end of the line, looking over his shoulder to see if any late arriving patrons might join the tour. No one appeared. He was becoming more certain than ever that this mission was destined to be a failure, then smiled inwardly that at least he had the $25,000 fee in hand, successful mission or not.

The tour began at the rear of the cathedral, the docent admirably speaking in a bold, yet reverently hushed tone, proudly showing off the wonders of what was, to him, a very sacred place. Charlie paid little attention to what was being said. By ten minutes after the hour, the group had reached the middle of the nave, the midpoint of the pew sections for the faithful. Charlie took two steps back from the group, then another as the docent turned to call attention to a significant detail in the ceiling. As the group proceeded forward, Charlie slipped into a pew and sat down, leaving room on both sides for a contact person to use. He looked around. No one was headed his way. He made himself as comfortable as possible, setting his over-sized briefcase on the floor where the kneeler was folded up. He was looking toward the altar while mentally picturing where the Hertz counter could be found.

He felt a swish, almost ghostlike, behind him, turning to look, he saw one of the nuns approaching his right side. Behind him, another of the nuns was kneeling, so that her habit brushed against his head. Instinctively, Charlie looked to his left. The third nun closed on him with a smile and sat close to his side. Along the edge of the white halo encircling her face, Charlie could see a wisp of blonde hair.

"Hi, Charlie."

"TK? Is that you?"

"I was hoping we could have some more fun when you came back to town, but you went and chose a church for our meeting. How boring."

"Why are you all dressed up like this," asked Charlie, once again catching the hint of honeysuckle perfume.

"Well, I couldn't very well be naked in here, could I? Although, I must confess in front of the Almighty, I have nothing on under this thing. Here, I'll show you." She grabbed Charlie's hand and slid it through a wide pocket opening at her hip. Charlie could instantly feel that she was telling the truth.

"Oh, my God," whispered Charlie.

TK shook her head, "No, I'm actually a goddess, Charlie. I thought you knew that. See, if you stayed in town a while, I could prove that. Well, maybe me and my sisters here." The other two nuns giggled.

Charlie surreptitiously and reluctantly withdrew his hand. TK gasped, "Oh, I liked what you were doing. I wish you hadn't stopped."

"We're in a Cathedral, TK, not in a bedroom, and I think we're supposed to conduct some business," said Charlie, trying to regain control of the situation.

"Can't you spend the night with me and my sisters? I told them how much fun you can be." The other two bowed their heads and said, "Amen, amen."

Charlie gulped almost audibly, "I need to leave later this morning, either with the package or without. So, I beg you, if you have the package for delivery, I'll take it now."

"Oh, poo! You always want to do only the right thing." Motioning to the nun behind him, TK said, "Sister Rachel knows a place in a hidden confessional up toward the front where we can all go for a little fun."

"Mm, hmm!" whispered Rachel into Charlie's ear, "I've visited it in the past. Even had a Monk lose his virginity in there with me."

Charlie could only shake his head, "Ladies, Sisters, I must insist that you stop all this. We're becoming conspicuous. Let's conduct business and all go our separate ways."

The nun to Charlie's right said, "TK, you promised we'd fuck him all night long. What will we do now?"

TK said, "I've got lots of vodka and batteries at my place. We'll have to make do."

Charlie tried to shake the image out of his mind. "Can I please have the package?"

"Charlie, you're officially a bore," said TK. "Naomi – I mean Sister Naomi, please give him the package."

From under the robe of her habit, the nun on his right produced a large manila envelope about two inches think. She handed it to Charlie and said, "It probably smells from my perfume. I'm naked under this thing, too."

Sister Rachel whispered in his ear, "So am I."

Charlie dropped the package into his lap and raised his head, "Oh, holy crap! I won't be able to stand up for a while, now."

TK leaned in on his left and whispered in his ear, "I somehow have the feeling we're going to meet again, Charlie. If that's the case, please do plan on spending a night or two, and not in a goddamn church." She kissed him gently on the ear, secretly slipped a business card with her phone number into his jacket pocket, and departed the pew. The other two nuns whisked away rapidly, and there Charlie sat, trying to regain his composure and stabilize his breathing. After about 10 minutes, Charlie was able to rise and head out towards the Hertz car rental a few blocks away. It would be a long drive to think about what had just taken place.

He focused on getting out of Manhattan quickly and putting as many miles as possible behind him before he stopped at the first exit past the Pennsylvania State Line. He checked his cell phone – another text message from Amir Habood. He had been remiss in not seeing his old friend. He returned the text suggesting they meet tomorrow or the next day for lunch. Then he sent a text to Rita and Pete: "All is good. On my way back. Lots to talk about when we next gather." He smiled and said to himself, "Yes, there is an awful lot to talk about. I wonder if I should tell them everything, or leave some things to their imagination?"

• • •

The Thespian Grill

Angelo DiFranco was nervous and shaken, unusual for the consigliere known for his calm in even the most dangerous of situations. His demeanor was noticed by the Dobermans as he entered the front door of the Thespian Grill. If Angelo was troubled, the Dobermans knew there was danger nearby. They checked their weapons to make sure they were loaded, then blocked the front door as Angelo bolted for the office in the rear of the restaurant.

He pounded on the door, ignoring the guard sleepily sitting nearby, who jumped up nearly knocking over his chair. The guard said, "What the fuck? Angelo! Knock it off! He's got Marie in there!"

"Oh, shit!" said the consigliere. "I forgot that was this afternoon. He's gonna kick my ass. But this is really important."

The intercom next to the guard chair buzzed. Rocco's voice came through loud and clear, initiating with a litany of curses and vindictive promises to dismember any and all who were outside the door and promised to stuff their appendages in unnatural places. The green light did not come on.

Angelo looked at the frightened face of the guard and said, "Go take a cigarette break. I'll wait here until he's ready to see me. Better if you're not around to take the heat." Not bothering to offer thanks, the guard raced to the exit, fumbling for his cigarettes as he went.

Angelo took the chair where the guard was sitting, and assumed that role. He could not control his restless leg from tapping up and down. His news was big. Huge. He used the minutes to try and settle himself so he could convey what information he could in an organized fashion. He needed to be as calm as possible and to slowly drop one bombshell after another so that Rocco could follow the flow easily. He didn't want to risk Rocco blowing his top and doing something foolish until the clear picture was known, and even Angelo didn't have a completely clear picture. This was going to be tricky. Some of what he had just been told was not for Rocco's ears. Angelo was about to walk a very taut high wire and there would be no net.

Almost twenty minutes went by when the green light went on and the automatic lock clicked open. Angelo looked to the back of the bar where the guard was now hiding and motioned to him to re-take his chair. He took a deep breath and entered Rocco's office.

Rocco thankfully had a smile on his face, but he still lit into Angelo, "What the fuck was so goddamn important that some asshole was poundin' on my door? What's going on out there? Where's my guard? Somebody poundin' just when Marie and I were ... talkin' things over."

"My fault, Rocco, not the guard's. I'm the asshole. I was in a hurry to give you some important news," said Angelo.

Marie was just coming out of the bathroom, smoothing her hair and re-applying lip stick. "I'll get outa here in a minute, fellas. Just let me grab my things."

"Actually, Marie," said Angelo, "maybe you oughta stick around outside for a few minutes. Some of this involves you."

Marie stopped in her tracks and glanced at Rocco who nodded to her. "Have a drink at the bar. I'll call you back in a few minutes." Rocco sat behind his desk as Marie exited, "What's this all about, Angelo? What's so important you try to beat my door down?"

Angelo asked, "Mind if I sit down?" Rocco nodded. "I talked to Pauly Basili. Lots of information. Let me put it into some sort of order. First, I found out that Charlie Franklin is on another job for the Cardinal. There's some talk that it's actually an extension of his first mission."

Rocco said, "Jesus Christ! What the hell is Charlie doin' for him? I thought he just went to pick up a package last week."

"It was closer to two weeks ago, but yeah, that's what he was doing. Cardinal wasn't happy with what was in the package, so Charlie's giving it another shot."

"We oughta tell Charlie not to trust that red-hatted asshole. He's up to no good."

Angelo nodded, "I think Charlie knows that. From what we hear, he gouged the Card for trip number two, getting a big payday. Anyway, it seems that the Card is after something valuable – at least something valuable to some other folks. He's planning on trading whatever it is for something else."

Rocco asked, "Who's he trading with?"

"That's where it gets a bit tricky. What Pauly told me is there's someone in Italy that would be willing to grant the Card some special favors if they could acquire a specific item. Pauly wouldn't say who, or where the person is, but I think if we put the pieces together, we can guess it's someone in Rome, possibly inside the Vatican."

Rocco shook his head, "That fat punk is way outa his league, don't you think? He never used to act that way back when he was just a Bishop. Sure, he had us do him some favors under the table, but nothin' like this."

Angelo shrugged, "People change, Rocco. You're right, this is far more involved than what he did in the past, but something's got him going."

"So how does Marie fit into all of this?"

Angelo said, "Well, that's where the Basili Family gets involved. They have people in Italy that asked them to intercede and slow down what the Cardinal is doing, or possibly stop him entirely."

"Jesus, are they gonna rub him out? That will explode on us here big time. That's worse than taking out a police chief or a politician. Holy crap!"

Angelo waived his hands, "No, no. They know that would be too big a deal for us and for them. The FBI would get involved, there would be investigations – no, no rub out. They just want to make his life a living hell, that's the way Pauly put it. The package that Charlie is picking up won't have the materials the Cardinal wants. It's going to be a nice photo album of the Cardinal and Marie in bed together."

Rocco burst into laughter, "Does Charlie know about this?"

"Don't think so. He just thinks he's making a second attempt at picking up what the Cardinal wanted in the first place."

"Holy shit! That's actually kinda funny. Charlie gets a big payday and delivers a pile of poop on the Cardinal's desk. I love it."

Angelo nodded, "Well, there are ramifications to all of this. First, Marie is probably through being the Cardinal's girlfriend. She may be at some physical risk if she goes back to him after he gets the photo album."

Rocco nodded, "You're right. We'll call her back in and send her somewhere nice for a while to stay outa his way. Maybe somewhere where I can join her from time to time."

"Sure, sure," said Angelo. "How about the villa in Las Vegas? Nice place, you like it there, private and quiet."

Rocco smiled and nodded, "That's perfect. It is quiet there. I'd like to make her scream a bit to break up the quiet." His mind was in a future reverie.

"The other thing is, we need to get the equipment out of the Cardinal's nest. Won't be good to have any investigators locate the smoke detectors with the cameras once he sees the pictures."

"Oh, shit. You're right. He's liable to call the cops and the chain back to us will be easy to trace. When's Charlie delivering the package?"

"Later tonight, I think. I've got the electrician on stand-by assuming you'll agree."

"Shit, yes. Get him in there right away."

"I told him that he'd have to make it a cold-call, saying that the units he just installed were found to be defective, a fire hazard, or something. That should allow him to get in quickly."

"Good. I don't care if he leaves bare wires dangling, just get those cameras outa there."

"I'm on it," said Angelo standing to leave. "You want to break the news to Marie, or you want me to do it?"

Rocco smiled, "No, send her back in. I'll tell her she's gonna have a really nice vacation in Las Vegas. Is that great restaurant still open in Caesar's?"

"You mean Rao's? I think so. Best Veal Parmesan I ever had."

"Ain't that the truth. I'm gonna go out there this weekend just to make sure Marie's comfortable."

Angelo added the last and most important news. "So, Pauly Basili says his old man thinks highly of you."

"No shit? I've never met the guy!"

"Someone who knows both of you must have dropped a dime on you. You should consider it an honor."

Rocco's chest pushed out, "No shit! Maybe I can use his backing to make a move on those bastards on The Hill. Town's not big enough for both of us."

"I thought you and Frankie Triunno were old friends," said Angelo, pretending to be astonished.

"Yeah, whatever. He'd do it to me if he had half a chance."

• • •

The Package Arrives

Charlie drove straight to the chancery, arriving just as the sun was setting in the mid-summer sky. He wasn't worried about having any backup. After all, he already had the cash from the Cardinal and didn't expect any incidents. He'd just deliver the package and leave. He parked at a meter across the street from the chancery gate just as a light blue service van was pulling away. The side of the van was painted with a logo for 'Ace Electrical, Alarm Specialists'.

He hit the buzzer at the gate, and after a short delay, the gate buzzed back admitting him. He was met at the door by the Monsignor. "No need for pleasantries, Monsignor Leonard, here's the package. I assume I can leave it with you and not deliver it personally to the Cardinal."

The Monsignor's lips tightened, "Correct. I will see that the Cardinal receives the package straight away. May I ask if you opened it?"

Charlie gave him a wry smile, "I remember the rules, Wesley. No, I did not open the package. What is in your hands is exactly what I received." He turned to leave, then turned back, "Oh, by the way. There may be a faint smell of perfume on the package. I'll let you two try to figure out where that came from."

The Monsignor's mouth hung open as Charlie exited the gate and returned to the rental car. Charlie started laughing to himself, which turned into a full guffaw as he drove away. He could only imagine the conversation between the Monsignor and the Cardinal over the smell of perfume on the package.

He returned the rental car at the Hopkins Airport Hertz counter then took the shuttle bus to the parking lot to retrieve his car for the drive back to his apartment. It was less than 18 hours since he left, but it felt like he had been away a week. He was exhausted from the short night, the early flight, and the long drive back to Cleveland. He wasn't looking for any tails, so he didn't notice that a car had followed him from downtown to the airport and was now following him home. Even if he had noticed it, he would be unable to identify the two men dressed in black in the front seat.

Charlie got to his apartment and knocked on the door with the safe knock before opening, just in case Rita was home with her gun. She was not. He kicked off his shoes and opened a beer, settling into his favorite chair. For once he was pleased to have the place all to himself, quiet and calm, and glad that Rita was enjoying herself with her friends. He closed his eyes and began reliving the events of the last several hours: the flight, the lousy coffee, the darkened cathedral with the rosary lady and the sad old man, and finally the nuns. Not really nuns. Who were they? Sure, one was TK Constantine, but who were the other two, Rachel and Naomi? He thought he could still smell the faint fragrance of honeysuckle. Then he fast-forwarded to the Monsignor and the Cardinal: what were they discovering in the package? It had felt similar to the previous package he delivered – documents in a heavy binder all wrapped in plastic and taped on all corners. Did the Cardinal get a whiff of the perfume from Naomi? Not the same as TK's scent, but just as enticing. His eyes remained closed as his thoughts scattered over the day's action and his head laid back until he fell asleep.

Outside the apartment, the car that had followed Charlie from the airport sat idling with the lights off. A small, dark-haired man dressed in black approached from the sidewalk and got in the rear seat. After a few minutes of lively discussion among the three men, the car slowly pulled away into the dusk.

• • •

The Cardinal and the Second Package

As soon as Charlie left the chancery grounds, the Monsignor rapidly yet carefully carried the package into Cardinal Maroney's office. The Cardinal was busying himself with a map of Rome laid out on his desk. He said, "Is that electrician finally gone from my chambers? I can't believe he put in a fire detection system that was itself a fire hazard. That's almost too ridiculous to believe."

The Monsignor was almost breathless, "Yes. Yes, he's gone. Just as he left, Mr. Franklin arrived." The Cardinal looked up from the map. "Here is the package," said the Monsignor, holding the parcel in both extended hands.

The Cardinal leapt to his feet and carefully took the package in both of his hands, sliding it away from the Monsignor. "I will take this into my private rooms. Please ensure that I am not disturbed."

The Monsignor bowed, "Yes, Your Eminence."

The Cardinal locked the door to his chambers and sat at the table with hands shaking. He thought to himself, Finally. Finally, I have what I need to make the next step. It has been an arduous journey with too many pitfalls, too many odd challenges that made it look like success was eluding me. But achieving greatness never comes easy. Once this deal is consummated, I shall need to clean up loose ends. Wesley, yes. He'll need to be dealt with. Perhaps I'll take him with me at the beginning. I'll need someone trustworthy for a little while. Perhaps he will do, but eventually he will have to disappear. He knows too much, even though he doesn't know the half of it. It may be easier for him to be lost in a place unfamiliar to him, like Rome. It will make excuses for his absence more plausible. "Yes, that's a good plan, I'll find someplace to send him," he said aloud, thinking about the map of Rome. "There are dangerous people and dangerous places there. Too bad Wesley doesn't know his way around very well."

He began unwrapping the tight package, being ever so careful not to mar any of the interior. The plastic was thick, and difficult to cut through. He had a sharp blade, but in his shaking hands, he had to be cautious. While peeling back the layers of plastic, he continued to consider ways to protect himself. Franklin will be more difficult, he reasoned, even though he knows less than Wesley. Nonetheless, his involvement makes him a liability. I've dealt with liabilities in the past, what's one more? Perhaps the dossier George is preparing on Charlie's girlfriend will be enough to guarantee Franklin's silence. But one never knows about such individuals. Just when you think you've got them trapped, they squirm free and become even more of a threat. What was it that father always said? Ah, yes, 'Never wound an enemy. Go for the sure kill.' Yes, I'll need to go for the sure kill against Mr. Franklin. I'll need to find an ally to make that happen. Perhaps the gentlemen from Boston, perhaps Mr. Rocco. As the wrapping continued to peel off, he said aloud, "I'll decide how to deal with Charlie Franklin later, once my power increases. I'll have many more allies then, and if there's time, perhaps it can be someone better than those close at hand."

The plastic gave way. He peeled it back in several thick sheets. Eventually, a thick leather binder was in his hands, almost identical to the first binder he had received. He pulled back the cover. It was very tightly wound, almost as though it had not been opened in thousands of years. The leather straps holding the pages together felt aged, ready to crack apart if too much pressure was exerted. Gingerly, he opened the cover farther, exposing a blank sheet resembling ancient papyrus. The Cardinal jumped up and turned off the harsh table light, almost forgetting how sensitive the documents could be. He carefully examined the papyrus to make sure there was no hidden or lost lettering on the page. Then he lifted the page to expose the second sheet, the edges of which looked like more parchment. What he saw made him gasp. It was a full color picture of himself, naked on his bed, with Marie caressing his genitals. The next page was an extreme close up of the same photo, this time focusing on the smallness of his penis.

He kept turning pages, hoping the first few pages were some sort of obscene joke. But each page was an 8 x 10-inch full color picture of him and Marie pasted onto paper resembling ancient parchment, worn or torn on the edges. Each photo showed the two in a variety of compromising sexual positions from several different angles, his face fully visible in each. There were four dozen photos in all, not all from the same day or at the same time. At the end of the photos was a final page with the words '*fruor ipsum*' printed in a script suggesting Roman calligraphy. He scrambled to the Latin / English dictionary on the shelf. As near as he could translate, the phrase meant '*enjoy yourself*'.

He ran to the bedroom scanning the walls and the ceiling for some clue as to where the cameras were hidden. He looked up in shock, collapsing into a heap next to the bed as he saw bare wires hanging from the ceiling where the smoke detectors had been. He ran to retrieve the photo album, trying to line up the photos with the angles accorded by the smoke detectors. There was no doubt – the smoke detectors had been the camera locations.

He grabbed his secret burner cell phone, to contact Marie Carlisle to warn her that these terrible pictures could end up in public view and could cause both of them career-ending embarrassment and public condemnation. He almost placed the call, then stopped – could it be that Marie Carlisle knew about the photos? Was this album her doing? Was this possibly some sort of perverted love letter to show her affection for the Cardinal? He had heard of women who took naked photos of themselves to send to their lovers as a way of exciting them. His mind warped on that notion for a few minutes before coming around to the thought that if it was from Marie, it was not likely an affectionate message, but rather an attempt at blackmail.

His heart flipped quickly from thoughts of love to thoughts of hate. He began to reason that the little tramp was setting herself up for some sort of payday. He'd sooner see her dead. But then, how did she manage to get the photos taken? She didn't install the smoke detectors. It was that damn electrician. And how did the photos make their way to Merke Edelstein? No, it was unlikely that Marie was involved, he rationalized. But if not her, then who?

Who had hired the electrician? His head turned in the direction of Monsignor Wesley Leonard's office. Could that little wimp be plotting against me? Did he think he could fool me? He and his lover George would jump at the chance to take over the chancery funds. It was Wesley who complained that the payment to Mr. Franklin had used up all the funds. There would be very little left for the two of them to use for a lovers' get-away. But how did Wesley get the photos to Ms. Edelstein?

What about Charlie Franklin? He didn't deliver the correct merchandise on the first attempt, then charged a king's ransom for the second pick-up, resulting in this book of garbage. He provided a description of Merke Edelstein intended to scare us off any thought of contacting her directly. What if the story about her was simply a ruse, and instead he actually made contact with Ms. Edelstein, working out a plan to milk me of even more money? The two of them cooked up this horrendous swindle intent upon draining me of all my money.

"Yes, that seems to make more sense than any of the other theories," thought the Cardinal. "But Charlie Franklin didn't get the cameras in here by himself. And perhaps it was Marie's willingness to perform for a camera that made her so athletic in bed. Are all three of them in on this together? After all, it was Wesley who vetted Mr. Franklin in the first place. He said he got the final recommendation from the Congressman, but I have no way of proving that, do I? And who was it that suggested Ms. Carlisle come to me for a private confession in the first place? I don't recall. But it is now apparent that none of my close associates can be trusted."

He poured himself a tall glass of Scotch and sat down in his easy chair to consider his options. If none of the three can be trusted, then none of the three can be told what was in the latest package. If they are guilty, they already know. If they are innocent, it must remain a secret at least until the guilty party is known. In the meantime, some vengeance must be visited upon those who can least be trusted.

The Cardinal revisited an idea he had developed some time ago, where he and Wesley would go on a little trip, one where George can accompany them. He nodded satisfactorily. Wesley would not see the plan through to its final conclusion. He was no longer trustworthy.

• • •

Wednesday, July 6:
Charlie frowned into his bathroom mirror. There was unfinished business. Package delivery or not, he had the unnerving sense that all was not right, and that his dealings with the Cardinal were not yet ended. As he finished his morning shave, he decided to take another run at the Summit County Records Department in downtown Akron. Something was still bothering him about the Maroney family, and he decided to follow a hunch that kept tickling in his mind. He dressed casually to avoid looking like an attorney. A suit makes people clench up, especially the often-put-upon records people. On the other hand, a pleasant smile, a kind demeanor yields better results. They are more likely to help you find what you're after if you don't look like someone who will ask them to testify.

Rather than taking the freeway, Charlie chose the surface road route. A slower trip gave him more time to consider random thoughts, either accepting or throwing away theories. Plus, he could drive with the windows down and suck in the fresh morning air. Along the way, he stopped in Hudson for a cup of coffee at an old looking local diner. The place looked like it had been in the same location for decades. The waitress at the counter looked like she had been there for decades, too.

"What can I get you?" she said, as pleasantly as her boss told her to be.

"Your coffee any good?" asked Charlie.

"Best in town! And I mean that, we make a great cup of coffee."

"Well then, I better have some. Little cream, too."

"Here you go. Refills are free. Want something to eat?"

"I left home without breakfast, so I am kinda hungry," said Charlie. "Looks like you have some sweet rolls. They as good as the coffee?"

The waitress looked at the glass case holding the sweet rolls, then over her shoulder toward the owner back in the kitchen. "Truth is, those are several days old."

Charlie nodded and smiled, "How about some scrambled eggs and wheat toast then?"

She smiled and said loudly enough to be heard in the kitchen, "Coming right up, sir." And then, as she wiped the counter next to Charlie. "I'm adding bacon to your order. He made too much this morning and he told me to push it on everybody."

Charlie smiled. "That actually sounds pretty good."

As Charlie sipped his coffee, the only other patrons at a nearby two-top paid their bill and left. The phone rang in the kitchen and the owner started a conversation as he prepared Charlie's bacon and eggs. The waitress tried to look busy.

"Things always this slow?" he asked.

Sorting silverware the waitress said, "There's usually a strong early crowd, between 6:30 a.m. and about 9:00. Little light today being only a few days after the Holiday. It's now – what – 9:45, so things really slow down until about 11:30."

"Lots of locals, I'm guessing."

"Oh, sure. Especially the old timers, and there's lots of them. Some of the new crowd moving into town, those that have been here less than ten years, they don't stop in much. As long as the older folks don't die off, we'll continue to be busy."

"Lots of old families, then? Old money, too. Huh?"

"You got that right, mister. You seen some of those mansions around here? Big money. Don't know where they got so much, but they do. Big money," she said, shaking her head.

Charlie had the conversation going right where he wanted. "So, who's the wealthiest family in town?"

She thought for a moment. "Well, that's hard to say. I ain't their banker, mind you. I'm betting the Edmonds have got one of the biggest fortunes. They've got a place off Hickory Lane that looks like the land goes for a hundred acres. House must have 30, 40 rooms."

"Wow! Must be pretty famous in this town, huh?"

She shook her head. "No, not really. Most of the big-time-money folks keep to themselves. They don't like to be famous. That just causes too much attention to come their way."

"Order up," came the call from the kitchen.

She delivered Charlie's breakfast. "This looks great," he said. "So, isn't anyone in town famous? Looks like someone should be, given how much big money is here."

The waitress thought for a minute as she refilled Charlie's coffee cup. "Oh, yeah. There is one guy you've probably heard of. Cardinal Maroney, from up in Cleveland. His family has a big place just south of downtown. That is, what's left of the family."

Charlie dug into his eggs. "Lots of 'em dying off?"

"Sort of. The father of the clan died a few years back. His wife divorced him a dozen years ago or so before that and left for California, or someplace. The two boys are all that's left, the Cardinal and his brother. Boy, were those two somethin' when they were younger, always getting' into trouble either alone or as a pair. Couldn't hardly tell who was the instigator, they looked so much alike. Police would usually just haul 'em both in. Father always got 'em off before any charges could get stuck on 'em. Heard one of 'em got sick or somethin' and no longer lives on the family estate. Cardinal, of course, he's up in Cleveland. Could'a knocked me over with a feather when he went and became a priest. Brother's wife is around somewheres. I'm guessing she's the only one living at the place now. No one's seen her in a long time, though. Keeps to herself."

Charlie bit off some bacon. "Money's not everything, huh? Sometimes being healthy is better than being rich."

"You said it, mister, you said it." She walked off to clean the far end of the counter.

Charlie bit into the toast thinking to himself, "The divorced mother of the Cardinal and his sister-in-law – now there's a couple people worth looking into at the Records Department."

The breakfast was just what his stomach needed, and the diner conversation was just what his brain needed – a smart move on his part to stop in at the one place where gossip was a mainstay. On his way south out of town, he swung into the dead-end lane where the Maroney Estate stood. He slowly drove down the lane, looking at each of the large homes, not stopping at the Maroney place, but just taking it all in and clicking off a half-dozen photos of what he could see as he rolled slowly by. It appeared the grass had been recently cut. Seven residences were all there were on the well-manicured lane, each as large as the rest. The Maroney homestead looked exactly as it had during his last visit – no sign of any life anywhere. He noted the address as he left the lane quickly, not wanting anyone to become concerned enough to call the village police again.

His afternoon at the Records Department was fruitful. He learned a great deal, a lot more than he expected to learn. The matriarch of the family had indeed divorced her husband fifteen years ago, citing his philandering as the reason. The father had died quite suddenly of a heart attack at his estate. The circumstances of his death were suspiciously not readily available. When asked for them, the Records Keeper gave Charlie a queer look. He was the second person in the past few days to ask for the same information.

Charlie tried a ruse. "Oh, I'll bet that was my assistant, short red-headed guy?"

"No," the clerk said, looking sideways at Charlie. "Short, yes, but straight dark hair, almost black. Spoke with an accent."

Charlie finished his exploration through the Records Department and headed to the dead newspaper files. The Maroney family was notable for many reasons. The patriarch was not a nice man. He had cheated many out of money, as witnessed by the several civil suits brought against him. He was not philanthropic. No one was eager to name a school or hospital after him, and there would never be a Maroney Street, given the numerous tax evasion citations leveled against him. The news clippings hinted that the mysterious circumstances of his death could best be traced to the person who called the emergency squad: one Miss Bunny Hutch, assumed to be an alias since she disappeared about the same time that the coroner arrived at the scene. A search of the estate by family members revealed that several gold watches and loose jewelry left behind by the divorced mother were missing, although no one was quite able to confirm whether Ms. Hutch had taken them or not.

The sister-in-law to the Cardinal, Victoria (Vicky) Maroney, was apparently a recluse. No one had seen her for at least a year. She had not participated in the hospitalization of her husband, Sean Maroney. Charlie thought she was a bit young to be a recluse, records saying she was only 52 years old. And the photo he found of her in the driver's license bureau files showed her to be a blonde-streaked light-colored-brunette, and quite attractive, even by driver's license standards. "Where are you, Vicky?" thought Charlie.

• • •

Thursday, July 7:
"Amir! How are you, my old friend?" Charlie found Amir Habood tending the cash register at his father's restaurant, Habood's Foods.

"A thousand days and nights since we last clasped hands," said Amir Habood, throwing his hands into the air.

"Knock it off, Amir. You do a lousy imitation of Ali Baba. It's only been about six months. Yes, too long, but I've been busy."

"I have heard that is so. You wish a cup of coffee?"

"Absolutely, as long as the chef made it and not you."

Amir called to a staff member to take over the cash register and led Charlie to a semi-secluded table in the back of the restaurant. "Let me sit here so I can watch what's going on up front. Dad's visiting relatives in Detroit, so I'm in charge."

"Oh, man! I feel for you," said Charlie. "There was one day back in high school when I tended the register for a couple hours. He made me fork over 12 cents that he thought the register was short."

"Yeah, he does that to all the new help. Sets the expectations early. He told me that he makes the accusation once within the new employee's first few days, and they're never tempted to steal from him after that." Amir took a sip of coffee, "It's always 12 cents, by the way.

He doesn't want anyone hurt by his little gambit. He always returns the 12 cents and more in their first paycheck."

Charlie smiled, "I really love your old man. He taught me so much, and not just about running a cash register."

Charlie sipped the richly brewed coffee. For as long as he could remember, the same dark-roast coffee was a highly regarded feature of Habood's Foods. It was the pride of Amir's father, and of his father before him. The Habood family had emigrated to the United States from what was once known as Persia just as World War I was beginning. The entire family – those in Cleveland and those who settled in the Detroit area – were Chaldean, a sect often described as Arab Catholics. The Chaldeans had a reputation as hard workers with strong ethical values, endearing themselves to their customers and employees alike for their honesty and fairness. Such it was when they first came to the United States, and so it remains today.

Amir smiled, "Dad liked you, too, although he never wanted you to know it. He knew it would go to your head."

Charlie said, "What's that supposed to mean?"

"It means he knows you can be arrogant and self-centered. Too much praise from him would just make you worse."

Charlie faked a frown, "That's pretty harsh. Accurate, but harsh." He took another sip of coffee. "I'm really glad you reached out to me. I probably would have gone another couple of months without giving you a call, and that would be too long a time to go without enduring your insults."

"Yeah, I figured you needed a reality check. Especially given what you're into right now."

Charlie looked surprised. "What do you know about what I'm currently doing?"

"The mysticism of the East allows those who are blessed to see all and know all."

"Oh, knock it off," scoffed Charlie. "You're no more a mystic than I am a Major League pitcher."

"You really did stink as a Little Leaguer, you know," said Amir.

"But you couldn't hit any of my pitches."

"You never put any over the plate."

"So, what do you know about what I'm doing?" questioned Charlie again.

Amir scanned the front to make sure both customers and staff were satisfied. He also was making sure no one could overhear their conversation. "Two trips to New York to retrieve something for Cardinal Maroney. Neither successful."

"How do you know that? How do you know I went to New York, or that I was working for the Cardinal? And, by the way, the second delivery was successful."

Amir shook his head, "No, it was not successful, at least as far as the Cardinal is concerned. You will soon learn that he is still not happy."

Charlie's face was scrunched into a scowl, "How do you know about any of this?"

"Not all of my extended family lives here in Cleveland or even in Detroit. There are some – those that live on the razor-sharp edges of life – who reside in New York. Or in Paris. Or in Istanbul. What they do is not entirely illegal, but neither is it entirely within the law. They buy and sell and trade things that – well, let's just say some of the items they market are not technically theirs to possess in the first place. Nonetheless, there are times when they collaborate with the authorities of justice from many different countries, if for no other reason than to maintain a semblance of virtuosity. They contacted my father for a character analysis of our dear Cardinal, of those associates around him, and of those who were drawn into his web – you."

"Jesus Christ!" exclaimed Charlie. "I was so careful to keep my involvement quiet! Now some gang of crooks from Europe knows all about what I'm doing – do you think I'm in trouble?"

Amir raised his hand to calm Charlie, "Please do not refer to my family members as a gang of crooks. Further, if you were in trouble, my friend, we wouldn't be casually sitting here sipping coffee. No, this is one of those times when my far-off cousins are collaborating with the men of justice. Don't take that to mean they are working with the U.S. authorities, however."

"Interpol?"

"I cannot say any more than what I have told you, other than the parties involved know you are an honorable man, at least most of the time."

"What do they think of the Cardinal?" asked Charlie.

Amir chose his words carefully, "There is a general feeling that Cardinal Maroney is not a saintly individual. That is why the parcel which he seeks, the parcel which you have twice-failed to deliver, may never end up in his possession – unless, of course, it serves the purposes of the men of justice to make it so."

"But just yesterday I made the delivery. It was the package he was expecting."

"Undoubtedly, he received the package you delivered and, given your strange obsession with promptness, at the time and place it was promised. But I have been told the contents were not what he had hoped for."

"What is it that he's looking for? What did I just deliver?"

"The answer to that question is far too dangerous for me to know, and even more so for you to know. It is far better that you remain pure of heart and mind."

Charlie shook his head, "You know better than most people that I'm neither pure of heart nor of mind."

Amir smiled, "That is so true. I remember that time ..."

"Stop! OK, I get it. Let me fill in a blank or two in my own filthy mind. Tell me if I'm right. Your extended family is the group from which our dear Cardinal is attempting to purchase something of great value."

"They have some peripheral involvement, correct."

"They have collaborated with some mysterious 'justice league' to make sure he doesn't get it."

"Correct, unless the men of justice choose otherwise."

"I need to remain in the dark as to what the item is."

"That is in your best interest."

"Am I or any of the people I work with in danger?"

"I have not been told that you are, but I would suggest caution in your dealings with the Cardinal."

"Does the name 'Merke Edelstein' mean anything to you?"

Amir shook his head. "I have never heard that name before."

"Have you ever seen a short, dark-haired, thin guy who speaks a foreign language?"

Amir motioned to the restaurant. "You have described more than half of my clientele."

Charlie sighed, "Do your people offer any suggestions for what I should do now?"

Amir thought for a second. "They did say something that means absolutely nothing to me. Maybe it does to you. They said, 'Seek Victoria'. Do you know what that means?"

Charlie sat back and smiled. "I think I might. Yes, I think I just might."

• • •

Friday, July 8:

The Cardinal checked his calendar and pulled out his phone book. It was 2:00 p.m. on a Friday in early July, just a few weeks past the Summer Solstice. None of this would mean anything to anyone but the Druids, he supposed. But he was not going to contact a Druid, just someone who lived his life as a remnant of those long-past souls.

"Friar James? How are you, my friend? ... Yes, it is I, your former seminary classmate, Phelan Maroney.... Yes, it has been too long ... What's that? ... Oh, I sound more jovial than usual? Well, the times have been very good ... Oh, thank you so much! I do appreciate your attending the robing ceremony, I just wish we had more time to talk back then ... Yes, we should plan on dining together soon. The reason I'm calling ... Aha! Well, I would love to try some of that wine ... Your fellows made it themselves? ... How wonderful! ... Yes, as I was saying, the reason for my call – back when you attended the ceremony ... yes, it was a beautiful event, was it not? ... You mentioned you had a young novitiate who might be better suited to a more worldly vocation than the harshness of life your monastery offers. Is that young man still there? ... He is, huh. Well, here's the thing. I would hate to lose someone of promise ... yes, you mentioned that he had many diverse skills ... I would hate to lose someone like that without offering him the opportunity to explore the religious life in a more, shall we say, secular setting ... Well, I do have an idea. It seems that I will need an apprentice, someone to help me with some of the more mundane but very real issues facing the diocese ... Yes, you told me he was good with numbers ... took some courses in bookkeeping, you say? ... Why, that fits in perfectly to the plans I have for him ... Uh huh ... Do you suppose he'd be willing to be temporarily assigned to me for – oh, let's say – about two or three months? ... Yes, I suppose he does have to do whatever you tell him to do ... Of course, he would still wear his monk's habit for the most part ... Well, there may be a need to have him in street clothes from time to time, more suited to the jobs I might send him on ... of course, only for a short time, if you approve ... no, it's not essential ... well, I'll defer to your judgement on that."

The Cardinal continued making his sales pitch, "My thought is, once he experiences the work I'll put him to, he'll be ready to make a firm decision to either return to you for the rest of his life or make an adjustment in his vocation and perhaps apply for admittance to the Diocesan Seminary ... No, I'm not trying to steal any of your men ... I'm sorry if it seemed like that. It's just that when we have a good man, you and I, we should do all we can to find the right place for him to be ... That's right, find out where is his best fit ... Ah, I'm so glad you see it that way, too ... Yes, that will be fine. Send me his information and prepare him for the trip ... Brother Gerald is his name? ... I'll make a note of that ... Oh, you think that's best? ... Alright, I'll expect him in a few days, then. Let me know what bus he's on so I can have someone help him with his bags ... Yes, James, I'll be sure to keep you updated on his progress. I just think this is a wonderful way to broaden a young man's perspective and ensure that he makes the correct decision about his future before it becomes too late to change ... of course ... you are correct, it would be wise for me to send some of our young men your way to try the contemplative life before they get too far along as well ... uh huh ... Well, that just fine ... Yes, I will check my schedule and visit you for a retreat, and some of that fine wine you are so proud of ... No, I did not mean to imply that you are guilty of the sin of Pride, it was just an expression ... Okay, it has been a pleasure to hear your voice again ... Yes, and the peace of the Lord be with you, too. Goodbye."

"Ye, gods, the man is insufferable," the Cardinal whispered to himself.

He went to the outer office looking for Monsignor Leonard. "Wesley, are you here?" There was no answer. He proceeded to the Monsignor's private living quarters. "Monsignor Leonard, are you at home?" He heard a rustling and thumping in the bedroom. "Oh, Wesley, where are you?" he said in a sing-song voice.

A red-faced Monsignor burst from the bedroom tucking his half-buttoned shirt into his pants, followed by a red-faced and red-haired George buckling his belt. "Your Eminence, I did not expect you this afternoon."

"That's quite obvious, Wesley ... George. When you've gotten yourself put back together properly, please join me in my office." The Cardinal turned to leave, saying, "Not you, George, you can stay here if you wish."

George was ready to explode with humiliation. He whispered, "You said he was too busy to bother you this afternoon!"

"I thought he was," offered Wesley. "He's barely spoken to me in the past few days since the package from New York was delivered. I was sure he was concentrating on whatever it was that he received."

The Monsignor straightened his clothes and smoothed his hair, then rushed off to the Cardinal's office, finding Cardinal Maroney making notes on a pad of paper. "Your Eminence, please accept my apology for what you witnessed. I am at your mercy for a proper penance."

The Cardinal looked up, "Wesley, we all have weaknesses of the flesh. If only I could once again enjoy the company of Marie."

"Have you sent for her, Your Eminence?"

Cardinal Maroney frowned, "At this time, I do not believe calling her is in either of our best interests. No matter. Perhaps it is best that we offer up our current sacrifices to God." The Cardinal almost sounded sincere with his offering.

After a few moments of silence, the monsignor said, "You wished to see me, Your Eminence?"

"Aha. Yes, Wesley. I've been in communications with an old friend from my seminary days, Friar James. He is the Abbot of Bergamo, the

Trappist Monastery in Southern Ohio. He has asked us to tend to one of his sheep who is troubled by the contemplative existence at Bergamo. He wishes us to expose him to the more secular side of religious life. Perhaps he will find he is better suited to a different vocation. He will join us in a few days. Could you arrange living quarters for him?"

The Monsignor brightened at not receiving a tongue-lashing, "Why, of course! I shall be pleased to arrange a suite for him."

The Cardinal shook his head, "No, not a suite. Let's remember that in the monastery he had only one small room with a bed and a sink. They call them 'cells', and they're not much larger than prison cells at that. Let's not make him feel awkward or sinful with too much luxury. A small room will do."

"Yes, sir, I will find appropriate lodging here in the chancery."

"Excellent. His name is Brother Gerald. He'll arrive by bus. I'll give you the particulars when I have them so you can arrange for a proper meeting. By the way, I'm told he is something of a mathematical genius. Do you think we could give him some of your bookkeeping duties to keep him occupied?"

Monsignor Leonard hated doing the books, so he was only too eager to relieve himself of that duty. "If you think that would be best, I will show him the books when he arrives so he can begin working on them."

"That's wonderful. Now, the private fund from the offering plate – we'll need a way to explain that to him."

Wesley smiled, "I've always told myself that by separating the funds as we do, we are establishing a treasure chest to assist the most needful of the diocese, and we can therefore assist them in secret, preventing any possible embarrassment to the recipients. I would think that would swell his heart with pride."

The Cardinal smiled wickedly, thinking that Wesley was truly a weasel. Aloud, he said, "Yes, that sounds perfect. But for the time being, let's keep that fund to ourselves. No need to trouble his sensibilities with that nuance right away. I look forward to you mentoring Brother Gerald upon his arrival."

Wesley turned to leave, then stopped, "Does Brother Gerald have a last name?"

The Cardinal replied, "Upon entering the Trappists, a monk gives up his entire past, and signs what amounts to his own Death Certificate. The former person ceases to exist, as does his last name. As far as I know, Brother Gerald no longer has a last name."

The Monsignor tilted his head, turned to leave and said, "How strange. How very, very strange."

The Cardinal folded his hands as the Monsignor shut the door of his office. He thought to himself that everything was beginning to fall into place. The monk would take over much of what Wesley was doing, making it possible for Wesley to disappear for a while – perhaps a long while – perhaps an eternity. He smiled to himself as he envisioned just how Wesley's departure could be explained. Yes, and George, too. He couldn't have one of them running around looking for the other and asking questions. So, George could accompany Wesley on the unique journey he had in mind.

Now he had to concentrate on the other two who were possible accomplices in the embarrassing book he had received: Charlie Franklin and Marie Carlisle. If the two knew each other, dealing with them would be more difficult than dealing with Wesley. But what if they didn't know each other? Then he could use one against the other without them even knowing it. That was more palatable. Was it possible they did not know each other? Marie had asked 'who is more important than me' when she last departed his bedroom, seemingly not knowing of the Cardinal's arrangement with Mr. Franklin. Charlie had never even hinted at knowing that the Cardinal had a girlfriend. Certainly, that would have been a chip he'd have put in play to show his dominance over the prelate. No, the signs all began to point to the fact that neither Marie Carlisle nor Charlie Franklin knew of the other's association with the Cardinal. He thought he could use that to his advantage. He just had to figure out how. But therein was another problem. If Marie and Mr. Franklin were not collaborators, someone else was very much involved, someone who was responsible for compiling the book of photos. The Cardinal sensed danger – and decided that he had to be even more dangerous in response.

• • •

Saturday, July 9:

Charlie quickly discovered Saturday morning was not to be a day for sleeping in. First, Pete called at 7:00 a.m., shouting into the phone that he was bringing donuts over and would be there in 20 minutes. Then, no sooner had Charlie put his head back down on the pillow for a short snooze than Rita came banging into the apartment tossing her overnight bag in the corner.

"Hiya, Charlie! Still in bed?"

Rolling out of the covers, he yawned, "Not any more, I guess."

"I'll go put on some coffee." From the kitchen she shouted, "Hey, I sang a set at the 'Danube' last night. Felt just like old times."

After washing his face and brushing his teeth, Charlie joined her in the kitchen, still hitching up his pants. "Just tell me you're current with your union dues," he said.

"Yeah, yeah, yeah. I won't make that mistake again. God, I missed singing, you know?"

"I suppose Nick was there," Charlie deadpanned.

Rita turned and gave him a hard look, "We said no questions asked. But for your information, Nick headed to Florida where his buddies are putting together a new band. So, no, he wasn't there."

"Sorry to hear that," he said trying to sound sincere but failing miserably.

Rita turned the tables on him. "By the way, we haven't discussed how the deal went down in New York. Was TK Constantine there again?"

"Oh, that's right, you haven't been around to hear my juicy stories, have you?"

The door buzzer rang. It was Pete with the donuts. He laid them on the table and grabbed a cup of coffee. "I need this."

"Sure. Everyone should have a cup of my coffee before I get any. And you haven't been around to hear my juicy stories, either, have you? Everybody bailed on me all at the same time," said Charlie.

"What the hell did I walk into? Are you two fighting? You're welcome for the donuts, shit head."

Charlie felt sheepish, "Okay, I'm sorry to both of you. I just woke up and both of you are way too awake while I'm still trying to focus. What are you both doing up so doggone early?"

Pete said, "I finished all of my cases yesterday. Made a boatload of money. I'm as happy as can be."

Rita said, "I had a nice little vacation from everything, sang some of my old songs, and I'm as happy as can be."

Charlie sat down with his coffee at the table and picked up a donut, "You two sound like characters straight out of a Disney World ride. It's a bit much this early in the morning."

The other two sat down as Rita said, "Aww, poor Charlie. All alone and crabby. Okay, tell us all about your New York adventure. Did you get the package delivered to the Cardinal?"

Between donut bites and coffee refills, Charlie related the events from St. Patrick's Cathedral, including the proposition from the three nuns, and the subsequent delivery of the package to the Cardinal. He told them what he learned at the Hudson coffee shop and the Akron records department. Then he filled them in on his lunch meeting with Amir Habood.

Pete reached for a jelly donut and placed the last glazed donut in front of Rita. "Wow! Naked under her nun's habit? Very kinky."

Rita shot him a look. "That's the first thing on your mind? Naked nuns, not the warning from Amir? Remind me never to ask you about your wet dreams. You are without a doubt a dirty old man."

Pete wiped jelly off his face. "I'm not that old. Besides, that was the most interesting part of his story. How often does someone get propositioned by three nuns in a Cathedral? Sounds like the start of a bar joke."

Charlie smiled, "I must admit, that was pretty bizarre. But I'm with Rita on this one. The message from Amir has more concern and intrigue buried in it. It's been several days since I made the delivery, and I haven't heard a word from the Cardinal. If Amir was right that the package didn't contain what he wanted, the Cardinal has got to be seriously steamed. Why would he not accuse me of a bait and switch?

He paid me a boatload to get him his package. If the contents were not right, why no screaming from him?"

Pete poured more coffee for all three of them. "Okay, what if Amir was wrong? The Cardinal got what he wanted and he's 'as happy as can be', just like Rita and me. He'd want to avoid talking to you, even avoid recognizing you in the street. Maybe that's all there is to it."

Rita asked, "Why were you meeting with Amir? Were you just catching up on old times?"

Charlie said, "That's just it. Amir messaged me twice within the past several days saying we needed to meet. I thought it was just that, to catch up after not seeing each other for a long time. But it didn't take but a couple minutes for him to get into the serious discussion, the reason he wanted to get together."

"So, he wasn't just making up a story, was he? There was an intent to clue you in with the information he had." Rita nodded, "I think we have to take his message to heart. We have to assume Amir's extended family is, at its most basic level, somehow associated with 'Merke Edelstein', at least on the perimeter."

Pete added, "Amir said that they are working with some form of justice authority, whether in Europe or the United States. That means someone broke the law, or is about to."

"What does that mean for Charlie now? Does he just walk away and forget about everything involving the Cardinal?" asked Rita.

"I don't think he can," said Pete. "Some sort of law enforcement is onto this case. Charlie is involved. Maybe his nose is clean, but we don't know that the law is convinced of that. And if the Cardinal is stewing in his juices about receiving a bogus package, he'll eventually come back at Charlie." Pete addressed Charlie directly. "You've got to be prepared for whatever may come from him. I don't think he's going to be so pleasant anymore. He's going to feel like you bilked him out of over $30,000 with the two deliveries, and he'll come at you hard. And, not to add undue alarm, he'll be very dangerous." Pete looked from Charlie to Rita. "He'll be dangerous to all of us. We have to assume he knows about each of us and that we three have been involved, so he'll think we're all complicit."

Charlie frowned, "That's about how I see it, too. The longer he waits, the more likely it is that he's planning something and he'll attack hard. If the package contained blank paper or old newspapers or something, he'd have been after me immediately. But he hasn't called. If Amir is right, then the package was not what he wanted. But he hasn't reached out to me, so I'm thinking that whatever was in there may be more than blank papers. As silent as he's been, I'm guessing the package contained something he doesn't want exposed – maybe something personally embarrassing. And if that is true, he is as dangerous as Pete says, and we all have to be very careful."

Rita said, "Remind me not to go to church anytime soon."

"As if there was any chance of that," chided Pete.

Rita sloughed off Pete's comment. "So, what do we do now, Charlie?"

"There are some holes we need to fill. The more we know, the stronger we can be to combat whatever comes next," said Charlie. "I wish we could just walk away, but Pete's right – we're still in the middle of this thing."

Pete said, "What holes are you looking to fill?"

"Let's list them," said Charlie:

"First, there's something odd about the estate in Hudson. Someone is paying to keep it manicured and livable, but no one seems to be there. Who is caring for it, and why are they doing so?

Second, where is 'mommy dearest', the Cardinal's mother, and what does she use for money? I'm assuming she got some alimony or a settlement from her husband, the elder Maroney, maybe even something from the old man's will. I think the more we know about her, the better.

Third, the brother, Sean, had a wife named Vicky. I'm assuming that is the 'Victoria' mentioned by Amir's contacts. She's only in her early 50s, too young to become a recluse. Where is she, and why has she been so absent from the scene?"

"I've got one I'd like to add," said Pete. "Where is the old man buried? Sometime you can learn a lot from visiting a cemetery."

Rita shook her head. "Pete, you are both sexually perverse and now openly morbid. I keep learning way too much about how your mind works, and it's very disconcerting. But I have a querry that I'd also like to add: The Italian Guy and the other one dressed in black. Are they still around, and who sent them?"

Pete sheepishly admitted, "One more thing—there's been three rough-looking young hoods hanging around the Terminal Tower the past few days. Their noses perk up when I come into view. I think we may have another set of fans. They're in their mid-20s, early-30s and look like they've had their face flattened a few times. Boston baseball caps."

"What the hell? We'll have to start selling tickets and printing up programs," said Charlie. "The Italian Guy may have been researching records down in Akron just like I was given the clerk's description. And now there's a new crew to add to our list of interested parties? Okay, I guess we have to add them to our list of unknown actors."

Rita said, "Well, we've got to start filling in these holes, otherwise there'll just be more to deal with over time."

"Right. We've got five or six questions we have to work on. Let's divvy them up as best we can. Rita, to keep Pete away from haunting around a few graveyards, could you find out where the Cardinal's father is buried? We can then see if his headstone carries any clues. Then, if possible, find out what landscape company works the estate. Maybe we can figure out who pays them."

Charlie continued, "Pete, since you seem to be free from other work and 'as happy as can be', could you research what became of 'mommy dearest' and what she's living on? Seems right up your alley."

"I'm going to try to locate Vicky Maroney," said Charlie, "where is she and how is she getting on in life. She certainly isn't worried about poor Sean, since she's never visited him. So, what's her story?"

"What about the Italian Guy and Pete's new set of Red Sox fans?" asked Rita.

Charlie said, "We can't very well go to the police. They will ask too many questions. And, so far, neither the men in black nor the Bostonians has done anything illegal. They've just be watching us. As disconcerting as that is, we can't very well expect the authorities to do anything about it. Until one or the other makes a move, we'll have to just be cautious and aware of our surroundings. We should stay in contact, even if it's just a quick note or voice-mail to say we're safe. No one goes more than 24 hours without checking in, OK? And stay alert and as safe as possible. We've got to be mindful of the Italian Guy, the Cardinal, and now these Bostonians."

Pete said, "I think Rita better bunk out here for the time being. This place has better security than her hippie hide-out on the West Side."

"I'm not even going to get upset over that crack, Pete, because it's accurate. I'm just going to hunker down here."

Everyone nodded that they had their assignments, would report new learning as soon as they had it, and that they would stay in touch with each other as the threats began to mount. "Thanks, guys," said Charlie. "Now if you don't mind, I'm going to take a shower."

"Okay, I'm outa here," said Pete, giving a squeeze to Rita's hand. "Everyone, please try to stay safe."

• • •

The Las Vegas Villa

Rocco was still asleep when the phone rang. He had arrived in Las Vegas late Friday afternoon, and after a full night of hard liquor and wild lascivious acrobatics with the voluptuous Marie, he was still groggy, and not just from jet lag. He was only vaguely aware that the phone rang twice before Marie answered it in the kitchen where she was making coffee. He rolled over into Marie's pillow, giving it a hug as he recalled where he was and what last night was like. "Minga, she has more tricks than a magician," he thought to himself. He opened one eye to see sunlight piercing through a gap in the curtains, then shut his eye quickly and rolled to the other side of the bed.

"Rocco, honey, do you want to talk to Angelo?" whispered Marie, bringing the phone into the room.

"Ugh! What time is it?"

"It's about 9:30, sweetie," she said as she sat on the edge of the bed.

"Goddammit, it's way too early. Tell Angelo I'll call him back later."

She spoke into the phone. "Didja hear that Angelo? ... OK, I'll tell him. Bye."

"He says it's kinda important, so call him back as soon as you can." She nestled in close to Rocco's back letting the small silk robe slip open exposing her nakedness.

Rocco reached over and, discovering bare flesh, was suddenly awake. "G'morning, doll. Aren't you a wonder to wake up to."

"I've got coffee brewing in the kitchen, if you're interested."

"I'm interested in you," he said, sneaking his hand between her legs. "But maybe some coffee is a good idea first. What'd Angelo want?"

She rose and pulled Rocco's hand, helping him out of bed. "He didn't say, just that you should call him back as soon as your awake. Said it was important, but it seems everything is important to Angelo."

"That's 'cause he's good at his job. He knows not to bug me unless he's got somethin' important. But he shouldn't be callin' me this early."

"It's after noon back home, Rocco," she said pouring him coffee.

"Yeah, well, after a long flight he should know better."

"What airline did you come in on," Marie asked.

"No airline. I don't do airlines. Got this guy I did a favor for, he owns a private jet company. All I gotta do is give him a call and I can go anywheres I want, whenever I want. Comes in real handy."

"Geez, that's pretty cool. Want some pecan rolls? I bought them yesterday when I heard you were coming."

Rocco drained his coffee cup and said, "Maybe later. I'm gonna take a shower and give Angelo a call back. Otherwise, he'll have a conniption fit if I don't get back to him quick-like."

"I'm going to take another cup of coffee out to the pool," said Marie. "Join me when you're done."

Rocco grinned at her lustfully, "Don't bother puttin' on a bathing suit."

Marie smiled spicily, "Oh, my! Someone might see me! What if the pool boy happens by?"

"You can fuck him when I'm gone. If he's out there when I come out, I'll put a bullet between his nuts and another between his eyes."

Rocco finished toweling off after the shower and dialed Angelo. "What's so damn important that you gotta bother me so early this morning?"

"Sorry, boss. I lost track of the time delay. Hope the trip was good and the villa is OK."

"Yeah, yeah, uneventful trip – love that Lear Jet – and the villa is ... well appointed, if you catch my drift."

Angelo chuckled, "Good. Good. Listen, I just heard from Pauly Basili, you know from Brooklyn."

Rocco was suddenly very attentive, "Sure. What'd Pauly want?"

"His old man, Giovanni, he wants a sit down with you."

"Jesus Christ, what for? We ain't lookin' for any trouble! Did we piss them off, or somethin'? What's this all about, Angelo?"

"I didn't get the impression that there is any animosity in the request. Quite the opposite. It sounded like Giovanni wants to meet with you and sit down as equals. The way Pauly put it, I got the sense that the old man is offering to meet with you in mutual respect, probably because we sent him the pictures he wanted."

Rocco wrapped himself in a large, terry-cloth robe. "I dunno, Angelo. Those New York families are big time compared to our operation. He's got, what, maybe a dozen or so button men, several lieutenants, a whole army if he needs it. What do we got? Two, maybe three made men, a couple lieutenants, and a small gang of goof-ball goombas hanging around. Doesn't quite put us on an equal footing requiring mutual respect."

"Size isn't everything, Rocco. We run a tight organization. We've got contacts."

"Size isn't everything? Maybe you should ask Marie how she feels about that."

Angelo laughed, "You two getting along OK?"

"Marone, Ang. She is one sweet ..." Rocco looked toward the pool. "Anyway, when's this meet supposed to happen?"

"I told Pauly you were out of town for some R & R. He said to let him know when you would find it convenient. How's that for respect? You get to choose the date. He did say it was regarding something of importance, and that the sooner you could make it would be preferred."

"Geez, that really does sound like maybe they think we're equals. That's very considerate of them. Tell you what, let's set it up for tomorrow. No, wait – day after tomorrow. I need some more time out here with Marie. She said she'd show me a new trick, and god knows, she's got some fine tricks."

"You're making me very jealous, Rocco. OK. I'll have the plane come and get you day after tomorrow at about 9:00 a.m., and take you straight to New York. Will that work?"

"That'll get me into New York at what time?"

"Ahh, roughly 6:00 p.m. I'll ask Pauly to set up the meet at a safe restaurant. You want any muscle nearby?"

Rocco thought for a minute, "If you say I'll be safe, I should be fine alone. It'll be my sign of respect to show that I trust him. Besides, Giovanni's not gonna want to start somethin' on his own turf. Bad for business."

Rocco hung up the phone and headed to the pool. On a large, pillowed chaise lounge, Marie wearing only sunglasses lay on her back, shimmering with freshly applied baby oil over her entire body, legs spread and knees raised. Rocco bit his lip, "Jesus Christ, she's gonna send me to an early grave, but what a way to go."

• • •

Sunday, July 10:

Brother Gerald bowed almost half over from the waist, hands clasped in a prayer position, as the Monsignor led him away from his initial meeting with Cardinal Maroney. Abbot James wasted no time in sending him on his way. Leaving the Monastery after Sunday services at dawn, he was now in the chancery at 4:00 p.m. with a small satchel of personal items. The Cardinal smiled at the tonsure on his head, his brown monk's robe and bare, sandaled feet as Monsignor Leonard showed him to his room. The Cardinal was more certain than ever that Brother Gerald would be the perfect answer to his needs. He decided to get a breath of fresh air in his rosary garden, not bothering to bring any beads with him. He needed time to mull over his plans, thinking them through again and again, making minor adjustments and timing everything out. Timing—the critical element to the plan's success.

He circled the garden a third time when he noticed someone apparently watching from across the street through a gap in the hedges. The short, dark-haired man dressed entirely in black moved on when the Cardinal spotted him. Had he been there all along? The Cardinal neared the hedge to peer in the direction the man had gone, but he was now out of sight. It was strange, but the Cardinal again focused his thoughts on his plan. Timing. Yes, that would be the key. And given current events, he needed to push things forward very soon.

The Monsignor led Brother Gerald to the work office, and brought out the main books for him to review. The Monsignor said, "The Cardinal wishes that you familiarize yourself with these books and records. It is his intention that you manage these for the diocese for the next few months. Normally, I do the books, but the Cardinal has pressing business to which I must give my undivided attention."

Brother Gerald nodded to the Monsignor.

"Should you have any questions, do not hesitate to ask."

Brother Gerald nodded again.

The Monsignor was becoming perturbed, "I hope you understand, it is essential that you take great care in assuring the accuracy of these books."

Again, a nod, even more strenuously this time.

Exasperated, the Monsignor said, "You've taken a vow of silence, haven't you?"

A nod.

"Did not your Abbot tell you that it may be necessary to speak from time to time, given your role here in the Diocesan Chancery?"

The monk took a pencil and wrote on a note sheet, "Only when absolutely essential."

"Oh, my lands. I don't think I share the Cardinal's confidence that this arrangement will work. Look over the books. Dinner is served at 6:00 p.m. in the Dining Room to the left of your room – I beg your pardon, your 'cell'."

The monsignor left Brother Gerald to examine the books. The monk was, indeed, a wizard at mathematics. His training as a bookkeeper prior to entering the monastery served him well. It took him only a half-hour to recognize that the books were slightly off, possibly not the result of a purposeful misdeed, but not correct, either. There wasn't a large deficit unaccounted for, perhaps 2% per week or slightly more. But in a diocese the size of Greater Cleveland, that amounted to several thousand dollars a week, and could easily reach a quarter million or more by year's end.

The monk sat back. How could that be, he wondered? Certainly, neither the Monsignor nor the Cardinal would want there to be any irregularities. The errors he discovered were crude. If the Cardinal knew he had a lot of money in the bank that did not show up in the books he would be able to make improvements to several old churches in need of repair, or buy books for indigent students in the diocese. There were any numbers of good uses for a quarter of a million dollars a year. And that was just for the past year. How long had the same errors been made to the books? An accumulation of just a few years could mount up to millions!

Perhaps it was simply sloppy bookkeeping. Yes, that must be it, he thought. He smiled thinking it was definitely a gift from God that he was sent to the Cardinal to assist him in straightening everything out. He decided not to write a note to the Monsignor or the Cardinal about the discrepancy just yet. He'd show them only when he figured out how and where the error had occurred. He smiled inwardly, certain that they both would be very well pleased.

The Cardinal was preparing for dinner. He was consumed by the thought that he had to deal with all the people most likely responsible for the photo album he had received: Monsignor Wesley Leonard who permitted the electrician to install the cameras; Marie Carlisle for her unfaithfulness to him – he labelled it her 'infidelity'; and Charles Franklin for his purposeful delivery of a book of scandal. There were three possibilities: none of them knew anything about the photos; only one or two of them knew about the photos; or all three of them knew about the photos.

He had placed two calls to Marie from his burner cell, but she had not answered either. He hesitated leaving a message for fear that a recording of his voice could be used against him. If she saw that he had called, wouldn't she have responded by calling him back? The lack of response led him to believe she was complicit in some way. The

Cardinal had a special place at the estate for people that were unfaithful.

As for Mr. Franklin, the time was rapidly approaching to call him to task. George had completed the dossier on the secretary / girlfriend, Rita Herns, whose real last name was Hernandez. There was enough damaging information included in the report about her extended family to prevent the pursuit of her dream to be an attorney, and might lead to her family being deported. If Mr. Franklin wanted to prevent the dossier from being made public, he'd have to make the missing-but-still-desired documents appear. Cardinal Maroney didn't care how Charlie might do it, his demand would be to just make it happen.

If both Marie and Charlie Franklin were in on it together, well, they'd both have to pay, each in their own way.

As for Wesley and George: they had both botched up several parts of the scheme and certainly were involved in the hiring of the electrician. Even if they hadn't been directly involved in the treachery, they deserved punishment for stupidity. And since they knew at least a little of the Cardinal's plans, their penance would have to be eternal. He smiled, thinking how much he enjoyed using religion-inspired words in double-entendres. The Cardinal fully expected he would have to jettison the Monsignor in the future, but events were happening so rapidly that it appeared the relationship needed to end sooner than anticipated. He had to be coy, however. He couldn't have Wesley and George panic before he was ready to act. Plus, he needed George to put his Boston friends to work.

• • •

Monday, July 11:

Rita dug through old records and contacted the cemeteries in the area surrounding the Maroney homestead, but kept coming up empty. She shifted gears and began contacting funeral homes.

She decided on an unusual approach when calling the undertakers:

"Hello, I'm representing the legal estate of a family who wishes to remain anonymous at this time. I'm sure you understand. One of the principals of the estate is approaching the end of his time on earth.

We're searching for a reputable funeral professional who has experience in preserving the confidentiality of the family name and providing secrecy for the ceremony. Do you have such experience? ... Oh, you do? May I inquire how long ago the service in question took place? ... I see. We are also exploring options for interment. Can you suggest any such options beyond a common public cemetery?"

And so on. A few backed away immediately. But most saw the potential for a financial windfall and were only too happy to make suggestions. A few sounded like they actually might have been involved in the burial of the senior Maroney.

Then she turned to finding landscape companies. It didn't take long to find the one willing to take credit for what Rita described as "such lovely grounds, it looks like a park", using the address that Charlie had given her. They took the time to give her a full run-down of the property:

"Yeah, we take care of that place. Big piece of property, takes a long time and a big crew ... Oh, thanks. We think we do a pretty good job out there ... Yeah, that's very good turf ... Uh huh, some of the bushes are pretty rare for this climate ... Well, beyond the house itself there are a couple out-buildings, and then that cement structure way out back ... I'm not sure what it is ... What's that? ... Oh, I suppose it could be a mausoleum, I'm not sure ... No, I never see anyone out there while we're working ... Listen, do you want us to take a look at your property? ... Sure, we could do an estimate ... Ah, well, the cost for that one is confidential ... well, we prefer a person's name, but like that one, we could just bill the trust, even though, you know, that can get complicated ... You see, if we do the work and the trust chooses not to pay ... no, hasn't happened, but it's a risk, know what I mean, no one to contact ... Sure, call us back whenever you want an estimate."

Thrilled that she had come up with the answers to her parts of the puzzle, Rita spent the rest of the afternoon casually unpacking her suitcase from her days away, sorting what needed to go to the dry cleaner.

• • •

Pete started with the divorce records between Mr. and Mrs. Parker Maroney. He discovered that Mrs. Maroney is the former Patricia O'Brien. After the divorce, she decided to re-take her old name, preferring to leave the Maroney name in the dust-heap of the divorce court. According to the filings, there was no alimony, only a simple one-time payment of $5 Million plus re-ownership of lands originally owned by the O'Brien family.

Pete mumbled, "Here's five mill, lady. Thanks for playing, and don't let the door hit you in the ass." Now he needed to find out where Patricia Maroney nee O'Brien has gone. Charlie told him to look toward California. He tried to find where other members of the O'Brien clan might have settled. He was talking to himself out loud now. "Holy crap, who knew how many O'Briens live in this country?" This would not be a quick and easy search. But Pete had his methods, and a lot of contacts in a lot of cities.

Five million dollars sounded like a lot, but with housing costs in California plus trying to live in the same luxury as during her married life, that wouldn't last long. She was 61 or 62 years old at the time of the divorce. Unless she had some family or friends she knew there, people who could be a support group, it is doubtful she would go all the way to California alone. Even if she was the independent sort, a big move such as that would stress a person who was already stressed by a divorce.

Pete wondered if, similar to her philandering husband, Parker, she might have her own sugar-daddy. There were no rumors of any such dalliances on her part, and given Parker's reportedly mean-spirited nature, one had to assume he'd have countered her divorce request with one of his own claiming her infidelity, thereby saving the $5 million settlement. But if there was no male companion, why go to California?

Where had the tip about California come from? Pete checked his notes – the only mention of California had come from the waitress in the village diner in Hudson – not the most confidence-building piece of evidence. He decided to broaden his search, recalling that the Maroney's owned a lot of property throughout the Northeast. He wondered if any of the property might have once belonged to anybody named O'Brien.

Deeds and property ownership are public record, but sometimes locating the one piece of property you're looking for can be a needle in the proverbial haystack. After two hours of not so painstaking research, he found his needle. Just outside Syracuse, New York, there was a property once owned by the O'Brien Clan. It was deed-transferred to the Maroney Clan around the time Parker and Patricia were married, then re-deeded back to an O'Brien in 1997, the day before the divorce decree was finalized.

"Bingo!" said Pete. "I found the old family homestead. Now, who do I know that used to work on the *Syracuse Post-Standard?*"

• • •

Charlie decided that working from his office would give him the quiet he needed to concentrate. Victoria Maroney had not been seen around the estate for some time. If Charlie went back to Hudson or Akron to dig into local stories or gossip, his repeated presence would be noticed, and might raise suspicions with anyone who still had contact with the Cardinal. He didn't want anyone to know he was looking into the Maroney family, so finding Vicky would require some other methods.

He found the marriage license for Victoria Dempsey and Sean Maroney in on-line records. She's a Dempsey, huh? Don't know what that means, but at least we have that info, said Charlie to himself, recognizing she might be using her maiden name to protect her whereabouts.

Interestingly, Victoria Maroney was one of the named Trustees for the family estate, along with a few others, two of whom were attorneys from a high-priced law firm in Akron. Virtually all of the other documents on the Maroney Trust were confidential, requiring a password to access them on-line.

Charlie detested social media networking systems. He was skeptical of them, and old school enough not to trust them. He reasoned that if he could track someone through some sort of communications network, then others could track him just as easily.

But on the off-chance that accessing the internet might lead to Victoria / Vicky Maroney / Dempsey, he reluctantly decided to sign on to Facebook. Giving himself a fictional name and choosing not to add a picture, he began searching for any entries from a Victoria or Vicky Maroney, then for Victoria or Vicky Dempsey. Those names were fairly common, and because of that, lots of potential hits came up. Eventually, one seemed to fit.

She called herself Vicky Demps. She included her picture in her Facebook registry, and it was a match to the driver's license photo of Victoria Maroney which Charlie had copied from the County Records Department. Vicky Demps and Victoria Maroney were one and the same. He went through all of her postings and, surprisingly, there were a lot. She was not so much a recluse after all. Several other people were communicating with Vicky Demps, either sharing jokes, offering advice, or setting up some girl's nights out. While there was no clear evidence as to where Vicky was living, whether in Northeast Ohio or elsewhere, it was evident she was not hiding away all by herself. The latest entry talked about a pending plan for Vicky and friends to fly to Las Vegas for a long weekend away. "Wow. She's not too worried about her Alzheimer-stricken husband," said Charlie. "If I can't find her in a city of a couple million people, maybe I can narrow the search down if I can figure out which hotel the group of girlfriends are booking in Las Vegas." He looked around, realizing there was no one there to hear his musings.

Charlie stepped away from his PC, and suddenly realized he was starved. He locked the office door and quickly decided on a cheese steak sandwich from the Thespian Grill. He left through the front exit, suddenly realized he forgot his wallet, and spun around to re-enter his office. It was just a glance, a quick did-I-really-see-that moment, but a block away behind him, he thought he saw a couple guys with ball caps quickly reverse course and swing backwards around the corner. He stopped momentarily, unsure whether to pursue or be pursued. He decided to let them pursue him, if that was their intent. Maybe they are the Red Sox boys mentioned by Pete. He recovered his wallet, set the office alarm, and returned to the street for a casual walk to the

Thespian. It would be interesting to see if they would dare come in. The Dobermans could make mince-meat of them easily.

Try as he might, he did not spot his tails during his walk to the Thespian Grill. Charlie went to the back of the bar where Rico Carponi was again reading the current day's tout sheet. As usual, there was an open seat on either side of The Carp.

"Hey, Carp, how's it going?"

Rico never even looked away from his track studies. "Got a good feeling about a horse in the 7th race."

"Should I bet it?"

"Not with me. I'm not taking any action on a fixed race. How's things with you, kid?"

"Busy. Got a lot going on."

"Yeah? You still fixin' things for the Bishop?"

Charlie said, "He's a Cardinal now, you know. And I think I'm done with him, unless he calls again."

"Pfff. Bishop, Cardinal, all the same other than the costume. Heard tell he's got a monk working for him now. Brown robe, sandals, no socks ... the whole bit. Another costume. Those kind give me the heebie-jeebies. Kind of obnoxiously religious. Know what I mean?"

Charlie smiled, "So, do nuns give you the chills, too?"

Rico put down his sheet. "Yeah, now that you mention it. Always did, even in grade school. Had my knuckles cracked by one who got me with a ruler. Could'a broken bones, but she didn't care."

"What made her do that to you?"

"Meanness. Plain old meanness. Said my handwriting wasn't no good. So, she cracked my knuckles. Couldn't even pick up a pencil after that. I think she was pissed that I'm left-handed. 'Sign of the Devil' she used to say." Rico picked up the tout sheet again. "Hey, did you ever figure out who was tailing you a few weeks back?"

"No, I have no idea. He disappeared for a long time. But just today I think I spotted someone new outside my office. Pretty strange."

Rico looked over at Charlie over his glasses. "Ain't you the shits? Not just one, but two different tails? You better be careful, kid. A short-term, one-time tail is one thing. But if you've got pros taking interest in you for several weeks ... well, just be careful."

Sally the barmaid came by and took Charlie's lunch order. Charlie came back to the conversation with Rico. "Thanks for your concern, Carp. I'll try to stay clear of trouble." He looked toward the entrance and said, "How come the 'Dobermans' aren't guarding the front door?"

Rico looked up. "Rocco's out of town for a few days. The boys are taking some R&R, too."

"Isn't Angelo still here?"

"Yeah, but he won't need no protection. Unwritten rule: consiglieres are off-limits to hits."

Charlie asked, "Where'd Rocco go?"

Rico put down the tout sheet and looked at the ceiling, not directly at Charlie. "You know, sometimes it's bad business to ask too many questions like that. But since you've done valuable work for Rocco – or so I've been told – I'll tell you just this once. Got a babe he's shacking up with in Vegas. Then got a call for a sit down in New York with one of the families there."

"Whoa. That sounds serious. You think trouble is brewing?"

"You never can tell with these kinda things," said Rico, picking up the tout sheet, "but Rocco is considering it a friendly sit down, a possible business arrangement, sign of respect and all like that. But for me, it's kind of a 'wait and see'. Don't let the barstool feel too comfortable, if you catch my drift."

"Gotcha." Charlie started munching on his lunch. "Vegas, huh? How's he getting out there and back? I can't see him flying commercial."

Rico gave him a hard stare, "You ask too many questions. Anybody ever tell you that?"

"Sorry. Never mind. It's just that I'm following one of my own leads, and I think I'll be needing to go out there soon, too. Just curious about the best way to get there."

Rico looked away and said, "Call the United counter and book your own flight."

The Brooklyn Connection

Rocco's private plane arrived at Teterboro Airport just past 6:30 p.m. Monday evening. He was met by Pauly Basili with a stretch limousine, the transportation to the dinner meeting with Giovanni Basili, the godfather of the family that controlled most of Brooklyn.

"Sorry I'm a bit late, Pauly. Headwinds or somethin'." He produced a wrapped and bowed package. "Got your father a fine bottle of Anisette. I hope he likes it."

Pauly smiled, "I'm sure he'll appreciate it. And we want to thank you for coming out to meet us. I thought maybe Angelo DiFranco might join you."

Rocco said, "We didn't want to be presuming – presumpting – you know, the invite was just for me, we was thinking. Besides, I flew here direct from Vegas where I was taking a little vacation, and Angelo's still in Cleveland, so ..."

"That's OK," said Pauly. "I'd just like to meet him sometime, that's all. Seems like a good guy, smart, too. Maybe in the future."

"Yeah, sure, he'd like that, too, I'm sure. In the future."

The conversation waned. Then Rocco remembered. "By the way, Angelo's hoping we might score some good Italian bread while I'm here. Not many good bakeries left in Cleveland."

Pauly smiled, "How about I prepare a package for him that you can take on your flight back?"

"Yeah. That'd be great. Not to put you out, or anythin', but we'd both appreciate it."

The limousine made excellent time crossing Manhattan into Brooklyn and pulled up in front of a small Italian Restaurant on a quiet street. Two men appeared as if from out of the ground and opened each of the rear doors, left and right. The shock and fear on Rocco's face was obvious.

"Our men. It's alright," said Pauly. "Nice little restaurant. The veal is excellent."

Rocco was ushered into a small private room near the rear. At the back of a round table, set for four, sat Giovanni Basili, perfectly groomed white hair, white moustache, expensive grey suit. He was obviously a man who deserved respect. "Welcome to Brooklyn, Mr. Parmissano," said Giovanni, extending a hand while remaining seated.

Rocco accepted the handshake, then kissed Giovanni's hand reenacting the time-honored greeting Angelo had recommended, "I am honored that you called me to join you for dinner. Please accept this small gift of Anisette from all of us in Cleveland, a token of our respect."

Giovanni smiled, "Sit, sit. You've come alone?"

Pauly took one of the other seats at the table and explained to his father that Rocco had come directly from Las Vegas where he had been vacationing.

"Nice of you to give up vacation time to meet with us. So, how are things in Cleveland?" asked Giovanni, as Pauly poured Chianti into each of their glasses.

"All seems fairly quiet. Business is good, could be better, but not too bad," said Rocco, sipping his wine as antipasto was delivered to the table by quick moving and silent waiters.

"You get along OK with the Triunno's?"

Rocco demurred, "We got a decent agreement to stay outa each other's way. Yeah, things are alright between us."

"Good. Good," said Giovanni. "Better to keep the peace so everyone can prosper. We don't wanna see no more cars blowing up, *capisce*? Too much of a big boom brings out all sorts of local and federal investigations and nosy reporters."

It took Rocco a minute to understand what Giovanni was talking about. "Oh, you mean when that Irish garbage man got hit? That was my grandfather and father what did that. Yeah, even my dad said that was probably the wrong way to handle it. Better to do him like Hoffa."

"You like veal? I hope so. I already placed the order before you got here. They serve a *perfecto* Scallopini here."

"Fine, that's fine. Whatever you recommend."

Giovanni nodded, "Pauly, shut the door." When the door was closed, Giovanni continued, "The reason I asked you to come here, Rocco, is we've received concerns. Some of our friends from overseas are watching what's happening in your city." Rocco's face was locked in a mixture of horror and fear, not sure whether to cry, run, or beg forgiveness for whatever he had done. Giovanni continued, "I'll get right to the point. You got a new Cardinal running your churches over there, don't you?"

Rocco was taken aback, "Uh, yeah, Cardinal Maroney. First time we've had a Cardinal in Cleveland. Got promoted about nine, ten months ago, or so. Maybe a bit longer." Rocco had imagined several reasons for the call from the Basili Family, but Cardinal Maroney was not even on the list of possibilities.

"Well, these friends of ours are concerned that this Maroney fella is ... how shall I put this ... not a very holy man, and I don't just mean schtuppin' that girl. They think he's trying to do something that is not what someone in his position should be doing. They've asked us to look into it. And since you are tight there, maybe you could help."

Rocco was eager to please, "Sure, sure, I'd be happy to help in any way I can. I sent you the pictures, didn't I?"

Pauly refilled Rocco's wine glass, smiled and interjected, "Yes, you did, and we appreciate that. It seems you had some concerns about Maroney already, since you had those pictures."

Rocco puffed up a bit, "Well, early on he asked us to do him a favor, which we did. But that gave us the idea we needed to have something on him in case things got screwy, so Angelo came up with the idea to install some cameras. When you asked for dirt on him, we had it right away."

Giovanni said, "Angelo's a smart guy. Keep him close and happy," waving his finger toward Rocco.

Rocco nodded, but the comment made him suddenly wary. "We had to pull the cameras right away when we heard that he was gettin' copies of the photos. Didn't want him figurin' out where they came from."

Giovanni said, "That was wise."

Giovanni raised his hand and all conversation stopped with a knock on the door as the dinners were brought in. Once the door was again closed, Giovanni continued, "We understand there is a man he hired to do some, let's call it—collecting—for him. Are you aware of this?"

Between bites Rocco replied, "Yeah, he got a guy named Charlie Franklin to pick up some stuff for him a couple times. From here in New York, I think. You know about that?"

Pauly asked, "What do you know about this Mr. Franklin. Is he a trustworthy guy?"

Rocco said, "Yeah. He's OK. I've used him in the past to do some special stuff for me. He knows how to keep his mouth shut. Yeah, he's trustworthy. But like I was tellin' Angelo, he's too good to be wasted on bein' a delivery boy, and that's what the Card was usin' him for. He's better at fixin' stuff – keepin' things quiet like, you know."

Giovanni put down his fork. "The Card?"

Rocco smiled, "That's what Angelo and me, we call Cardinal Maroney. Kinda a play on words – like a comedian, a card, ya know? He makes us laugh, he's so stupid sometimes. Like hookin' up with Marie ..." Rocco was beginning to squirm and knew he was talking too much.

Pauly asked, "Is that the girl in the pictures?"

"Marone, she is a sweet piece. Wasted on that fat ass. We sent her to him to ask for a confession, thinking he might like her. You seen what he gave her as penance." Rocco was drinking his wine too fast, a sign of his nervousness.

Giovanni said, "So this Charlie Franklin guy – you can work with him? He's legit and someone you can trust?"

"Yeah. Like I says, he's done work for me in the past. Good guy. Trustworthy, like Pauly asked about. Independent like. He's not part of any family. Works on his own. Either takes a job or leaves it alone, dependin' on whether it fits with his own idea of morals. He's done some work for local politicians – you know, buryin' some of the things they don't want known. Takes jobs where he can get them if he can stay out'a trouble himself. He's a lawyer by trade, so he knows his way around the law and tries to keep his nose clean most of the time." Rocco suddenly felt like he had talked way too much, and took another bite of veal and a sip of wine.

Giovanni turned to his son, "Pauly, run him through what we got in mind."

Pauly refilled Rocco's wine glass, "Like the Godfather has been saying, our friends from overseas have concerns. They need to stop your Cardinal from doing the bad things they're pretty sure he's doing. The parcels that this Charlie Franklin fellow picked up for him were part of that, though neither of the two pick-ups were what the Cardinal wanted."

Rocco laughed, "Yeah, I imagine what was sent in the latest package upset him pretty good. That was choice."

"Yes," deadpanned Pauly. "I'm sure he was pretty upset. But now our friends think it's time to let him make his move. They're going to release the stuff he's after, and watch what he does. That's where you come in."

"Where you can be a big help to us," added Giovanni.

"Right," said Pauly. "We want you to put this Charlie Franklin on a retainer, so to speak. He'll be working for you, even though the Cardinal will think Charlie's working for him. That way, Mr. Franklin can report to you on the Cardinal's every move, and won't feel like he's revealing private information about an employer."

Rocco said, "Charlie wouldn't rat on whoever he's working for, so yeah, I can see how this will work. He reports everything to me, even though he's doin' stuff for the Cardinal."

"Exactly. And you make careful records of whatever you learn," said Pauly.

"Then you send us the reports," said Giovanni. "Real regular-like. We want to hear from you often, even if there's nothing to report on a given day, tell us that. We'll have a regular communication link."

Pauly said, "We think it's best if Angelo DiFranco calls me daily. Better to have the two consiglieres talking while keeping you two bosses out of the limelight, just in case things go south for any reason."

Rocco nodded, "I get it. Sure. I'll get to Charlie tomorrow morning and set this up. The third pitch is the one that gets the batter out."

Giovanni raised his fork, "What's that mean?"

Rocco said, "It's a baseball term. The third pitch. Like the third package he'll be getting. Never mind, I know what I need to do. We're sorta a team, now. My organization and yours. We'll work together to make the Card show his cards." Rocco laughed at his own little pun. No one else did.

"And have Angelo contact my Pauly, here," said Giovanni with some skepticism.

"Sure. Sure. Angelo. I get it. Say, what do you think Charlie's retainer ought to be? He's gonna see this might be a dangerous assignment. Could get pricey."

Pauly said, "Our overseas friends see this as a fairly serious endeavor. They appreciate your cooperation, and they assume they need to make it worthwhile for both of you. They are offering to send you a quarter-million. Some for you, some for Mr. Franklin. You negotiate the best deal you can get with Mr. Franklin. How's that sound."

Rocco nearly choked on his last bite of veal, washed it down with a big swig of Chianti, and said, "*Mama mia*! OK, sure, that will be ... that's very generous ... please tell your friends I appreciate ... I'm appreciative, very ... and will do whatever they wish. And I thank you for the opportunity to prove my worth to you, as well."

"*Bene*," said Giovanni. "You liked the veal, huh? Good. It's nice to have a friendly dinner with good people. We'll plan to do this again sometime. But now, and I hate to end this so quickly, but I have someplace to be. The limo is outside to take you back to your plane, OK?"

Pauly said, "There's a couple loaves of good Italian bread on the back seat."

Rocco was smart enough to know that he'd been dismissed. Smiles and handshakes all around, and he was whisked back to the airport.

Giovanni and Pauly sat back down to polish off the wine. "He's dumber than we thought he might be," said Giovanni Basili.

Pauly shook his head. "I'm surprised how dumb he is. How'd he ever become the leader of his crew?"

Giovanni said, "Handed down from his father – both thick-headed bullies. No one else with the muscle to clear him out. He'd never accept our option for the future."

"No, I don't think so. But as long as Angelo DiFranco is there, we'll get what we want. After that, we'll see."

Rocco sat back in the plush seat of the executive jet as it taxied toward take off and thought, Two hundred and fifty G's! What a haul! Wonder how little I can get Charlie to take for this. I'll talk it over with Angelo.

Angelo. What the fuck? They kept talking about him. Angelo is smart, Angelo gives you good advice, better keep Angelo happy. Shit. Angelo better keep me happy! That's the way it works, *capisce*? Keep him happy, my ass! What's he up to? I gotta keep my eye on him.

As the plane took off, Rocco's eyes closed and he slept off the wine buzz all the way to Cleveland.

• • •

Charlie's Apartment

While Rocco was flying and sleeping his way back to Cleveland, Charlie, Rita and Pete convened at the apartment where each reported on their findings.

Rita said, "So, it appears that the trust is paying the landscapers to keep the estate looking like an occupied location. But there is no evidence that anyone is living there right now. I suggested I might like the same kind of payment arrangement for my property, and he swallowed pretty hard to avoid that idea."

Pete asked, "What kind of property do you have?"

"I have none, Pete, you dope. I simply suggested to the guy that I represented someone who had a similar-sized estate to the Maroney digs."

"Any luck finding the elder-Maroney's whereabouts? Was he cremated and scattered to the winds?" asked Charlie. "That would be my guess."

Rita said, "I don't think so. I get the impression he was entombed – out in the backyard."

Both men looked up in surprise. Pete said, "Whose backyard?"

"Yeah, we're going to need a bit more data on that piece of speculation," said Charlie.

Rita smiled, "Okay, try to follow along, gentlemen. First, none of the cemeteries have any record of a 'Maroney' buried on their land."

"Don't you mean buried 'in' their land?"

"Shaddup, Pete. You know what I mean," continued Rita. "In, on, above or below, none of the reputable burial grounds have anything on a Parker Maroney. And you gotta think that someone that important would have more than a simple headstone. He'd have a huge statue or crypt with his name in big, bold letters. So, it would be hard for any cemetery to have amnesia about such a celebrated guest, if you get my drift."

"I'm following you, even if Pete is stuck at six-feet below," said Charlie.

"Then I contacted the up-scale mortuaries or funeral homes where important clients might be laid to rest. Generally, a tight-lipped bunch. But when I once again faked my representation of a soon-to-be-departed wealthy client, their memory cobwebs started to clear up. I told them I wanted a confidential burial, no news media, private affair and all that. I asked if they had any recommendations or experience in such an event."

"Pretty smart move, Rita," admitted Pete.

"Yeah, well, no one would admit it outright, but there was one pretty high-class joint that said they had made an interment on a person's estate. Seems you need a permit to do something like that, and this funeral director said he knew how to grease the skids to make such an event happen."

Even Charlie had to laugh at that one. "The mental image of 'greased skids' with a casket on them will forever be in my mind."

"Well, ha-ha to you, too. Both of you can stop your laughing. Anyway, flash-forward to the landscaper – he complained about having to mow around the out-buildings and especially around one big cement structure way in the backyard. It's surrounded by bushes and small trees, but he needs to maintain the path to the door. I think that's a mausoleum or crypt, and I think that's where the old man is buried."

Charlie looked at Pete, saying, "It is speculative, but it would answer a lot of questions about the old man's whereabouts. Could be a family crypt, for others as they pass away."

Pete said, "It makes a lot of sense. Jeez, once they're all gone, that crypt is gonna make it very difficult to sell that property. I certainly wouldn't buy a place with someone else's bones in the backyard."

Rita said, "How do you know there aren't Native American bones under the foundation of your place, Pete? They were here for thousands of years before your ancestors, and their remains could be anywhere."

"You trying to spook me? You're succeeding," mumbled Pete. "That kinda stuff gives me the heebie jeebies."

Charlie shook his head, "Now I'm glad Rita drew that assignment instead of you. Good job, Rita. Even if it is circumstantial, you've put together a reasonable assessment on where the old man is likely buried. I'm guessing we'd be hard pressed to get into the backyard to investigate without the local cops being called. So, there we are. Pete, is it possible the former Mrs. Maroney is in the crypt with her ex-husband?"

"Ha! Wouldn't that be the nuts? Both of 'em in there screaming at each other for eternity!" Pete couldn't control his morbid sense of humor. "No, I don't think so. I got creative and followed my nose on this one."

"That's a pretty big pointer you've got there. Hope you didn't trip on it," said Rita.

"Cute. You know what they say about guys with big noses," said Pete.

"Yeah," said Rita, "they've got big noses."

"Alright, you two. What'd you find out, Pete?" asked Charlie.

"The California tip didn't make a lot of sense. There is no indication Patricia Maroney nee O'Brien had anybody in California to go to, no reason to be that far away from family and friends. You remember we learned that the Maroney family owned property all over the Northeast? I got to thinking, what if the O'Briens owned property in the Northeast, too? Cha-ching! Seems there was a place in central New York, near Syracuse, that the O'Briens transferred to the Maroneys as Parker and Patricia were getting married. Like some sort of dowry, or something. Then, the day before the divorce, the same piece of property was transferred back to one P. O'Brien. Seems Mrs. Maroney was only too eager to shed her married name. She reclaimed the old homestead. Nice big house on it, from the description I have, plus a fairly large farm run by a conglomerate."

"How did you confirm that she's there?" asked Charlie.

"I got an old friend who was the former sports reporter for the local paper, the *Syracuse Post-Standard*. He was only too happy to earn a C-note to do some digging for me. Seems 'Patty' moved back to town about 15 years ago, pleased to be back with her old friends and a few remaining cousins in her old stomping grounds. No one seems to know why she came back. They don't know much about a divorce. Nor do they know she's got a famous son who's now a Cardinal."

Charlie said, "How interesting. My waitress got it all wrong about California, then?"

"Not sure whether Patty ever went out there. Maybe to Palm Springs for R&R, but she certainly didn't stay. She's been on the farm for quite some time."

"Okay, I gotta ask," said Rita. "We made up this story about Merke Edelstein being a recluse on an estate in Upstate New York. And here we've got Patricia O'Brien being an almost recluse on a farm in Central New York. Is this too much of a coincidence? Is it possible that Patricia and Merke are the same person? Pete, didn't you say that the Maroney Family had a treasure of art and artifacts scattered all over the place. Is the Cardinal trying to get his hands on something they already own, but is in the possession of his mother?"

Pete and Charlie both sat back looking at each other. Pete said, "We made up the murky Merke story. So, that part is a myth."

Charlie added, "The Cardinal doesn't know who Merke is, so it's unlikely that she's his mother."

"If they already owned the piece, why would he spend big money to get it? He'd just grab it away from mommy dearest."

"And the involvement of the Habood clan doesn't seem to fit."

Rita interrupted their logical back and forth, "If there was so many items in the Maroney treasury, is it possible the Cardinal didn't know they had it? Did Patricia make it available to the black market to augment the paltry $5 million she got from the divorce? If she knew she had something her son wanted, but never told him about it, she could still be a link in this thing."

"That would be pretty cold-blooded of her – making her son pay for something the family already owned," said Pete.

Charlie asked, "What do we know about the family relationship? Any affection for each other? How did the boys react to the divorce?"

Pete replied, "Nothing about that in my research, either lovey-dovey or mean and nasty. Let me follow up on that."

"Rita, how'd you like to have breakfast in Hudson tomorrow? Go back to our chatty waitress and see if we can get anything more out of her. I'd go – the coffee's pretty good – but I think it might be suspicious if the same guy starts asking questions again."

"Sure," said Rita, "I could use some bacon and eggs. And maybe girl-to-girl she'll be willing to sling some dirt about the Maroney folks that she wouldn't to you."

"If you think you can get her to open up, see if she knows anything about the mausoleum in the backyard."

Pete added, "I'd like to do some digging in the Syracuse area to see if there's any skeletons in closets out there."

Charlie said, "I think it's a long shot, linking Patricia and Merke, but it's worth a little leg work to learn more about the family."

Rita asked, "What did you find out about Vicky Maroney? Where's she been?"

Charlie flipped notebook pages. "Here we are. Victoria 'Vicky' Maroney is the former Victoria Dempsey. She seems to be living in Northeast Ohio, but her exact address is unknown. It almost sounds like she may be sharing an apartment with a girlfriend. She has a Facebook presence under the name 'Vicky Demps'."

"What the hell, you on-line with Facebook?" asked Pete. "I thought you hated that social media stuff."

"Get with the times, old man," said Rita. "Everyone uses Facebook."

"Shit, I can't hardly remember phone numbers. I don't like it or trust it." Pete shook his head.

"Nonetheless," said Charlie, "she's using it. Can't tell from what's on it much about her whereabouts. It seems that she and some of her lady friends are planning a 'girls' trip' to Las Vegas real soon. I'm thinking I might be able to find her out there if I get a hint which hotel they'll be staying in."

Rita said, “You think you’ll be able to locate her in a hotel with thousands of guests? Needle in a hay stack.”

“Yeah, I know. But right now, she’s one of millions of people in Northeast Ohio. Shrinking the odds to one in a thousand sounds better. What do you think, Pete?”

“I think there’s a lot to be learned from Ms. Vicky ‘Whatever’, but you’re gonna look like a perv jumping out at her from behind a palm tree in Vegas. Not a good way to make her talk.”

“I agree,” said Rita. “She’s going to be there with her girlfriends. Plucking her out of the pack will be strange, if not impossible.”

Pete nodded, “Yeah, it could be that the only way to make a connection would be if another woman made the introduction, or did all the questioning. Much less intimidating. Maybe Rita should be the one to do it.”

Rita said, “Ahh, I don’t know. I can be kinda direct, you know?”

Both Pete and Charlie shook their heads, “No. Direct? What does she mean?” “I can’t imagine why she’d say that.” “What’s she talking about?” “She doesn’t intimidate me, how about you?” “No, never.”

“Oh, shut up, you two. You know what I mean. This needs to be done smoothly, almost subtly, so she doesn’t even realize it’s happening. I’m not subtle.”

“Well, you got us there, Rita,” said Charlie. “’Subtle’ is not a word I’d ever use to describe you. So, where does that leave us? If it has to be a woman, we’d need someone who could disarm Vicky, almost charm her without her knowing it.”

“Well, I’ve been charmed by plenty of women, but I don’t think there’s any of them I’d trust with this job,” said Pete.

“I can think of someone who’d probably be great at it,” said Charlie, “but I don’t know how to contact her.”

“Who you thinking of?” asked Pete.

Charlie looked askance at Rita, “TK Constantine was able to knock me off my game.”

Rita snorted, “I think any woman who got naked in front of you could knock you off your game. I don’t think that approach will work with Vicky.”

"It was more than that. She has a way of controlling a conversation, twisting the topic in ways that make you respond to her questions more than she responds to yours. I think she could make Vicky tell her things that she wouldn't tell anyone else. But it doesn't matter since I have no way of contacting her and she probably wouldn't want to work for us anyhow."

Pete said, "The way you describe her sounds like exactly what we need. But doesn't she work for Ms. Murky?"

"She did for the two deliveries, but I don't think that's an exclusive gig," said Charlie. "I get the impression she works for some sort of specialized delivery outfit. If that's the case, there wouldn't be a conflict of interest working for us. But like I said, no contact info."

"The only conflict of interest might be in your pants," said Rita, "or in your jacket pocket. After I did my research into landscapers and funeral parlors, I gathered up clothes for the dry cleaners. I took in that awful sport coat you wore too many times in a row, the one you wore last to New York." She reached into her jeans, pulling out a business card. "You forgot to take this out of your pocket."

Charlie took the card, "Where did this come from? I've never seen it before."

"She must have slipped it in while you were feeling her up," smiled Rita.

"What is it?" asked Pete.

Rita grinned, "It's TK Constantine's phone number. She's obviously hoping Charlie will call her sometime."

"Jesus H. Christ, Charlie, how could you not know she slipped it into your pocket?"

"It was a bit hectic in St. Pats that day, if you'll recall."

"Anyway," said Rita, "this deal in Las Vegas calls for a subtle female approach. From what you've told us about TK, she may be capable of pulling this off with Ms. Vicky without anyone ever catching on. If it's important enough that we learn what Vicky knows, TK may offer us the best option to learn whatever we can."

"Do you think she'd work for us, Charlie?" asked Pete.

"I don't know. She does what she does – at least the two times I met her – for financial reward. She said she gets paid handsomely for her work. I can't imagine she'd do this for the fun of it."

"Maybe you could offer her some hot sex, sweetie, that seemed to work before."

"Rita, please. As I was saying, she'll demand some payment. I don't think her work for Merke Edelstein was an exclusive arrangement. Hell, it's doubtful she even knows Merke. I don't suppose there's any reason for her not to get involved."

"She does seem to have the subtlety needed for this," said Pete. "Could a woman be drawn in by her?"

Rita said, "I hate to admit it, but I think she may be the girl for the job."

"Son-of-a-gun, Rita, that's a very mature way of looking at things. And I'll go out there to keep her company," suggested Pete.

"Not on your life, big guy! One victim is enough for Ms. TK Constantine. Charlie has a built-in relationship, so to speak. He needs to go out with her to make sure she gets the answers we need," said Rita. "You stay here with me. We'll hold down the fort."

Charlie said, "Sorry Pete. TK already caught your toupee act and didn't care for it. Rita's right. You'll be more valuable here. I'll try giving her a call in the morning."

Rita looked over at Pete, "You've got a toupee? I gotta see this!"

"It was only one of my many disguises. I think I may have thrown it away."

"I've seen your place. You never throw anything away," said Rita.

Charlie smiled and secretly wondered when Rita had seen Pete's place. Charlie had been there only a few times, himself.

PITCH NUMBER THREE

Tuesday, July 12:
Some Tuesdays are more eventful than others. Some Tuesdays, it seems like everyone is headed in the same direction with a unity of purpose, like a flock of swallows swooping and turning as if choreographed ahead of time. On other Tuesdays, everyone seems to scatter like crows escaping a farmer's shotgun blast, bumping into or sailing over each other in their frantic and frenetic escape. And on some Tuesdays, you just can't tell the difference.

At 9:30 a.m., Monsignor Leonard burst into the Cardinal's office with a telegram just received at the Chancery door. It read, "I surrender. Your package – the real one—will be ready for delivery in one week. Employ your same delivery man, no substitutes. Await instructions. – M.E." The Cardinal read it twice, then said to the Monsignor, "Bring me the dossier on Ms. Hernandez and rally the boys from Boston."

At 9:38 a.m., Charlie settled into the leather swivel chair in his downtown office and placed a call to the number on the business card. He said, "Good morning, TK. This is Charlie Franklin. I have a job opportunity for you."

At 9:46 a.m., Rocco Parmissano invited Angelo DiFranco into his office at the rear of the Thespian Grill. "How ya' doin' Angie? Listen, we got some things we need to do with the Basili boys. We're gonna be like a team, workin' on somethin' together. Us and them. Big time stuff. But I need to make sure everyone who's involved is loyal. And I mean really loyal. Even you. *Capisce?*"

At 9:48 a.m., Pete, sitting in his underwear in his apartment, got off the phone with his friend from Syracuse. He said, "I think it may be worthwhile for me to make a run up to Syracuse to check out the homestead myself. Whatdya think?"

Rita responded, "I gotta run to Hudson for breakfast. Let's talk about it this afternoon."

At 10:25 a.m., responding to a knock on his locked office door, Charlie found Rico Carponi chewing on an unlit half cigar and wearing his old dirty rumpled hat. "Carp! What are you doing here? I didn't think you knew where I worked."

Rico said, "Just dropping something off for you. The Indians got a day game today. Rocco wants you should join him in his box seats."

Charlie took the ticket offered to him. "Wow. I'm kind of busy today. Is this important?"

"Naw, I just left my seat where I make my dough on stupid bets to offer you a pleasant day at the ballpark. Whadya think, numb nuts? When Rocco asks for something, it's not for just a casual game of rummy. Be there. Game time is 12:05." He turned to leave, then stopped and said, "Hey, kid, have a hotdog – with lots of Ballpark Mustard. That stuff is great."

Game Time

At 12:01 p.m., Charlie walked down the ballpark steps toward Rocco's box seats. He smiled and wondered why the grass at the ballpark always looked greener and brighter than any other place. He spotted the two Dobermans, each five rows back, one to the left and one to right of where Rocco sat. Charlie nodded to the nearest one to make sure he was recognized, then slipped into the row where Rocco sat munching on popcorn.

"Hi, Rocco. Thanks for the ticket."

"Charlie! How are ya'? Glad you could join me. Great day for a ball game, don't ya' think? I like to get here early and watch 'em warm up."

"It sure is a nice day. Sunny and mild. No rain forecast. This really is one of the prettiest ballparks in America. Doesn't look like much of a crowd, though."

Just then, the National Anthem began. Rocco talked right through the song. "This is a make-up game for a rain-out. Makes for a late arrivin' crowd, businessman's special like this, noon start. If no one else shows, they don't know what their missin'. Baseball's always good, no matter whether the team is great or lousy." He munched some popcorn, "Remember back a few years when they was a great team? Couldn't find a ticket, even from a scalper. What was it some four hundred straight sell-outs? Damn! That was fun. Now, maybe they're not gonna win no pennant this year, but it's still fun to come to the games. They'll be better next year. I love it down here. Got season tickets. You like baseball, Charlie?"

The home team took the field and the warm-up pitches were almost done. "Yeah, I like baseball, Rocco. Great American sport."

"Did you play as a kid? I did. Loved it."

Charlie said, "Yeah, I played Little League. My friends tell me I stunk. I don't think I was that bad."

"What position did you play? I liked third base. Lots of action and I got to use my arm to throw out runners."

Charlie said, "I'm a lefty, so positions were limited. I played a lot of outfield, where the coach said I could cause less damage. I preferred pitching, though. Got to do it a few times."

"Pitchin'? Great! Then you can answer a question that I have. I got my own theories, but I'd like to hear what you think."

"Okay, what's the question?"

The game began as Rocco kept up his questions, watching the action and talking out of the side of his mouth. "Ground out. Good start. Okay, we got a new batter up. What's the most important pitch of this at bat?"

Charlie said, “Umm, fastball?”

They were close enough to the field to hear the umpire say, “Ball one.”

“Naw, I don’t mean the type of pitch – fastball, curve and like that. I mean which pitch is the most important in this at bat?”

The umpire said “Strike.”

“Oh,” said Charlie. “Well, I suppose it’s the first pitch of the at bat.”

“Why? Why do you say that?” asked Rocco.

“Well, the first pitch sets up all the rest. If it’s a ball or strike, whatever.”

A fly ball went deep to right field, caught at the warning track. Second out of the inning.

“See, I don’t agree with that. Watch this next batter, then tell me what you think,” said Rocco. “This guy’s a good hitter, that’s why they got him battin’ in the third position. Always put one of your better hitters battin’ third.”

The third batter was, indeed, a good hitter, averaging .317 on the season, according to the scoreboard. The first pitch was low, for a ball. The second was outside, also a ball. The pitcher was trying to be careful with such a dangerous hitter. The third pitch was also low.

“See that?” said Rocco. “Now the pitcher’s in real trouble. He’s gotta bring heat right over the plate.”

As if on cue, a fastball was grooved down the center of the plate and was sent deep in the gap against the wall for a double.

“Okay. Perfect. Now, which of those was the most important pitch?”

Charlie said, “Well, it certainly wasn’t the last one.”

Rocco looked at him, “I’m tryin’ to make a point here. Don’t be a wiseguy.”

“Sorry,” said Charlie, slightly alarmed. “I’m not sure, Rocco. You don’t think it’s the first pitch. I kinda still do. But I’d love to hear your theory.”

Rocco nodded as the next batter grounded out to end the inning. “Okay, here’s what I think. If the first pitch is a strike, a slight advantage goes to the pitcher. If it’s a ball, the slight advantage goes to the batter. That’s simple. If the second pitch is the same as the first, now the pitcher or batter has a better advantage, a real strong advantage. If, however, the count is one ball and one strike after two pitches, neither has the advantage. So that brings us to the third pitch. You follow so far?"

"I'm with you, Rocco."

"In my opinion, the third pitch determines the ultimate result of the at bat. If the count is 2 and 0, the pitcher has to bring somethin' to keep himself in control of the batter. If the count is 0 and 2, the batter is in deep shit, 'cause the pitcher can throw him anything and he has to protect against a strike out. If the count is 1 and 1, the pressure is on both of them to produce. The third pitch! That's what I think is the most important in each at bat."

"Wow," said Charlie. "I hadn't thought of it that way before. I'm going to bear that in mind whenever I'm watching a game." Charlie thought it best not to question Rocco's logic, nor how it fit in when a batter put either of the first two pitches in play. He was here as a reluctant guest, not as a buddy talking baseball strategy.

"Now, you take your situation."

"My situation?" asked Charlie, failing to see any logical progression from baseball pitches to Charlie's life.

"Yeah. You already threw two pitches. And you got two strikes."

"When did I do that?"

"Your work for the Cardinal. You delivered two packages. He didn't like either one. The first was a slider at the knees, the second was a nasty curve ball. Two strikes. Nice."

"Rocco, you know I won't tell anyone who I do or do not do work for, so I'm going to have to say I don't know what you're talking about."

"I know, Charlie. That's what makes you a good guy in my book. Let's just pretend I know what I'm talkin' about. Soon, you're gonna get a chance to deliver a third pitch to the Cardinal. You're up on him. You have the advantage. He's gonna try and take back that advantage, and that's why we're meeting today."

"I don't follow, Rocco."

"Stay with me on this. You're a smart guy. You'll figure it all out. But here's my deal to you. For this third pitch, you won't be workin' for the Cardinal. You'll be workin' for me."

"What do you mean, I'll be working for you?"

"You're an honorable guy, Charlie, you won't tell anyone who your clients are, and you won't tell anything about what you do for those clients. It just sorta happens, right? So, if you was to be workin' for the Cardinal, you couldn't tell me nothin'. But if you was bein' paid by me, well then you could tell me what's happenin', right?"

"I suppose that is correct."

"Right. So, if I paid you to do whatever the Cardinal wanted you to do, you could tell me all about it, right?"

"That's a bit convoluted, Rocco, but technically, you are correct."

"Good. So, here's the deal. I'm hiring you right now. I'm putting you on a retainer. I'm tellin' you to do whatever the Cardinal asks you to do, and report back to me on everything. Every day, whether he calls you or not, whether he makes a request or not. Everything. And I'll pay you real good for your work. OK?"

"This sounds kind of dangerous, Rocco. The Cardinal is not a nice person, and I think he's capable of acting viciously, vindictively. May already have done some bad stuff. To do what you're asking, I may be sticking my neck out pretty far on such a deal."

"I expected you would say that, so I'm gonna give you a big retainer, sweet enough to take some of the sting off your mind. How's 50 Gs sound?"

"Jesus, Rocco. Now I'm worried that it may be more dangerous than I originally thought. But you've just hit my sweet spot. We have a deal."

"Great. Here's how it's gonna work. The Cardinal is just now hearing that the package he has been wanting will be available for pick up in one week. He'll be told to send the same guy – you – to pick it up. I have no doubt the Cardinal doesn't trust you anymore, so he's gonna hold somethin' over your head. After all, you've got two strikes on him. He's got to be careful. But here's the beauty part – you're gonna groove him a change-up."

"Help me understand what you mean."

"The package will be the real deal, what he's been wanting all along. The third pitch will be one he can hit for a homerun."

Charlie considered how much he could tell Rocco about what had previously taken place. "You seem to know I've already given him two packages. I have no idea what the contents of either were. You're telling me he didn't like either one. If someone has been giving him bogus parcels, I don't know who it is or why. But you say that now they'll give him what he wants. Who are they, and why would they concede to his request at this time?"

Rocco shifted in his seat, momentarily cheering for a home team score. "Charlie, there are some big people – I mean BIG people – on the other end of this. I don't know all of it, and frankly you shouldn't know either. For your own protection. If they want us to see the whole picture, they'll tell us. Until then, take the 50 Gs and do as you're told. All I know is, these big folks, they want to see what that fat ass tries to do with what he's gonna receive."

"Not that I'm admitting anything, but if I've been working on delivering packages to the Cardinal, I would probably imagine that Maroney wants to try and trade the parcel – whatever it is – for something else he really wants."

Rocco looked directly at Charlie and smiled, "See? I knew you were a smart guy! Whatever you learn from this point forward, communicate it to Angelo. We'll send the information on to the other interested parties." He reached into his pocket, "Use this burner phone. Angie's number is in it."

"Okay, I'll keep in touch with Angelo every day. Does he know I'll be calling him?"

"Yeah. He's in the loop. You know Angelo? Whadya think of him?"

"I've only met him a few times. Seems like a smart guy. Helps you a lot, doesn't he?"

"Yeah. Yeah. It's just ... sometimes a guy like me can't be too careful, know what I mean? Yeah, Angelo's a good guy."

Rocco got up to leave, signaling the Doberman's to be up and ready. "Stay here and watch some more of the game. I gotta get back. Have a hot dog or two. Enjoy." With that he was off, leaving Charlie to mull over what had just happened.

• • •

At the Office

Charlie's mind was still whirling when he returned to his office. He left the game in the middle of the third inning, not even sure what the score was. "The third pitch," he chuckled to himself. "I'm not sure if Rocco is goofy or brilliant. I'll have to think on that one when I have some down time."

He decided to check on Vicky's facebook account, to see if there was any more chatter about Las Vegas. There was. Her girlfriends were finalizing plans to go out over the weekend, planning to stay at the Bellagio. Today is Tuesday, Charlie calculated. If I'm going to make a connection with Vicky out there, I'll have to make plans quickly. He booked a suite at the Bellagio, then began to call TK Constantine. He stopped in mid-dial, remembering his new assignment, and picked up the burner to dial Angelo DiFranco.

"Yeah? Who is this?" answered Angelo.

"Angelo, this is Charlie Franklin. I was told to call you and keep you updated."

"Oh, sure. What do you have? Did the redcap contact you?"

"No, not yet. Listen, I've been trying to cover my bases, not trusting him very much."

"That's smart. What have you got?"

"I'm looking for leverage by digging into his family – you know, his brother, father, mother."

"Okay, so what?"

"There's some weird things. I've got a lead on his sister-in-law, who's on the legal paperwork for the Maroney estate in Hudson. But she's been unseen for some time. She may know things and might be willing to talk. If so, that could be a help to me – and to you and the folks you're working with. But that means I'd have to go to Las Vegas this weekend to catch up with her. I just wanted you to know I'd be away for a few days."

Angelo sighed into the phone, "Jeez, I don't know. The redcap will be contacting you soon. But the package delivery is still a week away. You think talking to this babe will give us some leverage?"

"Might be. I hope so. I'm also looking into the Cardinal's mother, just in case."

"Where's she at?"

"Somewhere near Syracuse."

"Fuck, Charlie, we can't have you running all over the country chasing old women. We need you here."

"No, no. Someone else is covering that angle for me."

"You got a team? Didn't know that."

"Not really a team. Just some people who can do a little leg work without getting too involved," said Charlie, trying to protect Pete and Rita from Angelo's eyes.

"So, you need to hop to Vegas – for how long?"

"Say Friday through Sunday. Should be enough time to make the connection."

"Uh huh. Wanna fly a private jet?"

Charlie tried to control his shock, "Umm, what do you mean?"

"Rocco's headed out there on Friday morning for some R&R, coming back Sunday afternoon. You can hitch a ride with him."

"He won't mind?"

"I'll clear it with him. But you'll need to make your own hotel arrangements. He needs, um, some privacy where he's staying."

"Okay. Let me know the flight details." Charlie hung up the burner phone, and picked up his cell to call TK Constantine.

Angelo Calls Brooklyn

Angelo went to his car for privacy and dialed Pauly Basili. "It's me ... Yeah, Charlie Franklin's in ... Don't know how much cash Rocco's giving him ... Uh huh ... Listen, this Charlie guy is looking for leverage on the target, needs to follow some leads this weekend ... yep, he is a smart guy ... anyway, he'll be out of touch for a few days, I thought it would be OK ... no, shouldn't interfere with anything ... yeah, I'll grill him on what he gets, could help us out, too ... Sure, you'll know what I know ... By the way, what did you say to Rocco? He's acting kinda strange, even for him ... well, it's like he doesn't quite trust me anymore ... No, I'll stay close to him ... need to calm him down ... Really? That soon? ... Okay, I'll ramp up the preparations here ... I'll watch my back, don't worry."

• • •

Everyone's in Motion

Rita returned to Pete's apartment to find him packing an overnight bag. "Planning on blowing town?"

Pete said, "Syracuse. Just one or two nights, I hope. How'd things go at breakfast?"

"Interesting little place, that café. I found a lovely table with quite a few gossipy old ladies. They were only too happy to have a younger person willing to listen to them, so they were very eager to spill what they knew. Well, I guess the Bloody Mary's I bought them helped loosen their tongues a bit."

"What did you learn?"

Rita flopped down on Pete's bed as he struggled to pack. "Not a lot of love lost for the Maroney family, and not a lot of love inside the family, either. The town biddies were happy to dump on both Patricia and Parker as disinterested parents for infecting the town with their sons' awful behavior. The boys, lacking parental guidance or affection, got into any number of scrapes, only to be bailed out by daddy's money. The boys only got worse the older they got. One old woman was incensed that one of the boys actually became a priest, let alone a bishop or cardinal. It's funny, but they kept saying they couldn't tell one from the other, they looked so much alike. Anyway, if you can locate Patricia in Syracuse, you might be able to get her to spill something on her son, the Cardinal."

Pete was half listening while finishing his packing. "Charlie called and wants us to meet early this evening in my office. Says he wants to take advantage of the security system I've got. Sounds like he's got some big news."

"Huh. OK. Do we have time for a little afternoon delight?" she said, sliding behind Pete and giving him a big hug.

• • •

Charlie was just closing up his office door when the red-headed young man got off the elevator, momentarily panicked at running into a live human being. "Here. This is for you!" he shouted, turning left and right, searching for the quickest stairway exit.

Charlie took the manila envelope and pointed to the left where the staircase door was located. The young man literally jumped at the door and fled down the stairs, giving himself several bruises from the sound of the bumps and crashes he made.

Returning to his office, Charlie slit open the envelope to find a cryptic note and several pages ripped out of a binder. The note read, "This is only a portion of a dossier we have on your girlfriend, Rita Hernandez. You will do as I say, or it will become public and likely destroy her future. I will be in touch soon. Do not cross me again as you have twice before." There was no signature, but the reference to 'twice before' made it clear who had sent it. He slipped it all into his briefcase and headed toward Pete's office.

• • •

It got to be 6:30 p.m. before Pete and Rita got off the elevator in the Terminal Tower. As they turned the corner toward Pete's office, they found Charlie sitting on the floor outside the door sipping on a cup of what was now cold coffee.

"Jeez, Charlie," said Pete, "you been waiting long?"

"I know I didn't stipulate a time, but I was beginning to wonder if someone had shut off the elevators."

"Oh, boohoo, Charlie," said Rita. "Did you bring us any coffee? No? How very thoughtless of you."

Pete said, "Alright, alright. Let me get the door open." Two keys, then a code on the pad permitted entry without setting off the alarm. "I assume it's my amazing security system that attracted you to a meeting here, huh, Charlie?"

"You have no idea, Pete," said Charlie as the door opened. "We've got a lot of ground to cover, and my office may no longer be so secure."

Pete and Rita threw each other a look with raised eyebrows. Pete led them into an inner room, the door of which was hidden by a bookcase which swung open after Pete touched several hidden buttons. "In here," he said.

"Cozy," said Rita as she took in the mostly bare surroundings of the 10-foot-by-10-foot room. A small round table with four chairs dominated the center. In one corner, on an angled desk, a lap top sprung to life as the lights were turned on. Above the lap top, two small video screens showed the view from the cameras aimed down either hall. "Holy crap, Pete, this looks like it's straight out of Langley."

"You don't need to be in the CIA to acquire high-tech security," crowed Pete. "And Charlie seems a bit tense this evening, so I figured we'd use this safe room. By the way, your cell phones probably won't work in here. There's an old-fashioned land line hidden in the wall if we need to make a call."

"Very impressive, Pete," said Charlie. "In all the times I've come to your office, I didn't know this room existed. But I'm glad it does, because this time it's necessary."

"You're starting to frighten me, Charlie," said Rita. What's up?"

"Grab a seat and hold onto your hats. We are now working for Rocco Parmissano."

"What?!?" they both shouted at once. "When did that happen?" continued Pete.

Charlie gave them a run-down of the conversation at the baseball game and the subsequent call to Angelo DiFranco.

"Did the Indians win? Just asking," said Rita.

"Sorry, I didn't stay past the third inning. So, we'll still be doing whatever the Cardinal asks us to do, but given the retainer from Rocco, we now report to him, or at least I report to him via the burner phone to Angelo. Any questions about any of that?"

"Lots," said Pete, "but go on. I sense there's another shoe you want to drop."

"There is." Charlie reached into his brief case. "Just before I left the office, the red-headed guy gave me this before scrambling away at full gallop down the stairs. It's from the Cardinal. It's a portion of a dossier on you, Rita, with some nasty implications about you and your family. If this gets out, it could cause a lot of trouble for your folks, and ultimately, for you." He handed her the documents for her to examine.

After a few minutes of review, she said, "Holy crap, Charlie. This stuff is only half true, but even that half could get them thrown out of the country. We can't let this get out." She was suddenly in a panic, shaking her head as her whole body began to shiver.

"I agree. Before we get too upset, let's remember that we now work for someone who can help make sure that the information on these pages – and whatever else the Cardinal may have – is never seen by anyone."

Pete sat back. "Wow, talk about serendipity. Does Rocco know about this document?"

Charlie shook his head. "So far, Rocco doesn't even know you two are working with me. I made a little slip to Angelo that I had others doing some leg work, but I don't think he knows either of your names. Depending on how the Cardinal wants to play this, I may need to 'out' Rita to them, to help protect her. For right now, I think we keep this to ourselves." Turning to Rita, "But for your safety, I think it would be wise for you to move out of my apartment, keep away from yours, and stay with some friends for a while. Keeping your distance from me is probably a good idea."

Rita looked at Pete, who said, "I agree with Charlie. Whatever the Cardinal has, let's take it seriously. We can make this go away, but right now the Cardinal holds all the aces." Turning to Charlie, Pete said, "I see why you wanted to meet in a secure location."

"Yes, but I'm not done with bomb shells. Given this communication from the Cardinal, I'm going to be given instructions for picking up a third package for him, only this time it will be the real deal."

"Whadya mean, 'the real deal'? What's that mean?"

"Rocco called it 'the third pitch', making some sort of baseball analogy, and said it would be the documents that the Cardinal wanted in the first place. Whoever is controlling all of this, call them Merke Edelstein or whomever, wants to see what he'll do with the real goods. My suspicion is they want him to make a move so they can then stop him from doing whatever he's got in mind."

Pete said, "Jesus Christ, this got real serious real quick. There are so many dangerous pieces at play, I find it hard to believe that nobody gets hurt. In fact, I think there's a lot of somebodies who could get real hurt and real bad – starting with us!"

"I'm glad it's not just me who sees it that way. Yes, this has gotten very dangerous. I sensed that when Rocco gave me a $50,000 commission."

"Fifty grand?!?" shouted Pete. "Where'd he get that kinda loose dough?"

"His numbers business could cough that up in a day or two, but I'm thinking he got a donation from whoever it is he refers to as 'Big People' who are calling the shots. Yesterday he flew to New York for a sit down with another family. Then today I get called to the ballgame where he promises me 50 Gs. Doesn't take a rocket scientist to draw a line between the two. He's only giving us a portion of whatever they're paying him to pull this off."

Rita stopped re-reading the dossier pages. "We've got to protect my family!"

Pete held her hand. "We will, honey, we will."

"I know this has been a lot, but there's more," said Charlie.

"Good god," said Rita. "I can't imagine what more there could be."

Charlie said, "I got ahold of TK Constantine. Turns out she's a very mercenary individual, willing to work for whoever can meet her asking price. She'll do the questioning of Vicky in Las Vegas this weekend. She wants $2500 per day, plus expenses. I accepted her offer. We can use some of the money from Rocco to pay for her per diem, plus the flights. It turns out Rocco is taking a private jet to Las Vegas on Friday, and Angelo said I could hitch a ride with him, so I won't have to pay for my own flight."

Pete shook his head. "You sure Vicky and her friends are going this weekend? Who goes to Vegas in July? Must be over 100-degrees in the day, and almost that at night."

Charlie said, "They're headed out Friday morning. The facebook postings talked about cheap rates for hotels and flights. I'm guessing they'll drink all night and sleep all day."

Rita coughed while failing at suppressing a smile. "Uh, regarding TK's per diem, you didn't mention the cost of her hotel room. Shall we presume that's a shared expense?"

Pete came to Charlie's defense, "Given the circumstances, I think it will look better if TK seems to be attached, not just a single girl working the halls of the casino."

"True," said Rita. "The better hotels in Vegas are cracking down on the working girls. Can't have her ejected from her room as a prostitute, even if ..."

"Hey! Let's cut her some slack. She's on our team now." Charlie leaned forward, "I need both of you to consider this and give me your opinion. I'm supposed to contact Angelo as soon as the Cardinal reaches out to me. These pages from the dossier on Rita would be considered reaching out. But I haven't called Angelo yet. Do I tell him about the threat to me through Rita? If I do, then both Rocco and Rocco's New York contacts will know all about Rita. If they do anything to protect her, she'll likely owe them. If I don't tell Angelo about the threat, then we'll have to deal with the dossier ourselves, with no protection from the mob guys. And I may be taken to task for not telling them everything. What do you two recommend, especially you, Rita, since this affects you directly?"

Rita lowered her head as she thought her way through the options, finally nodding to herself. "Tell Angelo everything. Protecting my family is worth the risk that I may owe the mob boys something in return. I can deal with that. Actually, Charlie, you may end up owing them something, too. Are you OK with that?"

Charlie smiled, "I've done work for Rocco before. If I end up owing him or the boys in New York, I can manage. I was more concerned about how you would feel about it."

"That's very kind of you. Thanks. Let's be straight with them, and hopefully they'll be straight with us. What do you think, Pete? You haven't said anything."

Pete tapped the table as he gave his opinion slowly. "Rita, you aspire to be an attorney someday soon. Rocco and the boys would love to have a lawyer owing them something. I understand your concern for your family, but keep in mind that this could come back to bite you in the ass someday. Don't be too flippant about it."

Rita said, "I get it. I understand. I still want the added insurance that those guys could provide. I've been kicked in the ass before, I've been bitten in the ass before. I know how to apply bandages."

Charlie said, "Okay, done. Do you two have anything to add to this little soiree?"

Pete said, "While you're off gambling away the rest of the 50 Gs, I'll be driving to the small town of Pompey, New York, just south of Syracuse, where Patricia Maroney nee O'Brien is holed up. My newspaper buddy hasn't been able to get much on her, other than an address of the place, which he thinks is a pretty big house on a pretty big working farm. I'm hoping someone in the town can maybe stir up an invitation from dear old Patty if I tell them I'm doing a newspaper story on farming communities like theirs."

"Nice twist. Maybe you'll even get an article for some Sunday supplement," joked Charlie.

"A pox on you and your children! Sunday supplement, my ass!"

Rita jumped in. "Hey, down in Hudson I learned that the Maroney clan is not deeply admired and they're not an affectionate bunch. The parents, Parker and Patricia, are roundly despised and reviled by many in the community for raising two pretty much hateful children, who the locals believe became such hellions because they were raised in a loveless house. And one thing keeps creeping into conversations – the locals couldn't quite tell one brother from the other because they looked so much alike. Don't know why that bothers me, but it does."

Charlie said, "You know, that's not the first time I heard that. Pete, if you get to Ms. Patricia, quiz her a bit about that. Maybe we're missing something." He stood up, "Unless there's something else, let's break up this session. Rita, pack up a bag and find a friend to stay with for a while. Pete, travel safe to Pompey. Oh, and one more thing: I think the Boston Boys are still in play. I caught a glimpse of them the other day watching my office – at least I think it was them. Anyway, everyone be careful."

Pete said, "You got it. If you see guys wearing Red Sox ball caps, be wary. Boston's not scheduled to play in Cleveland for several weeks. Watch out for the Italian Guy, too."

• • •

Wednesday, July 13:

George was near tears. His cousin and the other men from Boston terrorized him, made fun of him, dismissed him, in their words, as a fairy. It fell to Wesley to give them direction. He hoped they would follow his orders. They paid attention to Wesley because of the Roman Collar he wore which alerted their unnatural fear and slow-witted mental progression: a priest equals confession which equals sin which equals hell which equals fire and facing the devil. Therefore, it was always best to obey a priest.

The monsignor closed the door of the small conference room where he met with the Southies in their hideout, the yet unopened men's homeless shelter. George chose to wait outside. The diocese had put a quarter million dollars into the renovation of a former hotel in a broken-down part of downtown, offering thanks to all the wonderful businesses and individuals who had contributed to the re-construction. A public accounting of the $1.25 Million actually donated was never considered necessary by the Cardinal or Monsignor Leonard, who oversaw the charitable campaign and the hiring of the several disreputable contractors.

"Gimme a beer, hey!" said George's cousin to buddy #1.

"Next time you go to the packie yourself, idgit," replied #1.

George's cousin stood up aggressively, "Yah bettah just back off on that kinda talk."

"Sit down, all of you, and be quiet. You can fight when this job's over," the Monsignor demanded. "I need to know what you've learned so we can plan our next steps."

George's cousin said, "We been tailin' the guy and his girl, although they're kinna slippery, no?"

Buddy #2 added, "Aw, that girl's wicked hot, though, yeah huh. I'll just follow her, maybe bring her here some night, yeah?"

"Don't be such a chahdahhead! We dough wanna get arrested again so soon," reasoned #1. "Anyways we donn even know where she is right now. This lunkhead lost her when she got on the pike," pointing at George's cousin.

The Monsignor shook his head, "Do you know where Mr. Franklin is?"

The cousin responded, "We got his office and his apartment all looked at. We know da' ins and outs. He's got some bald-head guy keeps meetin' up wit' him. Big guy, like a boxah. If he's in the pitchah we may need to make him bloody, no?"

"Umm, no. No," said the Monsignor haltingly. "We must stay focused on Mr. Franklin and the girl, Rita Herns. Let's not start something with anyone else. Especially if we don't know who it is." Nonetheless, Wesley made note of a new-to-him person involved. "But if you can tell me the name of the bald man, that would be helpful."

Buddy #2 said, "I'm good wit' dat. Anyway, I'd need a bigger knife to take him down. I'll stick to dat frickin' sweet babe, yes suh."

"Yeah, but if he gets in the way," offered #1, "well, we can't be responsible if sumpin happins cuza his actions."

The Monsignor was irritated at George for bringing these three almost uncontrollable hoodlums from Boston into the picture. He needed to find a way to make them take only one step at a time, to stay focused. Singular thought was not their strong suit. "Look. I can get you some cash if you just do what I ask, but do nothing more. Find out where Charles Franklin and Rita Herns can be found at any given moment. When it becomes necessary, I will tell you to eliminate one or both. But you are to do nothing until I tell you to do so, understood? In the meantime, here's $500 for food and expenses. You must keep a low profile and stay out of sight."

George's cousin said, "Sweet! We can get some killa beer wid' dis dough!"

• • •

Friday, July 15:

7:30 a.m., and Charlie was waiting at the Executive Jet terminal at Burke Lakefront Airport. The terminal seats were plush and comfortable, the jet would be, too. Nonetheless, flying with Rocco Parmisanno meant Charlie had to be alert and as charming as possible. After all, Rocco had agreed to let him share the flight. It would not do to antagonize his benefactor who was also, for the time being, his employer.

Waiting for his benefactor to show up for the flight scheduled to depart in 15 minutes, Charlie slapped his face a few times to wake up. He had taken an early cab, not wanting to be the last person to arrive. Pete was in mid-state New York searching for the Cardinal's mother, Rita was hidden away with a friend, and his newest associate, TK Constantine, would meet him at the hotel in Las Vegas. Everyone was accounted for, but Charlie still had a nagging feeling he was missing something – something very important.

Angelo did not seem troubled by the news of the Cardinal's threat. He said he would do what he could to protect Rita and her family from exposure. His casual aplomb was amazing, accentuating why he was such an asset to the volatile Rocco. Angelo mentioned that the Cardinal was likely at his most dangerous point, driven to distraction awaiting instructions from the mysterious Ms. Edelstein. Charlie could not disagree. The threat of danger seemed to come from every direction, whether it was Rocco, the Cardinal, or the various groups tailing him or his associates.

At five minutes before departure, a groggy-looking Rocco strode in, waving for Charlie to join him as he proceeded straight to the waiting jet outside the door. Within minutes and without a word, their bags were stowed, their seat belts buckled and the engines roared to life as they taxied to the runway.

Charlie checked his watch as the jet lurched forward at breakneck speed – exactly 7:45 a.m. It felt as if they were almost vertical as they crossed ten thousand feet in what seemed a flicker of time. Charlie looked at Rocco in his seat on the right side of the plane. Rocco was nearly asleep. The plane started to level off as the co-pilot came to the passenger compartment offering coffee.

Charlie gratefully accepted a cup that was freshly brewed just prior to take off. Rocco closed his eyes and didn't respond. Charlie looked around, taking in everything for the first time. The jet had only eight leather over-plush seats, four on each side. A small restroom was in the rear. Individual 5-inch video screens were available to each of the eight seats, offering a variety of viewing options. The home screen offered a view of the flight path on a map simulation, with air speed, altitude and ETA superimposed. Charlie liked watching the flight in motion. Despite the three-hour time difference between Cleveland and Las Vegas, the screen calculated they would arrive at 8:35 a.m. Even though there would be the inevitable head winds, the executive jet was far faster than any large airliner, shaving more than an hour off the estimated commercial flight time.

Experimenting with the electronic seat controls, Charlie discovered that his seat could recline, spin, even massage his lumbar region. He sat back with his coffee and closed his eyes. There would be very little communication with Rocco this morning.

• • •

Syracuse, NY

At 7:55 a.m., Pete met up with Abraham Taylor at a coffee shop in Syracuse. The night before the two had dropped in at several local eateries and taverns in the Pompey area, hoping someone might know Patricia O'Brien. There were two promising leads, one at a grocery store and the other at a local tavern.

"Look, Pete," said Abraham, "you're going to have more success with that old lady grocery clerk without me around."

"Are you kidding? You charmed her."

Abraham shook his head. "That wasn't affection in her eyes, and you know it. All she saw was a huge black man hovering over her. No, you go talk to her alone."

"But the guy at the bar, Abe. He liked you."

"He knew I played football at the 'Cuse'. And he recognized my name as a sports reporter. But he wasn't too thrilled to have me standing behind him. You pick up on these things after years of discrimination, Peetie."

"So, what are you saying, you gonna abandon me out here? Make me try and succeed on my good looks and natural boyish charms? Fat chance of that!"

Abe smiled and said, "Fat chance, indeed. You gained – what – thirty pounds since college? Forty? As for succeeding with your 'boyish charms', well, that didn't work on the girls in college as I recall, so I doubt it'll work now."

"What a mean thing to say. I'm hurt," Pete pretended to be insulted. "Those girls didn't appreciate what a fine fellow I was back then."

"What I recommend to you now is to be straight with these people. Tell them what you are able to reveal of the truth. You'll be surprised at what you can accomplish out here with the truth."

"Yeah, that ain't happening, Abe. Too many squirrelly pieces to lay out bits and pieces of the truth. Just raise more questions than I'm willing to answer."

"You're into some deep shit, huh?"

"Kinda. Hey, try this out for size. What if I walk in like a reporter ..."

"You are one."

"Uh, used to be. Anyway, what if I tell them I'm doing a story on big family farms, how important they are to our country, and other stuff like that. Think they'll talk to me then?"

"Make the pitch that the story will be about people just like them, but offer anonymity if they prefer it. Some won't want their name in print. This is a fairly tight-lipped farm district. They don't like making waves or causing trouble for their neighbors. They don't like outsiders prying into their lives. But that's just my take as an old sports reporter. I never wrote any stories about corruption like you did."

"You mean stories that got me fired."

"My sports stories didn't save my job, either, what with so many newspaper cuts everywhere. At least you wrote something important, not about some running back's blown out knee."

"I still think you should come with me. Your insight will be very helpful, plus you know the roads better than a GPS. You don't have anything else going today, do you? Maybe you could pretend to be my photographer."

Abraham thought about it for a minute. "You got a camera?"

"In my trunk. Looks like the real deal, too."

"Film?"

"Digital."

"Okay if I break it?"

Pete laughed. "We'll see how it looks draped around your neck."

• • •

At the Chancery

Brother Gerald finished a review of the financial books for the last year, even though no one had asked him to do so. He shook his head – too many irregularities. Whoever was tending the books had been very careless, missing thousands and thousands of dollars which would greatly strengthen the diocesan treasury and provide funds for much needed help with so many struggling parishes. He thought about writing a report to the Cardinal, identifying the amount of the missing funds. If only he could get ahold of the bank books, he could probably find what account the money was in. But those were under lock and key held by the Monsignor. It was frustrating.

He hoped that he could build the Monsignor's trust in him so the bank books could be examined. He was sure it would be fairly easy to find a record of the money, as it was likely a simple accounting error. After all, just because you became an ordained priest didn't mean you automatically became an expert bookkeeper.

Then he had a thought. He knew approximately how much money was mis-reported. With a little more work, his written analysis to the Cardinal could show where the money was most needed, which parishes would benefit the most from a windfall infusion of diocesan funds. He smiled as he reached for the several volumes with the complete history and records of each parish. He would not only provide the Cardinal with an increase to the treasury, he'd also provide him with a plan to put those funds to their best use. Sometimes having a vow of silence was a benefit, he reasoned. It allowed one to concentrate deeply at the task at hand. He began humming a Gregorian Chant, the only use of his vocal cords permitted by his vows. He loved Gregorian Chant.

• • •

As the plane began the descent into Las Vegas, the seat belt chime wakened Rocco from his nap. "Where we at?"

"About 15, 20 minutes out, I'd guess," said Charlie.

"That's great," yawned Rocco. "Where are you booked?"

"Staying at the Bellagio. That's where the lady will be that I'm trying to track down."

"So, what's this all about? Why d'ya need to talk to this lady? Angelo told me but I gotta say, I don't get it."

Charlie was starting to wonder the same thing, but thought spelling it out to Rocco might help put it straight in his own mind, too. "The Cardinal has a brother who was active in collecting ancient artifacts, just like the rest of the family. The brother is now in a nursing home, suffering from Alzheimer's. But he has a wife who is on the record as a trustee of the estate, which probably includes all those artifacts. We've been unable to find her to get her take on what the Cardinal may be up to, since he seems to be after one special artifact. And like I told you at the ballgame, I think he's trying to trade it for something else. If we know what that something else is, we've got leverage on him. So, since we know that his brother's wife is on a little vacation out here, we're hoping to quiz her a bit and build that leverage."

"Who's this 'we' you keep talkin' about? I thought you worked alone," asked Rocco.

"What? Oh. Well, I do sometimes have some minor assistance on finding things out. Primarily it's Rita, my receptionist. I think of us as a team, even though she doesn't really know all that much about what

I do. Despite that, the Cardinal is trying to threaten her and her family with exposure. I told Angelo about that." Charlie was kicking himself for almost exposing his team. He hoped Rocco could be put off the scent. "What brings you out here? Angelo said you were getting some R&R?"

Rocco smiled at the thought. "Yeah, some R&R. Good way to put it." His mind was clearly focused on something pleasant. "A while back I made ... ah ... a deal with a guy, a business transaction, you might say. A trade, you might say. I did him a favor which he appreciated. As thanks, he gave me the keys to a villa in the valley. Nice place. Quiet. Got its own pool. I let some people stay there sometimes. Someone's there right now, who I'm gonna join up with. Yeah, that was a good deal for me, and the guy got to live another day."

Rocco and Charlie complied with the pilot's instructions to raise seat backs. Rocco said, "Well, good luck with your search for the broad. Hope you get somethin' outa her. Uh, we're taking off Sunday at 4:00 p.m. Be at the plane if you want a ride back."

Rocco was successfully distracted, imagining whatever he might soon enjoy while the plane made a smooth approach, landed, taxied and shut down. He raced off the plane into a waiting limousine and was off without another word or any acknowledgement to anyone. Charlie found a black town car looking for a passenger and headed to the Bellagio. It was still only 9:05 a.m. when the town car dropped him off. He used his charm and a palmed $50 bill to convince the hotel check-in clerk that he was eligible for one of the suites prepared for early arriving guests.

Keys in one hand and roller bag in the other, he turned toward the elevators when he noted a bushy-haired brunette in frumpy clothes waving to him from one of the circular red velvet couches positioned under the Chihuly ceiling sculpture just beyond the registration desk. He cocked his head and approached the young lady. "Do I know you, miss?"

"Hi, Charlie! It's good to see you. Sit down a minute."

"TK? What's with the disguise?"

"What, no kiss? No 'glad to see you'?"

"Why, of course I'm glad to see you. I just didn't recognize you. What are you doing?"

"My job, silly! I'm supposed to figure out who I'm looking for, right? So, I've got a list of the ETAs for all planes coming from Cleveland, estimating the amount of time it takes to get luggage and transportation, then making a note of three ladies in their early fifties who look like they're ready to have a blow-out bash in Vegas. The first plane landed just about a half-hour ago. If they were on it, they'll be here in the next ten or fifteen minutes, plus or minus. If not, the next plane's ETA is at 10:50 a.m."

"Are you going to be a brunette this weekend?"

She leaned closer to him, "Shh! This is a wig. I thought you were smart enough to know that."

Charlie nodded, "I figured it was, but why are you wearing it?"

She sighed, "Oh, Charlie. You can be so dense sometimes. You see, when I spot the three ladies come in, I'm going to jump in line right behind them to overhear their conversation. Later when I approach the one that we want to question, I'll be my natural blonde. I don't want her to recognize me as the eavesdropper from this morning. Simple, see?"

"Got it. Yes, very smart of you. Where are your bags?"

"They're at the bellhop claim stand."

"Here's a key to our suite, number 1705. Give me your check ticket. I'll have the bellman bring up your bags. After I unpack, I'll come back to you with a cup of coffee. Okay?"

She smiled devilishly at Charlie, "I'm so glad we'll be sharing a room, and coffee would be heavenly. One cream."

"It's a two-bedroom suite, TK. You'll have your own space." He stood and said, "Coffee coming shortly."

She licked her lips, "We'll have to talk about whether we sleep in my space or yours."

Charlie blew out his breath as he headed to the bell stand, muttering to himself, "I don't know what I was thinking."

• • •

Pompey, NY, South of Syracuse

Pete and Abraham pulled up to a gated driveway. "You sure this is the place?" asked Pete.

Abe said, "You talked to the old lady at the grocery store. She said it was out here, somewhere, with a gate on the drive. And the guy at the bar said it was the place with brick pillars on either side of the entrance. There are the brick pillars. I haven't seen anyplace else even close to that description."

Pete got out and peered through the heavy bushes. "Pretty big place back there. Not what I'd call a 'farm house'." He stepped back. "Speaker box over here. I'll push the button."

A man's voice came over the speaker, "May I help you?"

Pete said, "Uh, yeah, um, yes, I'm looking for Patricia O'Brien. Is this her residence?"

"Who are you?" came the voice from the box.

"My name is Peter Wasniak. I'm a free-lance writer doing a piece on the importance of the small farmer to America. Miss Eleanor at the grocery store gave me Ms. O'Brien's name as someone I should speak to."

A long pause, followed by, "One moment, please."

Pete waited by the box for a few minutes when the gate suddenly swung open. He hurried back to the car and they drove through the opening. Now in plain sight, they could see a large, rambling stately manor, two-story in the middle, single level to either side. Easily 4000 square feet of living space, maybe more, constructed of white brick with a green roof. Several smaller and larger barns, all painted white with matching green roofs surrounded the large house. Conspicuously, a two-story silver metal building with an enormous HVAC system visible on the roof was partially hidden behind the residence and between the barns. The driveway was almost a half-mile long flanked by fields of corn and soybeans along its entire length, then circling around a flagpole in front of what was looking more like a mansion the closer they got.

"Now, that's intimidating," deadpanned Abe.

A man came out the front door and approached the car. He was neither the owner nor a butler, but seemingly something in between. "May I see your identifications?"

"Sure," said Pete, fumbling for his old Press I.D. which thankfully did not have an expiration date. "This is Abraham Taylor. He's from Syracuse. He's here to take pictures, provided that is permitted."

The man eye-balled Abe holding up the camera, and said, "We'll have to see about that." He inspected Pete's I.D. and asked, "Tell me again about this story you wish to do."

Pete did his best to make the fake story sound real, embellishing as he went, saying he expected it to be printed in "Parade Magazine" with likely pick-ups in several other well-known weeklies. As his I.D. was returned through the open window of the car, Pete got out as if invited to stretch his legs. Abe followed suit. Pete concluded, "As you can understand, it's important to talk to the real heroes and heroines of the farming community."

The man stepped back, "Perhaps I can answer all your questions."

Abe started taking pictures of corn, the house, the flagpole.

"Sure, sure," said Pete. "I have no doubt you can answer a lot. Are you Mr. O'Brien?"

He looked at Abe with some concern, "No, I'm Ms. O'Brien's business manager. Can he stop taking pictures?"

"Gotcha. Knock it off, Abe. Gotta get permission to publish photos anyhow. Well, is Ms. O'Brien available for an interview? I promise we won't take much of her time."

Suddenly, a white-haired woman with a cane came to the front door. "Who are these people, Walter?" she said.

Walter said to Pete, "One moment please, and no photography," glancing hard at Abe. He went to the door and spent a few minutes in animated conversation with the woman, returning to say, "Ms. O'Brien will grant you an interview. No longer than twenty minutes, please."

An hour-and-a-half later and after two servings of iced tea and cookies, Pete and Abe departed leaving a flattered and amused Patricia O'Brien and her still skeptical business manager, Walter. Meanwhile, Pete's notebook was full of quotes and notes and, despite his occasional fumbling, Abe's camera held several dozen photos of Ms. O'Brien, Walter and several of the outbuildings and barns.

"Did you get what you were after, Pete?" asked Abe as they passed out through the gate.

A visibly excited Pete said, "Oh, buddy, did I ever. Did I ever!"

• • •

Angelo's Plot

Angelo's call to Pauly Basili was, as usual, succinct. "He's in Vegas ... Yeah, Charlie Franklin's there, too, but they're not together ... Nah, he only knows the topline facts, shouldn't be an issue ... No, nothing direct from the red cap ... Yeah, so far only the threatening note ... I'll let you know if I hear anything ... Rocco's being entertained ... Talk tomorrow unless something comes up ... No, haven't finalized plans here yet ... I'd like this to get a little farther along before ... Uh huh ... I see ... Okay, I'll speed things up ... Yes, that would make it easier on this end, too ... Okay, send my best to your father ... *Ciao*."

• • •

Rita was both nervous and bored, a calamitous mixture for her. Her hot, Latin blood wanted revenge on the Cardinal, even though she knew she had to stay out of sight. She wanted to warn her family, but she only knew part of what the Cardinal had on them, and she didn't want to panic them without knowing all of it. At one point, she put on her shoes and packed her gun, intent on having a face-to-face with the Cardinal. But she followed the lesson taught by Charlie and reinforced by Pete: 'When you decide on a plan of action, stop and consider what happens if you succeed. What will the ramifications be?'

If she had confronted the Cardinal, whether she killed him or not, the police would likely be called. She would have to explain that she was being threatened with exposure. The police would want to know the manner of the threat. If she told them the truth, that would be just as bad as if the Cardinal made the dossier public. If she told them a lie, it would all come out anyway as reporters would dig deeply into her past. The 'ramifications' were too horrific to ignore.

So, she put her gun away and sat down on an ancient couch in Pete's apartment, all alone and stewing, biting her nails, glowering at midday TV silliness. She was both alarmed and thrilled when her cell phone rang.

"Any word from Charlie?" asked Pete.

"Oh, God, am I ever glad you called. I'm going stir-crazy. No, haven't heard a word from Charlie. Where are you?"

"On my way back. Should be there about 6:30 or 7:00 tonight. What're you cooking?"

"I'm not cooking anything! You need to get back here and feed me. All there is in the 'fridge is beer and stale cheese."

"There's bread in the pantry, and some peanut butter, I think. Should still be edible. That and a beer is a pretty good lunch."

"Oh, my, that sounds so appetizing. You seem pretty chipper. Did you have success?"

Pete shouted into the phone. "Sweet Jesus, yes! I even got some pictures to go with it. Why don't you order some food to be delivered around 6:30. I'll tell you all about it when I get in."

"Okay. 'Tai Dragon', sound good?"

"Sure. Whatever you want."

• • •

Charlie and TK in Vegas

Charlie returned to the registration area with two coffees and sat down next to TK. "Any luck so far?"

"My only luck is that you remembered one cream. Ah, that tastes good. Next plane is due to land in a few minutes. If I was to place a bet – get it? Place a bet in Vegas? – Anyhow, I'm betting they'll be on this next plane. Took off from Cleveland around 9:00 a.m. That's not too early for those girls to be up and at the airport, and it won't get them here too late to have a lot of fun. That's the plane I'd be on, so I'm betting that's the one they're on."

"If you're right, they'll be to the hotel in about 30 or 45 minutes."

"Uh huh. Hold my coffee while I go to the restroom. I can only hold it so long."

Charlie took in the scene of the Bellagio Registration area, something he had never done before. He wondered why he had not paid attention to it in the past. Of course, when checking in a person usually concentrates on showing identification, getting the room key, asking and answering the receptionist questions, gathering bags and locating the proper elevator. On top of that, the ringing slot machine chimes and muffled murmur of the nearby casino almost works against admiring the beauty and elegant extravagance of the hotel lobby. And so, too often, guests breeze right by the color and brightness and opulence on display. That was what Charlie had done when he arrived earlier, but now he had a few minutes to soak it all in.

"You look like a Nebraska farm boy who's never seen anything but corn stalks before," said TK upon her return.

Charlie smiled, "Sometimes I feel that way. I don't often have the luxury to just sit and watch people go by, and imagine what went into constructing a place like this."

She sat and took her coffee. "Now, you be a good boy and get lost. Go play some slots or something for a while. Can't have you be seen by our ladies, either. Check back in an hour or so. If I'm not here, that means I made our mark and I'm up in the room."

Charlie did as he was told. TK was good at her job. She knew how to get things done and understood her role in this mission. He was enjoying working with her rather than being the foil on the other end of whoever had sent her in their past meetings. Nonetheless, he was still wary of her, since her loyalty had not been completely earned yet, and he was not sure that she was working only for him. Unfortunately, that was a chance he had to take under the circumstances. Unless she was an informant for someone else, the only people that knew she was working for him were Pete and Rita. He had not mentioned TK to Angelo or Rocco. So, if something went sideways, it would only expose the treachery of TK.

An hour later and $150 poorer, Charlie wandered back to the couches in the registration area. There was no sign of TK. He headed up to the suite. He felt foolish knocking on the door of his own suite, but to do otherwise seemed inappropriate. He walked into the common living area, a bedroom entrance on either side, and said, "Hello? TK? You here?"

She walked out of the bedroom on the right, toweling off her short blonde hair after a shower, naked and tanned body glistening as if covered with a fine dew. "There you are! I thought you maybe had a hot streak at the tables. Pour me a vodka out of the minibar, would ya'?" She dropped the towel and continued slowly walking toward the center of the living room.

Momentarily stunned, Charlie lurched for the minibar to do as instructed. "She's doing it again," he thought. "I'm supposed to be in charge here." He cracked open a vodka and poured it over ice. Then he grabbed a bourbon for himself and did the same. Turning around she was within inches of him, throwing her arms around his neck.

"Thanks. I really need that after a very full morning." She pressed herself into him and gave him a deep tonguing kiss. "I'm so glad we're working together. I was hoping we would get a chance to be partners." She took the vodka and sat down over the edge of the couch, legs spread over the arm rest.

Charlie remained standing and sipped his bourbon. "Did the ladies show up," he managed to croak.

She smiled, "I told you they'd be on that flight! I win the bet! That photo of her driver's license that you sent me helped. She looks a lot better than that image, thank heaven for her."

"What's our next move?" Charlie found it unnerving to stand over such a naked beauty, trying to establish a plan when all he wanted to do was take her to the bedroom.

TK casually sipped her vodka then rubbed the cold glass on her nipples. "They're planning on sightseeing this afternoon, then hitting the casino after dinner. I think the best idea is for me to start making small talk with 'Vicky' – that's what her girlfriends call her – at either a slot or table where she sits down this evening. That way I can charm her into opening up, if not by tonight then certainly by tomorrow."

Charlie couldn't take his eyes off the vodka glass. "Sounds like a decent plan," he said, his voice uncontrollably husky and raspy. He took a deep swallow of the bourbon.

"So, I win the bet. I knew which flight they'd be on. Time for you to pay up."

"I don't recall making a wager. What is it you think I owe you?"

She stood up and grabbed his hand. "Come with me while I think of something," and led him into the bedroom.

• • •

In the Chancery

The Cardinal sat in his residence considering his options. Why had he been sent two packages of embarrassing material? That was a mystery to him. And why, quite suddenly, had Merke Edelstein apparently capitulated, promising to send the real material in a third package? That was equally puzzling. He had placed a few calls to Marie Carlisle, but none were ever returned. He would have told her about the compromising photos if she had called back, both to warn her and to gauge her response. But the lack of a return call told him all he needed to know. Reluctantly, he decided his relationship with Marie was over and she could no longer be trusted. Nonetheless, he could not bring himself to delete her number from the burner phone, solely due to lust.

The message from Merke Edelstein said to await further instructions, but that Charlie Franklin would again deliver what she promised would be the real deal. At this point, he distrusted both Merke and Charlie Franklin but had no other options than to do what the message said. But when – if – the deal was finally complete he would deal with Charlie Franklin severely. At the very least, he had to ruin Charlie's girlfriend's life. Such treachery as he imagined Charlie had done demanded firm retribution. Not as a future warning, but simply for self-satisfaction and vindictiveness. He knew he would have incredible power soon and he would use that power to settle scores with anyone who crossed him. In the meantime, George's Boston relatives were wandering about. Bringing them here was not the best move, he now realized. But at least they could track Franklin without implicating anyone except perhaps George. When the time comes that they are unnecessary, Maroney would assist in their departure to Canada. A well-meaning call to the Mounties warning that a certain group of three men were armed and dangerous would no doubt settle things nicely.

Wesley and George would, of course, need to be eliminated as well. Once he had the artifact in hand, they would become a needless liability. They knew too much, even though they only knew the basic outline of his plan. He still might need some physical assistance once they were gone, but he would get that from elsewhere. They had bungled so many things already he was certain they would continue to make errors, likely at a time when only the most masterful subtlety would do. No, they were proving to be a liability – intolerable. They had to go, and he had a very clear idea how he could make that happen without too much difficulty and with no evidence.

The Cardinal smiled to himself. The thought of finally tying up loose ends made him breathe easier. But then, he thought about Brother Gerald. The monk had proven to be reliable at the tasks given to him, but he was almost too close to the center of things. Cardinal Maroney hated second guessing himself, but he now thought bringing Brother Gerald into the chancery may have been a bad idea. Then again, the Brother's vow of silence would prevent him from saying anything, and once all the pieces fell into place, he could be sent back to the monastery where he could pray away any concerns he had for the rest of his life.

Dialing up the Monsignor on the intercom, the Cardinal said, "Monsignor Leonard, could you join me in the outer office, please?"

After a few second interval, the Monsignor responded, "Your Eminence, I will be in shortly."

The Cardinal and Monsignor arrived in the outer office at almost the same time, Maroney taking his seat behind the desk and in front of the mirrored cross while Wesley stood at attention.

"Sit down, Wesley. How are things going?"

Wesley sat gingerly on one of the chairs facing the desk. "Why, I think everything is going well. George delivered the message to Mr. Franklin, per your instructions. His cousin and the others are tracking Franklin's movements, and that of his secretary. We are all awaiting your further direction." Wesley scanned the room, wondering if the recording devices had been turned on. It had been two days since the Cardinal had spoken to him in confidence.

"And how do you think Brother Gerald is doing? Is he adjusting to his role here?"

Wesley started to relax at the casualness of the conversation. "Brother Gerald is minding the books well. He's also looking at the summaries on each of the parishes in the diocese. I believe he's planning to surprise you with an analysis of how to best manage each of their needs."

The Cardinal smiled. "How very thoughtful of him."

The Monsignor gave a wry grin. "Although he's very tight-lipped about it."

"Wesley, that may be one of the best jokes I've heard in the last month," said the Cardinal before chuckling out loud. "We haven't had a chance to spend much time together lately. Let me tell you what I see as our next steps." He sat back in his leather chair and Wesley finally relaxed his posture. "Once Mr. Franklin has delivered what we believe will be the correct package, we will need to retrieve a small treasure hidden by my father at the estate. That treasure will restore our financial well-being. There is some weight, some heft to the treasure, which means I'll need both you and George to accompany me to retrieve it. I'm guessing we'll be able to accomplish the retrieval in one afternoon or evening – hopefully we can go there in a few days, depending upon Mr. Franklin's timeliness of delivery. That's why I was asking about Brother Gerald. We'll be leaving him alone for the day, and I don't want him to feel overwhelmed, or to dig into things he should not see. Likewise, I want George to have a bit of advanced warning so he can be prepared to go as soon as the time is right."

"Most thoughtful of you, Your Eminence," said the Monsignor, "most kind. I'll alert George – he'll be pleased as he sometimes thinks you don't value his contributions – I'll tell him to be ready at the drop of a hat. And I'll monitor what Brother Gerald is doing, explaining to him that the reason you want him here is to handle things should we be absent. I'm sure he'll be honored with your trust."

"Wonderful. That's wonderful. As soon as I'm sure of the delivery, we must be ready to put our plans into action."

The Monsignor asked, "Plans? Do you have another plan in mind?"

The Cardinal waved the thought away. "Simply a figure of speech, Wesley. Tell George to make sure that his cousin and friends stay put in the shelter when they're not tracking our adversaries. I want to be sure of the whereabouts of the Boston Boys. That will be all for now. See to George and Brother Gerald."

As the Monsignor departed, the Cardinal returned to his private quarters and made a long-distance call on his burner phone to a person in Rome he met while vacationing during the weeks leading up to his elevation to Cardinal.

"Allo?" said the voice in Rome.

The Cardinal responded, "It's me, Maroney."

"Are you aware it is almost midnight here?"

"Sorry. The package is almost here."

"You have it in your possession?"

"Not yet."

"Then you do not have it at all. You should not call me until you do have it."

The Cardinal whispered, "I simply want your assurance that the plan is still in place."

"There is no plan until you have the package. I understand there have been problems, Si?"

The Cardinal tried to cover his frustration. "I'll have it shortly. But you should have begun introducing my name. Will there be openings?"

"Perhaps. Depending upon timing. Bartolo of Argentina is ill. He may need to step down. Richtermann of Denmark approaches 80. Perhaps one other."

"So, floating my name has been a good start. How is the health of His Holiness?"

"He suffers. His time is not long."

"All the more reason to put my name in for the Conclave."

"Hush! Speak not so directly. You know how rare it is for a newly appointed Cardinal to jump up in stature so soon. If not handled delicately, this could – how you say – fire back."

"Backfire. Yes, I get it. But as you have noted, the timing is almost perfect. We will both profit from our success, so I suggest you do all that you can."

"And I suggest that you might consider sweetening the pan."

"Sweetening the pot? You've already received a great deal, plus a promise of so much more in the future."

"The future is unknown. What I do know is I am sticking out my head and neck for you. I need more reassurance that I will not be forgotten, and I prefer my reassurance to be in advance."

The Cardinal blew out his breath. "This is ridiculous. Why should I give in to such blatant extortion?"

"Why, you ask. Why then should I make such risks here for you? Perhaps you would prefer that I not put your name up for consideration."

"Never mind. Let me think. Alright, I will send you a painting. A Vermeer. A friendly gift to a friend. It is quite valuable. I'm sure you will be pleased. Will that suffice?"

"Ah, you are so kind, *mio caro amico*. I will look forward to receiving it. *Buona note*."

The Cardinal stared hard at the phone as the call was disconnected.

• • •

Pete's Apartment

Just before 5:00 p.m., a hard knock on the door startled Rita. "Wow, Pete! You made good time. I haven't even ordered dinner yet," she said as she opened the door.

Three men dressed in black rushed in, one covering her mouth and nose with an ether-filled cloth, another pinned her arms behind her back. She recognized the third as a short, thin man who said with an Italian accent, "Treat the signora carefully. We must have no mistakes, no blood."

Rita said into the ether cloth, "The Italian Guy," just as she passed out.

Pete arrived at the apartment a few minutes after 6:00 p.m. expecting a starving Rita and, if he was lucky, some half-eaten Asian delicacies from the Tai Dragon Restaurant. What he found was nothing. No Rita, no food, not even any evidence that Rita had ever been there.

The apartment was spotless. No dishes in the sink, only a half-full dishwasher. No food on the counter, itself wiped clean. The bedroom was equally spotless – bed made, his rumpled clothes not on the floor but in the hamper, closet door shut. It was never shut. He took a deep breath and opened the door, expecting the worst. Instead, he found all the clothes neatly hung and properly separated – pants in one section, shirts in another, jackets toward the back.

"What the hell," he said, "has a team of cleaners been in here?" He searched the rest of the small apartment. It didn't take long. No sign that Rita had ever been in the place, let alone just a few hours ago. He sat down at the table, itself wiped completely clean of food particles, dust and finger prints. He went back through his recent call with Rita. She had been in the apartment since Charlie told her to find a place to stay with a friend. She was there when Pete left for Syracuse, her bags stuffed in a corner, open so she could grab whatever garments she wanted. He had seen her hand gun in one of the sleeves of the bag, so he knew she was armed. He looked to the same corner – no baggage nor any sign that a bag had ever been there.

He went to the bathroom. Surely, she would have left some evidence of her occupancy there. There was nothing in there which looked to be a feminine left over. The garbage can was empty. He held his breath as he pulled aside the shower curtain. The shower was dry and wiped clean, with not even a random hair in the tub or on the floor.

It was too clean, too neat. Someone else had been in the apartment and had sanitized the place, making it impossible for anyone to prove that Rita had ever been there. Pete considered his next steps. He was not sure he had any. He placed a call to Charlie.

"Pete? I saw it was your number. What's up?"

"Sorry to bother you in your search out there, but we have a situation here."

"Not a problem. We're waiting for this evening to approach Vicky. TK has a plan to draw her out. What's your situation?"

"Rita's missing."

"What do you mean 'missing'?"

"She was staying at my place. I talked to her just a few hours ago on my drive back from Syracuse. Now she's not here."

"She was at your place? I thought she was spending a few days with a friend ... Oh."

Pete said, "Yeah, so I need to have a talk with you about that. But in the meantime, she's not here. No sign that she's ever been here. The place has been wiped clean, like a bunch of Merry Maids took it on as a life's project. Even fingerprints have been erased."

"You sure she didn't just go over to one of her girlfriend's place?"

"I'll be checking on that next, but frankly, given what I see here, that's not the case. I think someone grabbed her."

"Goddamn! The Cardinal?"

"I haven't had a lot of time to think it through, but somehow I don't think he's up to such a feat. Rita's tough. And she's got her gun. If it was the Cardinal, there'd be blood on the floor and cops circling the building because of the gun shots. Plus, what does he have to gain from abducting her? He's got the dossier to hold over your head."

"Dossier or not, he might want the added protection of holding Rita personally to guarantee I do what he wants."

Pete asked, "Should we call the cops?"

Charlie thought for a moment, "With no signs of a struggle, I don't think they'll touch this. Maybe after 72 hours we can say she's a 'missing person', but how could we convince them otherwise without blowing everything up? That will put her at a greater risk."

Pete said, "I'm usually hard-edged about this kind of thing, but I gotta admit, this has got me pretty shaken. How do we figure out where the Cardinal has her – or if he has her?"

Charlie said, "Stay calm. Call her friends just to make sure we're not jumping at scarecrows. I'll give Angelo a call to tell him what's up. Maybe he can help."

In the background, Pete heard a sultry voice, "Dossiers and scarecrows? Sounds kinky."

Pete smiled wanly, "You with your lady friend?"

"Uh, yeah," admitted Charlie sheepishly. "We're just about to head out for an early dinner."

"Okay. Enjoy. But call Angelo first. Let me know what he says."

"Pete, when I call Angelo, I'm going to have to tell him about your involvement in this thing. So far, he doesn't know that you've played a part in any of this. You OK with that?"

Pete thought for a minute, then said, "I'm a big boy. I can handle it. Do what you have to do."

• • •

Angelo DiFranco looked at his ringing phone with resignation. He answered the call with some disgust. "What, you got what you need already?"

Charlie replied, "Hi, Angelo. No, that's not why I'm calling. There's something that came up back where you are."

"Something from the red cap?"

"No, well, maybe. My assistant Rita has disappeared. I'm thinking maybe the Cardinal had something to do with it."

"Rita? Disappeared, as in how?"

"Once we received the threat about the dossier, I suggested she go stay with a friend for her safekeeping. But now, she's not there."

"So, maybe she went for a walk."

"I wish that were the case. But it appears the apartment she was at has been swept clean, fingerprints and all. The person she was staying with says it's cleaner than he's ever seen it since he moved in."

Angelo was surprised. "She's shacking up with some guy? I thought she was your squeeze."

"Used to be, I guess. Long story. Anyway, can you put out feelers to see where the Cardinal took her?"

"Who's this guy she was with?"

Charlie was worried Angelo would ask that. "Uh, he's a guy I've been working with, Pete Wasniak."

"Wasniak! The newspaper guy? Whadya mean you're working with him, of all people. He can be a real trouble-maker, a real thorn in the ass."

"I try to keep everything to myself, but even the best of us need help sometimes. I've got Rita and also occasionally Pete. But he's not a newspaper man anymore."

"Once a nosy newsman, always a nosy newsman. So, you got a team, huh? I kinda thought you ran a one-man show. What other secrets have you kept from us?"

"Never meant for it to be a secret, Angelo. I'd have told you if you asked. I just liked to portray the image of a lone ranger."

"Bad analogy. The Lone Ranger was a lawman. And I already knew Wasniak and you were close. I called him to get his take on your tail. Let's get back to Rita. When did all this happen?"

"Must have been in the last few hours. Pete talked with her while he was driving back from Syracuse. Then when he got home, she was gone. And – like I said – the apartment was sanitized. Pete's a bit shook about it."

"Any weapons involved? Any blood anywhere?"

"Rita's got a handgun. No blood, no sign of a struggle."

"Okay. I'll look into it. Tell Wasniak I might want him to come in here for a sit-down. You know, just to make sure we're all playing on the same team."

Charlie heard the click as Angelo hung up. He blew out a long breath and called Pete to give him the warning that Angelo would be calling him.

• • •

Pete made the last of his check-up calls to Rita's friends, then pulled out his notebook. He scanned the notes from his meeting with Patricia O'Neal Maroney, but couldn't concentrate on any of the words he had written down. He was too worried about Rita. Together, Pete and Rita had come to the opinion that Pete's place would be the safest hiding spot for her. They didn't think anyone knew about Pete's involvement in the case, and very few people had any idea where Pete lived. It seemed to be a natural safe location. Plus, there was their growing affection for one another.

He came to the conclusion that somewhere along the way he had been careless. Someone knew he was working with Charlie, someone knew Rita was staying with him. He cracked open a beer and tried to think calmly and logically, opening his notepad to a blank page where he listed all the possibilities.

He had called a few of Rita's closest girlfriends while Charlie was calling Angelo. None of them had heard from Rita or knew where she might be.

If someone suspected his involvement with the case, it was still true that very few people actually knew where he lived.

Even Charlie had not known Rita was staying with him.

The Cardinal may have the dossier, but he didn't seem to have either the inclination or the muscle to pull off an abduction. Even if he had, there was nothing to be gained from taking Rita hostage. It might actually have fouled up his deal with Charlie.

From what Charlie said, Angelo claimed to know nothing about Rita's disappearance.

That meant someone else – someone unknown – was likely involved in taking Rita. There were a couple possibilities now that some guys from Boston were floating around. But from the few glimpses Pete had of them, they looked rather careless, not the type to sanitize his apartment after an abduction.

Pete tapped the notebook, then stiffened, and wrote in large, bold letters:

THE ITALIAN GUY!!!

He closed his notepad, drained his beer and headed out the door. It was time he paid a visit to Angelo DiFranco on his own.

• • •

Dinner in Vegas
Charlie and TK surveyed the menu, quickly arriving at a selection for dinner. "I am famished," said TK. "I haven't eaten anything since I left New York very early this morning. Thank goodness they're serving so early."

Charlie looked around, "Not many people in here. We must be among the first, even though it's not quite dinner time. I appreciate the fact that you didn't wear the nun's habit tonight, although I've not seen you so casually dressed before."

TK looked down at her stylish but modest outfit. "I'm dressed for Vicky, not for you. Kinda Midwestern, don't you think? Once we get the information you want, I'll change into something sexier just for you." Charlie shook his head. She changed the subject, "Back in the room, what was that phone call all about? Sounded like something important."

He looked at TK, still unsure he could trust her completely, and even if he could rely on her, better to keep her out of some of the close-to-home details. "Nothing important for our work here. Just some nagging issues back in Cleveland."

"I'm sure it will all work out fine. Now, tell me again – what's the deal with this 'Vicky' person?"

Charlie ran through a basic lie to lead TK toward the information he wanted. "Her husband's family is worried that Vicky is spending too much of her husband's money while he is in a convalescent home. She hasn't been to see him lately, but she is listed on the family estate paperwork, whether she knows it or not. The family is afraid she might sell the property out from under them if she were to discover her authority. We need to find out what her attitude is, whether she knows she has such strong fiscal access, and whether she ever plans on rekindling the relationship with her husband. The family is sensitive to what she might do, because her husband's brother is a highly regarded clergyman and the family name is notable. We need you to find out if she's just out to have some fun, or if there's a wicked plan brewing. I concluded she'd be reticent to talk to a man. Instead, I needed a woman who had the ability to subtly draw her out. That's you."

"That's such a cute story, Charlie, I almost believe it."

Charlie smiled and said, "That's the whole truth as far as you need to know."

The waiter interrupted to take their orders. When he left, TK rubbed her leg against Charlie's. "I take you to bed twice and you still can't trust me? What's a girl got to do to get on your good side?"

"As much as I enjoy your unrestrained sexuality, it doesn't necessarily foster absolute confidence in your undivided faithfulness. Let's remember, I'm paying for your ability to glean the truth from Vicky. Technically, I'm your boss on this job. As such, I probably already violated the non-fraternization rule."

"What are you, a lawyer or something?"

Charlie nodded. "Yes, I am a lawyer."

TK frowned. "I was so much more attracted to you before I knew that."

"I should have told you that back at the bar in New York. Might have kept you more chaste."

She shook her head. "Oh, I doubt that, Charlie. I'm just not that kind of girl."

"Let's focus on this evening. As you described it, you'll pick Vicky out and sit down next to her – either at a slot or a table – and casually start a conversation. Then what?"

TK leaned in and whispered, "I'll start with girl talk. Become gambling friends. Gambling friends are always willing to get better acquainted, if only to tell lies about their big wins or legendary losses. Eventually, we can move on to personal stuff. That sometimes takes time, not something that comes out right away, but certainly we can bump into one another again either later tonight or tomorrow where I can cry the blues over my bad boyfriend – that's you – and how I'm getting even with you by spending all your dough."

Charlie looked concerned. "And suddenly my radar is beeping red. Exactly how will you prove that to her?"

"Oh, look! The fountains just went off! How pretty! Thanks for bringing me here for dinner. This is terrific! I wish it were later in the evening, so much more romantic at dark." She batted her eyes at Charlie.

"TK, you do not have an unrestricted expense account. Don't get crazy."

As the food was served, TK said, "I do hope you brought some gambling money. I'd hate to have to dig into my own purse."

The waiter began delivering their courses, and conversation lagged between bites and views of the fountains.

When dinner ended, Charlie said, "Well, let's go to the cashier cage so I can get some gambling money for you." He added sarcastically, "I'd hate to have you digging into your own purse."

TK pulled him in the other direction. "First, let's go to the Blackjack Tables. I need to refresh myself on the rules."

"What are you intending, to get some chips by batting your eyes?"

She gave him a scowl. "Now, you stop that and just be a good boy!" Charlie had already become the bad boyfriend. They got to the tables where TK went directly to the pit boss. "Hi, Johnny! Good to see you."

The pit boss gave a surprised smile. "Miss Constantine! I was told to expect you. I have your rack right here. Please sign the receipt." He handed her a chip rack with five yellow chips and twenty-five black chips, a total value of $7500. "Please let us know if you wish us to access more off your account."

"Thanks, Johnny. I think this will do for now. I'm just here for a short stay."

"Very good, Miss Constantine. A pleasure to see you again. Good luck to you."

She turned to face an astonished Charlie and said, "I'm ready now. What would you like to play first?"

• • •

Pete and Angelo Meet

Pete slowly walked down the stairs into the Thespian Grill dining room. It had been a few years since he entered the place, back when he was still a reporter. He wasn't all that welcome back then, and he wasn't sure what his reception would be this evening. He paused to look for anyone ready to throw him out. A few tough-looking men were stationed near the rear doors, but no one seemed to pay him any particular attention. He recognized Rico 'the Carp' Carponi sitting at the back of the bar and made his way into a seat next to him.

"You don't wanna sit here," said the Carp.

Pete settled into the bar chair. "Why not?"

"That seat's reserved for someone else."

"Oh yeah? Who?"

"Someone other than you," snarled the Carp as he turned away from Pete.

"What'd I ever do to you?"

"You wrote a story about fixed races at Thistledown a few years back. Ruined my business for months."

Pete nodded. "You recognize me, huh? I'm not here to cause trouble. I need to see Angelo DiFranco. Know where he might be?"

"He's not sittin' next to me, now, is he?"

"Look, Rico, I'll be glad to leave you alone if you just point me in the right direction. Charlie Franklin always says you're a straight shooter. So, shoot me straight."

The Carp looked over his shoulder in Pete's direction, "You know Charlie?"

"He and I are associates. We sometimes work together. Like now."

The Carp slowly rotated his stool toward Pete. "I like Charlie. He and I get along okay. He did me a small once, no charge. Okay, assuming you're not feeding crap to the Carp, I'll shoot you straight. You ever met Angelo?"

"Nah, I don't think so."

"Probably better that way. Anyhow, he's holed up in the boss's office, back over my left shoulder. There's a guy sitting in a chair next to the office door. Tell him your business. If Angelo wants to see you, he'll let you in. If not, the guy in the chair will show you out. Hope you brought your own bandages."

Pete laid a $20 bill on the bar. "Have a drink on me," and walked slowly toward the office door. The Carp watched him go, then called to the barmaid. "Hey, Sally! How about a Manhattan-on-the-rocks!"

The guard at the office door was at full alert as Pete approached and held out his hand as he stood up. "Where you think you're goin', Mack?"

"I need to see Angelo."

"I don't know no 'Angelo'. Go away. This here's a private area."

"Tell him Pete Wasniak is here to see him."

After looking Pete over for a few seconds, the guard motioned to a second guard in the darkened corner who came up silently behind Pete and quickly frisked him. After a nod from the second guard, the first picked up an intercom phone. "Visitor. Says he's Pete Wasniak ... OK." The green light clicked on, and the guard opened the suddenly unlocked door. "In here."

Angelo sat comfortably behind the big desk, Rocco's desk. "I was going to give you a call, Mr. Wasniak. Sit down. We need to talk."

Pete remained standing, "Where's Rita?"

"Rita, who?"

"You know who I'm talking about. You talked to Charlie Franklin. You know that his associate, Rita Herns, is missing. Now, where is she?"

"Peter, Peter, Peter. Always the tough guy reporter. You're a bit out of your element here, you know? You don't stand there and make demands of me. That's not how we're going to play this. I'm telling you nicely, sit down. We'll both talk, polite like. Otherwise, I'll have to assume you mean to do some harm here. That won't go well for you. Now, sit! Down!" Pete realized he had overplayed his hand. He sat down.

"That's better," smiled Angelo. "Let's start over. You want to know where Rita Herns is. I want to know that we're both on the same team, you and I. Here's how this is going to work: you tell me everything you know about what you and Charlie – and this Rita girl – are working on, all the details. Then I will tell you what I know. That is, provided you don't leave anything out. If you do leave something out, I won't share what I know. And I know a lot, so don't try to skip over anything because, geez, I may already know the truth. And skipping key pieces of information – that won't look so good, now will it? And when we're through sharing what we know, we'll be on the same team, right? So, if we're on the same team, I can help you and you can do something to help me, don't you think? That would be a good thing. Two guys helping each other. What do you say?"

Pete sat back and looked at his hands, considering how best to handle the situation. He needed help in locating Rita and keeping her away from harm. He felt responsible for whatever fix she was in. He had no other options, nowhere else to turn for help in finding her. He was stuck and he realized he'd be working with a gangster. It gnawed on his sense of righteousness.

Angelo broke the silence saying, "I'm thirsty. You thirsty?" He picked up the intercom and said, "Bring me a bucket of ice, a bottle of my Anisette, and two glasses." He looked over at Pete and said, "Shall we begin?"

• • •

At the Tables

Charlie played a few hands of blackjack with TK. She was much better at it than he was. As the late afternoon drifted toward evening, TK said, "I think it's about time you make yourself scarce. The ladies from Ohio will be showing up soon. I'll begin to work my magic with them. Come look for me around 10:00 or so. If things are going well, I may need to show them my 'bad boyfriend' whose money I'm spending. But don't approach me unless I call you over."

Charlie said, "I need to go up to the room and make a call to my associate in Cleveland. Then I may wander across the street for a drink. I'll look for you around 10:00." TK leaned in and gave him a kiss. The scent of honeysuckle was strong.

Back in the room, he tried calling Pete. No answer. On a whim, he tried Rita's phone. It was not in service. His worries increased. Both his friends were unreachable, and he was three time zones away. He thought about calling Angelo, but realized that to do so would indicate panic, and he needed Angelo to trust his ability to stay calm under pressure. Besides, if Angelo had anything, he would call Charlie. He called Pete one more time and left a cryptic message: "Wondering if you got anything. Call any time if you do." He waited a half-hour, then another. No return call from Pete. Tiring of pacing the floor in his room, he headed to a casino across the street to have a drink, allowing

TK to have the entire Bellagio Casino floor to contact Victoria 'Vicky Demps' Dempsey Maroney.

Time passed slowly, too slowly. Charlie kept looking at his watch every few minutes, even peering at the second hand to make sure the watch was actually working. Worry etched his face. First Rita disappears, and now Pete's not answering his phone. Maybe this whole idea of chasing after Victoria Maroney was a huge waste of time. Maybe they'd get nothing out of her that could help solve the riddles. He mentally kicked himself for running off to Las Vegas when his partners most needed him to be with them. He stared at the ice in his cocktail glass as if the dissolving cube was a fortune teller's crystal ball, able to conger up an answer.

Had he come out here, had he worked up the plan in the first place, just so he could be with TK Constantine one more time? She had charmed him like a witch offering candy to children. Her touch, her scent, all worked on him like a spell. Every time he met with her his mind turned to jelly. He shook his head. She was not someone he'd want to spend the rest of his life with, but she was certainly someone he enjoyed being around for short episodes. She was smart, talented at her work, disarming in a most unusual way. That was what made her perfect for this assignment.

Why did they all decide this was a good idea, chasing Vicky out to Las Vegas? The dossier – that was what kept them going after more clues. They had all agreed that they needed something on the Cardinal, something that showed his corruption or his evilness, or ... something, if only to provide protection for Rita against the dossier. That is why they are pursuing all the possible leads. That is why Pete went to Syracuse, that is why Rita went into hiding, that is why Charlie came to Las Vegas. The fact that Pete was not answering calls, that Rita was missing, pointed out that they were likely closing in on the truth. He would not be able to help Pete or Rita even if he was back in Cleveland. He was better off finding out all he could from Vicky first, then he could rush back to help his friends with something in his hip pocket. He nodded to himself, "Maybe I wasn't just being stupid with this idea after all."

"Did you say something, sir?" asked the bartender. "Another scotch?"

"It wasn't scotch, it was bourbon, and yes, pour me another." Checking his phone to see that no calls had come in, and gazing again at the slow-moving watch, he took his drink and idly wandered around, playing several inexpensive slot machines until he could stand it no longer.

At a quarter to ten, he went back to the Bellagio casino floor, wandering slowly, trying not to be seen too soon. He circled around the outside of the gaming area, checking the aisles as inconspicuously as possible – which, he realized, ended up being quite conspicuous.

Nearing the High Roller area, he heard loud, screeching laughter. Several ladies were talking and laughing at the same time, drowning out the soft tinkling of a piano coming from the Petrossian Bar. The ladies were not at a gambling table, they were surrounding the piano player. Four women, each with a half-empty champagne glass, went from leaning on the piano to collapsing into over-stuffed couch cushions, roaring with laughter. One of the four was TK Constantine. And another was Vicky Dempsey Maroney. On the table in front of them was an empty champagne bottle, upside down in one ice bucket, with a second bottle being passed around to fill up their glasses. Between the ice buckets were two plates of mostly eaten and very expensive Petrossian chocolates, and two small demitasse goblets of even more expensive caviar. The ladies were having a fine time of it, and TK was encouraging them all the way.

Charlie decided to sneak out to the cab stand, then enter as if he'd just returned from somewhere else. As he passed an aisle away from the piano bar, he heard TK's voice, "Hey, Charlie! Come here!" He turned and tried to look like the bad boyfriend he was supposed to be.

"Look! I made some new friends! These are Susie, uh, no, that's not right, uh – oh, hell! These are my friends. I'll get their names right later. Anyhow – you see the champagne and chocolate and the caviaaahrrr," she purposely dragged out the word. "Thanks, sweetie, you bum you! I've put it all on our room. You're paying for all of this, you piece of ... I shouldn't say bad words in public, should I girls?"

They all shook their heads and screeched with laughter. One of them said, "Should we let him join us?"

TK said, "Girl's vote. Yea or nay? I say Nay!" All four chorused, "Nay, no, unh uh." TK wobbled to her feet, "You lose, loser! Go up to the room, or something. Leave us alone," as she waved him away and fell into the couch cushions. More laughter followed after him as Charlie, the bad boyfriend, headed for the elevators.

He was fairly certain that TK had just put on one of the best acting jobs he had ever seen. The sampling was small, but he believed that TK could hold her liquor. Then again, she had been up since the early hours to catch her flight. Maybe she was totally looped. Champagne can do that to a person. The same was true for the other three – up early, drinking away the day, and their body clocks now on 1:00 a.m. Eastern time. He hoped they had not put too much onto his room charge. He estimated that what was already on their table was costing him about $1500.

Charlie had one more idea, an outgrowth of the theory bubbling in his head since his visit to the Summit County Records Department. He gauged the time difference as he placed a call. The person at the other end would not be happy. But Charlie suspected that, by the end of the call, the clarity he received would be worth what he might owe the informant.

Around midnight, TK entered the suite and found Charlie asleep on the couch. She sat down on the floor near his head, and rubbed his cheeks. "Hey there, boss man," she whispered, "I hope I didn't hurt your feelings."

Charlie's eyes opened, but by the stupefied look on his face, it was obvious he had no idea where he was. "What ... where ..."

"You're in Vegas, Charlie, remember? I'm TK Constantine, remember? Oh, jet lag has got you good."

He rubbed his face with both hands. "Wow. I am out of it." Focusing on TK's smiling face, he said, "Did you have any luck tonight?"

"Yeah, I won a couple hundred. Showed Vicky how to play Blackjack."

He sat up. "I don't mean gambling. Did you get any information out of her?"

"Some."

"Well?" Charlie was getting impatient.

"You know what's worse than knowing nothing, Charlie? It's knowing only a little. If I told you what I know now, it will send you in the wrong direction. I'd prefer to give you the whole story with no loose ends. That way you'll get it all at once and not be misguided. I'll get more from her tomorrow, but right now I'm tired and going to bed. Alone. See you in the morning." She got up and went to her bedroom and locked the door.

Charlie sat on the couch for several minutes, seething. He could pound on her door and demand to know what she had learned, but he worried someone might call security. That would not do. What little he knew about TK Constantine was that you had to play the game by her rules. He had no way of forcing her to talk. He finally got up and went to his own bedroom and angrily fell asleep.

• • •

Saturday, July 16:

As the sun rose Saturday morning, several people were in motion at the same time. The Cardinal called to the Monsignor to join him for coffee; Angelo placed a call to Pauly Basili in Brooklyn, New York; and Pete called for room service after waking up in a hotel room in downtown Cleveland. It was still only 5:00 a.m. in Las Vegas, but a restless Charlie Franklin showered away his grogginess, preparing for a long day. As instructed, he placed a follow up call to the same overseas number he had called in the late hours last night. After dressing, he went to the coffee shop, returning to the room with two large coffees. He knocked on her bedroom door and called out, "TK! Time to get up!" Two could play her game just by slightly twisting her rules.

• • •

Leaving the door to his personal residence ajar, the Cardinal awaited the Monsignor's arrival. "Where is that little twit," he mumbled, "he always has some excuse for being late. Probably disengaging from George." His morning began sour, and this delay did nothing to improve his glowering mood. "I should have listened to those who said he was too young to be a monsignor, but I needed someone I could manipulate, and Wesley Leonard fit that bill perfectly. In retrospect, it is possible I could have done better." Finally, he heard doors opening and the shuffling of footsteps as the Monsignor approached the residence.

"My apologies, Your Eminence, but I was signing for this envelope that just arrived. It's addressed to you."

"Who's it from, Wesley?"

The Monsignor examined the large envelope. "There is no name on it, but it appears to be from New York City."

The Cardinal quickly grabbed it from the Monsignor's hands. "Give me that!" He tore it open and found a note typed in single space placed between two pieces of cardboard. It read:

"Your expected artifact will be delivered by midday Monday, July 18. Be available. We have contacted the same Mr. Franklin used for past deliveries. He will deliver the artifact. Do not attempt to contact him yourself, or the delivery will not take place. In exchange for the parcel, you will remit all evidence, whether written or electronic, which may indicate or imply that Mr. Franklin was ever involved in this or previous missions. You will also provide Mr. Franklin with any and all incriminating documents, whether written or electronic, regarding any person or persons with whom Mr. Franklin is associated. Failure to comply with these instructions will lead to your ultimate and untimely demise. – M.E."

"Well, this is a rather intimidating note." He hesitated, then handed it to the Monsignor to review. "You might as well see this, too, since you've been so involved. I believe we're being threatened. What do you make of it?"

After reading the note, the Monsignor said, "Why does she refer to the package as an artifact? Is that what it is? Also, Ms. Edelstein seems to have knowledge of things she should not know. It appears she knows a great deal about Mr. Franklin, about the dossier, possibly even about the recording system in your office. Given the wording, I would speculate that this note was written by a lawyer. How certain are you that this message was sent by Merke Edelstein?"

"Valid point, Wesley. It does have the scent of Mr. Franklin on it, does it not? If I were him, I would send something just like this. However, we do not have the luxury of making that assumption and acting on it. We are firmly wedged between the proverbial rock and hard place. If we assume this letter is the work of Mr. Franklin and we are wrong, the golden opportunity we seek might disappear forever. If we simply comply with the instructions as they have been given to us, we will lose all leverage over Mr. Franklin, and perhaps lose control of the entire venture. Either way, there is a serious risk."

The Monsignor's face took on the look of a Cheshire Cat. "Begging your pardon, Your Eminence, but at one time we reached the conclusion that, at the end of this venture, Mr. Franklin would have to be dealt with in some eternal method. May I be so bold as to say that time is rapidly approaching?"

The Cardinal shared the Monsignor's grin. "My, Wesley, you do have a vicious streak about you, do you not? Are the boys from Boston up to the task? We'll want them to act just after the final delivery. Tell them to make it seem like a random tragedy, perhaps a mugging or robbery gone bad. Also, a while back, you made contact with Mr. Rocco Parmissano on our behalf, did you not? He helped us with that matter regarding the Knights of Columbus, as I recall – that loan we needed. Could you contact him again? This time, I should like to meet with him myself in private to, let's say, hear his confession. Meanwhile, please put the Bostonians in motion as soon as the package is in our hands."

The Monsignor demurred. "I never spoke to Mr. Parmissano directly, it was always through an intermediary. But I could attempt to set up a private meeting between the two of you, a confession as you call it. He is a devout person who should be honored to meet with his Cardinal."

"Excellent. Please do so. I believe the gentleman can rid us of this nemesis, Charles Franklin, even if the Boston boys fail. Since the parcel is due to arrive midday Monday for which I will make myself available, see if you can arrange the confession to occur on Monday morning as well." The Cardinal started to rise, then sat down again. "By the way, we might as well collect all of the materials requested by Ms. Edelstein, or whomever sent the letter. Gather the audio tapes, the dossier, any camera shots that were taken. We'll turn them over upon confirmation of the package – not before."

"Yes, Your Eminence. Umm, about the visit from Mr. Parmissano – if he agrees to rid us of the nemesis, he will likely require a donation to his favorite charity. Our treasury is still a bit thin, given past transactions."

"I'm glad you brought that up, Wesley. You recall I said I'd need you and George to help me recover a small treasure at the estate? Well, let's plan to retrieve it on Monday afternoon, after the package is delivered. By then I'll know Mr. Rocco's donation request and we can use what we find to embellish his favorite charity. Assume we will be away all afternoon and into the evening, giving us a plausible excuse should Mr. Franklin have his accident during that time. And tell George to dress in work clothes – you too – as the location is likely a bit dirty. Since we'll be away from the chancery, bring me the treasury bank books. I'll put them in my safe so Brother Gerald doesn't happen across them by accident."

Wesley nodded and left the office. The Cardinal sat back in his leather chair and took stock of where things stood. The artifact would soon be in his possession. His contact in Rome would use that knowledge to secure his advancement into the Conclave of Cardinals. In the meantime, Charlie Franklin and his friends would cease to be a problem. A properly sized donation would guarantee that Rocco Parmissano would agree to kill him if the boys from Boston were inept. Either would be acceptable.

Wesley and George would likewise cease to be a problem. The Cardinal would take care of them personally. That meant that, aside from whatever Rocco Parmissano might be able to figure out, the only person who knew the full extent of the plan was Alphonse Lucatello, an Italian Cardinal and the Vatican Treasurer, Maroney's contact in

Rome. But Cardinal Lucatello needed Maroney to deflect the money-laundering charges he was facing, and because of that, there was very little chance that he would turn on Maroney. Even so, Lucatello would be surprised to know that he'd be committing suicide shortly after Maroney was empowered. Maroney felt it was all coming into focus very neatly.

• • •

Angelo and Pauly

Angelo DiFranco's call to Pauly Basili was not unexpected. Pauly said, "You got my message explaining what we know, and that everything would be okay, right?"

Angelo replied, "Got it. Had a nice talk with this ex-newspaper guy. He's got the sweets for the missing girl. Figures I'm the only one who can help, so he'll be easy to deal with. We can use him to feed some stories after the change-over."

"*Bene*. That's a nice twist. He won't say nothin' to this Charlie fella?"

"The newspaper guy is holed up in a hotel downtown. I told him no communications with anyone for the next 48 hours. After that ..."

"That's good, it shouldn't be more than two days to finalize everything."

"That's okay, I can hold him off a little longer if need be. What else?"

"Rocco's back Sunday night, right? Leave word for him that Giovanni wants him to go deep sea fishing early next week. The weather will be perfect for some big tuna on Monday, that would be the best."

"That soon?"

"Yeah. My dad talked with old man Triunno. He gets it and he's fine with everything. Come Monday after Rocco leaves for New York, you should give Frank a call to make sure he's fully plugged in, too. Don't need no mess ups now."

• • •

A Suite at the Ritz

Pete Wasniak sipped his coffee and picked at the remaining bacon from his breakfast in the hotel room arranged by Angelo at the Ritz-Carlton in downtown Cleveland. Pete was registered as Rocco Parmissano, on Angelo's instructions, to insure he would not be bothered. Pete was not at all sure registering as Rocco was a good idea, as there were plenty of people who would prefer Rocco was no longer alive. Sitting alone in the hotel room pretending to be a mob boss with no guards gave him a queasy feeling.

Pete was still nervous about recent events despite Angelo's assurances that Rita would be found in good health. He wanted to reply to Charlie's calls, but was told that any communication with him might jeopardize Rita's safe return. Pete felt torn between his loyalty to Charlie and his concern for the girl he had grown to love. Angelo told him Charlie would eventually understand, and that Angelo expected to contact Charlie this morning to calm him down. So, Pete turned on the TV and watched Saturday morning nonsense shows: a DIY home improvement segment, a country cooking show, and finally Sports Center. None of it registered. Anticipating another call from Charlie, he reluctantly turned his phone off to prevent it from ringing. Angelo said Pete would be cooped up in the hotel for no longer than two days. This was going to be a long 48 hours.

• • •

The Suite at the Bellagio

TK Constantine finally responded to the pounding on her bedroom door, wrapping herself in one of the hotel's over-large bathrobes. She glowered at Charlie as she accepted the cup of coffee.

"Listen, sweetie. I don't do well at 5:00 a.m. What the hell are you thinking?"

"It's just after 8:00 on your internal body clock. Time to get the day moving."

She shook her head. "I guarantee the Ohio girls are still sleeping off the champagne – as I should be doing. There's nothing to be gained from being up this early."

"Hmm. That so? Well, then you can tell me what you learned last night from Vicky."

TK slumped down on the couch. The bathrobe separated revealing her soft tanned flesh underneath. She sipped her coffee. "I suppose I was a bit curt with you last night, huh? Okay, you win. But I'm going back to bed after I fill you in. You can either join me or not. Your call."

"You're such a joy to be around at this hour, I'll find it hard to resist your offer."

"Save your sarcasm for later, lover. I officially revoke my offer." She re-wrapped the robe concealing her body. "Here's what I know so far, and some of this is coming from the girlfriends, not directly from Vicky. Seems her husband is not ill, but is off on some sort of financial boondoggle – that's what Vicky called it – that's lasted far too long for her liking. Her girlfriends think she should divorce him, but she said she's getting so much money in monthly living expenses that she can't afford to walk away until he scores it big with whatever he's doing."

Charlie's face twisted as he tried to understand. "Her husband isn't sick? Isn't in some private clinic?"

"Not from the way she puts it. She's not sure where he is, although she's fairly certain he's banging some young girl. She has a sense about these things since it's happened before."

Charlie said, "If she's waiting for a profitable windfall from hubby, she's not aware that she pretty much has financial control over the estate."

"I'd say she has no idea. She seems fairly certain that she needs the monthly stipend to continue in her lifestyle."

Charlie sat back in his chair, sipping his coffee and recalibrating his thoughts.

"Jeez, Charlie, I think I can actually hear those gears meshing in your mind. The noise is deafening. I'm going back to bed."

"Wait. You are meeting up with her again today, aren't you?"

"They're going shopping this afternoon. They want some more chocolates and champagne tonight. I said I'd meet up with them around 8:00 p.m. if not before. I told them I really want to hurt my 'bad boyfriend' financially, so I'm buying. They'll be there."

"I wish you'd have come up with a cheaper way to get back at me."

She stood up and headed for the bedroom. "They said I should have an affair with someone else while I'm out here." She turned toward Charlie, "You're starting to make that seem like a better idea than chocolate and champagne. Don't wake me up again!"

Charlie decided to get an early breakfast. Still before 6:00 a.m., there wasn't much happening on the main floor of the casino as he threaded his way toward the buffet dining room. A few late-night revelers stumbled their way toward the elevators on their way to bed. An old man pushing a walker searched for a gaming table that was open, though none yet were. A floor manager struggled to convince an old woman slot-player, withered and grey-haired and hooked up to an oxygen tank, that lighting her cigarette could have explosive consequences.

The breakfast buffet was not yet displayed, so Charlie wandered out to the pool area for some cool, fresh morning air and early sunlight. Even at that early hour, the July temperature was pushing the upper 80s. He sat in a shadowed lounge chair to collect his thoughts. If Vicky's husband was not in a nursing home, where was he? None of Charlie's team chose to verify that Sean Maroney was actually one of the patients in the facility. Could it be that such an assumption was wrong? They believed they knew something, but perhaps they did not have it as straight as they thought. Vicky said her husband had been gone for some time. TK will need to find out how long he has been gone. And where was the money that Vicky received each month coming from? Did she receive a check, a direct deposit to an account? That would be a tricky ask, but TK seemed to be adept at getting people to open up about things they ordinarily would not talk about.

Some of the information he learned in the last 24 hours was coloring in the outline of the picture Charlie had drawn in his mind for the past several weeks. His overseas contact had redrawn the lines and said that 'all is not as it seems', which allowed Charlie to add pastel hues to the picture. It was no longer just a paint-by-number deal. It was complex enough to be a Rembrandt.

What was it that Rocco had said? The third pitch was the most important? Rocco didn't really know baseball strategy, but he did accidently stumble into some wisdom from time to time. Soon, Charlie would be asked to deliver a third package to the Cardinal. This time it would be the 'real deal', whatever the 'real deal' was. And the Cardinal would use that package as trade bait for something bigger, something he wanted very badly. This trade would not be as one-sided as flipping Rocky Colavito for Harvey Kuenn. This would be a big-time swap with huge implications on both sides. Something Rita and Pete had casually mentioned was stuck on the baseball like a smear of Vaseline, making that third pitch jump more than a Gaylord Perry slider.

His cell phone rang. He answered quickly, hoping it was Pete. "Pete? Is that you?"

"Pete? No, Charlie, it's Angelo. Hope I didn't wake you."

"No, Angelo. I've been up for some time. Any news on Rita? And it seems I'm also missing Pete Wasniak."

"Yeah, I know. I've got Pete on ice for his own good. We had a nice long chat. He's being taken care of quite well. We even reached an agreement that he would assist me in a future venture. Nice fella, that Pete. Kinda bull-headed, but I get that. Told him to not contact you for a couple days, so his whereabouts remain secret – just in case. Everybody will be fine real soon."

"You've got him on ice? What is that supposed to mean? And what about Rita? Have you found out what happened to her? Who took her?"

"You know, for someone who's off on a holiday, you sure don't trust the people you left back in your home town. Let's not forget – you're working for Rocco at this moment. *Capisce*?"

Charlie had forgotten that fact, but persisted nonetheless, "I get it Angelo. But you are my only contact back there, and I'm concerned for my people."

"Your people? You act like you got a huge staff or something. Don't worry. Everyone is fine. Everyone is safe. Now, listen up real good for a minute. When you get back Sunday night, someone will meet you at the airport. He'll give you a package, something the Cardinal wants really bad. Monday around midday, you take it to the Cardinal, personally. He'll be expecting it. In return, he'll give you the dossier on Rita, plus any evidence indicating that you and he ever met. You're welcome. When you're done, call me. I'll give you your next instructions."

Charlie looked at his phone. Next instructions, he thought. "What, am I like a schoolboy, now? Instructions one step at a time?"

"Don't get pissy, Charlie. This is for your own good. Sometimes if you know too much too soon it's not healthy. You don't want to get unhealthy, now, do you? But let's talk about Las Vegas. What did you learn out there, anything?"

Charlie bristled silently, "Okay. You got me at a disadvantage. I'll admit that. Yes, there is something. The Cardinal has a brother, name of Sean Maroney. Supposed to be in a nursing home with Alzheimers. The thing is, his wife says he's not ill at all, but instead is off on some money-making scheme. We need to find out whether he is or isn't in a nursing home."

"Yeah, I'm already on that. Like I said, Pete and I had a nice, long conversation. He told me all about this Sean guy. So, there's an inspector paying a visit to the home he's supposed to be in. Seems the State of Ohio likes to send inspectors to those places on Saturday's, when the staff is smaller. I should know something later today."

Charlie was impressed. "Wow. That's great. Now, tell me about Rita."

"Didn't I already tell you everybody is safe? Now, go fuck that chickee you took out there and leave the tough stuff back here to me."

With that, the call ended. Charlie was left staring at the dead phone. He spent the next several minutes staring at the blank phone, then decided to try someone else for information – someone nearby.

• • •

At the Chancery

Brother Gerald believed that hard work was a blessing, and the only respite to a full day of work was to pray. At the monastery he was assigned a garden to tend which he enjoyed immensely, although he was not very good at maintaining it. Working the earth with his hands felt pleasurable, the cool moist soil a salve to his soul. If only he could learn to grow the vegetables as assigned. After a series of failures, the abbot took pity on him and gave him a potato patch. No one could fail growing potatoes, or so the abbot thought. But even that proved difficult for someone who was a born mathematician and expert bookkeeper, but a remarkably terrible farmer.

Nonetheless, Brother Gerald enjoyed being outside. So, when a respite from the diocesan books was necessary, he took pleasure in roaming the rosary garden outside the chancery – meditating on his God, on his role at the chancery, on his life as a monk. But meditating laid bare his most personal faults and problems which plagued his soul. The key problem, as he saw it, was that he took too much pleasure in things. He had learned from the other monks that life's pleasures should not be enjoyed too much. The life of a monk was to sacrifice. Even taking too much pleasure by sacrificing too much was somehow wrong – at least that was what they taught him. He learned that a monk should not partake in too many actions which brought him pleasure.

Others had done so, at their peril. To rid themselves of the awful sin of excessive pleasure, many of his brother monks resorted to the primitive and nominally forbidden practice of self-flagellation with a home-made discipline, a cat-o-nine-tails. They would offer up their self-administered pains as penance for taking too much pleasure in their life. But, then, some took pleasure in the pain – it was all very confusing.

He strolled the chancery garden, smelled the flowers, said his mandatory breviary prayers. As he walked, his thoughts drifted to what the abbot had said upon his assignment to the Cardinal's staff. "Consider your vocation," he said. "Determine if the contemplative life is right for you. If you find your work at the chancery is fulfilling a need presented by God, and fulfilling a need in your soul, then you must make the difficult choice to adjust your vocation."

Adjust? What did the abbot mean? Perhaps, Gerald thought, perhaps I am having a vocational crisis. I have seen it happen to others before me. They left the monastery, presumably to be more effective in the busy world by which he was now surrounded. He wondered if it was acceptable to God for one to abandon the monastery for an active life in the secular environment of parishes and priests and the faithful laity. Would he find too much pleasure in such a role? Or would serving the Lord in this fashion bring the Lord more pleasure than if Gerald remained a monk? The Lord should be permitted to have pleasure, too, should he not? "Do that which will please the Lord, not yourself," said the abbot.

Brother Gerald circled the garden slowly, then again more quickly, and yet a third time almost at a trot. He was making up his mind. He would take the opportunity to adjust his vocation, as the abbot put it. He would become a lay brother, and aspire to become a parish priest. He saw the need for more parish priests as he reviewed the diocesan roster. He would give over his life to saving the parishes that he knew were suffering from lack of funds. He had seen in the reports that there were many such parishes in deep financial trouble. The thought of helping them, of saving them, excited his heart and soul. If only he could find the bank records so he could show the Cardinal how to do it.

He stopped his trot in mid-step – I know how to do it, he thought to himself. I will make a phone call to the abbot, breaking my silence vow, of course, and announce my vocational change. He will be pleased that I've reached a decision. I believe that is why he sent me here, to come to grips with my vocation. He suspected – no, he knew – I am ill-fitted to the monastery, to the monastic life. Brother Gerald smiled. He continued the thoughts. Once I have the abbot's permission to follow the Lord's will, I can call the bank on the phone and request the documents I need to complete my report. The Cardinal will be so very pleased. He decided to wait until Monday to make the call to Friar James, the abbot at Bergamo, permitting both the abbot and Brother Gerald to have a peaceful weekend before going through what might be a complicated process of disengagement.

• • •

Breakfast in Vegas

Charlie finished the last of his omelet and poured one last cup of coffee. He shook his head, thinking that working for Rocco Parmissano meant dealing with Angelo DiFranco, which Charlie found more than a little bit stifling. At least with Rocco, Charlie could work on his own, following his own theories. Rocco was so full of himself he barely saw what others might be doing. But Angelo was a different story. He was highly intelligent and street savvy. He could read people, almost able to know what they were thinking. He was never at a loss in handling even the most difficult situations. Additionally, since he had the fate of Charlie's friends in his hands, he could control Charlie easily and skillfully. Angelo was no fool, and was not someone you should try to fool. While it was difficult working for him, at least Angelo was able to somewhat mollify Charlie's concern about Pete and his worries about Rita, even though the exact details were missing. Furthermore, Angelo seemed to share Charlie's speculation about Sean Maroney, even though the theory that Charlie had developed remained unspoken.

After finishing a full breakfast and the better part of a pot of coffee, Charlie headed back to the room with his theory firmly taking hold. There had been several clues, each independently leading nowhere, but taken collectively they pointed in one seemingly absurd direction. There were still some loose threads looking for a needle, but even those, as if drawn by static electricity, wanted to connect to the primary thought.

He returned to the suite quietly as to not awaken the easily angered TK, only to find her fully dressed and enjoying a room service breakfast at the coffee table in front of the couch, watching an animal show on TV.

"Did you know that there is such a thing as a blue wildebeest? You probably call it a gnu," said TK.

"Good morning to you, too, sunshine."

"There aren't a lot of TV choices unless you want to watch a pay-for movie. And I'm not in a movie mood right now. Want some bacon?"

"I already ate. You mind if we talk a bit?"

"Why, Charlie, I always love talking to you. What's on your mind, sweetie?"

"You weren't so talkative earlier, so I thought it best to ask permission now. You feeling better?"

"Golly, you take things I say too much to heart. You're way too sensitive. Anyone ever tell you that?"

"Who's Merke Edelstein?"

TK seemed shocked by the question, a piece of toast stationary before her lips. After several seconds she said, "I've never heard of him."

"Merke Edelstein is a woman. And you do know her, or of her. You have a 'tell', TK, and I just spotted it. Now, who is she?"

"I know lots of people, Charlie. I may have met this person in the past, but I can't seem to place her right now."

"She was the person behind the last two packages you gave me. That jog your memory? Who is she?"

Rising to look out the window, TK said, "What kind of day is it?" Pulling the drapes aside she exclaimed, "Wow! That sun is bright! Wanna go swimming? I've got a nice little string bikini I can wear."

"No swimming. You're on the job and I'm paying you, remember? Who is Merke Edelstein?"

"What difference does it make? You got the packages. I got paid. I assume you got paid. Past business. Let's talk about the future," as she gave Charlie a sexy look and moved toward him with her arms open.

As she approached, Charlie grabbed the wrists of her outstretched arms. "Not now, lover. Who is ..."

"Why the third degree," she interrupted and pulled herself free from his grip. She sat back down in front of her almost finished breakfast. "I'm eating now."

"You can talk and eat. This is no joke. My friends are in some sort of danger and if you have information that can help them, I'll get it out of you."

TK smiled at him. "That sounds like a threat. Not a good play when you know you need me to get information from Vicky."

Charlie sat opposite her, grabbed the remote and shut off the TV. "Yeah, well, Vicky may be less important right now. Another avenue is opening up. So, you want to tell me about Merke?"

TK sat back and gazed out the window as she considered her next move. Finally, she lifted her hands as if arrested. "You know, sometimes knowing too much can be worse than knowing too little. But I suppose it is time that I fill you in on one piece of the puzzle. Don't know if it will help you or hurt you. Depends on what you do with the information, I guess. But understand, I don't want you hurt. You're a nice guy, who sometimes does nice things for good people – and sometimes does bad things for bad people – I get it. Me? I'm sorta the same. I like to think the people who employ me are the nice kind. That may be foolish, but it helps me sleep better." She sighed and seemed to argue with herself, then finally said, "Your Merke Edelstein isn't a person. It's an organization."

Charlie's face twisted to understand what he had just heard. "What? What does that mean, an organization?"

"Just that. It's not one person, but a group of people, working together to accomplish a set goal, one case or step at a time. The goal is to make money. Maybe calling it an organization is too formal. There aren't any meetings or offices or anything – much more loosely knit. The organization prefers that outsiders think Ms. Edelstein is a single person, one individual. And because the various people who work together are each independent operators, so to speak, they don't run the risk of all of them falling into the hands of law enforcement if one of them goes rogue or does something stupid. Some of the people involved are genuinely good people with good intentions. Others participate strictly for the money no matter what is necessary to achieve the end result. Each serves a purpose to the whole. They collaborate when needed, as long as they don't think such collaboration would be too risky to themselves or violate their own personal idea of righteousness. Each of them works independently at whatever their business may be and only work together when their particular skill is required for the mission. Any Merke Edelstein organizational efforts have a share-the-wealth proposition for each one involved. It's a pretty lucrative deal."

TK continued. "You see, Charlie, not all good people are entirely good all the time, and not all bad people are entirely bad all the time. Each member realizes they depend on the courage, integrity and honor of the others. Yes, integrity and honor, even among those who may have selfish motives or may be intrinsically lawless. That's what makes Merke Edelstein so effective. Everyone must play by the rules if they want to share in the wealth. Of course, if someone cheats on the organization, they're out of the club, so to speak, and they run the risk of retribution from the cooperative, which can have some very dire consequences. Neat system."

Charlie sat stone-faced, wondering how much of the story he should believe. "What kind of projects does this group take on?"

TK demurred. "The kind that make money. Lots of it. Sometimes they sell things: items of value, information; sometimes they provide support, in one way or the other. Generally, it's all done legally, whenever possible. Sometimes retribution is called for, which can be messy and is best left to those who specialize in that craft. But as long as there is a profit, nothing is off limits."

Charlie still had his doubts, asking, "How do you know all of this, and how do I know you're telling me the truth?"

TK smiled, "You don't. You don't know if I'm telling you the truth. But I'll ask you to not share what I've said with anyone. Because just telling you puts me in jeopardy of a retribution from the cooperative."

Charlie pursed his lips, "So, are you a member? Are you one part of Merke Edelstein, just like the men in black who have been following me?"

TK grinned, "Member? Who said there were members? I don't know how you came to such a wild accusation, Charlie. I have no idea who these little green men in black may be."

"Cute. They are not little green men, but they are likely associates of the group, just like you."

"How could I be part of such a group? Little old me? What could I possibly offer them?"

"The ability to lie convincingly. That's what you can offer them. And the ability to get things done. I've been trying to figure out why I like you so much, why I admire your techniques and competence, and why I distrust you all the more because of it. I think I understand now. You are me. You're younger and prettier, but you are a fixer, just like me. We do the same kind of work, sometimes for good people and sometimes for bad people. But we both do our best to keep a moral compass nonetheless. If I were to set up my own version of a Merke Edelstein-type scheme, I'd want someone just like you to be part of it."

"Sort of like a third pitch in baseball, huh, Charlie?"

"What did you say?" he almost jumped out of the chair.

"Baseball. You know, the game? A good pitch is one that fools the batter. A bad pitch is one that fools the catcher. But the best pitch is a 98-mile-an-hour fastball that catches the edge of the plate – strike three. That's the 'moral compass', the ethics of baseball, that third pitch."

Charlie sat back hard into the chair. "Just how much of all this do you know?"

TK reached for her coffee cup and took a swallow. "I know less than you think, and more than you'd imagine. But I do know that Merke Edelstein could use a good attorney based in the Mideastern United States. They've got one on the East Coast, but they're always looking for new talent that fills a void."

Charlie shook his head, "Is that some sort of a job offer?"

"Depends on whether you think it was or not. If it was, would you be interested?"

"How can I say whether I'm interested in something that I know so little about, especially since I don't know whether I was offered a position or not?"

"That's just it, Charlie. No one is quite sure what it's all about. If they did, they'd be a liability, don't you think? Everyone participates, if they can do so without a conflict of interest, when called on by another member. They gauge whether to take the assignment or not. Those who choose to participate share in the reward. The others do not."

"Who calls the shots in such an organization? There has to be someone in charge, right?"

TK stood up and stretched, "Of course, silly. Merke Edelstein is in charge."

Charlie decided it was time for a bourbon. It was just after 12 noon back home, so why not. "Who's this mysterious East Coast attorney? Am I permitted to talk to him to see how he keeps his law license through all of this?"

TK headed for the bar and grabbed a vodka for herself, "Sometimes you can be such a misogynist, Charlie. The lawyer is a woman, not a man. Maybe she'd like to know how you've kept your law license after everything you've been through. Maybe she is ... just like you."

Gears clicked in Charlie's brain as he sipped on his bourbon. He spun toward TK with surprise on his face. Of course. It suddenly made all the sense in the world. Her ability to verbally jab, to change subjects in mid-stream, to push aside questions she didn't want to answer. "You?"

TK smiled and gave Charlie a peck on the cheek, "Columbia Law School, class of 2009, 12th in my class. But I certainly need advice from time to time."

• • •

Just Another Evening in Vegas

Charlie and TK spent the rest of the morning trading confused questions and cryptic answers as they each tried to conceal personal secrets while allowing the other to glimpse ever-so-gently into their souls. The more they discovered, the more they wanted to know, and the less each was willing to reveal. Mutual frustration spilled over into the start of affection and eventually into lust. They chose to use the free time of the afternoon for a more intimate exploration of their mutual desires.

By late afternoon they were exhausted and starved. Freshened up for the evening, they headed to Caesar's Palace for an early dinner, hoping to avoid Vicky and her friends. Once again over dinner, TK set the agenda for the evening, reviewing her plans and the expectations for Charlie.

Rocco Parmissano was intent on enjoying a meal at his favorite Italian restaurant, Rao's, before leaving Las Vegas, and he also wanted to play some Craps. Marie Carlito was eager to get out of the villa as well, just to be out and among other living human beings. The villa was nice, but she was bored just lounging at the pool and tending to Rocco's carnal desires. She was thrilled to be headed to a nice dinner in Caesar's Palace and dressed well for the occasion.

Just as Charlie and TK were leaving Caesar's to return to the Bellagio, they met Rocco and Marie, just arriving.

"Hey! Charlie! What the hell! You like this place, too?" said Rocco.

"Hi, Rocco. Yes, we just finished an early dinner. Good to see you out and about."

"Glad I bumped into you, kid. Got a call from Angelo a little bit ago. We need to leave earlier tomorrow. Say about 11:00 a.m. I gotta go to New York Monday morning. Fishing trip with, uh, some friends. So, we leave early. Got that?"

"Yeah, sure, Rocco. I'll be at the plane on time. Thanks for telling me. By the way, this is my friend, Tanya. She's helping me on this case."

Rocco looked TK up and down. "Very nice, Charlie. You got good taste. Uh, this here's Marie. She's my friend, too."

TK shook hands with Marie and said, "You look lovely, my dear. If Rocco is as bone-headed as Charlie is, you have my sympathies."

Rocco frowned, "What the hell? Why're you bustin' my chops? What's up with this dame, Charlie?"

"No offense intended, Rocco," said Charlie. "She busts everyone's chops. Especially mine."

Not amused, Rocco said, "Yeah, well, be at the plane on time if you want a ride. Otherwise, you're on your own." Walking into the restaurant, Rocco muttered, "Smart-mouthed bitch."

TK had a Cheshire cat grin on her face as she watched the couple depart. "I suppose he's right. I am smart-mouthed." Turning to Charlie, she said, "And I can be a bitch, too, don't you agree?"

"Let's leave that discussion for another time, shall we? We need to get in position for your meeting with Vicky." As they walked back to the Bellagio Casino, Charlie repeated TK's instructions. "I'll stay at one of the Roulette tables not far from the Petrossian Bar, but far enough away as to not be too obvious. You will try to wrap up your inquiries by 10-ish, and try not to get too drunk. I'd like to debrief tonight since I'm leaving early tomorrow. Is your flight back to New York at a reasonable hour?"

"I'll be fine, boss. Don't worry about me, boss. I'm a big girl, boss."

Charlie groaned, "He's right. You are a smart-mouthed ... young lady."

"Would he have left town without you had you not bumped into each other?"

Charlie thought for a minute. "Yes, I believe he would have. Rocco's not the brightest bulb in the pack. Until tonight, I'd wager he didn't even remember I had flown out with him. Yes, he'd have left and remembered somewhere over Kansas that I was supposed to be there."

TK said, "Once again, here's how I'm going to play it tonight with Vicky and the girls: I'll be weepy, morose, feeling bad about the way I treated you. You've been so very nice to me on this trip and bought me this lovely diamond bracelet." She shook her wrist in his face, "Like it?"

Charlie's jaw dropped open, "Did you ...?"

"Don't worry. I brought this from home. But it is beautiful, don't you think? Anyway, last night you were a jerk, so they opened up about their own jerks. Tonight, you're a wonderful guy, so they should tell me about their own wonderful guys. That way I'll get the full spectrum of what they think about Vicky's husband, and, hopefully, the rest of his family. That's what you want, right?"

"Sounds perfect to me. Should I come and look for you?"

"No. When I think I've pulled as much information out of them as seems possible, I'll jump up crying and run off to find you to make amends. Then we'll head straight for our room." She grinned, "And leave them stuck with the bill."

Charlie smiled, "Did I ever tell you you're an evil little lady?"

"Don't make me laugh, now, I'm trying to build up to being weepy."

Arriving at the Bellagio Casino floor, the two separated, Charlie heading for a secluded Roulette table while TK slumped her shoulders and hung her head, entering the Petrossian Bar. Charlie loved playing Roulette, and had a routine he followed every time he played. With just average luck, he could go for a couple hours without losing or winning a fortune. Sometimes the wheel was bad, and he had to reload his chip supply. At other times, and this was one of those times, the spinning wheel shined like a golden carrousel, the white marble clattering along and dropping into all the right spots. His $500 investment doubled, then redoubled. He was betting house money which magnetically attracted more house money. Before too long, he had overcome more than the previous night's champagne charges and was heavily in the black.

At about 10:15 p.m., a commotion caught everyone's attention as a weeping TK ran toward him, one of Vicky's friends tailing a safe distance away. She threw her arms around Charlie and kissed him everywhere she could, as he struggled to tell the Roulette operator to cash him out.

"Oh, darling! Can you ever forgive me? Please say that you still love me," cried TK.

Only too happy to agree, Charlie threw his arms around her, "Of course I do, silly! I'll always love you." Grabbing his winning chips off the table, he said, "Let's go to the room."

Vicky's friend, satisfied that all had gone well for the distraught TK, smiled and trotted back to the Petrossian to report on the success and to have some more champagne. Someone was going to have a big bill to pay in the morning.

Back in their room, TK provided a report. "It seems that Sean, Vicky's husband, went off on his money-making scheme just a few months before his brother, the Cardinal, became ordained, or elevated, or whatever you call it when you become a Cardinal," said TK. "Vicky hasn't seen him since, and only heard from him occasionally at first, then nothing for the past several months – other than one note saying he's doing well, along with a receipt for a healthy deposit into her checking account. Their marriage has been rocky for years, and they frequently spend long periods apart, so she didn't find it too unusual this time, other than it's starting to become kind of permanent, she thinks."

Charlie asked, "Does she ever communicate with her brother-in-law, the Cardinal?"

"She only mentioned him in passing. Seems he's a real pompous ass, never approved of Vicky or her marriage to Sean. Even though the brothers were close at one time, for the past decade or so, they've been a bit estranged, rarely speaking to one another. Which she found very strange for twins."

"What? Twins?"

"Yeah. Apparently, Sean and the Cardinal are twins. Didn't you know that?"

"Holy Sweet Jesus! I suspected that, but needed confirmation. I love you, TK! You just put all the pieces of the puzzle together."

"Well, duh! That was my job, wasn't it?" She made a mental note that for the second time that evening, Charlie said 'I love you'.

• • •

Sunday, July 17:

Sunday morning, 10:45 a.m., and Rocco was already in his seat when Charlie boarded the plane. "'Bout time you got here, buddy boy, I was getting' ready to tell 'em to take off without you."

Charlie fastened his seat belt just as the engines began to whine. "Hell, Rocco. I barely had time for my morning coffee. Had a few too many drinks last night." Which was true. After TK had finished her briefing, the two of them raided the mini-bar and emptied most of it. The rest of the night was a blur, a very pleasant and mostly naked blur.

"Ha. You was dickin' that bitchy blonde broad, wasn't you? You need to slap her around a bit, keep her in line. Otherwise, that mouth of hers will get you both in trouble."

Charlie grunted, "I'll keep that advice in mind."

"You do that, smart ass," said Rocco. "She should know better than to talk to your boss that way." Charlie kept trying to forget that he was working for Rocco these days. "Now that you've had this little vacation, I expect you'll keep me informed on everything goin' on with the Red Cap. Some important people are dependin' on me to provide the latest dope on the guy. So, you need to do your part. That's what I'm payin' you for, *capisce*?"

"Yes, sir," nodded Charlie. "Do you want me to still use Angelo as my contact?"

"Uhh, yeah, that's right. Angelo. I gotta go to New York tomorrow. Very important. Some big-time people are gatherin' to do some deep sea fishin'. Me included. So, you keep Angelo informed, he'll fill me in."

"Will do, Rocco. Will do." Charlie was hoping he'd actually have something he could report.

The plane was airborne a minute later, climbing rapidly over the surrounding mountains. Both Charlie and Rocco leaned back in their seats. "I'm gonna catch some Z's, so don't try talkin' to me," said Rocco. "I had a long night, myself," he chuckled and closed his eyes. Charlie was thrilled to follow suit. Settling back into the soft leather seat, he reviewed what he knew – which was now quite a bit – and how he would handle things back in Cleveland. His only remaining concern was separating himself from the Rocco arrangement. One doesn't just walk away while working for a mob boss, especially one as volatile as Rocco who had forked over a $50,000 retainer. Nonetheless, Charlie had an inkling, a sixth sense, that a separation might be easier than one might expect. Leaning back, he was asleep in seconds.

Either the change in the pitch of the engine noise or the downward tilt of the nose of the plane or both roused Charlie from his deep sleep. He looked over and saw that Rocco was looking out the window as the downtown Cleveland skyline came into view. It was approaching 6:00 p.m. Eastern time.

Rocco said, "Ball game's over. The stands are empty. Only a few stragglers havin' one too many beers in the local bars. Too bad. Love seein' the stands full for a baseball game. But the game is over. Last out's been made. Someone won, someone lost. Can't tell who."

Charlie thought that was the most wistful, almost poetic thing he'd ever heard Rocco say – the game is over, last out's been made, someone won and someone lost, can't tell who. And the plane descended to a soft landing.

Rocco leapt out of his seat just as the engines turned off. Without so much as a word to anyone, he grabbed his bags and headed to the car where two Dobermans stood watch.

Charlie thanked the pilots and headed out through the terminal to look for a cab. He was startled to see a livery driver in black jacket and hat holding a sign that read, 'Mr. Charles Franklin'. He approached the driver who kept his hat down tight. "Follow me, Mr. Franklin."

Charlie thought the driver looked vaguely familiar, and recognized him when he turned around to open the rear door of the town car. "Amir? Is that you?"

"Shut up and get in, Charlie."

Doing as he was told, Charlie said, "What the hell is going on?"

Amir Habood started the car and headed toward Charlie's apartment. "There is a package next to you on the seat. You are to deliver it tomorrow."

Charlie looked at the seat and saw the package, similar in size to the first two delivered to the Cardinal. "Since when do you moonlight as a limo driver, Amir?"

"I'm doing this as a favor. My father asked me to do it. It was requested by my distant family."

"Holy crap, Amir. We're into some deep shit, here. You shouldn't be involved."

"I am not involved. I'm simply ensuring that you are properly transported to your apartment. You are responsible for your own safety. I'm not in the protection game. Others will do that."

"What's that supposed to mean, 'others will do that'? Who is supposed to provide my protection?"

"Do you know what you are to do tomorrow? Has someone given you instructions?" asked Amir.

Charlie was getting peeved, "Amir! We're old friends. Why are you treating me like this? Not even a 'how the hell are you' from you."

Amir grinned in the rearview mirror, "So, how the hell are you?"

"Oh, go fuck off! I'm fine – tired, but fine. And to answer your question, yes. I know what I am to do tomorrow. How much do you know? Should I tell you what I'm supposed to do?"

"No. Please do not tell me anything. All I was asked to do was to tell you to deliver the package tomorrow. I wasn't told who you are delivering it to, although I can surmise from our previous conversation. And I don't know what you are to do after delivery, but I was told to make sure you remembered, and to call in if you didn't. That's all I know, and I don't want to know any more than that. As you say, you are into some deep shit, pal. I really don't want to get my shoes dirty, too. They're kind of expensive."

"Atta boy, Amir. I wouldn't want that either. Too many people I love are already in some sort of trouble. Don't want to add you to the list."

"Now, all that being said, you know you can count on me if you really do need help. I'm not any heavy muscle, but I can handle a knife better than most."

Charlie chuckled, "Amir, you are a ray of sunshine on a gloomy day. Keep your knives in the kitchen. What you're doing now is as far into this as I would want you to be. And I don't think I'm going to need a 'blade man' moving forward."

A few minutes and some small talk later, Amir pulled into Charlie's apartment parking lot. He got out and looked around as he opened the passenger door. "Looks quiet. Don't forget the package. My dad will cut off my ear if I screw this up."

"Might improve your looks, Amir. I got the package, and my luggage. No, no, Mr. Liveryman, don't bother. I'll carry it myself."

"Why, thank you sir, fuck you very much."

"You don't really expect me to tip you, do you?"

Amir bowed, "Ah, you are so kind. May the gods reward you with dysentery."

"Be safe, my friend. And give that outfit back to someone who knows how to drive."

THE PICK-OFF PLAY

Monday, July 18:
Monday can be a cruel day. The first day of the week always carries so much promise, but it never seems to live up to its potential. You hope it will deliver a warm breeze and a bright sun, but then it smacks you with a raw wet wind straight into your face no matter which way you turn. This particular Monday was circled on many people's calendars for many different reasons. And the way the day developed for each person, on each calendar, depended a great deal on their own actions and their own expectations. Some will end up cursing their fate. But fate will have little to do with it. Some will end up blessing their luck, but luck is just another word for fate. There is an adage that says, "You make your own luck", and that is so true for all those who circled this day as an important one. They each have made their own luck, sealed their own fate, and have no one to blame but themselves. Yes, Monday can be cruel. Oh, so cruel.

• • •

At 7:30 a.m., Angelo DiFranco placed a quick call to Pauly Basili. Assuming the call might be tapped, the conversation was circumspect. "He just got wings. Should drop in around 8:45 or so. Grumpy at being up so early."

Pauly replied, "We'll give him a nice reception. Everything set up on your end?"

"No issues here. Had to put down one of the dogs that was very fond of him."

"Okay. Unfortunate, but sometimes those things happen. Sends a necessary message. Unless you hear from me otherwise, call your new friend on the Hill around noon."

Angelo replied, "Will do. Got a meet with the St. Louis ballplayer later this morning. He wants something. I'll let you know if it's significant."

"What about the delivery boy and his playmates?"

"I'm setting up a play date for later. They'll all be fine."

"Some of my overseas friends are curious. Want to be sure everyone is as clean as a whistle," Pauly cautioned.

"I'll make sure of it. *Buona fortuna*," said Angelo as he ended the call.

• • •

After cooling his heels and unable to wait any longer, Charlie arrived by cab and rang the buzzer at the chancery at 9:30 a.m., much earlier than anyone anticipated. Monsignor Wesley Leonard opened the door and permitted his entrance.

"I have something for the Cardinal."

"You may give it to me," replied the Monsignor, "I'll see that he gets it."

"Nothing doing, wise guy. This goes straight to Maroney, or I walk."

The Monsignor looked away. "You needn't take that tone, sir. Follow me."

Charlie didn't move. "No. Not in his office. We wouldn't want your recording devices turned on, now, would we?"

The Monsignor was puzzled. "Where would you like to meet?"

"Let's go to the altar boy's sacristy in the Cathedral. Nice and quiet there, don't you think? And have Maroney bring the exchange package."

Monsignor Leonard hesitated and considered options. Finally, he pulled out his cell phone and dialed the Cardinal. "He wishes to meet in the Cathedral sacristy, altar boy side ... yes ... alright ... he's asking for the exchange package ... right."

The Monsignor put away his cell phone. "The Cardinal will join us momentarily. Allow me to show you the way."

He led Charlie on a serpentine route through the chancery and through a passage way connecting the residence area to the Cathedral proper. A well-worn, dark, narrow and dusty curved walkway led behind the main altar to the altar boy's sacristy, similar to the one Charlie had known as a youth.

Charlie looked around and smiled. "This takes me back to a time long ago." He touched the old, worn wood of the table in the center of the room.

"You were an altar boy?" said the Monsignor, less a casual question and more an accusation.

Charlie gave him a smug smile, replying with the same sarcastic tone. "And you're an ordained priest?"

The Cardinal burst in through the same passageway. "Let's get this over with. Give me the package."

"Good morning to you, Your Eminence. You put your package on that end of the table, I'll put mine at this end. We'll walk clockwise toward our respective packages and examine the contents. When we're both satisfied, I'll exit through the church door, and you'll go back through the catacomb."

The Cardinal scowled and glared at Charlie, then sneered at the visibly shaken Monsignor. "Agreed." Charlie and the Cardinal each placed a package on their end of the table, then slowly made their way to the opposite end, taking possession of what the other had left.

The Cardinal tore through the plastic wrapping, throwing it onto the floor, then gently opened an obviously ancient leather binder, crumbs of dried leather falling off the edges, exposing a document that to Charlie seemed thousands of years old. The edges of the pages showed signs that it was once a curled document. Each page now encased in a plastic sheath, the writing could have been Greek, Hebrew, Aramaic, or some other Near Eastern language.

Charlie's view seemed to confirm Rita's suspicion: flattened out and secured in a special wrapping, it was a scroll. Rita was right all along. In the meantime, he busied himself examining the contents of a large manila envelope in front of him. He found what appeared to be the original dossier on Rita, a second copy, several audio tapes identified and dated as his conversations with the Cardinal, and three video recordings of their encounters.

The Cardinal cleared his throat. "I believe I finally have what I have been seeking. I trust that you are equally satisfied?"

Charlie nodded. "I am. From this point forward, I will deny ever having met you, or having worked for you in any capacity. I know nothing about the contents of the package now in your possession. And you, sir?"

The Cardinal almost spit on the floor, as he responded. "I, too, deny ever having met you or asked you to do anything for me, not that you were very good at it. And I know nothing of the contents of that envelope in your possession."

Charlie resealed the envelope and said, "I wish I could say it has been a pleasure. It has not." He turned and exited through the door leading to the main body of the church.

"You go to hell!" shouted the Cardinal as Charlie bolted through the open door, the sound of his words echoing into the Cathedral nave.

The Cardinal mumbled, "Put the boys from Boston in motion," as he and the Monsignor returned through the tunnel back to the chancery. Several minutes later, when all the echoes and sounds had faded away, Brother Gerald silently crept down the stairs from the attic of the altar boy's sacristy. He had been re-sorting the cassocks by size. Yesterday, he had noticed the disarray, and took it upon himself to fix the problem without asking permission. No one knew he was there.

He slowly peered around the now empty room, strips of torn plastic on the floor. What had he just witnessed, he wondered? He recognized the Monsignor's voice, and that of the Cardinal. They were unmistakable. He didn't know the man of the third voice. But whatever had just transpired sounded awful. Sinful. Could he justifiably keep silent about what he had heard? He thought not. But who could he tell? Did his vow of silence mean he should not report this to someone? He made his mind up to call the Abbot this very afternoon. He'd announce his crisis of vocation, and ask his advice about the strange discussion in the sacristy.

At about 9:15 a.m., the limousine dropped Rocco at a private boat dock on the New Jersey side of the Hudson river where Giovanni and Pauly Basili waited next to a 32-foot fishing boat.

Giovanni extended his hands. "About time you got here, Rocco. We're ready to cast off!"

Rocco bowed and accepted his hands. "Thank you, Godfather Basili. This is indeed an honor. I hope I didn't keep you waiting too long. I've been travelin' a lot lately and maybe I'm not as fast as I yusta be."

Pauly said, "We're just glad you could join my dad. Tuna fishing has been good these days, about five miles out. You guys have fun." The boat began to pull out.

"You not coming, Pauly?" asked Rocco.

"Somebody's got to mind the store. Dad will introduce you to the other guys on the boat. *Ciao.*"

At 10:15 a.m., Charlie called Angelo as he stood on the street outside his office building. He was so anxious to find Rita and Pete that he chose to not go inside. He wanted to do something productive, to be actively involved in whatever was happening. "You said to call you after I made the delivery, Angelo. You said I'd receive my next instructions. The delivery is done. I'm ready to go."

Angelo asked, "You done already? I said midday. Any problems?"

Charlie replied, "Not for me. He got what he wanted, I got what I wanted. And, by the way, thanks for making sure of that."

"Yeah, wasn't me. But you're welcome, anyhow. Listen, there's a lot of moving parts right now. Go to your office, put that stuff he gave you in safe keeping, and wait there until I call you back. Early afternoon, probably."

Charlie was excited. "What? You expect me to just cool my heels until you call me? What about Rita and Pete? You said they'd be OK after the drop."

"Hey! Settle down. Grab a box of donuts or something. Your friends are in safe keeping. You'll join them later, if you're nice. Now, just do what I say. Got that?"

Charlie grumbled. "Seems I have no choice."

"That's right. You don't. Remember that. Everyone will be safe if you just follow my instructions. I haven't steered you wrong yet, have I?"

The line went dead as Angelo abruptly hung up. Charlie considered whether he should ignore the advice and go out and do something, anything. He tried to review his options. But he soon came to the conclusion that he had no choice. It was true, Angelo hadn't steered him wrong yet. If staying put somehow meant he was protecting Pete and Rita, then he had to do what Angelo said. It tore him up inside, but he went into his office and sulked. There were no calls on the answering machine, and nothing else he could do. He reviewed everything he received from the Cardinal, then locked it in his safe. He turned on the PC only finding trash e-mails. He had to satisfy himself with solitaire. Later, he heard a short but loud commotion outside in the rear parking lot. Assuming it was the garbage men, he returned to solitaire.

• • •

At 10:30 a.m., Cardinal Maroney retrieved his burner phone and placed a call to Rome. "I've got it," he said, before the person on the other end could say anything.

"It is in your possession?"

"Yes. It is exactly as promised," the Cardinal gushed.

"Bueno. I am meeting with the Cardinal Camerlengo shortly. I will once again suggest your ascension. He was not unreceptive the last time I brought it up. Keep your phone with you. I may need to call."

"My, that is wonderful. I thank you, my friend."

"And the gift which you mentioned the other day?"

The Cardinal tried to control his frustration. "Of course, of course. It has been packaged and shipped. You should receive it later today." He changed the subject quickly. "How is Bartolo of Argentina?"

"Ahh, it is so very sad. I hear he is nearing the end of his time on earth. The heavens will soon claim him as a new angel."

"Excellent," growled Maroney. "A vacancy will exist soon."

"That is such a harsh response to the imminent passing of a fellow Cardinal. Perhaps you should temper your enthusiasm should you get a call from the Camerlengo."

Maroney spoke with a chastened voice. "You are correct, my friend, so it shall be. May God in his mercy grant Cardinal Bartolo some soothing hours as he prepares for his great reward."

"Si." And the line went dead.

Maroney hung up and muttered, "And may the hours be short. Take the old goat already!" He smiled to himself, thinking that, in the future, every Cardinal, every priest, even the most casual church attendee would be amazed when they witness him making connections with other governments, other nations. In his mind, the Vatican was to be the centerpiece of a new world order – not simply a religious hegemony. All the nations of the world will beg to be part of the new structure – his structure. He even envisioned being proclaimed the new Holy Roman Emperor.

The intercom buzzed, "Your Eminence, the gentleman is here for his private confession."

"Thank you, Monsignor Leonard. I will meet with him in my outer office, I believe."

The Monsignor replied, "He has requested a more private setting, Your Eminence."

Surprised, the Cardinal said, "I see. Perhaps my chambers will be more acceptable. I will unlock the door." He grabbed the purple sash required for accepting a confession, just to keep the ruse complete should any prying eyes view the scene. The Monsignor led Angelo DiFranco into the room.

"Thank you, Wesley. You may leave us. Please have a seat in one of these chairs, sir, as it is far more comfortable than the old-fashioned Confessional Booth." As both men sat opposite each other, the Cardinal continued, "You are Mr. Parmissano, I take it?"

"No, Father. My name is Angelo DiFranco. I work for Mr. Parmissano. I serve as his ... uh ... Chief of Staff."

"I see. Where is Mr. Parmissano? I thought it was he for whom I'd provide confession."

"He had other business to attend to outside the city. I understand you wished to make a request of him."

"Yes, well, only if he was willing to make an offering after his confession. I'm not sure you can ..."

"I am authorized to provide assistance, an offering, on his behalf, Father."

The Cardinal wryly smiled. "You should refer to me as Your Eminence. That is the proper address for a Cardinal."

"You're a priest, right? Yeah, then I'll call you Father. Now, do you have something you want or not? I'm very busy with Rocco being away. I'm here on his behalf because I know you've been partners in the past. But just to be clear, I'm the one who made that dispute with the Knights of Columbus go away. So, if you just want to play word games, I'll be on my way." Angelo made a move to get up.

"No, no. Please. Sit. You see, I've never actually met Mr. Parmissano. Others have interceded on my behalf in our prior dealings. Therefore, I'm overly cautious to jump right into this request. But since you seem to be the power behind the throne, so to speak, I'm prepared to move forward with you."

Angelo sat back. "Okay, then. What can we do for you?"

The Cardinal chose his words carefully. "I've had someone working on a secret project for the last several weeks. It now appears that he has become treacherous, and threatens my work, and that of the Almighty."

"I take it that this project is not only yours, but the Almighty you speak of is God. It's God's project, too."

"That's right. That's correct. And, well, as you might imagine, we shouldn't permit someone to challenge the will of the Lord."

"Uh huh. What do you think should happen to this treacherous person?"

"I don't make this recommendation lightly, because one sin cannot overcome another sin, but the Bible does say 'an eye for an eye', and this fellow will make a ruin of everything unless we make it easier for him to meet his eternal judgement sooner rather than later."

Angelo raised his eyebrows. "You want him wacked, is that it?"

The Cardinal demurred. "That is rather crudely put, but if one person's death makes the world a better place, who is to judge God's will?"

"Gonna cost you," said Angelo without batting an eye.

Unable to raise the discussion to a gentler plane, the Cardinal said, "How much?"

"25 Gs, more if he's a well-known figure."

"I doubt too many people will miss him, so I expect $25,000 will suffice."

"In advance."

The Cardinal nodded. "That's acceptable. Do you know what a Krugerrand is?"

"Sure. South African gold coin."

"Right you are," smiled the Cardinal. "I have a few five-ounce gold Krugerrands, quite rare, mind you. Each one worth approximately $7000 in today's gold market. What do you say to accepting four of them as a, uh, 'donation' for doing God's work? Depending upon market fluctuation, those four coins will return anywhere from $28,000 to whatever gold sells for on the day they are redeemed."

Angelo considered the offer. "I'll need to check with my money guy to verify that valuation, but if it checks out, that sounds like a deal. Who's the mark?"

The Cardinal leaned back and said, "He's a two-bit lawyer and con man, Charles Franklin."

Angelo's expression never changed. "Okay, I think I've heard of him. Works alone, right? Yeah, he's a 25 Gs guy. Your four coins will buy the deal. You want a public display, or a discrete disappearance?"

"I hadn't considered that," said the Cardinal, rubbing his chin. "I suppose something discrete. We're not trying to send a message to anyone with an exposed body."

"And you want this done soon, right? You get me the Kruger's, we'll set it in motion. Call me at this number when I can get the coins." He handed him a business card with only the number and nothing else printed on it. "Anything else we can do for you?"

"No, my son, you've taken a great weight off my mind."

"Pleasure to be of service, Father." Angelo left quickly through the same door he had entered.

A few minutes later, the Monsignor knocked on the still open door of the Cardinal's chambers. "He's gone, Your Eminence. Did his confession go well?"

"Yes, it did Wesley, yes, it did. Can you and George be prepared to leave just after lunch? Remember to wear work clothes."

Wesley smiled. "We are ready, sir. Looking forward to it." And he turned and ran to tell George.

The Cardinal said to himself, "Me, too, Wesley. Looking forward to it."

• • •

Out in the Atlantic

It was 10:45 a.m. before the boat slowed and switched to idle.

"Marking fish here, Mr. Basili!" shouted the Captain.

"Wonderful. Sometimes we need to go out a little farther like this to find the school of fish," Giovanni Basili explained to Rocco. "Get the rods out!" he shouted to the other men on board.

Everyone scrambled toward the aft of the boat where a single fisherman's fighting chair sat mounted in the rear, a few feet from the stern. Heavyweight reels affixed to long, stiff fishing rods were placed in the left and right gunnels, as bait was carved by experienced hands.

"You ever go deep sea fishing like this, Mr. Parmissano?" asked one of the mates.

"No, nothin' like this," gushed Rocco. "Totally new deal for me."

The mate shouted, "Hey, Mr. Basili! We've got a rookie here!"

Everyone laughed hearty fishermen laughs, as Giovanni said, "Then he gets the first fish! Come here! Get in the fighting chair."

Rocco bounded toward the stern of the boat. "Should I wear a life vest thing, like the rest of you?"

One of the mates said, "We're going to belt you into this chair. You won't need a floatation device. You're not going anywhere unless the chair goes with you."

"Belt me in? I dunno. I don't like bein' confined."

Giovanni said, "If you're not belted in, a big fish will take you and the rod straight into the ocean with him."

Rocco raised his arms as he was tethered to the chair across the chest and waist. Other thick leather straps were positioned on the arms of the chair. In all the hubbub, he didn't pay attention to the heavy anchors and chains placed on either side of the chair.

"We got a fish on the starboard pole!" shouted a mate. "Get ready, Rocco. You in nice and snug?"

"I think so. I can barely move!"

Shouts of "set the hook", "man the gaff", and "clear all ropes" added to the melee and confusion as Rocco watched each of the mates run back and forth.

"Prepare the fisherman!" came another shout, at which point two mates locked the straps around Rocco's arms and the chair, and the anchors and chains were snapped onto his ankles.

"What the fuck," screamed Rocco.

"Small fish. Good eater though. Reel it in," said the mate.

Giovanni stood face to face with Rocco, and said, "Rocco, you deserve an explanation. You see, what we are – you and me – the kids call us Old School. They want us to modernize, to not be such Moustache Pete's like our predecessors. You and I, we're in the way. So, I'm going to retire and Pauly is taking over our operation here. Much more modernized, less like the old syndicate of our fathers. In Cleveland, Frankie Triunno is taking over for his father, who is also retiring. I'll do more fishing, old man Triunno likes to play golf, got a place in Florida, I understand."

"What about my operation? You can't just ... "

"It'll be OK. Angelo will take over. Actually, he already has taken over. He and Frankie are working out a nice collaborative arrangement. And they'll be working under Pauly who will still be headquartered here. Nice. Like a big corporation. Makes a lot of sense, don't you think?"

"Okay, okay, but why can't I just retire, too?"

"Do you really think you could? Just walk away? Nah. We don't think so. Plus, there's this thing with the Triunnos."

"What thing?"

"You remember when your guys blew up the Irish garbage man? Well, a couple members of the Triunno family got gunned down by the Irishman's goons. Retribution. Big mistake. One was Frankie's uncle, the other Frankie's older brother. Shoulda been your guys. You didn't offer them a condolence, did you? Didn't attend the wake. Didn't even send flowers. Anyway, no one has paid for that insult. Somebody has to pay for that, no? The Triunno Family thinks so. They said it should be you."

"Why me?" cried Rocco.

"You been a prick, Rocco. You don't work out deals with them nice like. You hold a heavy fist over them, steal their numbers territory and now you're even ready to start a war – there's a whole list of things they presented to the Council."

"The Council knows about this?"

"Of course," said Giovanni. "You don't think we'd do this without permission, do you?"

"*O Dio mio*," cried Rocco, in almost a prayer.

"It also didn't help that your Cardinal is causing lots of problems, right under your nose – and you even helped him!" Giovanni threw up his hands. "Bah!"

One of the deck hands came over and said to Rocco, "Here's the deal. This chair weighs about 75 pounds, and it doesn't float. Each of these anchors attached to your ankles weigh 50 pounds. That's a total of 175 pounds. You'll go to the bottom pretty quick. We're in 200 feet of water, along the North Atlantic gulf stream. The current will eventually wash you toward the Arctic Ocean. You won't suffer long, and your body will probably be eaten up quickly by crabs or sharks, so it's all cool."

"Fuck you! Fuck you all!"

"Pull the pin on the chair and throw the anchors overboard," said Giovanni.

The two ball-anchors plunged almost simultaneously. Rocco screamed as knee tendons snapped and bones separated and shattered from the sudden weighted jerk. The chair vaulted over the stern railing into the Atlantic, leaving a huge splash which washed over the rear deck. About 30 seconds later, a large air bubble broke the surface. Then there was silence.

Giovanni said, "Okay, Captain, bring up the replacement chair and take us to where there's some good tuna fishing. We wasted enough time here."

• • •

The New Structure

At about half past noon, Angelo called Frankie Triunno.

"Frankie! How are you my friend?"

"Good to hear from you, Angelo. How's things with you?"

"No problems worth mentioning. I want to make amends and settle an old issue with you. As I recall, Rocco strong-armed the numbers take from the Glenville area away from your family, along with other stuff from that general area. That was bad business. I want to return that territory to you today. I spoke to Louie V. who's been handling the area for us. He'll turn over all the books to you this afternoon."

"Angelo, that is a wonderful gesture. I appreciate it."

"Louie will give your man any help he might need – or, if you'd prefer, Louie is okay with the idea of transferring to your control. He knows the area, and he'd like to continue doing what he's doing. He usually gets 10% of the take for himself, but you can negotiate that with him if you want to keep him."

Frankie laughed pleasantly. "Yeah, I know Louie. Send him by to see me. I'll be glad to add him to our group. The territory and the smarts to run it, all to me? What do I have to give you, a first-round draft choice?"

Angelo said, "How about you pick up the tab for the first of our monthly organizational dinners with Pauly Basili?"

"Done," said Frankie. "How's that church business working out?"

"Should be wrapped up in a few days, a week or so at the most. Thank the stars you're not in the middle of this. Messy business. We'll play hell keeping it out of the news."

"Got a plan?"

"Yeah, got some people know their way around who can fix media stuff pretty good. They have their own reasons for making the story go away, so we'll see how well they do."

"Okay. Let me know if I need to keep my head down," said Frankie as he hung up the phone.

• • •

Brother Gerald Makes his Call

It was just after lunch when the Cardinal, the Monsignor and George left the Chancery in a car, telling Brother Gerald that he was to mind the store until their return later this evening. All three were dressed in work clothes. The red-headed man, never introduced to Brother Gerald before, snickered as the three walked out the door, obviously amused at the idea that Brother Gerald could manage the Chancery on his own.

He sat in the accounting office staring at the phone. He allowed his hand to rub the receiver. He picked it up once, then immediately dropped it on the cradle, as if it was a hot coal. He argued with himself that he was about to make a decision which could not be undone. Breaking his silence, breaking his vow – these were actions which would forever change his life, whether for good or bad he could not imagine. But now it was much more than simply changing vocations, not that such a change was so simple anyway. No, now he had to admit to listening to something untoward. He had witnessed a sin – at least he thought it was a sin. Whatever had transpired in the altar boy's sacristy was certainly not a heavenly act. The smell of corrupt activity hung in the air of that room like putrid incense. It had to be reported. The only person he could trust was Abbot James.

Would the Abbot understand? Would he believe him? Would there be too many shocks all at once for the Abbot to take in? First, Gerald talking against his vow; second Gerald announcing his desire to change his vocation; third, reporting sinful activity by the Cardinal and the Monsignor. It was almost too much for Gerald to even think about.

Bravery. It was all about bravery. Abbot James once said that all monks are brave, just through the act of being a monk. It was brave of them to forsake the world to serve the Lord in silence and solitude. Would the Abbot think it equally brave to forsake the silence and solitude for a life which served the Lord in the secular world? Gerald had been unable to sleep last night, worrying over this moment. The cushioned mattress in the chancery was almost too comfortable after the straw mattress of the monastery, making a deep sleep seem almost wrong. Yet it was not just the thought of his change of vocation that gave him concern. He knew he might never sleep again if he didn't tell the Abbot what he heard earlier this morning.

Bravery. He picked up the phone and dialed the number for the Bergamo Monastery to speak with Abbot James.

• • •

The Boys from Boston

Earlier, in the rear parking lot of Charlie's office building, an old station wagon rumbled to a stop. The three men inside were waving their arms, disagreeing with each other as to how to proceed. The driver waved a gun around, while the one in the back seat made cutting motions with a knife. They got out of the car, slamming doors, pretending to look like dangerous thugs, building up the courage to enter Charlie's building. The driver with the gun returned to the driver's seat while the other two attempted to enter the locked back door of the building.

That's when Charlie heard the commotion. Maybe thirty seconds of noise, no more than a minute, then quiet. He didn't even look out the window. If he had, he'd have seen two men dressed in black exiting from the locked door of his building, shoving the two thugs down the steps, quickly rendering them unconscious. The driver struggled to exit the car as the men in black slammed the car door on his head, taking his gun. The three now unconscious men were thrown into the back of the station wagon, their arms and legs tethered together behind their backs like hog-tied calves. The two men in black stood by until two Doberman types arrived a few minutes later. The Dobermans got into the station wagon and drove off. The only sign that any of this even happened was at the edge of the parking lot curb – a dusty old, worn ball cap with a red letter "B".

The call to Angelo came around 2:00 pm. The Dobermans told him they drove the station wagon to an auto demolition yard, where it was immediately put in the crusher while the now conscious occupants objected for a short time. The flattened remnant, dripping oil and other fluids, was loaded onto a railroad car with a dozen other wrecks, headed for a smelting plant in Pittsburgh.

• • •

Facing Facts

Charlie had played far too many games of solitaire on the PC, changing to an actual deck of cards to take up more time. Finally, just before 3:00 pm, Angelo called and told him to go to suite number 1004 in the Ritz-Carlton Hotel. A key to the suite was waiting at the front desk in Charlie's name. Angelo said that all of Charlie's questions would be answered in the hotel, and not to bother him until tomorrow. Charlie doubted that he'd get all the answers he wanted. He had more questions swirling in his head than could ever be found in a hotel room. Angelo didn't say who else would be in the room, but Charlie expected someone would be, if there were to be any answers at all. The uncertainty of what he was walking into made him very cautious.

There were only six sets of double-doors on the tenth floor of the hotel, each entering into a suite. He found 1004 and carefully inserted the key into the slot. He thought he could hear many voices inside. Could it be the Bostonian punks? The Italian Guy and his mob? Charlie's best option was to catch the occupants by surprise. Flinging open the door, he burst in. Five people surrounded a round table, with cards and poker chips strewn about.

"Hi, Charlie! About time you got here," said Rita.

Pete jumped up. "I was really starting to worry about you!"

Charlie's mouth hung open. "YOU were starting to worry!?! What the hell is this?"

The three others sitting at the card table were all dressed in black shirts and pants, and one of them was the slightly built man known to Charlie as The Italian Guy.

"C'mon, have a seat over here. Let me introduce you to these sweet guys," said Rita.

"Sweet guys? Isn't that the fellow you named the Italian Guy?" said Charlie.

Rita looked over at the man and said, "Oh, yeah, but he's not Italian. He's Swiss. That's Dominic, this cutie is Wilhelm, and that's Hans, who thinks his two pair will beat my flush, don't you Hans?"

Pete said, "Sit down while I pour you a drink. We'll let everyone explain as soon as Rita takes Hans' money."

Charlie thudded into a chair while Rita raked in her chips and Pete offered him a strong Bourbon on the rocks. Pete said, "I think you're going to need this when the stories start coming out."

"Perhaps I should start," said the slightly built man, his accent thickly Italian sounding. "My name is Dominic. You and your friends have identified me as The Italian Guy. An apt *designatione* given my accent. But Rita is correct. I am actually Swiss, as are Wilhelm and Hans. I can speak English, but Hans and Wilhelm are best in Italian or German, or a relatively obscure dialect of Romansh. We have been watching you during your dealings with Cardinal Maroney. You see, he has been a suspect to our group for several months."

"Your group? But, you're not Interpol, are you," guessed Charlie.

"That's what I guessed, Charlie," said Pete, "but I was wrong."

"Si. A good guess," said the man identified as Dominic. "Your man Pete, he saw me very quickly as a tail which made you all suspicious of my actions. I apologize for that. We mean you no harm. We actually wish to protect you – all three of you."

Charlie smiled a knowing smile. "No, you're not Interpol, but your group has a similar footprint, does it not? Your people are spread through many countries, mostly in Europe, but lately over an expanded map."

"Take a drink, Charlie, a deep one. This will knock your socks off," said Pete.

Dominic continued. "Mr. Pete, I believe Mr. Charlie has already identified us." Directing his comments to Charlie. "You have no doubt heard of the Papal Swiss Guard, known in Latin as the *Cohors Helvetica*. They are the protectors of the Pope in all his public appearances. The Swiss Guard has many functions beyond those protection duties seen when the Pope appears. There is also an investigative wing, for which the physical entry requirements are not as strict as for those of the Papal Guard."

Rita said, "Did you know that to be in the Papal Guard you had to be Swiss, 5-foot 9-inches or taller, be single and under 30 years old?"

Charlie had figured out many of the answers to his questions, but let Dominic provide his explanation. "With those restrictions, you could not be in the Papal Guard, I assume."

Dominic said, "Sadly, I am too short. But I – we all three of us – have just the right capabilities to be a member of the investigative wing. We are members of what is called the Constantine Guard."

Charlie looked toward Pete. "Did I just hear that right?"

"Wait. It gets better," said Pete. "Take another swallow."

Dominic continued, "As we continued to observe your efforts, and as we orchestrated to bring the matter with the Cardinal to a head, we felt we needed to add protection to each of you. You, Mr. Franklin, were heading to Las Vegas. Mr. Wasniak was likewise out of town headed to the middle of New York state. And Ms. Hernandez, Rita, was alone and possibly vulnerable to the Cardinal and the men he had hired. We suspect the Cardinal is capable of much evil, and we felt the need to offer her protection. Miss Rita is, how you say, a firebrand, no? She was suspicious of me, and she possesses a firearm. Therefore, we felt it best to make her rescue more of a rapid abduction. We have apologized for the intrusion and any fear we may have caused her."

"And they got me this suite, and a nice steak dinner, and took my phone because they knew I'd try to call you or Pete," said Rita, waving the now returned phone.

Dominic continued, "When Mr. Wasniak returned to town, he recognized that Rita was not in his apartment. We planned to bring him here immediately, but before we could meet with him, he went to Angelo DiFranco for assistance. Angelo then sent him to us."

Charlie threw up a stop sign, "Wait. You do realize you're in league with a gangster, right? Angelo is in the mob, you know. Does Angelo know who you are?"

Dominic frowned, "We do not approve of or forgive the actions of some of our associates. Mr. DiFranco did not know who we represented until informed by others from New York City. Not all bad men are entirely bad, just as not all good men are entirely good."

"Where have I heard that before," deadpanned Charlie. "That's great. Both Pete and Rita came under your protection while I worried myself sick out in Las Vegas. How come I didn't get any protection?"

Dominic smiled, "Oh, but you were protected. We did not judge that the Cardinal had tentacles that far away, but we couldn't take any chances."

Charlie said, "I hardly think Rocco was going to provide me any protection out there. He barely remembered I was there."

"I do not speak of Mr. Rocco as your protection. Rather another of our associates. She goes by the name Constantine."

"You think TK Constantine was my protection? I find that hard to believe," said Charlie, shaking his head.

Dominic leaned back against the couch, "It is fortunate that no action on her part was necessary. She is most lethally trained. Not by us, mind you, but she can be formidable when challenged." He reached into his pocket, "She assumed I might see you, and asked that I give this to you should I ever have the opportunity." He handed an envelope to Charlie.

Charlie found a hand written note in the envelope:

"Dear Charlie,

By now you know that I'm not just a glorified delivery girl. I'm glad you finally know the truth. I really did enjoy our time working together. Perhaps circumstances will find us collaborating again someday. You never know with Merke Edelstein. By the way, in case you're wondering, TK Constantine is not my real name. If our paths cross again, I may tell you what my real name is. Or not.

You really are a nice guy. Stay safe. And I love you, too. — T.K."

He laid the note in his lap and drained his drink. "Hit me again, Pete."

Dominic said, "We also assisted in eliminating a threat from the Cardinal, the men he hired from Boston."

"When was this?" asked Charlie.

"Earlier today. They were outside your office preparing, we believe, to do you serious harm. Hans and Wilhelm subdued them, and Mr. Angelo's men took them away."

"Angelo's goons got them? Well, I'm guessing they won't have a pleasant or lengthy future." Charlie wrinkled his face, "Shouldn't we be calling them Rocco's men, not Angelo's men?"

Dominic turned away. "I am told that Mr. Rocco will no longer be in charge of his business in this city. More than that I do not know."

Charlie said, "More than that you do not want to know."

• • •

The Maroney Treasure

The Cardinal, Monsignor Leonard and George arrived at the Maroney Estate in Hudson just before 3:00 p.m. The Cardinal took the precaution of alerting the village police that they would be on property to prevent any unnecessary patrol car visits while they were working there. Maroney led the group to what appeared to be a falling-down work shed. He entered numbers onto a key pad beside a substantial metal door disarming the security devices, shutting off all alarms and security cameras. He opened the large shed door and wheeled out a four-seat all-terrain vehicle with a small wagon attached to the rear. He put some assorted tools in the wagon: a spade, a long pry bar, a sledge hammer and several smaller tools. He added three flashlights and several pair of work gloves. He pocketed a bulky leather satchel hanging on a nail in the shed.

"The ATV has seats for each of us, gentlemen. No one will have to walk or run to where we're going. I must warn you, however, the ride can be quite bumpy, so do hang on."

The Monsignor asked, "What is it we'll be doing? All of these tools – I didn't anticipate we'd be doing construction."

"I told you we might get dirty. Don't worry, it shouldn't strain you too badly, Wesley."

A wide-eyed George took one of the rear seats and clung to the roll bar for dear life as the Cardinal started the engine. It took three tries for the engine to turn over. "Hasn't been fired up for some time," said the Cardinal. "Little rough at first. But we'll need this and the wagon to carry the items we retrieve." Eventually the Cardinal got the ATV to lurch forward and he drove it behind the main house down an incline toward a tree line a half-mile away.

"Is all of this part of your property, Your Eminence?" shouted the Monsignor.

"And then some, Wesley. Those distant woodlands are on our land for perhaps another quarter-mile. But we're not going that far." He steered the ATV almost to the woods, then veered to the left toward a copse of trees and bushes which partially covered a stone structure. He pulled up in front.

"I trust you boys do not spook too easily. This is my father's mausoleum. We need to go inside."

George looked back up the hill, "Why, you can't even see the house from here, nor any other buildings anywhere."

"That's why my father chose this spot. He didn't want strangers peering at him during his eternal rest." The Cardinal opened the leather satchel and removed a large, ancient looking key. "Rather dramatic, isn't it?" said the Cardinal as he showed the key to the two men. "But it was intended to work well. We shall see."

The cardinal donned a pair of work gloves and cleared some vines away from the deeply set steel door; he then inserted the key into the door. After a few jiggles, the key turned and, with a shove, the thick door opened inward.

"Get the flashlights," instructed the Cardinal, "let's look around in here."

George and Wesley glanced at each other with wide-eyed alarm as they turned on the flashlights and followed the Cardinal in. The interior floor of the mausoleum was poured concrete, 16-feet wide by 20-feet long. In the center was a massive carved stone funereal lid, itself 8-feet by 12-feet, raised some four-feet off the floor on a cement wall resembling a bier.

The three shined their flashlights this way and that, assuring themselves that no woodland residents had made the place their home. The Cardinal broke the silence. "I'm relieved to see that the construction has held firm. It was built with very thick walls to prevent entry accept through the keyed door. Here is what we need to do. My father's casket lies ten-feet down, beneath this carved lid. The space is small, but manageable for two persons. The casket lies on a hollowed-out cement catafalque. In the hollowed-out area under the casket are a dozen burlap bags. Each bag weighs approximately fifteen pounds. Do you know what is inside those bags?"

The Monsignor said, "You referred to your father's treasure. Is that what is there?"

The Cardinal chuckled, "You are correct, Wesley. And it is in the form of gold Krugerrands. Each bag is a fortune in its own right."

George began to whoop and jump about. "Then let's go get them!"

"Patience, my boy. First, we must slide this lid aside by a few feet to give us access to the area below. It is quite heavy, but once we get it moving, it will open sufficiently to permit careful entry under the catafalque. Closing it again once we are done will be much easier with the pry bar. Go get the tools, men."

The Cardinal took the sledge hammer and approached the front of the lid. Almost hidden from view were two large metal spikes fitted into holes in the lid and corresponding holes on the frame wall. He pounded on the bottom of the left spike, forcing it upward exposing the flattened spike top. "Grab the spike, Wesley, and pull it out. Well done. Now, you two do the same on this one here, and then the two in the rear. Leave the spikes below where they were removed so we can replace them later."

When the Monsignor and George finished removing the spikes, the Cardinal explained, "The area below is air-tight. This lid is perfectly designed to make it so. We'll slide the lid from the rear because that's where the ladder is. We can use this tool to help us." The three all went to the rear of the lid and pushed hard, the Cardinal manning the pry bar. Remarkably for its weight, the lid slid without too much strenuous effort by the three men. They pushed until a three-foot opening was exposed. "That's far enough," said the Cardinal. Each of them turned their flashlights into the darkness below.

"There, you see? My father's stainless-steel casket. Impervious. Not even the smell of death. Look over here. See the ladder? It's just below the lid level. Five steps down to the treasure. Now, make sure you have your flashlights. One after the other climb down. Be careful, now." Once both had entered the casket vault, the Cardinal instructed, "Look under the casket to the catafalque. See the opening? That's right. See if you can locate the bags."

Wesley and George warily snuck on hands and knees under the casket. "I found one," shouted George. "Here's another," shouted Wesley. "Oh my gosh! They're very heavy," said Wesley.

"Yes, they're quite heavy. Don't strain yourselves," said the Cardinal. "Bring them out one at a time to the ladder and hand them up." They did as they were told. One, then the other brought the heavy bags to the ladder where the Cardinal took them and laid them beside the exterior wall. The more they found, the slower they moved, as the excitement of finding the treasure was replaced by the exhaustion of the hard work. As the tenth bag was lifted to the Cardinal, he said, "Just two more, boys, two more. Look hard."

"I don't see anything else in here," shouted Wesley from under the catafalque. "Go help him, George. Get under there and use your flashlights. Those last two are for you boys as payment for your hard work." The two scrambled further into the opening, searching for the last two bags while the Cardinal grabbed the pry bar and moved to the front of the lid. Placing the pry bar at the base, the Cardinal gave a great shove and the lid began to slide back into place.

Shouts and screams came from below as the grinding sound of the moving lid registered with the two men below. One final push closed the lid in place as the Cardinal heard what sounded like snapping twigs. He quickly replaced the front anchor spikes, locking the lid in place, then hurried around with the flashlight to the rear. Lying next to the rear spikes were the tips of three fingers. "Oh, Wesley. Look what you've done. Your hand must have reached the top just as the lid slipped shut. Tsk, tsk. That's got to hurt," said the Cardinal as he replaced the rear anchor spikes.

The Cardinal put the ten bags of Krugerrands onto the ATV trailer, gathered up the tools, and examined the interior of the crypt one last time. The screams and cries from below were so muffled by the heavy cement that they were less than whispers.

The Cardinal said quietly so that only he could hear his voice, "Boys, did I say there were twelve bags? I made a mistake. There were only ten. Sorry about your luck." He smiled with satisfaction, "And so, I must bid adieu. *Requiesce in Pace.*" He roared in laughter as he closed and locked the door of the crypt, retracing his path up the hill in the ATV.

• • •

The Suite at the Ritz

Charlie could not disguise his Cheshire Cat grin. Rita recognized the look. "Why do I sense that you knew all of this before you arrived?"

"Well, I didn't know Brother Dominic's name," admitted Charlie. "At the beginning of the week I only had a theory. Puzzle pieces fell into place, a distant acquaintance provided confirmations – and I learned something in Las Vegas from Victoria Maroney. Well, I guess to be accurate, from TK Constantine, or whatever her real name is. What she learned from Vicky confirmed my suspicions. It has to do with the two brothers, Sean and Phelan. Phelan is the Cardinal."

"We may already know what you're about to say," offered Pete. "Dominic has been filling us in."

"Really," said Charlie. "So, you know they're twins?"

Pete nodded. "Yep, one born on September 30 at 11:58 p.m., the other born on October 1 at 12:04 a.m. We missed making the connection when we checked their birth dates."

"Well, hell! You didn't need me to do any investigating at all! We just needed Dominic and his boys to come out of the woodwork earlier."

Dominic raised a calming hand. "Do not misunderstand. My team did not reach our conclusions until we were able to compare notes with

Pete and Rita. I must ask you now if you concur with our supposition that one is masquerading as the other?"

"Yes, I do. I have no proof of that, nor do I fully understand the motive, but I believe the man now claiming to be Phelan Cardinal Maroney is actually his brother Sean Maroney."

Pete said, "Sweet Mother of God, what's his end-game?"

Dominic motioned the other two men in black to sit back down as they started to rise. "Mr. Pete. Please refrain from speaking of our Holy Mother in a profane manner. Hans and Wilhelm are sworn to protect her good name with all severity."

Pete leaned backwards. "My apologies. Won't happen again, I hope."

"Mr. Charlie, we have put several pieces of the puzzle together, and we think we know the purpose of man posing as the Cardinal, his motive, as you call it. It is most dastardly. We cannot mention our conclusion at this time. But steps are being taken to thwart him."

Charlie nodded his head. He knew the pieces well, having turned them around in his brain several times. He put himself in Sean Maroney's fake red slippers and looked at the world. What he saw was purely evil. Dominic was correct – it was dastardly. "Okay, then. I'll ask you the same question I asked TK Constantine – who is Merke Edelstein?"

Rita said, "Oh, I got this one. I bet I know!"

Pete shushed her, saying, "First, I gotta tell Charlie something that's been eating me." Turning to Charlie and handing him a fresh glass of bourbon, "Man, I'm sorry about this, and I should have told you sooner. It's like this ... um ... oh, hell. Rita and I are together these days."

Rita said, "What do you mean, 'you're sorry about this'? I think we're happy together."

"No. I mean I'm sorry to tell him like this. Because you two ..."

Charlie interrupted. "Pete, it's cool. I had that figured out a while ago, too. I'm happy for you, both of you. Probably better for you, Rita. But just one thing – will you still be my receptionist?"

"Nope. I'm going to work with Pete, study and finally take another shot at the Bar Exam. You need to find someone else to do your busy work. The stuff you get involved with drives me crazy."

Charlie smiled and said, "You know what? You're right. Better for us all. Now, Dominic, Brother Dominic, I believe. Please excuse my vulgarity, but just who the hell is Merke Edelstein?"

Dominic smiled. "She is a complex person, is she not? At times she is here, then she is there, then she disappears completely and is no one and everyone all at the same time. Did not Ms. Constantine give you an answer to the riddle? Did you not believe her?"

"She said Merke Edelstein is not an individual but rather is the name given to some sort of an organization. It seemed to make some sense, but I just don't know ..."

Rita interrupted. "What is that supposed to mean? She's not a real person? I was guessing it was old lady O'Neal."

Pete was equally amazed. "You mean we – and the Cardinal – we were chasing around looking for a person that didn't exist? That's just crazy!"

Dominic said, "Perhaps that is what Ms. Edelstein wants. She wants confusion, she wants people to not quite grasp what she is about. She wishes to see, not to be seen. Is she a person? Is she a group of people? Is she simply a concept, an idea, an image, a phantasm? Would it matter greatly if you understood it all? Would you feel better about your life?"

Charlie looked squarely at Dominic. "You're not going to give me a straight answer, are you?"

Dominic smiled and returned to his seat at the poker table. "You already have the answer, Mr. Charlie, if you wish to recognize it. But I should caution you – all three of you, really. Knowing what you think you know can be dangerous. Tell no one. And if, at some time in the future, someone calls asking a favor, or for help with a project, that person might be calling on behalf of Merke Edelstein. And, barring any personal conflicts, your assistance may be expected. Nothing you would be asked to do would be outside your abilities, nor against your presumed conscience. Of course, it would be up to you to decide to participate or decline participation."

Charlie said, "So, am I to assume that we are now part of this mysterious group known as Merke Edelstein? Just like you, and TK Constantine, and even Angelo and the mob?"

Pete said, "Don't forget Amir and his family."

"That's a pretty strange meld of people, Dominic. Both good and bad intentioned folks. Does that mean there are no morals in Merke Edelstein, that 'the end justifies the means'? Gangsters do the dirty work while the Papal Guard does the pretty work, and everyone is just fine with that?"

Dominic's cell phone rang. He answered it without saying a word. After listening for a few minutes, he said, "*Bueno. Si. Ciao.*" He hung up and ordered Wilhelm and Hans to their feet. "We must go. All three of you, stay here for your own protection. The danger is real and growing more imminent, and we do not know where it may come from. Please trust me, you must remain in this suite. We will return presently."

• • •

The Cardinal and the Krugerrands

The Cardinal was driving back toward the chancery, the trunk of his car laden down with the bags of Krugerrands. He stopped at an intersection and turned on his burner phone. He had missed a call from his contact in Rome. He pulled over and returned the call:

"*Mio amico*, where have you been! Pack your bags. The Camerlengo wishes to speak with you directly as soon as possible. The Vatican plane is due to land within a few hours in Cleveland. Check your e-mail for details. Be prepared to leave at once. This is magnificent, my friend. This is what you ask for! Bring the artifact with you. *Ciao*!"

Maroney let out a huge breath. This was it! This was what he had been trying to achieve! It was to be only a matter of time for everything to fall into place. Perhaps events were happening sooner than expected. With well-executed plans, timetables can accelerate. He thought of the fortune in his trunk. He needed to find a safe place for it. He wouldn't have time to secure all the bags of coins in the chancery, not if he expected to meet the Vatican plane. He didn't trust leaving it in the chancery garage. Too many others might have access to it.

Leaving it at the airport was not an option. His mind raced, trying to think of who could best guard his fortune. There was only one person who kept coming into his mind. He reached into his pocket and pulled out the card from Angelo DiFranco.

A half-hour later he met Angelo at an old warehouse in a worn-out part of downtown Cleveland. Angelo opened the freight door allowing the Cardinal to drive in. He parked the car in a far corner and locked the doors. The Cardinal handed Angelo five Krugerrands, retrieved from the trunk earlier. "I appreciate your assistance in this matter, Mr. DiFranco, which is why I'm giving you five coins rather than the agreed upon four. You will take care of the car, and the man we spoke of earlier?"

Angelo nodded and examined the Krugerrands. His money man had informed him they were not worth the $7000 each estimated by the Cardinal. Rather, they were valued at nearly $10,000 each. "That's good. Smart of you to pay me now. The car and the hit. I'm not even offended by the tip."

The Cardinal didn't quite know how to respond. "Um, er, fine then. I'll be back for the car when I return from a short trip. You're sure it will be secure here? No one will bother the vehicle?"

"You've got the keys, so no one will take if for a joy ride or anything. This warehouse is our building – my building now – for storing items we don't want outsiders messing with. I've got pretty tight security on its contents. You don't have to worry."

"Excellent. Again, I do appreciate your assistance."

"C'mon, I'll drop you at the Cathedral. I assume that's where you're going."

"Yes, I have to pack quickly. My flight leaves very soon."

"Where you headed," asked Angelo.

"Church business. I'm afraid I can't say much more. Please give my regards to Mr. Parmissano."

"With any luck, you'll see him before I do," Angelo said with a cordial smile.

• • •

For a few minutes after the three Swiss Guards left, Pete, Rita and Charlie sat silently looking at one another. Then Charlie checked his team for doubts, "Okay, is anyone buying this crap? Does anyone really believe these three are part of the Swiss Guard?"

Rita said, "Who else do you think they are? You seem to have more info than you're letting on. I'm usually the skeptic in this crew, but I gotta say they've convinced me."

Pete jumped in. "There has been nothing that they've done or said that makes me think they're not telling the truth. I know it seems far-fetched, but this whole deal has seemed absurd from the beginning. The Cardinal; his brother with Alzheimer's; the package that wasn't, wasn't, then was the real deal; the blonde, TK, or whoever; this Merke Edelstein person or organization; Amir's family; the guys from Boston, who may or may not be out there somewhere; the involvement of Rocco's crew – none of it makes any sense. So, why not a trio of Swiss Guards?"

"You left out the twin Maroney's, old Mrs. O'Brien and Vicky Dempsey Maroney. Throw them into the gang of people that make this whole thing bizarre," added Charlie.

Pete said, "That's right! I haven't told you! Old Mrs. O'Brien, the mother of the Maroney twins, has been living in style while selling off various parts of the family's artifacts. She said she's been selling them to several different buyers, some from the U.S. and some not. She thinks some of the items may date back thousands of years. I got the impression there may be contraband in the stacks of stuff. There's a huge warehouse on her property – looks like a big barn – where it's all stored. Properly cared for under humidity control with appropriate heating and cooling. She's got a guy acts as her manager. I think he may be a nephew, or something."

"Did you see any of it?" asked Charlie.

"No. All off limits. Her manager slash nephew got very irritated when I asked if I could take pictures of the inside. But given the timing of what she said was her most recent sale, which just so happened to coincide with the start of the Cardinal's quest, there's a fairly good chance the Cardinal was after something he didn't know his family already owned."

Charlie wryly asked, "Did she mention any scrolls?"

"What are you driving at?"

"When I delivered the final package this morning, the Cardinal and I played a little you-show-me-yours where we each examined our take in the trade. I got your dossier, Rita."

Rita jumped for joy, "Oh, my God! That's wonderful. No chance he kept anything back?"

"Don't think so. I'll give it to you to examine."

"So, what's this about a scroll," asked Rita. "That was my guess a while back."

Charlie said, "I could only glance at what he was looking at, but it sure looked to me like pages cut from a scroll. Corners all curved up, crumbling edges, hand scribed in ancient looking letters, looked like the real deal."

"Wow! What could he possibly do with a scroll? Do you think he'll try to sell it to the Church?"

Charlie shook his head. "He's already got a lot of dough. I don't think this is about a money deal. But a trade – that's what we've been thinking, right? And the trade could be a big one. If your three poker buddies really are part of the Swiss Guard investigative branch – and I also believe they may be – I'd say we need to look at the very top rung as his trade goal."

Pete said, "You got our attention. Tell us what you're thinking."

Charlie palmed a round glass decoration off the end table as he started his analysis. "Rita did some research on when our Cardinal was elevated. She figures it was some ten or eleven months ago." Charlie idly grasped the orb with two fingers over the top. "She said that although there are over 200 Cardinals in the world, only 120 are ever appointed to the conclave, the voting group that elects a Pope." He twirled the orb in his left hand, regripping it in his fingers. "Those 120 have to earn their way in, through age, longevity, or by some special act or noteworthy accomplishment." He flipped the orb into his other hand.

Pete said, "Discovering an ancient scroll and giving it to the Vatican would be pretty special."

"Exactly," said Charlie. "But would someone go through all of this just to be on an election board? Not likely. Let's look at one step further." The orb was now being flipped from hand to hand, like a baseball. "Since the 1300s, no one has been elected Pope who was not one of the 120 conclave voters. For the past 700 years, the electors have chosen someone sitting among the 120."

Pete scoffed. "You think he's after the Pope's job!?! What for? Why would anyone want that thankless position!"

"Well, Pete, you might not want it – I certainly wouldn't, either – but consider that the Pope can control all of the jewels, money, art and artifacts in the Vatican. He sets the rules. He has immense power. He can parley the power of the Vatican into a more dominant political force than it is today. Remember, at one point in history the Church ran the modern world – Holy Roman Emperor and all of that under Charlemagne. If the Pope was as corrupt as the Medici's, he could control many countries where religion is bigger than politics, and commit any number of atrocities without worrying about arrest since the Vatican is its own country – his country. And, just as a safeguard against a bunch of holy types turning up the heat or trying to pull the plug on him, he can set up an off-shore account and purchase an island where he can live out his days in extreme luxury." Charlie tossed the orb into Pete's lap.

Rita shook her head, "But he's already wealthy. The family has so much already. Why would he need to do this?"

"Remember, the old lady has all of the artifacts. That's what Pete discovered. That's where a lot of the wealth is tied up, and he can't very well sell those out from under her. And Vicky has signing rights to the estate. She may be his wife, but it seems both of them would just as soon end their relationship. If that comes to pass, she'll fight hard for all of it, given Sean's proclivity for extra-marital friendships. He may be wealthy, but not Vatican wealthy. Pushing his brother aside makes some perverted sense if he's after more wealth and power than several middle-sized countries. If the real Cardinal does have Alzheimer's, pushing him out of the way would be easy. If, on the other hand, he's paying people to keep his brother on ice, he really could use excessive wealth. Imagine being the Emperor of the World, or something like that. There are many nations who would welcome what they imagined to be a benevolent world ruler."

Pete and Rita looked at each other as Rita said, "It's so crazy, but it does explain a lot of what's been going on."

Pete said, "There's got to be another step in there somewhere. Even if he gets to be one of the 120, how does he guarantee that he gets elected? That's got to be one of the toughest elections to try and fix."

"You're right, Pete," said Charlie, accepting the orb tossed back to him. "There's got to be more. But what if the scroll – if that's what it is – is not meant to be a present to the Vatican, but rather something held over their head? What if the contents are so volatile that it could melt the whole Catholic Church if it became public? Having that in his hip pocket could sway a lot of voters. And being the first American Pope would buy him so much good will here, they'd have a hard time fighting him, no matter what evil deeds he might perpetrate."

The three sat contemplating the ramifications. The whole concept was daunting.

Charlie tossed the orb to Rita. "Now then, I think we need to get out of here. Who's with me?"

Pete shook his head. "Where would we go? Your office or mine, your apartment, my place? If you're right, our fake-Cardinal is just about at his most dangerous point. I kinda like the protection of our Palace Guard."

"You do realize that they're armed, don't you," said Rita. "Pete's right, I like it right here for the time being."

Pete said, "Look, you've been working with Angelo, right? Angie-baby sent me here, and he sent you here, too. If you want to leave, why don't you give him a call to get his opinion."

Charlie looked at his watch. It was now just after 5:30 p.m. He realized that Angelo would not appreciate another call. Pete was right.

Charlie couldn't think of any one place that was more secure than Suite 1004 of the Ritz-Carlton. "Well, if we all agree to simply staying put, can we at least get some food from room service? I'm starved and tired."

• • •

The Cardinal Visits the Vatican

Cardinal Maroney quickly donned his red robes and threw together a bag for his trip to the Vatican. He had no idea how long he'd be gone, but figured he could purchase extra items in Rome, if need be. He was headed toward the door where a cab was waiting when he bumped into Brother Gerald.

"Your Eminence, may I speak with you a moment," said Brother Gerald.

The flustered Cardinal said, "I'm in a big hurry, Brother Gerald. Later, perhaps – wait – why are you speaking? Your vow of silence?"

"That's just it, Your Eminence. I have spoken to Abbot James. I'm changing my vocation to a secular one."

"Well, that's fine. Lovely. But really, I must go now."

Brother Gerald said, "But I have heard things, troubling things. What you said in the sacristy ..."

The Cardinal dropped his travel bag and his face flushed with anger. "I don't know what you are talking about, Brother Gerald. I don't know what you think you heard. When I return from my trip we can sit down and discuss it with your new-found voice."

"But I have already spoken about it with Abbot James. He is concerned as well."

"Jesus Christ!" exclaimed the Cardinal. "I don't have time for this right now. Just – just sit tight. We'll talk later."

"Perhaps I should speak with the Monsignor?"

The Cardinal chuckled. "Yes! Excellent idea! You and he can have a nice long conversation. I'm sure he'll be along shortly. Just stay put until he arrives. Goodbye!" With that the Cardinal rushed to the cab on the way to meet the Vatican plane.

Brother Gerald spoke to the door as it slammed in his face, "It's just that Abbot James said he would contact his superiors in Rome about what I overheard."

• • •

The Suite at the Ritz

Pete turned on the TV, "Indians game is just starting. Pass me another beer, will ya' Charlie?"

"Another for me," said Rita. "I'm not sure I've ever had such a great cheeseburger."

"Tasty, yes. Not as good as the hamburger served at the Thespian. I think we were all just very hungry," said Charlie. "But I'm still concerned that we're just – "

The door burst open and the three Swiss Guard investigators entered, with faces showing concern, anxiety and disgust. Dominic looked at his three guests and said, "You have eaten? That is good. Now you will all come with me, please." He said something in Italian to his two fellow guardsmen, motioning to them to sit down. The anguish on their faces lessening as he spoke.

Dominic left his men in Suite 1004 while leading Charlie, Pete and Rita to the hallway. "I'm glad to see you're finally letting us out of confinement," said Charlie.

Dominic looked up at him with a firmly set mouth. "What you are about to witness is no joking matter, Mr. Charlie. This is to show you that the work you did on this case was toward justice." At the door of Suite #1006, he knocked once, waited a few seconds and knocked again. He then used a key card to enter. He led the three to the bedroom on the left, where shades were drawn and two nuns, dressed in white nursing garb, tended to a man in a hospital bed, a tube providing fluids attached to his arm. He looked emaciated and drawn, badly in need of a shave.

Dominic pointed to the man. "This is His Eminence, Phalen Cardinal Maroney. The man you have been dealing with is his brother, Sean Maroney."

"Oh, dear God, will the Cardinal be alright?" asked Rita.

One of the nuns said, "It will take some time, but he will recover. He has been through a lot."

Pete asked, "Does he suffer from Alzheimer's?"

Dominic said, "Thankfully, no. He has been repeatedly dosed with strong sedatives which would give any non-medical person he encountered the suggestion that he did suffer from that mind-stealing disease. But he is actually quite healthy, albeit virtually starved. The three of you can take some satisfaction from knowing that, in some way, you helped save him."

Charlie shook his head. "I had suspicions, but I can't help but think I should have done something sooner."

Dominic put his hand on Charlie's shoulder. "You have been involved for perhaps a month, only that and not much longer. Your activity led us to follow certain leads, which, in turn, directed us to find him in that nursing home. Had you not performed as you did, it may have taken us much longer to discover his whereabouts – and that may have been too late."

"What about the people at the nursing home who did this," asked Pete.

"Come. Let us return to the other room where we can talk more freely," said Dominic. "I also must calm down my men who wish to administer Biblical retribution upon his brother."

• • •

Loose Ends: Marie Carlito

Marie answered her cell phone, surprised that the call was from Angelo DiFranco.

"Listen, Marie. Some things have changed here. Actually, lots have things have changed here. I need to know where your head is at."

"Whadya mean, Angelo?"

"You've been very loyal to this organization. We appreciate that. You've also been very close to Rocco lately. Tell me how you view your involvement with us."

Marie was street smart. She sensed that this was not simply a personnel review. "Angelo, I like being part of the crew. I think I add something that very few others have the ability to do. This has been a pleasant vacation out here, but, frankly, I'm bored. I'd like to come home. I don't know if Rocco will let me, but I don't see any future in being his girlfriend, if you know what I mean."

Angelo said, "Yeah, I get that. Did you want to marry him, or something?"

"Oh, God! No! That's not what I meant. Look, I'm just a couple quarters short of a business degree. I'd like to get off my back – literally – and help with the business. I know, that's probably weird, but ..."

"Not so weird, not weird at all. Actually, that's sort of what I was thinking, too. We need to put on a more pleasant face on what we do. Tell you what. Pack up, catch a plane back here, and see me at the Thespian. We'll talk it through when you get here."

"What about Rocco? You think he'll go along with any of this? He seems pretty attached to me."

Angelo said, "I don't think he'll be a problem anymore. Let's get you back here and get that degree."

• • •

At Suite 1004

The group in Suite 1004 sat spell-bound as Dominic finished updating them on almost everything that had transpired on this fateful Monday.

"... And so, with Mr. DiFranco's behind the scenes assistance, the governmental authorities permitted us to remove the real Cardinal Maroney from the facility while law enforcement arrested those facility administrators responsible for his illegal sequestering."

Charlie said, "The Monsignor at the chancery – he seems to be in this up to his neck."

Dominic said, "We agree that he is, to use your American police parlance, 'a person of interest'. However, he seems to have disappeared. We will continue to search for him. Frankly, he is of less importance than stopping the fake Cardinal Maroney from carrying out his plan."

Pete asked, "Where is Sean Maroney now?"

"The man masquerading as the Cardinal is on his way to Rome, where he believes he will be rewarded by the Vatican. What actually happens to him when he gets there, I am not permitted to say."

"But he committed a crime. He should not be rewarded for that."

Dominic said, "His crime, at least the one we know about, is a violation of Canonical Law. Once inside the Vatican, he will be judged there for that crime. No one outside the Vatican hierarchy is permitted to know how Canonical Law is upheld."

Charlie asked, "What about the artifact, what I think is a scroll?"

Dominic paused and said, "We know that he has an item in his possession which may be important and, if it is authentic, politically volatile." He paused again, and thought hard before answering. "Once the artifact is inside the Vatican, who knows what will become of it?"

Pete looked around at the other Swiss Guardsmen, "Beg your pardon, boys, but I just gotta say—Holy Shit!"

Even Dominic had to chuckle at that one. He concluded saying, "The physical danger for you three, therefore, has passed. You may return to your homes, to your lives. We will remain here until the Cardinal – the real Cardinal Maroney – is safely out of medical danger and can return to his duties, likely in a week or so. I will meet with you three just before we depart to clear up any – how do you say – lost ends."

Charlie said, "Loose ends. But I understand what you mean. I think we are owed such a final report."

• • •

Tuesday, July 19:

The morning sun was baking the runway in Rome as the Vatican jet carrying Sean Maroney, dressed in the red cassock and cap of Phelan Cardinal Maroney, pulled toward the private hanger. As he de-planed he was met by an honor phalanx of Swiss Guards in full decorative bright-colored uniforms and escorted to a waiting limousine as a special dignitary. His other luggage was transferred to the trunk, but he gripped his leather valise tightly, refusing to allow anyone else to touch it. After all, enclosed was the scroll, his entrance ticket to the conclave and, as he saw it, to the white cassock and mitre of the papacy.

Sean had been to the Vatican a few times before but only as a tourist. He was not overly surprised when the limousine veered into an underground parking garage under one of the side buildings. He smiled, realizing he was being taken to a place where no tourist had ever been, a place that few humans even knew existed. He was directed into a side doorway onto an elevator. But instead of going up as he expected he would, the guard pushed the down button.

The door opened and the guard silently pointed to a large steel windowless door with Latin words engraved. Maroney didn't bother translate the words, he simply pushed the door open, expecting a warm reception from the Vatican Camerlengo. Instead, he found himself in a damp, semi-darkened room facing three priests of the Dominican Order, black cowls hooding their heads – the Black Friars.

"Enter!" demanded the one in the center. The steel door behind him slammed shut as a large, muscular, masked guard partially clad in armor threw three locks on the door. Sean's mouth dropped open. He said, "Perhaps there has been a mistake. I am Phelan Cardinal Maroney, from the United States."

"We know who you are," boomed the voice of one of the Black Friars. "And we know who you are not."

The priest in the center shouted to another guard at the left side of the large room, "Pull back the curtain!" There was Alphonse Lucatello, Sean's Vatican contact, almost unconscious, naked from the waist up, arms outstretched and chained to the wall. "This man has confessed to your heinous crime. How say you?"

Sean felt his only defense was to deny. "I have no idea who that man is. Nor do I know who you are. I insist upon being taken to the Camerlengo. This is outrageous treatment for a Cardinal."

The Black Friar in the center stepped forward, "Yes, indeed, you should be told who we are. We three are Elders of the Dominican Order. Tell me, do you know the history of the Dominican Order? No? Allow me to explain. In the 13th Century, the then Pope determined that only Dominican priests had the proper, um, temperament to be judges of the Inquisition, of abuses of Canonical Law. Since that time, there have been many unfortunate changes, limits, as to what is permissible conduct by the Inquisition Judges. Those changes are enforced everywhere in the world. Everywhere, that is, except in the Papal States, meaning Vatican City, the Holy See. You are now in the Holy

See, and the crime for which you have been accused is a violation of Canonical Law. Therefore, you come under the judgement of the Black Friars of the Inquisition."

Sean shook with a chill even though he could feel the sweat pouring down his back. He chose to bluster his way out of what seemed to be a difficult situation, "Of what do you presume to charge me? I am a Cardinal of the Church! I have been invited here by the Camerlengo. You have no authority to keep me here." He turned toward the door, his way blocked by the armored guard, "Let me pass!"

The guard did not move. One of the other Black Friars stepped forward. "You will be pleased to know we are no longer referred to as 'Grand Inquisitors'. Our group is now named the 'Congregation for the Doctrine of the Faith'. This building you are in is the Palace of our congregation. I prefer the old name, don't you agree? Much easier to say, and more to the point, I think. But time marches on, it seems. Nonetheless, we remain committed to judging and punishing sinners – with the proper evidence, of course. And, at least here in the Papal State, we may still utilize several of our traditional methods for accumulating that evidence."

Sean turned to face the three, his intestines turning to liquid, "This is utter nonsense! I have committed no crimes. You are terribly mistaken. And you will all be subject to severe retribution when the Camerlengo finds out you have kidnapped one of his guests."

The Black Friar who seemed to be the leader said, "Perhaps we did not make ourselves clear, dear fellow. The Camerlengo is the man who sent you to us. He requested your presence here in the Holy See for this expressed purpose. He knows you are here, and he not only approves of the trial, he recommends it."

From the far wall, the semi-conscious Cardinal Lucatello suddenly blurted out, "They know all, Cardinal Maroney! They know all. They even have the painting you sent me. But for some reason, they don't think you are a Cardinal at all! Tell them the truth, my friend. Tell them so they will stop punishing me." His legs buckled beneath him. He was held upright only because of the chains tethered to his arms and wrists.

"Perhaps you should sit here, Mr. Maroney," said one of the Black Friars motioning to a hard-backed chair under a single spotlight.

Maroney looked at the chair and at the three judges. “Bring your valise. It must be examined and the contents properly recorded and filed. We also request that you take off the red vestments. Please do so willingly, Cardinal Maroney. We do not wish to physically abuse you ... at this time.”

• • •

The Warehouse Garage

Just after midnight, Angelo returned to the warehouse and popped the trunk of the Cardinal’s car. He whistled in astonishment at the ten burlap bags. He was not quite sure what he might find, but ten bags of gold coins would not have been his first guess. He put the bags on a dolly and wheeled them toward a wooden work bench standing against an inner wall. The back of the bench was made of heavy wooden planks reaching 12 feet up the wall, itself covered with hammers, wrenches and other tools needed for car repairs. Angelo pulled three innocent looking wooden dowels from the left side of the bench, then gave the front of the bench a shove. The whole assembly, backing and all, swung forward on a massive hinge. Behind the workbench was an eight-foot-tall door of a huge safe.

He rolled the tumblers to the correct combination and swung the safe open. He searched for an open shelf that wasn’t full of other items he found useful. Some shelves were laden down with stacks of cash (real and counterfeit in separate bins), other shelves had enough weapons and ammunition to start a small war. There was a small printing press, burner phones, hard drive discs and thumb drives, some identified, others new and as yet unused. Toward the back he found enough room to store the ten burlap bags.

He locked up and called Pauly Basili to report on what he had discovered in the Cardinal’s trunk. Then he contacted three of his men to join him at the warehouse. He gave them detailed instructions, which they followed to a tee. In the dead of night, they tied down the popped trunk of the Cardinal’s car, hooked it up to a tow vehicle and hauled it down to the valley created by the Cuyahoga River known locally as ‘The Flats’. Between two abandoned buildings from a now-defunct steel mill, they doused the car in gasoline and set it aflame. A few minutes after the men left, they heard the boom of the half-full gas tank exploding. All that would be found of the Cardinal's car was a smoldering hulk of the frame. The police would make assumptions, and add it to their unsolved stolen car cases.

• • •

Friday, July 29, Ten Days Later:
At the request of Brother Dominic – who finally identified himself as the Assistant Commandant of the Constantine Guard, the Investigative Branch of the Swiss Guard – Charlie, Pete and Rita returned to Suite 1004 in the Ritz-Carlton Hotel. It had been ten days since they last saw Dominic with his promise to clear up loose ends. As the three entered the suite, Hans and Wilhelm were lowering the blinds to block out the early evening bright sun, and Dominic was pouring everyone a glass of wine.

"Thank you all for joining us this evening," said Dominic. "When we last met there were still many things yet to be accomplished which meant that not all of your questions could be fully answered. Hopefully we can correct that this evening. Since Hans, Wilhelm and I will be departing in the morning, I recommend you leave no questions unasked. As long as we are able to speak about an issue, we will answer your queries."

Pete said, "I have just one concern – is Rita safe? And her family?"

Dominic had a wry smile on his face, "It is very thoughtful of you to be concerned about one of your comrades before yourself, Mr. Pete. An admirable trait. Yes, Ms. Hernandez and her family are safe from any of the persons or evidence from this event. As are you all safe. There is no permanent record of your involvement in any of these matters, except what may remain in your collective memories."

Charlie raised his wine glass and said, "Thank you for that, from all of us. In the coming days I believe we will all benefit from our non-involvement."

Pete added, "There has been a murmur among the news media, but they're following the trail of bread crumbs I left them. I fed them a story about an audit of the diocesan books, as Angelo DiFranco suggested. And they're looking for the Monsignor who may have run off with a bunch of dough. Also, it seems Rocco Parmissano has slipped away to parts unknown, leaving Federal Investigators searching for the person they believe influenced a friendly ruling by a local judge. So far, none of them have put together any reasonable explanations or connections for these matters, and most of the reporters will not write negative stories about the Church's irregularities unless solid evidence becomes obvious."

Charlie asked Dominic, "I don't suppose you have any information on the whereabouts of Rocco? Or even the Monsignor?"

Dominic said, "Insofar as it affects matters of the Church, we remain interested in finding Monsignor Leonard. The Cardinal's new Financial Aide, Brother Gerald is his name, discovered that there is a great deal of Diocesan money unaccounted for. The Monsignor can likely answer for the shortage. We will continue our search for him."

"And Rocco?"

"Presently he does not concern the Church. We know he had dealings with the man impersonating as the Cardinal, but it does not appear he was deeply involved in Sean Maroney's plot. We have decided to allow his associates or the law authorities to deal with him."

Charlie said, "I have heard from reputable contacts that his former consigliere, Angelo DiFranco, is now running the organization. That indicates to me that Rocco may no longer be walking among us."

Dominic said, "If that is true, we shall pray for his soul."

"How is the Cardinal, the real Cardinal? Has his health improved," asked Rita.

"Thank you for asking. Yes, he has made a remarkable recovery and is back in his offices in the chancery, working with Brother Gerald to undo the various wrongs perpetrated by his brother."

Pete said, "How can a brother do that to his twin? That is unspeakable. Where is that jerk, Sean?"

Dominic grew circumspect, "The Vatican has ways of dealing with those who violate Canonical Law. I am not permitted to go into great detail, but if you study the punishments doled out during the Albigensian Heresy of the 16th Century, you can then imagine what kind of fate such a person might expect. Impersonating a high cleric of the Church is ... must be dealt with severely." Rita made a visible shiver while Pete's mouth parted and Charlie let out a low whistle.

Charlie let all of that sink in. He asked, "What became of the artifacts Sean was holding? Was it a scroll, or something else? Will the Church display whatever it is?"

Dominic looked away before responding. "Scrolls, fragments of scrolls, artifacts from the time of Christ – they are bought and sold frequently. And just as frequently they are forgeries. When possible, such items are removed from access, thwarting the illegal trade market."

"Should we assume that what Sean had was a forgery?"

"By removing artifacts from unscrupulous marketing by wayward souls, the Church preserves an unbroken legacy of faithfulness." Dominic's non-answer received curious looks from Pete and Rita, and a knowing smirk from Charlie.

Dominic waved to Hans and Wilhelm to retrieve something from the back of the room. "There is one other matter to be discussed. Cardinal Maroney – the real Cardinal Maroney – is very thankful to everyone involved in his rescue. He is a fair man, and does not wish to retain any of the family wealth that led to all of this in the first place. He is divesting all of his claims to the property and wealth of the estate."

Dominic paced and continued. "His mother has the art and artifacts gathered by his father. Whether they were acquired legally or otherwise, the Cardinal's wishes are that she may retain them, cautioning her that the authorities may wish to become involved. The value of the art is likely several millions of dollars, which will allow her to live out her days in luxury."

"The Cardinal has deeded the estate and land in the town of Hudson to his sister-in-law, Victoria Dempsey Maroney. Although she and the Cardinal are not on good terms, and even though she may have had tacit knowledge of her husband's deeds, the Cardinal wishes to wash his hands of the estate. She may do what she wishes with the house and land." Dominic motioned to Hans and Wilhelm to distribute what they had retrieved. They handed one heavy burlap bag to each of his three guests.

"It appears that Sean Maroney recently retrieved a hidden a treasure acquired by his father. Where it was hidden, we do not know. The Cardinal has asked us to distribute portions of the treasure equitably to all who assisted in his rescue: one bag to the family of a local Arab restauranteur who was instrumental in the purchase of the scroll fragments that Sean desired; one bag to an Italian family in Brooklyn who aided in the delivery of the scroll fragments; one bag to Mr. Angelo here in Cleveland who aided us immensely in rescuing the Cardinal from where he was being held. Also, one bag to the monastery run by an old friend of the Cardinal, Abbot James, who provided the able Brother Gerald; and a bag is being given to the person known as TK Constantine who was helpful from the very beginning. The bags in your laps are your shares of the treasure. He has kept two shares which he is donating to the diocese to make amends for his brother's actions."

Rita said, "Oof! These are very heavy bags. What's in them?"

Dominic smiled, "Each of the bags contains fifty coins known as Krugerrands. Each coin is a five-ounce gold piece, so the weight of each bag is substantial. I apologize for the heavy weight."

Charlie said, "I'm not an expert on these things, but a five-ounce gold Krugerrand is worth a great deal, isn't it?"

"I am told," said Dominic, "that the value of Krugerrands adjusts daily with the price of gold. But the current estimate is that the bag each of you have received is valued at approximately $500,000."

"Holy shit!" screamed Pete. Looking to Hans and Wilhelm, he said, "Sorry, boys, but you gotta admit, that needed to be said."

"You have all saved the Church from an enormous scandal, at the very least. Cardinal Maroney – and the Vatican – are most thankful," said Dominic.

Charlie said, "Please extend our gratitude to the Cardinal along with our good wishes for his continued health. But your list of those sharing in the reward – there are both good and bad folks among them, and probably some people a bit in between. How do you reconcile that? Are they all part of this Merke Edelstein organization? And if so – as I asked you once before – does the end justify the means? You got your man, but were illegal means used to do so?"

Dominic said, "I believe there is some good in everyone."

Charlie replied, "And, conversely, there is some bad in everyone."

Dominic pulled up a chair and sat down. "That is a very pessimistic view of mankind, but at the same time implies some deeply philosophical thoughts which trouble you. Mr. Charlie, it seems your conscience is bothered by the events that transpired during the past month. So, let us review. Did you or your friends do anything illegal or immoral while working on this project?"

Charlie looked to Pete and Rita as all three shook their heads, "We may not have admitted our true intent during our investigations," said Charlie, "but there was nothing illegal about what we did."

Rita smirked, "As far as the immoral part, Charlie and TK will have to confess that themselves."

Dominic continued, "Are any of you aware of any illegal or immoral actions undertaken by any of the others regarding the resolution of this Sean Maroney matter? Our observations conclude that the only sinful actions were those of Mr. Maroney himself. Now, it is true that, in parallel activities, some of the participants may have transgressed in other areas. Those actions are between themselves and their conscience – or perhaps legal authorities. But any such transgressions were not associated with the resolution of matters involving the Cardinal. Therefore, your concerns, Mr. Charlie, about the 'ends justifying the means', are more a matter of whether bad people can assist in a good ending. Do you agree?"

Charlie thought for a minute. "I suppose you are correct. It's just that when you involve people of questionable reputation you never can be sure what they might do to accomplish the task."

"Quite so," said Dominic. "But neither should you pre-judge their ability to do good. Perhaps an analogy would be helpful. In America, you have a game which I have come to love, because it is a microcosm of life. There are nine players in the field, each with a special talent to play in a specific area on the field, but each with the same goal for the success of the group mission. You would not want someone who is an excellent Stop-short to put on a mask and catch pitches. You would not put a pitcher in the outfield. It is the same with each player and each position. The group cannot succeed without a specialist at each location. Now, occasionally, one of the players makes a mistake, an error. That is not helpful to the group's goal, but the error is on the part of the individual, not the team. The error is, therefore, on the individual player's conscience. The team is assembled to play well, and hopefully do no wrong."

Charlie said, "So, Merke Edelstein assembles a team and says let the ball fall wherever it may? Seems a bit cavalier."

"You forget that there is a common goal in mind. That goal tends to identify the players needed. And you continue to make the wrong assumption that there is one person known as this Merke Edelstein coordinating the players. To continue the analogy, it is a pick-up game, with players added or selected because they can add a special skill toward achieving the stated goal of success. As with pitches thrown, there is always a judgement. A pitch that is over the plate is a strike, one that misses the target is a ball. But then there is that third pitch, the one that is right on the corner of the plate, that might be a strike, or might be a ball. The umpire is called on to judge its rightness from wrongness. That third pitch – that is what makes life interesting, not so?"

"So, who's the umpire in this Merke Edelstein loosely knit organization that's not an organization at all? How does someone get in or out of the team, if it even is a team?"

Dominic's face twisted as he searched for a way to explain. "You first heard the name Merke Edelstein from Sean Maroney while he was pretending to be the Cardinal, correct?"

Charlie thought a moment, then nodded. "Yes, I guess that's true."

"And Sean got the name from the records of his deceased father, who used Merke to purchase artifacts for his collection, correct?"

"I suppose that's true, too."

"And that led you to the assumption that there is an individual – one individual – that orchestrates everything. Is that also correct?"

Charlie nodded. "Yes, but obviously that was an erroneous assumption. I just can't wrap my head around any other way of looking at it."

"Perhaps the deceased father made up the name, so that only he knew from whom he purchased items." Dominic looked at Rita and Pete. "Might either of you understand enough to help this fellow? I'm fouling off that third pitch." Dominic chuckled at his own joke.

Pete said, "Allow me to try. What if we say that tomorrow I'm contacted by someone who needs a ride to the hospital so he can visit his sick aunt. Along the way, we stop at a florist so he can buy her something nice, but before he can do that, we stop at the bank so he can cash a check for the money to buy the flowers. The team he needs is me and my car, the bank teller, and the florist, plus possibly the doctor or nurse caring for his sick aunt. Depending upon the day and the need, the people he needs can change. It doesn't matter to my friend that my car needs an oil change, or the bank teller is an embezzler, or the florist is a drunk, or the doctor cheats at golf. That's the team he needs that day for his sick aunt."

"Bueno!" said Dominic. "Whether the doctor cheats at golf is irrelevant to the health of the aunt. As long as he is a good doctor, that is what is essential. We will hope that he stops cheating at golf, but that is on his conscience."

Rita added, "And the fellow needing the ride gave the florist a fake name, Merke Edelstein. Anyone who tried to find the florist would search in vain." Rita groaned, "Is it just a coincidence that the initials are M.E.? As in me?"

Dominic clapped his hands, "Si! You've got it. Mr. Charlie, does it begin to make sense, now?"

Charlie smiled, "You didn't tell me that that third pitch was one wicked curve ball."

THE END

ABOUT THE AUTHOR

A new voice on the literary scene, Robert Allen Stowe borrows from his unusual past to create characters so real you can almost smell them. He writes about life as he's seen it, and he's seen it from many different angles, from the bottom to the top. This is his first published work but is sure not to be his last. There are too many tales yet to be told.

NOTE FROM THE AUTHOR

Word-of-mouth is crucial for any author to succeed. If you enjoyed *The Third Pitch*, please leave a review online—anywhere you are able. Even if it's just a sentence or two. It would make all the difference and would be very much appreciated.

Thanks!
Robert Allen Stowe

Thank you so much for reading one of our **Mystery** novels.
If you enjoyed our book, please check out our recommendation for your next great read!

K-Town Confidential by Brad Chisholm and Claire Kim

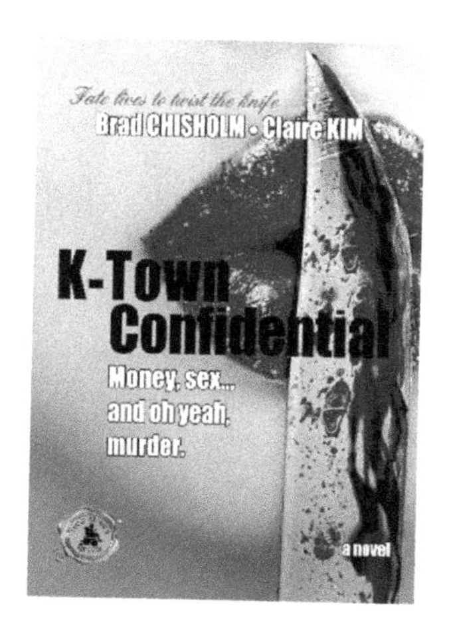

"An enjoyable zigzagging plot."
–*Kirkus Reviews*

"If you are a fan of crime stories and legal dramas that have a noir flavor, you won't be disappointed with *K-Town Confidential*."
–*Authors Reading*

View other Black Rose Writing titles at www.blackrosewriting.com/books and use promo code PRINT to receive a **20% discount** when purchasing.

CPSIA information can be obtained
at www.ICGtesting.com
Printed in the USA
LVHW010255270721
693746LV00001B/2